Stage Three: Be

Voices of the Sanctum, Volume 3

B.K. Bilicki

Published by B.K. Bilicki, 2024.

STAGE THREE: BE

First edition. October 31, 2024.

ISBN: 979-8227400864

Written by B.K. Bilicki.

Table of Contents

Dedication

To the readers – past, present, and future.
Hope you enjoy the ride.

———◉———

To the incredible Richard Godspell,
whose awesome cover art likely lured you in this far.

———◉———

To Danielle, Nick, and Chris,
for musical inspirations, the chance to perform the occasional
miracle,
and for generally keeping me on my toes over the last few decades.

———◉———

To Yv,
Three-for-three.

———◉———

To Monti, Kathy, and Brenna,
for giving an amateur hack the chance
to spread the weirdness around a bit.

———◉———

And to the multitude of characters, critters,
and other odd little concepts in my head.
Just shut up and wait your turns.
I'm editing as fast as I can.

Author's Note: Please see glossary of terms (Distil Arcanum III) and the recommended listening guide at the end of the story

Preface

A ll relationships had their occasional problems.
     And then there were Kana and Jamyn.

Jamyn's secret passion for Kana soon turned into a declaration of his love for her. As Kana was struggling to accept this revelation, her acolyte disappeared. Jamyn had been possessed by a creature who sought to use his proficiency with the Voice to free itself from a demonic bond. During Kana's search for him, Jamyn nearly killed her. In the end, Jamyn was freed, the enemy was destroyed, and the battle for Kana's heart had been conceded when she finally accepted his feelings for her.

Bruised and battered, the pair was returning home to the Sanctum. Healing and rest aside, there were numerous other tasks facing them. There were explanations to be given, apologies to be made, and a budding relationship to be properly addressed.

Chapter One: Lockdown

A glowing gate opened beside the bar and Jamyn stepped through the lit doorway. His arms were immediately pinned to his sides and his entire body rendered immobile by a series of powerful holding spells.

Qa and Evrok stood before him, their outstretched hands aimed straight at his head.

Jamyn stared wide-eyed at his former master and the rail-thin barkeep.

"Explain yourself, Mister Siska," Qa said in a measured tone.

Kana stomped out of the gate and the spells holding Jamyn shattered.

"Some welcome," she said, shooting both of Jamyn's captors a withering glare. "Hold your fire, boys. Jamyn's back to being one of the good guys."

"Maintaining the Balance," Jamyn blurted before he could stop himself.

She turned back to him and frowned. "I think you can stop waving the company banner for a bit," she said in a low growl. "You're lucky not to be *under* the Sanctum with everything you've been up to lately."

He grimaced and bowed his head.

"Nevertheless, I believe some explanations are in order," Qa said without relaxing his stance.

"And you'll get 'em," Kana replied with an impatient wave of her hand. "How about giving us a second to get our bearings first?"

Neither of the men appeared to be moved by her words.

She sighed heavily. "Okay, fine. The kid didn't attack me. He had someone hitching a ride."

"A demon?"

"Nah. Ever hear of an Aqiri?"

Qa finally relaxed his stance. "I have. A very rare and unique creature."

"A real pain in the butt, you mean," Kana said. She grabbed Jamyn's hand. "Let's sit down. This is probably gonna take a while."

Without waiting for a response, she pulled him right between Qa and Evrok to one of the large booths along the far wall. She sat down, then scooted over to make room for Jamyn.

He sat beside her but kept his gaze downcast.

Qa sat opposite them. Evrok, still regarding Jamyn warily, pulled a chair over to the table and sat down.

"Much more comfy," Kana said, settling into the cushioned seat. She looked back at Qa and cocked her head. "What were we talking about again?"

Qa smiled weakly. "As you are so fond of telling me, get on with it."

She grinned back at him. "Sucks, don't it?"

Jamyn spoke up, though his voice was now a ragged whisper. "Tell him."

"Right. Jamyn was under the influence of an Aqiri. The little bugger was using him to get free of a demon."

"An Aqiri attached to a demon?" Qa asked. "I've never heard of such."

"Yep. It was plenty pissed when it found out that it was stuck in the demon's realm forever. Dunno how it found Jamyn. Once it did, it realized that Jamyn could neutralize the demon's spirit enough for it to free itself."

"Neutralize it?" Evrok asked, speaking up at last.

Kana nodded. "Jamyn was bouncing around all over the place while you were busy napping. During one of the jumps, he ran across a lesser demon and was able to siphon away most of its aura. Nearly turned him human." She gave Jamyn a nudge. "He was able to finish the transformation himself, by the way. You made him and a young lady really happy."

His only reply was a brief nod.

"I recently talked to Locan about him," Qa said to her. "They're doing quite well, all things considered. Eddie's still incredibly protective of her. He's also getting much better at reining in his temper." Qa shook his head and chuckled.

"What?" Kana asked.

"*Eddie?*"

Kana laughed. "At least someone got the joke. It fell flat on him."

"Then Jamyn was able to destroy this demon?" Evrok asked.

"Only part of him," Kana replied. "It's kind of like what he did to you when he siphoned off your aura."

Jamyn looked to Evrok. "I'm really sorry—"

"But a demon's aura is different," Evrok said, rudely cutting off Jamyn's apology. "You know of the duality, correct?"

Kana cast a concerned look at Jamyn before replying. "Yeah, I know all about it. Demons don't have auras like ours. Theirs are separate and distinct entities. If one could wipe out a demon's aura, its physical body would become mortal."

"And no longer part of the demonic chain," Evrok added. "The body would lose some of its powers but also the inherent restrictions."

"Which is exactly what that dopey Aqiri was after. When Jamyn nuked Eddie's aura, the Aqiri realized that it could do the same to itself and get free from the chain."

"But then why did it attack you?" Qa asked.

At this, Jamyn slumped even further where he sat. He stared down at his lap until Kana cupped his chin and turned his head to face her.

"Stop beating yourself up," she said quietly but with authority. "That's *my* job."

"But I—"

She slid one finger up to cover his lips. "Not another word about it," she said, all the while trying to keep her expression neutral despite his forlorn visage. She looked directly into his eyes. "We good?"

He nodded once and briefly puckered his lips against her fingertip.

She gave his chin a gentle shake. "Troublemaker."

She released him and turned back to Qa. "Evidently Jamyn was somehow still giving the Aqiri grief once it took over. It figured that allowing Jamyn to see it attack me would crush his spirit once and for all."

"And did it?" Evrok asked Jamyn directly.

Jamyn drew his arms in closer as if he was trying to disappear within himself.

Kana glared at Evrok. "Back off, Squeaky. He's been through a ton of shit already and—"

Jamyn interrupted her. "No. I'll answer him." He raised his head and looked straight into Evrok's sunken eyes. He clenched his teeth, and his lip quivered in rage. "Yes, seeing myself tear Kana apart like that and not being able to stop it nearly killed me. When I got free and saw that she was still alive, I was able to repay it properly."

The sheer hatred in his soft voice sent a shiver through Kana.

"And the manner of its repayment?" Evrok asked, apparently unfazed by the young man's anger.

"I stripped every bit of magical energy from its body and then destroyed what was left."

"That girl I sent here," Kana said to Qa. "Shamara. She has an ability—"

"That she calls the push," Qa said for her. "Yes, Lob has told me all about it. He's thoroughly fascinated by it."

Kana smiled briefly. "Figured. Jamyn learned how to do it too and stomped the Aqiri with it. Actually merged its body with the ground while it was still alive."

Evrok sniffed. "Sounds like something Donta would do."

At the sound of the name, Jamyn's body stiffened.

Kana noticed his discomfort and resisted the urge to embrace him. "Hey, don't rag on Donta. He actually helped Tiris put me back together."

"It was him?" Qa asked in surprise.

Kana nodded.

Qa's gaze went thoughtful. "That would make sense. Tiris reported seeing a large black entity strip away a smaller one from your body. She said the small one actively prevented her from healing you."

"A favorite tactic of some demons," Evrok said. "Leave a shred of essence behind to ensure the victim will die before anyone can help them."

Kana frowned. "Nice. That would explain where Donta got the essence he used to track down where the Aqiri went."

"Which was..." Qa asked.

"Didn't get the exact address. One of the lesser infernal realms would be my guess."

Qa and Evrok shared a quick glance, then Qa turned back to face Kana. "He didn't enter with you, did he?"

"Nope. Got the info we needed near the entrance and then he sent me in after Jamyn. I'm guessing he came back here after that."

Qa released his held breath in a soft sigh. "Then he didn't enter."

"We would know if he had," Evrok said.

Kana looked at them both. "Okay, what's the problem?" she asked, her senses now on high alert.

"Nothing you need concern yourself with," Qa replied, his tone lightening. "I trust your abilities are fully intact again," he said, deftly changing the subject.

Before Jamyn could slump even lower, Kana wrapped an arm behind him and hauled him upright. "You duck down any further and you'll be on the floor," she said. "I told Qa what you did."

"What he did?" Evrok asked.

After another firm squeeze from Kana, Jamyn nodded. "When I retrieved her soul back on Letron 12-B, I unintentionally added part of mine to it. Whenever she tried to use magic, it reacted and cut her off."

"A soul-based variant of the anchor spell?" Evrok turned his gaze to Kana. "You of all people should know how dangerous something like that could be."

Kana snapped at him. "Piss off. I didn't teach him that. He figured it out himself."

"Ah. It's the Voice, then."

Jamyn looked back at him in alarm.

Qa chuckled softly. "How long have you known?"

"Long enough, no doubt," Kana said before Evrok could reply. "He's evidently had me pegged from the moment I walked through his door. I'm guessing it didn't take too much longer with Jamyn."

"Between the succubine and nearly obliterating Second Heirophant Keller, he wasn't really doing much to hide it," Evrok said. "Has he gained any control of it yet?"

"Hard to say," Kana replied. "Most of the times he's used it so far have been accidental."

Evrok frowned at Qa. "So, this is your latest."

Qa arched an eyebrow in question.

"Another of your pet projects that could destroy us all."

"Another?" Qa asked innocently.

"Indeed. Sitting right beside your first."

Kana scowled at him while Qa smiled. "You are incorrect, old friend. Kana was far from my first. If memory serves, I believe you yourself hold that honor."

Evrok nearly cracked a thin smile. "I stand corrected." Turning his attention back to Jamyn, he asked, "How do we ensure you will stop having *accidents*?"

"Look," Jamyn said in a rush. "I'm sorry, all right? I freaked out after the anchoring because of the Aqiri trying to possess me."

"Which led you to absorb my aura to fashion a crude gate through which you could escape," Evrok said, as if it was common knowledge. "I am not worried about the past. I am concerned about your potential for future episodes."

"That concerns all of us," Qa said. "I still believe that with the proper training and discipline, Jamyn will be just fine, and the Sanctum will be all the stronger for it." He gestured to Kana. "You have no better proof than Kana here."

"Not exactly a shining example, but I must agree."

Kana frowned. "So glad you approve."

"I did not say I approved. Merely that I agreed." Before Kana could fire back a scathing reply, Evrok stood up. "Qa, I require your assistance."

"With?"

"A matter of some importance that I have neglected until now."

Qa shrugged at Kana's inquiring glance and stood up. Together he and Evrok walked over to the bar and then slipped into the back room.

Kana watched them go and then turned her attention back to Jamyn. His expression was still clouded in gloom, and she shook her head. "Will you just snap out of it already? What the hell has got your ass dragging now?"

"I should just go home," Jamyn muttered, staring at the table.

"Why?"

"They're right," he said, waving a hand to where Qa and Evrok had been sitting. "I'm a disaster waiting to happen."

"That's why we're not waiting," she replied firmly. "You heard Qa. We're gonna train you and get your mind on straight so that you'll never have to have another *accident* again." She gave him a firm shove.

"What? You think I'm not up to it?"

"Kana, I—"

"Am being a royal pain in the ass and feeling *way* too sorry for yourself," she said for him. "You fucked up. Big deal. You said you read about every mission I've ever been on. How many times have I screwed up? If I got *my* shit under control, I'm pretty sure we can whip your ass into shape. Right?"

He forced a shrug. "I guess."

"You guess?" she asked incredulously. She jabbed a thumb into his side and then grinned fiercely when he turned to face her. "Who the hell do you think you're dealing with here? I'm not some little sissy like Donta. I am Kana-friggin'-Morel, the scourge of the Sanctum. If I say I can train you, you *will* be trained!"

He couldn't help smiling at her theatrics. "C'mon, Kana. Cut it out. You know what I mean."

"No, I'm pretty sure I don't. You think your fragile little mind is gonna snap and you'll be off terrorizing the villagers again. You forget that you stopped yourself this last time?"

"Huh?"

She fixed him with a wild-eyed glare. "How the hell do you think you got free of the Aqiri?"

Confusion overran his face. "I...I don't remember," he stammered. "I was just suddenly free of him. I figured that you did it."

"You did it, dumbass," she said, poking him in the chest. "Path somehow came out and knocked you away from the Aqiri with a wicked right hook to the chest."

He gasped. "Path? But how did she—"

"Ask her yourself, genius," Kana replied, gesturing to the seat across from Jamyn.

He turned and saw Path, his aspect of the Voice, sitting there and grinning back at him.

"Path! Why are you here?"

Path nodded to Kana and her grin turned into a genuine smile.

Jamyn faced Kana. "You called her out?"

In reply, Path kicked his shin under the table.

"Ow!"

Kana laughed. "No, I didn't call her out. You're the only one who can do that. But I guess she did have a little help."

"Why do you mean?"

"She can somehow interact with my aspect. She's sitting right next to her."

He looked at the empty space. "She is?"

Path seemed to giggle to herself before reaching a hand under the table. Suddenly a short, dark-haired woman appeared beside her. Path gestured to her with her free hand and then to Jamyn, silently introducing them to one another.

"Who are you?" Jamyn asked.

The newcomer seemed surprised. "He can see me now too?" she asked Kana.

Kana shrugged. "Evidently. Jamyn, this is Eva. She's my aspect of the Voice."

Jamyn stared at her in shock. "Um, hi."

Eva laughed. "Hi back. I'm Eva, like Kana said. It's short for Evasion."

"Is that—"

"Yeah, another one of her silly nicknames." She faced Kana. "How did we set up this little conference call?"

"Beats me," Kana replied with a shrug. "I just called you up when Path appeared. I can see her without you around now, which suits me just fine."

"Little brat." Despite her grumble, Eva's smile didn't fade. "Maybe it's because she's holding my hand." She disappeared and then reappeared a moment later. "Did I just blink out?"

"Nope," Kana replied.

"Not for you, you twit. You can see me regardless. I meant for him." She jerked a thumb at Jamyn.

"You did," Jamyn said.

"There we have it." Eva turned to Jamyn. "So, you're in love with Kana, huh? What the hell is wrong in your head?"

Path laughed silently and squeezed Eva's hand under the table.

"Lots of stuff, I guess," Jamyn replied, still off-balance from this strange conversation.

"Shut up, Eva," Kana said. "Do something useful for a change, like telling me how I can see Path."

"It's not my doing," Eva said simply. "Ask the boy toy." Looking Jamyn up and down, she gave him an appreciative leer.

Path looked shocked and leaned over, bumping into Eva's side.

Eva looked at her and laughed. "Oh, come on! He's all kinds of yummy!"

Path released Eva's hand. Eva disappeared to Jamyn's eyes, but Kana glared at her.

"Will you shut up?" Kana said, trying to keep her voice low.

"Doesn't matter now," Eva replied with a sulk. She raised the hand Path had been holding and waved it at Kana. "He can't see or hear me anymore."

Kana's angry retort was swiftly muted as Jamyn wrapped an arm around her and hugged her tightly. He rested his head on her shoulder. "We're sorry."

Kana was stunned. "We?"

"Path and me. She said she's sorry for allowing me to hear what Eva said. I'm sorry for us invading your privacy like that."

Path's head was now bowed as low as Jamyn's had been throughout most of their talk with the others.

"It's not your fault, Path," Kana said quietly. "Eva's suddenly got a big mouth on her. That's my problem, not yours." Turning back to Jamyn, she grabbed his shoulders and forced him to sit up straight.

He released his hold on her and his hands fell into his lap.

"As for you..." Her voice failed her. She swallowed hard and looked into his teary eyes. "Dammit to hell, you *are* gorgeous." She forced the words out from between her clenched teeth. His perplexed gaze made her chuckle at last. "I've thought you were hot since our first mission together."

"But you—"

"*Regardless* of all the other stuff that I got outta your head. Truth is, I've been beating the crap out of myself ever since then trying to figure out what to do about it. I knew you wanted me too, but you never acted on—"

Jamyn twisted out of her grasp and snared her lips in a passionate kiss.

She fell into it willingly and wrapped her arms around him in a firm hug.

Eva vanished as she was pulled back into Kana's mind.

Path disappeared as well, though not before releasing a childlike titter.

Jamyn smiled at last against Kana's voracious mouth and started to reach for her waist.

Before he could touch her, she grasped his hands in her own and held them together against the center of her chest. Reluctantly drawing away from their kiss, she rested her forehead against his and whispered, "Not here."

"I should hope not." Evrok's voice sounded directly behind Jamyn.

The pair jumped at his words. They looked up to see Evrok and Qa standing there, each of them holding a pair of mugs.

"Evrok realized he was being a dreadful host," Qa said with a bright smile.

"I am merely fulfilling a request Kana made before the sanction hearing," Evrok replied, placing a tall mug in front of each of them. Kana's drink was topped with a white foamy head while Jamyn's fizzed angrily at him. "*Two of the usual* upon your return, as requested," Evrok said, gesturing at the drinks. He and Qa returned to their earlier seats, and each took one of the mugs Qa had brought.

Qa raised his mug in a toast. "To the return of the wayward."

"Finally," Kana said, raising her drink.

Jamyn swallowed and lifted his mug. "To all of you for getting me back."

"To new beginnings." Evrok advanced his mug through the gap between all of theirs, clinking each of them. He took a sip of his drink, ignoring the glare Kana was now throwing his way.

Qa chuckled and took a healthy swig.

Kana and Jamyn looked at one another. Jamyn's faint smile helped chase away Kana's outrage at Evrok's words and she smiled as well. They brought their mugs together in an additional though quieter *clink* and each took a deep draught.

Kana lowered her mug and wiped the foam from her upper lip with the back of her free hand. "Now *that* hits the spot," she said with a pleased sigh. She muffled a small belch.

"Yeah," Jamyn said quietly before sipping more of his heavily caffeinated drink.

"So glad you approve," Evrok said, mirroring the comment Kana had made to him earlier.

Kana smirked. "You're a total jerk most of the time, but you serve one mean root beer."

Jamyn polished off his drink, put down his mug, and turned to the barkeep. "Evrok, I need you to do something for me."

"Given our recent dealings, a favor would likely be out of the question," Evrok replied while he continued to peer into the dark recesses of his own mug.

"This isn't a favor," Jamyn said, ignoring the verbal jab. "I need you to lock down my magic again."

Evrok raised his eyes to the acolyte. "Why?"

"Because until I sort out everything I've just been through, I don't want to run the risk of doing something stupid again."

Evrok considered his words. "A sound decision. But what guarantee can you give me that you won't attack me again? I must warn you that doing so would now be a grave mistake."

"I'm in control now," Jamyn replied. "That and I won't have an Aqiri trying to possess me this time."

Qa smiled. "We do have two First Seers on hand to subdue him should things go amiss."

Kana spun Jamyn around to face her. "Why are you doing this?"

"To be safe," he replied. "There are a lot of things I have to make right around here after this whole mess. I think it would be better for everyone if I can't cast until I know for sure that I can handle it."

Kana thought over his words and finally nodded in agreement. "Good plan."

Jamyn turned back to Evrok. "Please shut it off."

Evrok looked to both Qa and Kana before locking his sunken eyes upon Jamyn.

"Deny."

Kana watched closely as Jamyn's aura was clamped down. He sighed once and then his eyes rolled back. He pitched forward and landed on the table face-first with a dull thud.

"Jamyn!"

She hauled him upright and looked at his unconscious face. Immediately she hurled a furious glare at Evrok and shouted at the barkeep. "What did you do?"

"I locked down his magic, as he requested." Evrok spoke calmly, despite Kana's obvious rage. "Nothing more."

Qa was already casting a suite of spells over the lifeless acolyte. "Calm down, both of you. Jamyn's fine. He's just sleeping."

"*Sleeping?*" Kana asked. She fought to rein in her sudden anger.

"He appears to be suffering from extreme fatigue and dehydration." Qa continued to scan Jamyn's body. "I would guess that he hasn't slept or eaten since he left the Sanctum. His magic must have been the only thing that was keeping him awake and mobile."

Kana looked over Jamyn's blank face in concern. "You mean he's been going at it nonstop?"

"I believe so, judging by my scan." He paused for a moment. "Please check the back of his head. Something's not right there."

Kana turned Jamyn's head and ran her fingers through his hair. A large patch of clotted blood caught her eye, and she carefully found the bruised gash centered beneath it. "Ouch. Something clobbered him good." Her memory flew back to the police covering the site of the mugging. "That's right. The Aqiri said something about Jamyn getting hit in the head right before it could fully take him over. I'll bet this was from that." Another memory surfaced of her repeatedly banging Jamyn's head against the ground during their fight against the Aqiri. She grimaced and lightly ran her fingers across the wound.

"He'll be fine," Qa said, nullifying his scans. "He has a concussion but it's not bad. Other than that, he's got an impressive collection of scrapes and bruises." He pointed to a darkened spot beneath Jamyn's left ear. "What's that on his neck?"

Kana's eyes widened as she recalled the mark she had left there. "Probably another abrasion he got during the fight," she said as dismissively as she could. "It was pretty intense."

Qa nodded. "Then I will leave him to you. Take him back to his quarters. I believe a restorative potion and a few days of bed rest should do the trick. You should get some rest as well."

Kana held on to Jamyn and faced Qa. "But what about—"

"The Sanctum's concerns can wait a while longer. Go fix your acolyte, Kana."

Kana nodded in gratitude. "Thanks, Qa. Thank you too, Evrok." She cast a spell and the couple vanished.

<hr>

Evrok huffed in disbelief. "*Abrasion*."

"Come now, Evrok," Qa said with a chuckle. "It was a good lie." He finished his drink and sighed. "I suspect we'll have to put together a few of our own before this mess blows over."

"True. Another drink before then?"

"Of course, my old friend."

Chapter Two: Restoration

Kana and Jamyn reappeared seated on the couch in Jamyn's living room. His limp body flopped backwards, and she tightened her arms around him in a protective embrace. She carefully laid him back and then gazed at his peaceful face. She gave him a firm shake but he didn't respond.

"You are one sound sleeper, kid," she said, despite knowing that he was actually unconscious. "I could probably stuff your ears with lit firecrackers right now and it wouldn't even faze you." She released her grip on him, then brought her face close to his and lightly caressed his cheek. "But you've been a busy boy," she whispered, her lips nearly brushing his. "I'll let you rest for now." A familiar ache bloomed deep within her, and she leaned over to his ear. "But not for too long."

She gave him a quick peck on the cheek and then sat back to look him over. His clothes bore a multitude of stains and rips, and she was suddenly aware of a pungent odor emanating from him. She waved her hand in front of her face and wrinkled her nose.

"Whew," she said before muffling a cough with her hand. "The last of that magic you surrounded yourself with must be wearing off. You are *ripe*!"

She stood up and gestured and his body rose from the couch. His back and legs straightened, and his arms extended along his sides until he resembled a standing statue lying on its back. She beckoned and his rigid form glided smoothly behind her as she led him to the bedroom. He drifted past her until he hovered over the bed. She was about to lower him onto it when she stopped.

"No, let's get you cleaned up first. No sense spreading your funk all over the place."

She waved him on, and his body floated into the adjoining bathroom. She followed him in and then grabbed one ankle before his head hit the far wall. She pivoted his body in midair until he was upright and floating a few inches off the ground in front of her. She looked at his closed eyes, which were now level with hers, and she shook her head with a smile.

"Nah, I kinda like you looking up at me." His body floated lower until his booted feet just skimmed the tile floor. She nodded in approval and pressed a kiss to his forehead. Standing back, she looked him up and down.

"Now how should we do this?"

She considered just undressing him normally but discarded the notion. Instead, she lifted her hand, and his body floated up again until he was a full foot above the floor. One by one, articles of his clothing became ethereal and slipped down through his body. As they hit the open air, they became solid again and landed in a pile beneath him. Kana concentrated on her casting, carefully controlling the transformation of each piece to avoid watching his body slowly being revealed to her ardent gaze.

As his tattered pants joined the rest of his clothing, she enclosed the pile in a vacuum sphere surrounded by a barrier. She nudged the mystical ball with her foot to get it out of the way and it rolled into the corner. Her head still bowed, she took a deep breath to steady her nerves. She blew it out in a rush and grumbled. "What the hell's with you, Morel? He's naked. Big deal!" With this, she took a step back and her head snapped upright.

Despite the dirt and bruises and lingering aroma, her breath caught in her throat as she found herself faced with the most perfect male physique she had ever seen. Snapshots of her few glimpses of his body until now passed by her mind's eye. None of them compared with the carved perfection suspended in the air before her. He was a bit thinner around the waist and legs than she had envisioned, but the sharply defined muscles of his thighs and lower torso more than made up for it. His smooth upper body was exquisitely molded, and she licked her lips while she watched his chest expand and contract with every deep breath. She focused on his dark nipples and giggled when she saw that his left sat slightly higher on his chest than his right. This one minor oddity in the middle of such a flawless specimen suddenly struck her as impossibly hilarious and she clapped a hand over her mouth to keep from crying out. Momentarily snapped out of her awestruck gaze, she removed her hand from her mouth and slapped her cheek several times.

"Good God. What's with you, girl?" She laughed and shook her head. "It's only Jamyn! Young, foolish"—her eyes took another lap up and down his body and her voice dropped to a throaty chuckle—"totally fucking *gorgeous* Jamyn."

She purposely focused on his flaccid cock and grinned at the thoroughly unimposing lump of flesh. "So, you're a *grower* not a *shower*, huh?" she said, by now knowing well his fully aroused dimensions. She reached forward and hefted his wrinkled scrotum. "We'll have to work on that when you wake up," she whispered, coming close to his ear. She leaned in to kiss him when she got another good whiff of him. She coughed hard right in his face and then stepped back again. She released her intimate hold on him and fanned the air around her. "But first I have got to fumigate your ass!"

Waving him back, she maneuvered his body into the shower. She started to pull up her shirt but then stopped. She sighed deeply and pulled her shirt down again.

If he suddenly decides to wake up and I'm naked too, we're gonna get into it. He couldn't handle that in his condition.

She shook her head and smiled at him wistfully. "Always something, huh, kid?" She cast an elemental screen over herself, ensuring that water could not touch any part of her clothing or body except for her hands.

She stepped into the shower and turned the water on, keeping Jamyn out of the spray while she adjusted the temperature. Once it was to her liking, she pulled him into it and watched as the water sluiced down and around his entire body.

Focus on the task.

She repeated the thought over and over as she skimmed her hands over him. Slicking back his hair, she looked at his closed eyes to check for any signs of him waking. His eyes remained firmly closed so she shrugged and reached for the soap. Lathering up her hands, she started to scrub him clean. Her movements were quick at first but started to slow as she got the feel of him. She eased her hands over his chest, soaping him up while she traced her fingertips along the curves of his muscles. Before she knew it, she was toying with his nipples and leaning her body closer to his. She caught herself before she could kiss him and took a quick step back, growling at herself the whole time.

Dammit to hell! Keep it together, girl!

Her outrage at her lack of self-control sparked her into action. She launched into her task, efficiently scrubbing Jamyn clean from head to toe while not allowing herself another chance to linger. In moments, her acolyte was thoroughly cleansed of any trace of his recent adventures. She gave his body a final rinse and turned the water off. Stepping out of the shower, she pulled him along at her side. Grabbing a thick towel, she patted him dry, allowing only the briefest of pauses to admire his cock. It had responded to her vigorous handling and was now dangling semi-soft between his legs. She hung up the towel and then grasped his thickening shaft. "You had better wake up soon, dammit," she said, her voice a lusty rasp. She carefully tugged his cock to guide his weightless body back into the bedroom.

A quick series of manipulations later, Jamyn was lying peacefully in bed and covered with a blanket. "That fixes the smell and the sleep," Kana said with a pleased smile. "Now to get you that restorative." She leaned over him and pressed a kiss to his lips. Despite his lack of response, a burst of desire shot through her body. She flicked the tip of her tongue between his lips and slipped a hand under the blanket to stroke his chest. She was lightly dragging her fingernails over his abdomen when her mind shouted a heated reproach. In a rush, she forced herself to pull away from her lusty kiss before it became more than she could handle.

"Medical," she said through her clenched teeth. As much as she wanted to stay with him, he had to get that potion in him before his condition worsened. "I'll be right back," she whispered before planting one last tender kiss on his cheek. She stood up and hurried out of his quarters, locking the door behind her with a spell.

Kana hurried down the stone-lined corridors. Since leaving his quarters, her concern for Jamyn had steadily mounted until she was nearly jogging to her destination. The halls were curiously empty, and she glanced at a clock on the wall as she passed.

Middle of the night. Her steps quickened into a loping run. *Hope someone's still awake in there.*

Finally reaching the medical wing, she slipped through the door to find that most of the lights in the ward were switched off. Only the few emergency lights provided a dim illumination. She walked between the rows of empty beds.

What the hell?

Keeping her voice low, she called out. "Tiris? Leel? Anybody?" She turned the corner and entered the main office.

A small form leaped out of the shadows and collided with her. She stood her ground and cast a spell. Instantly the room was flooded with light, revealing a naked Leel sprawled out on the floor at her feet.

"Leel! What the—"

"Kana!" He sputtered, blinking at the sudden brightness. By his expression, she could see he was easily as surprised as she was.

Right on cue, a naked Tiris bounded into the room and tackled Leel. "Gotcha!"

Leel cried out before clutching her with a joyous shout. Without pause, he started to wrestle with his naked wife, the pair hooting and shrieking with wild abandon.

"Knock it off, you two!" Kana bellowed in outrage.

The naked gnomes stopped their amorous play and looked up at her.

"Kana," Leel said in a stern tone, "I would remind you that this is a place of healing. Kindly keep your voice at a civil level."

"Me?" she shouted in reply. "You two are making all the damned noise!"

Leel jumped to his feet and his body was suddenly surrounded by a churning blast of magic. "I would advise you once more to adjust your tone, Miss Morel." He was snarling at her now and holding his clenched fists tightly to his sides.

Tiris clambered to her feet and shot Kana a worried glance. "Stand down, Kana. You're obviously upset, but this doesn't have to get out of hand. Just calm down and tell us what you need."

Kana quickly realized her concern for Jamyn had caused her to lose her temper with the diminutive healers.

Shifting her gaze back to Leel's furious scowl, she composed herself and bowed low. "I am sorry for my outburst, Master Leel. I shall abide by your wishes."

Apparently unmoved, he continued to glare at her.

Tiris came close to him and grasped one of his tiny fists. She pried it open and held his hand tightly. "She said she was sorry, dear," she whispered into his ear.

"Take off your clothes," Leel said, his voice no less harsh.

"Um, I'm already naked," Tiris replied.

"Not you. *Her.*"

Kana's head popped up and she looked back at him in shock. She and Tiris shared a confused look.

"Why?" Tiris asked.

His features softened and he turned to face his wife. "She said she would abide by my wishes." He looked back at Kana and shrugged as his aura faded away. "It was worth a shot."

Tiris gave him a quick swat on his bare butt.

"Apology accepted, Kana," he said, his normal gentle voice returning. "What do you need?"

Kana stood up straight. "A restorative potion, Master Leel. Jamyn's been in a bit of trouble. He hasn't slept or eaten for days. Qa said he might have a concussion too."

His brow creased in concern. "And you didn't bring him here because..." Kana started to respond but he held up one small hand. "This is somehow connected to your recent injuries?"

Kana tried not to grimace. "Yes."

"I am thinking there is much more to your story, but it will have to wait. The patient comes first." Turning to his wife, he said, "Please bring me a coated flask from the shelf marked *Industrial*. A dual application, if you would."

He pulled her close and kissed her soundly, palming her ass as he did. She moaned into his mouth and stroked a hand over his stiffening cock. He pulled back from her and looked into her starry eyes.

"Go, my love," he whispered.

"On my way," she replied with a nod and a quick smile. In a flash, the naked gnome was streaking out of the office and into the darkened wing.

Leel turned to find Kana trying hard to look like she hadn't been paying any attention to them. "We're making you uncomfortable."

"No," she replied instantly. "Not at all."

"Please," he said, holding up a hand to her. He gestured and covered himself in an illusion spell to disguise his naked body. "It happens. We are quite aware of our reputation in the Sanctum."

"You love each other," Kana said. "Nothing wrong with that."

"Nothing at all," Leel replied with a courteous bow. "We are also the most skilled healers in the Sanctum, which is usually good enough to earn us a pass. However, I know that many disapprove of our, shall we say, constant and rather public displays of affection."

"It's not—" She cut off her thought.

Leel arched an eyebrow at her.

"It's just—"

He held up a hand again. "Kana, I know. Your concern for Jamyn caused you to lash out at us. But he has also frustrated you beyond reason, so seeing us together like that really sent you over the edge." He stepped forward, took her hand, and gave her arm a gentle tug. "Get down here."

"Why?"

"Because you're tall and all this talking is killing my neck," he replied with a gentle smile.

She smiled in reply and dropped to one knee beside him. "What?"

"Tiris and I both know of your, shall we say, *situation* with Jamyn," he said. "In some ways, we are nearly as perceptive when it comes to affairs of the heart and body as Mistress Daystar. There are reasons for that." He examined her face. "Qa has never told you about us, has he?"

"Told me what about you?"

"See?" he said, squeezing her hand. "I didn't feel your pulse waver, so I know you're telling me the truth. He's never told you why Tiris and I are so skilled in our field."

Kana shook her head.

"Since you're a First Seer now, I'll let you in on our secret. My darling wife and I are masters of chi creation."

Kana's eyes widened. "Chi *creation*? That's impossible!"

"If that were the case, you would be dead right now. We are able to generate and distill the basic energies found in all living beings. And we do this through..."

She realized he had left the question hanging so that she could answer. She started to speak but then held her tongue.

Leel nodded. "Go on."

"Sex," she whispered.

"Correct. The power generated through our lovemaking enables us to create the spells and potions and such so vital to our position. All the fondling and groping we're constantly doing is done in the pursuit of the craft."

"Well, not entirely," she said with a sly chuckle.

He laughed along. "No, not *entirely*. It does help that she's the most gorgeous creature I could ever hope to see. Being perpetually and passionately in love with her helps as well."

"Likewise, you short stack of studly," Tiris called out in a sultry voice from the doorway. They looked to the door and saw her standing there in a short satin robe of deepest blue. In her hand was a small flask that contained a tiny ball of pulsing white light. "And just what is the nature of your little heart-to-heart, my dear?" she asked innocently, gesturing at the pair.

"I've just revealed our great secret," he replied, letting his gaze wander up and down her form with a look of undisguised lust.

Tiris chuckled as she came forward. "Pssh. *Secret*. Anyone with eyes can see what we're doing."

"Anyone with eyes usually can't get very far past the sight of our constant pawing at one another."

She grabbed his ass through the illusion and pulled him to her. "Then I feel sorry for them," she said in a low purr. Turning to Kana, she asked, "Might I have my husband back?"

"Of course," Kana replied with a quick nod. She let go of Leel's hand and stood up again, looking down at the gnomes with a new sense of respect.

Tiris held up her parcel. "One flask, as you requested."

Leel took it from her and examined its glowing contents. "With a double dose?"

"Of course."

He peered at the light a moment longer then looked to Tiris. "Really?"

"Well, the first one was a little more intense than usual."

"Because it was really two." He held up the flask for her to see. "Note the slight flutter of the light."

She winced. "I see. I'm sorry." Thinking a moment, she smirked and hugged him tighter. "It's all your fault for winding me up so much beforehand."

"Then I apologize as well, but you should always check." Looking up at Kana, he smiled. "We want to cure our young Jamyn, not blow him up. Correct?"

Kana nodded. "I'm trying to avoid doing that right now."

"Then we'll go for *non-exploding*," he said, fixing his eyes on the captured light. He mumbled a few arcane words, and the light started to pulsate in time with his heartbeat.

Slowly it spread out in the bottom of the flask as if it had turned to a liquid. The glowing mass churned wildly, its color changing from white to dark green and finally to a murky brown. He yanked Tiris close and planted a crushing kiss upon her lips which she gladly returned. The potion flashed bright red for a second before revealing a turquoise brew that bubbled angrily. Pulling away from the torrid kiss, Leel gasped loudly.

When he finally caught his breath, he held up the now full flask for Kana to see. "One heavy-duty restorative potion. However, it's far too potent to be used all at once." Letting go of Tiris, he tapped the neck of the flask with his finger. A glowing ring of light encircled the neck and then faded. "There. Now it will only dispense the proper dose. Save the rest for whenever you need it next." He handed the flask to Kana.

She could feel the potion buzzing through the glass as if it was alive. "Thank you both," she said, cradling the elixir in her hands.

"Oh! One other thing," he said before she could leave. "It's gonna taste like garbage."

Kana laughed. "I know. I remember the last time I took one."

"No, this one is *really* bad. It's probably one of the most potent we've ever completed. It'll cure him in record time, but only if the first swallow doesn't kill him."

Kana stared back at him in shock. "It won't really—"

Tiris swatted him. "Of course, it won't!" She gave Leel's body a shake. "Stop worrying the poor girl!"

He laughed. "All right! I'm sorry! Just pinch his nose and pour it down. He'll be fine."

Kana smiled in relief. "Again, thank you both. For this and for saving my life." She bowed low before them.

"Thank *you* for the flowers," Tiris replied. "We enjoyed them very much." Leel gave her an affectionate squeeze and she giggled. "One of them a little more than the other!"

"You should thank Master Donta as well," Leel said.

"Donta?"

"I talked with Qa after the procedure."

Kana nodded. "Ah."

"She has something else to attend to first," Tiris said in a rush. "Go fix Jamyn!"

Kana nodded again and hurried off.

———➤●⤚———

Leel held his wife in his arms. "You *knew* that was a triple dose, you little trickster."

"Did I?" she replied innocently, though her hands were stroking down toward his cock.

"Let me guess. You wanted to help get Jamyn back on his feet so he can sweep Kana off hers."

Tiris pouted. "Guessing right the first time takes all the fun out of it."

"Oh, I don't know." He swept her legs up in one swift motion and held her close while she shrieked in delight. He nuzzled her small breasts through her robe. "I got it right the first time when I found you, didn't I?"

"The first time and every single one after that." She gasped through her rising passion. "You gonna keep doing me right, Leely?"

"Repeatedly and without mercy," he said as he peeled away her robe.

Chapter Three: Renewal

Kana's feet were a soundless blur over the stone floor, propelling her forward so quickly that she nearly bowled over an unfortunate couple out for a midnight stroll through the hallways. The pair had rounded a corner in front of her. Only a quick leap to the opposite side of the corridor saved her from a hard collision. She planted one foot on the wall and kicked hard, vaulting herself into the air above them. A quick midair somersault later, she landed back on the floor and resumed her blistering pace forward as if nothing had happened. The stunned couple could do nothing but stare at her in shock while she streaked off into the distance.

"First Seer tramples innocent casters," she murmured under her breath. "Film at eleven."

She lengthened her stride even further and a sudden cramp seized her right thigh. The burst of pain forced her to slow down at last and she frantically rubbed her leg with the heel of her hand. She clenched her teeth into a hard grimace and bit back a curse. Fatigue finally caught up with her as well and she yawned so deeply she thought her head would snap in half at her mouth.

"Whoa," she said, her steps faltering and her gait slowing to a shuffle. Looking to the flask in her hand, she smirked. "I could probably use a hit of this too." She came to a stop and leaned back against the wall, keeping up her massaging until the pain subsided. She lifted her leg and shook it tentatively before pressing on. "And a long bath and about ten hours of sleep," she said with a tired sigh.

Finally reaching Jamyn's quarters, she was surprised to find a note on the door. The slight aura around the paper told her that it was magically hidden from all eyes but hers. Pulling it off the door, she silently read it.

Once Jamyn recovers, a meeting with all relevant parties at your earliest opportunity would be wise.

Below the message was a small handwritten *Q*. She quickly pocketed the note and grumbled. "Thanks for pointing out the obvious, Qa. This mess is gonna take one hell of an effort to sort out." A deep breath was followed by an even deeper sigh. "And ain't that gonna be all kinds of fun?"

She released the lock enchantment on the door without dispelling it and went in. Closing the door behind her, she listened intently for any signs of life. Silence still reigned and she made her way into his bedroom. As she entered, a voice barely more than a weak mumble stopped her in her tracks.

"Hey."

She stared in surprise at the figure on the bed. Jamyn was still covered by the blanket, but he had scooted up the pillow to a semi-reclined position. His eyebrows rose as he fought to keep his eyes open more than slits.

"*Hey* back, you dope," she said, coming forward in a rush. "What the hell are you doing up?"

"Up?" He tried to push himself further up the bed but failed. "This as up I can do."

She stood beside the bed and frowned down at him. "All the more reason to still be asleep. You can't even get out a complete sentence."

"Sorr—" He quashed his apology with an annoyed grunt. "'Mokay," he mumbled quietly.

She shook her head and sat beside him. "Yeah. Sure, you are. Here." She reached under the blanket and grabbed him under his armpits. He protested weakly but she hauled him up closer to a sitting position. "Time for your medicine," she said, showing him the small flask.

His unsteady eyes regarded the turquoise liquid. "What's?"

"Restorative potion. Basically, jet fuel on the rocks." She tipped the flask against his lips. "Drink it slowly."

As the first drops hit his tongue, he jerked his head back, likely a prelude to spitting the concoction as far across the room as he could. Before he did, Kana placed an open hand against his bare chest.

"Don't. I know it tastes like shit, but you need it." Before he could argue, she leaned in and pressed a soft kiss to the top of his head.

He nodded slightly and started to sip the nauseating brew. Though the complete dose was little more than a mouthful, his facial gyrations made her feel like she was making him swallow a gallon of the stuff. The liquid agony ended, and she pulled the flask away. He swallowed repeatedly in what she guessed was a fruitless attempt to dilute the horrific flavor in his mouth.

"Yeesh," she said. "Must taste even worse than Leel said."

Jamyn forced a weak nod. His body started to slide back down the pillow.

Kana helped guide him until he was lying down again. "There. Now go back to sleep or I'll knock you out. Got it?"

His eyes were already closed but the corner of his mouth twitched upward.

She smiled at him and lightly tweaked his nose. "I mean it."

"Kana?"

She glanced up at the sound of Qa's voice. "Gimme a second, Qa." She leaned down over Jamyn's peaceful face and whispered, "Get better. That's an order."

Standing up, she hurried into the bathroom and closed the door. "What's on your mind?" she asked. "I just got your note."

"Good. I had hoped we would not have to act on this matter immediately, but it appears we may not have a choice."

"Let me guess. Donta's getting antsy again."

"To put it mildly. He accosted me as soon as I left Evrok's and demanded to know your whereabouts."

Kana sighed and leaned back against the vanity. "What did you tell him?"

"I informed him that, as far as I knew, you and Jamyn were safely within the Sanctum's confines. Oddly enough, this seemed to satisfy him. He stormed off without another word."

"Oh, crap. He's not on his way here, is he?"

"I've already considered that. My troupe informs me that he went straight back to his quarters and has remained there ever since."

"Good. If he would've shown up here..." Her voice trailed off and she reined in her feelings with another tired sigh. "Well, let's just say there would be one hell of a cleanup involved."

"Are you all right, Kana? You sound exhausted."

"Do I?" She stretched out and groaned at the aches in her back and arms. "Dunno why. Only had a near-death episode and a lovely little spat with my idiot acolyte and his Aqiri stowaway. That should be a walk in the park for me."

"Kana," Qa said in a serious voice, "please stop calling Jamyn that. He's going to end up with the same complex you strapped yourself with before joining the Sanctum."

"Just joking, Qa," she replied. "Get off my back. It hurts enough as it is."

"You should get some sleep too."

"I would but I'm busy yapping with you," she snapped back through a yawn. "I'll ring you once we're both conscious again." With this, she canceled the converse spell. Looking back at the closed door, she considered crawling into bed beside Jamyn. A tingle shot through her despite her fatigue, and she smiled at his probable reaction once he woke. She ran a hand over her face and shook her head with another yawn. "We'd probably fall asleep in the middle of it," she said with a brief chuckle. Turning her attention to the shower, she nodded in approval and started to pull up her shirt. "Best idea you've had all day, Morel."

———◉———

Jamyn's entire body felt as if it had caught fire. Shortly after Kana's hasty retreat to the bathroom, his body spasmed and every muscle clenched on its own, causing him to writhe in agony under the blanket. At the same time, an explosion of white light bathed his mind. The overload of sensations quickly battered him into submission, and he fell into a deep rejuvenating sleep.

Dreams started to coalesce in his mind's eye. He found himself standing in the center of an endless field of lush green grass. He was wearing his usual workout garb—a light blue sleeveless shirt, gray sweatpants, and running shoes. The sun was high overhead in a cloudless sky, and he smiled as its warmth poured down over him. For the first time in ages, his mind was untroubled, and he felt really good.

A young female voice called out behind him. "Hey, you."

He turned around and gasped. Path was standing before him, wearing an outfit similar to his along with a warm smile.

"Did...did you just talk?" he stammered.

"I think so," she said with a grin. She straightened up, cleared her throat a few times, and repeated her words. "Hey, you." She nodded happily. "Yep, that was me!"

"How can you talk now?"

"Simple. We're in your head. Here I can say whatever I want."

"Why can't you talk outside?"

At this, she frowned at him. "You haven't figured that out yet? C'mon, it's not that hard." She sighed at his ensuing silence. "A hint, then." Her expression became fearful, and she whispered, "*They're* coming!"

Jamyn's eyes widened at the sound of the familiar warning. "*Them?* Then you're—"

Path curtsied. "One imaginary friend, at your service."

He looked her up and down. "I didn't think you were a girl."

"You never thought I was anything other than the extra voice in your head," she said with a shrug. "And I didn't really have a gender or identity until I first appeared to you. I was hoping by now you would have connected the dots as to why I'm like this."

"I'm sorry, but no. With everything that's been going on—"

"You mean everything with *Kana*," she said with a teasing smile.

"Uh, yeah," he replied sheepishly. "That too."

"But we've got time now. Tell me why I'm in this form."

He looked her over again. "I'm guessing you're about ten."

"Because..."

"That's when I was introduced to magic."

"Very good. What else?" She made a show of batting her eyelashes at him.

He laughed. "Your eyes are obviously mine."

"I'm a product of your mind, so at least part of me has to come straight from you." She did a little pirouette and curtsied again. "Next?"

"And you're a girl because of her."

Path squealed in delight and clapped her hands. "He got it! I thought I'd have to drag that out of you."

Jamyn chuckled softly. "No, I figured that one out right away. You're supposedly a facet of my mind that gathers and interprets information on the Voice. Women have given me most of the answers in my life, so it makes sense that you would be female too."

"Hey, you're good at this!"

He pointed at her hair, which was now dark brown and cut in a short bob. "But what about your—"

"Ah!" She held up a finger to him. "I'm not gonna tell you that."

He frowned at her. "Why not?"

"Because that's cheating. You can ask her about it yourself. No fair asking me to tell you what's in her head." She absently twirled a strand of hair with her finger. "Or on it!"

"What about the fact that I wanted to be with her? She got that out of my mind. That's cheating too."

"Nope. That was all *your* fault. You let that id frenzy tell her all about your little secret crush."

"No, I didn't!"

"Yes, you did!" She laughed and started to dance gaily around him with long, skipping steps. "You let it slip that you wanted her and you two have been bouncing around the issue ever since."

"Well, it's all out in the open now," he said as she circled him. "She knows I'm in love with her and she's okay with it."

"And the rest?"

He swallowed hard. "We'll just have to wait and see."

She leaped up onto his back and draped her arms around his neck. "Guess so."

He hauled her legs up and shifted her into a more comfortable position on his back. "Why can you touch me? Out there, I mean. Kana said you shouldn't be able to do that."

"Lucky for you that I can though, hmm?"

He nodded. "Yeah."

She rested her chin on his shoulder. "I dunno. Maybe because I've been with you a lot longer than other more typical aspects. I've only dealt with Eva so far. She's only been in Kana's head since Kana first became aware."

"But because I was born aware, you're a lot more *real* to me than the others would be to their owners."

"Excuse me? *Owners?*" Path gave his thighs a quick dig with her heels. "I don't think so!"

"Companions?"

She hugged him. "Much better. So, we gonna get down to business here or what?"

"Business?"

"You think I'm just here to chat?" she asked before thumping her small fist against his chest. "You have some serious catching up to do."

"On..."

"Your little jaunt with the Aqiri." She dropped down off his back and landed on her feet. "Time to check out all the trouble you got into while he was in your head."

He glanced back at her. "I would usually do a replay to figure that out."

"And you're thinking it won't work with your magic locked away," she said. "Remember that we're in your head right now. You don't need magic here. Just start drawing on your memory and I'll help you translate what you see."

He reached a hand forward and a mass of churning blue light appeared in the air before them.

"Okay, then. Let's start right before the anchoring..."

———◉———

Kana groaned in appreciation as jets of hot water pummeled her back. She had already efficiently scrubbed away her accumulated grime and now reveled in a long hot rinse. All the tension and exertion of the last several days melted away and she pressed her hands to the walls of the shower to keep from following them right down the drain.

Ahh, that feels good.

She leaned her head back into the spray and ran her fingers through her short black hair, breaking up a few snarls and massaging her scalp as she did. Tingles ran down her spine and she shivered as contentment subtly changed over to a glowing desire. She kept her head under the spray and let her hands wander down over her chest, imagining the touch was now Jamyn's. She flicked her fingers over her stiffening nipples, drawing a low moan from deep in her throat. She hefted her breasts and gave them a gentle squeeze.

I should wait.

The feelings building within her begged to differ. Her thoughts went to Jamyn sleeping naked in the next room and her body shrieked at her.

No telling how long until the potion kicks in.

Her thighs started to tremble as she dipped one hand lower across her belly. She closed her eyes and gently stroked a nipple.

A quick one. Just to take the edge off.

She skimmed a finger past her trimmed mound and slid it between her slick lips. At the first touch upon her clit, her head snapped forward and she braced herself against the shower wall in front of her with her free arm. Instead of letting her passion build slowly, she jettisoned all restraint and went straight for the payoff. Her fingertip danced in small circles around her clit, endlessly teasing the slippery bud. The thought of doing this with Jamyn so nearby added to her growing excitement and she suddenly envisioned him walking in on her.

Her body spasmed and she came with a shuddering gasp. Her thighs started to press inward, but she forced her legs apart with an effort and planted her feet solidly on the floor. She continued to torment her flesh and fell forward, resting her head on the arm against the wall and gasping against the cool tile. Plunging two fingers into her pussy, she cried out in delight as she imagined it was him filling her from behind. Grunts and mewls filled the shower as her movements quickened, her second peak thundering in on the heels of the first. She bit her forearm and screamed as her orgasm crashed into her. Her entire body shook as it consumed her, and her knees threatened to buckle. She pulled her fingers from her sated sex and trailed her fingertips up over her belly, spreading her juices across it. Resting her forehead against the wall, she dropped her other hand down to cup her breasts.

"Holy shit," she said with a gasp as she gave her breasts a loving caress. Through the haze of her afterglow, her mind wandered back to previous sessions where she had fantasized about Jamyn. All of them paled to this one and she released an exhilarated laugh.

If just being closer to him makes it this much hotter, I'm in real trouble once we finally get together!

The stream of cooling water against her legs brought her mind back to the present. Turning off the water, she slicked back her hair and smiled. The shower and her ensuing play had refreshed her more than she had expected. Her brightened mood nearly had her humming to herself. Stepping out of the shower, she grabbed a towel and started to briskly dry herself. Looking down at her clothes while she toweled her hair, she shook her head.

"No sense putting that stuff back on. I'll pop back to my place to get something clean." She raised a hand to cast a teleport spell but stopped and glanced at the door.

Should see how he's doing first. Make sure he didn't blow up like Leel said.

Wrapping the towel around her body, she combed her fingers through her hair and opened the door.

Jamyn called out as she stepped into the doorway. "Hey, beautiful."

Kana stopped and stared at him in shock. Jamyn was no longer a pitiful unconscious heap curled up under the blanket. He was now sitting up and leaning back against the headboard with his fingers laced behind his head. A mischievous light sparkled in his eyes, and he smiled brightly at her. The blanket was pulled down, exposing his bare chest to her stunned gaze. She tried to speak but the sudden visual overload had somehow disconnected her brain from her mouth.

She gathered up the shattered bits of her composure. "Why are you up again?"

"Because I'm cured!" he said enthusiastically, raising his hands high in the air. He brought his arms back down and folded them across his chest. "Whatever that rot was that you gave me really did the trick. I feel as good as you look." His hungry stare roamed over her body. "Nice outfit," he said with a wicked leer.

She looked down at the towel wrapped around her. "This old thing?" she replied with a chuckle, her nerves swiftly banished by his infectious good mood. "It doesn't do a thing for my figure."

"Then take it off."

Her eyes widened even further at his request. "You're supposed to be resting."

"It'll help me relax."

A stir under his blanket seemed to disagree. She choked down a renewed surge of lust. "I think I'll keep it on for now." She tucked the top edge of her towel in a little tighter.

"Aww, c'mon," he said in a disappointed though teasing voice. He grabbed the edge of the blanket covering his lap. "Show me yours if I show you mine?"

She was surprised her eyes didn't pop right out of her head. "What?"

"No?" He pouted at her reaction and made a show of peeking beneath the blanket. "I'm pretty sure you should be insulted!"

Kana's thoughts immediately raced to the flask she had left with her clothing in the bathroom. "I am gonna kill Tiris!" she whispered, all the while trying not to leap at Jamyn and yank the hated blanket from him.

He casually lowered the blanket and placed his hands over the growing bulge in his lap. "Hey, if she's the one that mixed up that potion, then I owe her a big ol' kiss!"

"I'm sure she'd love that," Kana said with a brief sarcastic laugh. "I'm just wondering what else the little trickster put in there. That potion was only supposed to heal you, not change you into a raging horndog."

He turned a disbelieving eye to her. "It *did* heal me. I feel phenomenal! The hormones and other stuff?" He pointed at her and licked his lips. "That's all your fault"—he lowered his hand and absently rubbed his poorly-disguised cock—"mistress."

She tore her gaze from his lap and her mouth went dry. "How so?"

"You were a little loud in the shower," he replied softly.

She felt the color rising in her cheeks and cinched up her towel again just to have something to do other than squirm in place. "Ah."

"Thinking about anyone I know?"

His smug tone drew a muted growl from her, though it was one of mingled annoyance and desire. "*You*, if you must know," she said in a huff, going back on the offensive to avoid falling into a full retreat.

He considered her words and then gave her a bashful smile. "I hoped so." He straightened up where he sat. "Come here."

Her brow creased and her defenses shot up. "What for?" she asked, mostly as a nervous reflex. She shook herself to get her mind back on track and then stared at him solidly. "What do you want?"

"I guess this is where I'm supposed to say I want to make love to you."

A minor thrill shot through her, and she shrugged. "Then say it."

"I can't."

"Why not?"

"It's not really what I want."

Her heart sank. "No?"

"Nope."

"Then what *do* you want?"

His eyes locked with hers. "I want to fuck you."

Her knees went into full revolt at the sound of the raw sentiment coming from her previously unsure acolyte. All of her fantasies charged forward at the same time, and she did a quick two-step in place just to assert control over her legs.

"I see," she said, barely managing to choke the words out.

"You sound surprised."

"No," she replied immediately, then ran one hand back through her hair. "Well, yeah. I guess. But not by that. I—" Realizing she had been reduced to babbling, she clamped her mouth shut. His amused expression lit a fire somewhere behind the glowing inferno of her lust. "You sure that damned Aqiri isn't still in there?"

"The Aqiri?" he asked in an unbelieving tone. "He's deader than dead."

"And no one else is in there hitching a ride?"

He sighed heavily. "Kana, it's just me. What's with you?"

"Gee, I don't know. Maybe because the Jamyn that left the Sanctum to go on his little joyride would have died on the spot if he had ever—" She frowned and finished her thought. "If he had ever said aloud that he wanted to fuck me."

Jamyn's expression darkened. "Yeah? Well, *that* Jamyn was an idiot. *That* Jamyn knew what he wanted but didn't have the balls to come out and say it. Even knowing that you wanted it too wasn't enough to get him to spit it out."

"And this one doesn't have that problem?"

"What do you think?"

He tore the blanket off and tossed it to the floor. His rampant erection slapped up against his belly and he spread out his arms in disgust.

"Do I look at *all* unsure to you?"

Despite her surprise, she let her hungry gaze casually roam up and down his naked body. "No, I guess not. You look pretty sure to me." Noticing the look of outraged impatience growing in his expression, a smile spread across her face.

Finally got him on the defensive, she thought with a wicked satisfaction.

"So, you want to fuck me?" she asked lightly.

"More than anything." He forced the words out.

She grinned at how his cock bounced with every angry word. "Well, then," she said, raising her arms above her head in a catlike stretch. "Isn't that *sweet*?"

"Kana," he said in an agonized whisper. "Please."

The desperation in his voice tweaked her heart and she lowered her arms again. His eyes pleaded with her, and she swallowed hard. "Then I guess I should hold up my end of your deal."

"Huh?"

"Well, since you've already shown me *yours*..."

She untucked the upper corner of her towel and peeled it away slowly, keeping her arms tight to her body to keep the rest of it in place.

He leaned forward, his eyes wide and unblinking.

She raised her arms and let the towel fall away from her. Just as he was about to be granted an unrestricted view of her naked body, however, she snatched the towel again and tossed it right at Jamyn's face.

He cried out and swatted at it with both hands. Though he became momentarily entangled, he knocked it away at last and flung it onto the discarded blanket.

She laughed at both his wild antics and the way his jaw went slack as he drank in her naked glory. "You like?" she whispered, striking a sultry pose.

He uttered a small squeak of affirmation and started to scoot down the bed toward her, but she firmly held up one hand.

"Ah! Stay right where you are."

He lurched back to where he had been sitting and nodded quickly. "Kana," he whispered under his breath.

She traced one finger down the center of her belly and let his impassioned plea filter through her body, setting every nerve tingling. Her long legs carried her in a slow saunter forward and she silently cast a spell upon herself.

That takes care of that.

Reaching the foot of the bed, she leaned down and grasped his ankles. She gave them a light tug and he instantly slid his body down the bed until he was lying with his head upon the pillow. She nodded in approval and climbed onto the bed, moving her body with agonizing slowness over the quivering expanse beneath her. The heat rising from him added to her own. She kept her eyes trained on his while she continued to stalk over him like a panther closing in for the kill. Reaching his cock, she grasped it and gave it a gentle squeeze. His gasp turned into a feral groan as she gave him a long, slow stroke from tip to root. His body tensed and she quickened her pace, kissing a path from his navel up to his throat, all the while caressing his cock and marveling at how his girth filled her hand. Reaching his face at last, she considered his pained expression for a moment. She leaned down to his face, gave his cock a firm squeeze, and planted a chaste peck on his cheek.

He arched up with a maddened cry and snared her mouth in a deep, passionate kiss.

His desire fed hers and she responded in kind, thrusting her tongue into his mouth while she continued to slowly stroke his length. He reached up and lightly gripped her hips, easing her body further up over his own. She moaned into his open mouth and positioned herself over his rigid cock. They continued to fervently kiss one another, their exploration expanding to cover cheeks and chins and necks. The whole time Kana glided her steaming sex over his length, leaving slick trails of her essence up and down his cock.

Their combined passion now reaching dizzying heights, she held his cock up and slipped down just enough to accept the head inside her body.

His frantic kissing stopped in a heartbeat, and he stared directly into her eyes.

She grinned devilishly and eased herself down another inch, drawing delicious groans from each of them. His grip tightened ever so slightly, and she was caught by the mix of emotions in his wide amber eyes. Her body still adjusting to the intrusion, she held herself in place and tried to decipher his curious expression. Lust was obvious but it carried with it unexpected twin rushes of both surprise and panic. Her smile blossomed and she rubbed her nose against his while she lifted slightly and then descended to accept more of him within her needy body. The sudden move drew a faint whimper from him.

"You okay down there?" she whispered, punctuating her words with a wiggle of her hips. The move caused even more of his cock to slip up into her and the sudden lusty intrusion drove away all thoughts of playfulness.

He forced a nod and tugged at her hips, urging her on.

She started to undulate above him, alternating small retreats with longer advances and enveloping more and more of his cock with each new plunge until he was fully sheathed in her heat. Settling her weight upon him, she bore down and rubbed her clit against his pubis, sending a victorious thrill rocketing through her. She pulled up a space and descended just as quickly. The feeling of fullness momentarily robbed her of breath. Bracing her arms to his sides, she rose again in preparation for a long slow ride.

Her plans were dashed as he seized her hips and pulled her back down onto his cock. His brawny arms wrapped around her and yanked her body close, her breasts crushing into his chest and her face plunging into the pillow beside his head. He pulled back, drove into her again, and his entire body jolted as if he had been kicked. A burst of heat erupted deep within her, and he twitched powerfully several times. His movements stilled and he released a long, shuddering sigh.

Despite the fabric against her face, her eyes opened wide in absolute outrage. A myriad of thoughts blazed to life and shrieked inside her head.

He came? Already?

Denials sprang up one by one but were quickly smashed by the warmth spreading within her depths. Anger swiftly joined in, and she clenched her jaw in hate. After waiting for so long and with everything they had been through together, that their first encounter should be ended so prematurely seemed like the ultimate injustice. Her churning feelings all transformed into a glowing rage in a heartbeat and her mind screamed.

I'll kill him! I will fucking destroy this little—

Her internal diatribe was interrupted as he started to move beneath her. His pelvis dipped down and then came up again, easily sliding his cock into her wetness. A tingle cut through her growing fury just enough to alert her to something she had somehow missed.

His cock hadn't gone soft. It was still just as stiff at it had been when they had started. He speared her again and the ensuing tingle instead drew a disappointed sigh from her.

Now he's just trying to make up for it.

She tried to push herself up but his hold on her did not waver. He shifted his arms up and grabbed her shoulders from behind as he started to pump into her in earnest, his hips settling into a steady rhythm. Despite her mind's indifference, her body started to respond to his urgent thrusts. Suddenly, she realized he wasn't just mindlessly hammering into her. His strokes were varying in both depth and angle, as if he was methodically sounding her out. One particular thrust drew a ragged gasp from her, and his fingers clenched on her shoulders. She quickly found herself faced with dozens of similar attacks, his raging cock plundering her every hidden weakness. In mere moments, she found herself crying out in ecstasy, her shrieks muffled by the pillow. With her peak closing in, she didn't notice when one of his hands released her. He rumbled in her ear and started to passionately kiss and nip at her neck.

She screeched as his fingers found her clit and rubbed it firmly. Her orgasm ripped through her, causing her entire body to quiver against his. He growled in triumph and continued to ravish her, his entire being reduced to lips and cock and fingers, all of it focused with a fanatical intensity on Kana's pleasure. She cried out again, his thorough loving driving the breath from her, and she started to drink in huge gulps of air. He growled deep in his throat and drove his cock into her one last time before exploding again in her welcoming depths. The aftershocks coursing through him bounced her up just enough for him to free his trapped arm. He draped it over her back again and held her tightly as he planted a deep, wet kiss on her sweat-slick neck.

"I love you," he mumbled against her flesh before nuzzling her shoulder.

Kana fought to catch her breath. She panted heavily and finally drew enough air to whisper a quick, "Holy fuck!" into his ear.

He chuckled, jostling their tangled bodies. "Is that good?" he asked before playfully nibbling her ear.

She clenched down on his softening cock and moaned in reply. "It was a lot of things," she replied, her voice still a shaky whisper. "*Good* doesn't begin to cover it." She swallowed a few times and cleared her throat while her mind slowly reassembled itself. Once the haze cleared, she turned her head and nuzzled his cheek. "What the hell? You running a two-for-one special today or something?"

"Um, yeah," he said in an embarrassed voice. "Something like that. The first one always hits a bit fast, but the second one takes longer."

Intrigued, she pressed on. "That happen to you with everyone else too?"

"You're the first."

She kissed his cheek hard then lifted her head enough to see his face. "Wow. They never knew what they were missing!"

His body tensed but then relaxed again just as quickly. He looked deep into her eyes and shook his head. "No, you don't get it." He ran his fingers through her hair before letting them trail down the center of her back. "You *are* the first. Like, *ever*."

Chapter Four: Hearts and Minds

Kana studied his face for any sign that he was joking. He continued to gaze up at her in complete adoration and her brow creased in a flustered frown.

"First? *Ever?*" Her questions only added to his bemused expression. The words rolled through her mind over and over and she gasped when she finally deciphered them. "You're a *virgin?*"

Jamyn laughed at her reaction. Palming her ass with both hands, he gave it a gentle squeeze. "Well, I'm no expert or anything, but I think you just took care of that."

She continued to frown at him in disbelief, even though she was fully enjoying the feel of his strong hands caressing her. "There's no way!"

Despite having gone soft, his cock was still trapped within her body, and he nudged his hips up against her. "You can't fool me," he said with a languid grin. "I was there."

"Not that, you goof!" She pressed back with her full weight to pin his pelvis to the bed and swatted his hands away. "You're twenty-two! How the hell could you still be a virgin?"

"Really?"

"Really!"

He chuckled at her insistence. "Come on, Kana. It's not that hard to figure out. I was ten before I could even interact with people normally. The next eight years were spent catching up on school, graduating, and spending every spare second learning magic from my grandma. She died a little over two years after that and then Qa showed up. Spent another two-plus years studying my ass off in the Sanctum. Now I'm here with you. Do the math."

"You're telling me that you never—"

"No, I never. Sure, I noticed girls. I *am* a guy, after all. And, yeah, I did the necessary research to figure out what I was supposed to do with 'em, *if and when*." They shared a quick laugh, and she shook her head at his clowning. "There just wasn't the time," he said with a shrug. "That and—" His words cut off and he hesitated.

"And what?"

"Well, I never met anyone that I wanted to be with."

His timid revelation crashed right into her heart, and she fought to maintain her composure. Determined not to let him see her eyes misting up, she fell forward and hugged him fiercely.

Discreetly dabbing her eyes on his pillowcase, she asked, "And now you have, huh?"

He nodded and wrapped his arms around her. "What do you think?" he murmured before kissing the side of her neck. His flaccid cock finally slipped from her body and they both sighed dreamily, then started laughing together at the shared moment.

Bolstered, she looked into his eyes and smirked. "So, on top of being friggin' gorgeous, you're going for thoroughly adorable too?"

He fought a blush and failed. "Um, yeah. If you say so."

The return of her unsure acolyte made her insides quiver, and she swallowed the lump in her throat. A small part of her mind protested the absurdity of the entire event but her newly roused heart shouted it down.

"Yeah," she whispered. "I do."

He thought for a moment and then grinned mischievously as he gripped her waist. "If you'd like, I could piss you off every now and then. You know, just to even things out. Sound good, mistress?"

The wave of conflicting emotions churning within her slammed into her hard. This time the tears came faster than she could hide them. She bit her lip at his look of concern and took a quick gasping breath.

"Just stop," she blurted.

"What?" he asked. "What did I do?"

She tried to respond but the inner conflict had stolen her voice. Pulling against his hold on her, she muttered, "Let go."

He released her at once. She shifted and fell onto the bed a small distance away, lying on her side facing away from him. He carefully rolled over toward her, though making sure not to let any part of his body touch hers.

"Kana?" he whispered. "Are you okay?"

"I'm fine," she instantly replied, quickly wiping her eyes with the back of her hand. "Fine."

He didn't press her further. "Okay." He nearly touched her hip, but she pulled away before he did. "Kana, I—"

"Don't."

He bit back a sigh. "Okay. Sorry."

Her shoulders slumped and she blew out her breath in a frustrated rush, making her body look like it was deflating. Flipping over, she brought her face right up to his.

She growled, anger chasing away her tears. "No, dammit. You're not sorry. And if you are, you shouldn't be." She pursed her lips and touched her forehead to his, then took a deep breath to steady herself. "This time, *I'm* sorry."

"For?"

"I just am."

"But you haven't—"

"Shut up." Desperation turned her command into a feeble plea. She scrambled to put her thoughts in order, but her mind refused to cooperate. Giving up, she blurted the only thing that came to mind. "Just shut up and be in love with me and hope to Hell I don't do something stupid to screw it up!"

"Like what?" he asked without thinking.

Groaning in disgust at herself, she hooked a hand behind his neck and held his forehead tightly to hers. "Dammit, Jamyn. *Think!* The last time someone told me they loved me right after sex—" She purposely cut her statement short to allow it time to filter into her acolyte's brain. "It didn't work out so good," she muttered at last.

"Oh, right," he said with a grimace, his memory obviously kicking in. "Then I won't—"

"No!" she cried. She closed her eyes, squeezing out a trickle of tears.

"Kana," he said gently, "please tell me what's wrong."

She drew in a labored breath. "You were about to tell me you loved me, right?"

"Right. But if you don't want me to—"

"That's the problem, dammit!" she cried. "I *do!*" She opened her tear-bright eyes and stared into his. "I *want* you to say it. Especially now that I believe it." Her gaze wandered away from him and she mumbled, "I just have no idea how to react to it."

He pulled her body against his and wrapped her in a firm embrace. Stealing a quick kiss, he murmured against her cheek. "I get it."

She hugged him in return and nodded. "Thank you," she whispered.

She closed her eyes and snuggled into his embrace, grateful for his understanding. Pulling him closer, she molded her body to his and nuzzled his neck. A sudden nudge against her thigh brought her back to the moment and her body stiffened.

"Is that your hand?" she asked, already guessing that it wasn't.

"Um, no." He tried to shift his pelvis away from her.

The unexpected contact and his fumbling retreat drew a brief smile from her. "Gearing up for round three?"

"No!" he replied, finally moving his lower body away from her. "You just—" He bit his tongue and hoped she would let the matter drop.

Happy that she wasn't the only one stumbling over their words, she continued her teasing. "*I just* what?"

Defeated, he replied, "You just feel way too damned good in my arms."

"Yeah?"

He sighed and shifted forward again, trapping his growing erection between their bodies. "Yeah. Better than I ever dreamed."

The compliment warmed her, and she playfully traced her fingernails over his back. "Likewise." Her sense of humor charged forward, and she reached down and pinched his butt. "You're not really ready to go again, are you?"

A shiver raced through his body at her question. "Um, yeah. Pretty much."

His words triggered a quiver in her belly that emerged as a clipped laugh. "Sheesh. How much stamina have you got anyway?"

"When it comes to you, a lot," he replied, trying to keep his tone light to hide his embarrassment at her question. He felt the tip of his erection nudging up toward her navel and he squirmed in her grasp.

She loosened her grip and leaned back so she could see his face. "How would you know that?"

He looked back at her, a shade of guilt in his eyes. "You really want to know?"

She came forward and kissed him, her lips a long and soft caress against his. Drawing back at last, she nodded. "Yeah, I do."

He swallowed hard. "I spent a lot of time fantasizing about being with you."

"Ah. And took matters into your own hands." He started to turn away in shame, but she snared his lips for another kiss. When they came apart, she playfully nudged the tip of his nose with hers. "Glad

I'm not the only one," she whispered, punctuating her words with a quick wink. Seeing his awestruck stare, she asked, "You heard me in the shower, right?"

He nodded and clenched his teeth as his cock throbbed against her soft skin.

She grinned. "I'm surprised my fingers haven't permanently pruned in the time that I've known you."

They shared a small laugh. "Sounds familiar. I was worried I'd break it before I even had the chance to be with you."

"Putting in a bit of overtime polishing it for the big event?"

"More than a bit."

"And that's how you figured out it's a little fast out of the chute the first time around."

He groaned. "Yeesh. Nice."

"Hey, don't sweat it." She laughed at his flustered expression. Lowering her voice, she brought her lips close to his. "You more than made up for it afterwards."

"Glad you liked it," he whispered. Suddenly he pulled away with a jerk and stared into her eyes. "Oh, my God!"

"What?" she asked, stunned by his retreat.

"I-I came inside you!"

"Yep. Twice." She waggled her eyebrows at him. "I was there." Despite her joke, his expression drooped even further. "What's with you?"

"I...I didn't—" he stammered. "I mean, we didn't have any protection!"

Despite his growing look of panic, she laughed heartily.

"Like hell we didn't!"

She released him and then scooted her body away from his. Waving a hand in front of his face, she pointed down their bodies.

"Look."

She watched his gaze scan down her body but then linger on her breasts.

"Down a bit farther, boy," she said, beckoning him on with a quick curl of her finger.

He followed her hand down until it hovered over her belly. She flicked her fingers outward and a glowing sigil appeared on her skin just below her navel.

"Just because I wanted to fuck your ever-lovin' brains out didn't mean I wanted a permanent reminder of it."

He gasped in wonder when he deciphered the many radiant symbols. "A blocking enchantment!"

"Crafted for just such an occasion. I activated it right before we started." She reached forward and grasped his rigid shaft. She traced the tip over the patterns on her skin and rumbled deep in her throat. "I've been called a *mother* before but I'm not about to take on the job for real."

He tried to laugh but it came out as a broken groan. He brought one hand up to stroke lightly through her hair while the other cradled her cheek.

His cock throbbed angrily in her hand and left streaks of pre-come over her belly. "Round three it is," she said, his gentle caresses sending trickles of rekindled desire skittering down her spine. She skimmed her hand down his shaft and cupped his balls. "Hey. Time-out for a second."

He immediately stopped and drew back. "What did I do?"

She laughed at his sudden look of dismay. "Easy there, big fella," she said, giving his shaft a quick stroke. "I just had an idea. You game?"

He glanced down at her intimate hold on him and then looked back at her incredulously. "You have to ask?"

She cupped her hand over his glans and gave it a quick circular stroke with her palm that had him gasping. "That's the spirit!" she said with a wicked grin. "Follow me."

She released him and rolled onto her back. Lifting her legs high in the air, she flared them around in a wide arc and hopped up out of the bed. Looking back at him over her shoulder, she batted her eyelashes at him. "You coming?"

He scrambled across the bed and stood up behind her. "Lead on, mistress," he said, sneaking in a quick caress of her backside.

His cock was at full attention again and she gawked at it. Aside from a slight bowing out from his body, it stood straight up. "You ever been checked for high blood pressure?"

"My blood pressure's normal. Why?"

She nodded down at his cock. "He looks fit to burst."

He relaxed again and chuckled. "Yeah, he's always like that."

"And pointing straight north, hmm?"

"Yeah. Bit of a pain." She cocked her head, and he winked at her. "Gotta be careful not to shoot my eye out when I'm by myself and thinking about you."

A burst of heat ignited between her legs, and she grasped his rigid shaft. "Can't have that now." She tugged it gently to get his feet moving and then led him into the bathroom.

Upon entering, he noticed the vacuum sphere in the corner holding his dirty clothes. "What happened to my clothes?"

"I sealed 'em up before your shower."

"Shower?"

"Yeah. You were ripe when the magic around you dissipated. I got you into the shower and cleaned you up before I put you to bed."

His jaw nearly dropped. "We showered together, and I missed it?"

She stole one last stroke up his cock and released him. "You didn't miss much. I cast an environmental screen on myself and kept my clothes on."

"But mine weren't. You sneaking a peek beforehand?"

"Yeah, right." She pointed at his cock. "He was shy the whole time." Ogling his fully aroused dimensions, she whistled low in appreciation. "Glad he got over it."

"So, what are we doing in here?"

His question broke her stare, and she smiled. "Two things. We kinda ruined our showers."

His heated gaze swept up over her sweat-slick breasts. "Yeah, kinda. What else?"

She slowly backed into the shower. "How about seeing what you missed?"

His cock pulsed and he licked his lips. "Which time?"

"Well, like I said, your shower was kinda uneventful." She turned on the water and gave his entire body a slow leer. "Aside from the *spectacular* view." Easing back into the steamy spray, she smiled craftily as the water cascaded down over her. She ran her hands down over her slick breasts and tummy before leaning back against the wall. "Want to see what happened after that?" she asked, skimming her fingertips over her erect nipples.

"Please," he replied, entranced by her wanton display.

She closed her eyes and let her hands wander over her body, much as she had done earlier. Her body thrilled to the familiar touch, and she reached down to stroke her clit with one hand while the other cupped a breast. In moments, she was panting heavily and charging headlong toward another orgasm. She uttered a long moan and was answered by a ragged gasp from Jamyn. Suddenly remembering that she was putting on a show for him, she turned around and bent over to display her shapely ass while continuing to stroke herself. The first tingles of her peak hit and she nearly lost her balance as she tried to plant her feet.

His strong hands gripped her waist, keeping her upright. The firm touch was enough to propel her over the edge and she came with a shuddering groan. The groan turned into a screech of delight as he slipped his cock into her from behind, just as he had during her fantasy. She abandoned her clit and eased her fingers to either side of his shaft as he filled her. He entered her slowly, her warm heat embracing every inch, and he dug his fingers into her hips as he fought the urge to just slam into her. His thighs eased up against her ass and he released a rumbling sigh. Suddenly he drew back and plunged forward again, taking her with as much force as he dared. She cried out and he froze.

"Too much?"

She brought her arms up and braced them against the wall.

"More!" she said, her breathing ragged. "Please!"

<hr />

He quickly complied, long-stroking his cock back and forth within her. She started to drive her body back onto his, meeting his every thrust. Gaining confidence from her movements, he abandoned restraint and pistoned his cock into her writhing form. Her moans increased and soon she was vaulting headlong into yet another orgasm. Her body spasmed and her feet slipped out from under her.

His incredible reflexes kicked in and he stopped in mid-stroke. Bending forward, he wrapped one arm around her waist and the other just beneath her breasts to keep her from falling. Hauling her upright, he struggled for a moment to lift her up off his trapped cock. Rather than lose his own footing and send them both crashing to the floor, he eased her down his shaft until he was again buried inside her. She panted and whimpered as he held her there, her latest peak having reduced her to a quivering wreck.

"You okay?" he whispered into her ear.

"Mm-hmm," came her weak reply.

Taking small shuffling steps, he walked them both out of the shower. Once he was sure she could stand on her own, he bent his knees and crouched down, slipping his cock out of her. A faint squeak of protest escaped her, and he quickly stood back up to restore his hold on her body. As he stood there, a sudden elation lit up his being. He reached back and turned off the water, then wrapped his arms around her body just under her breasts. He hugged her firmly and rested his cheek against her back.

I love you, Kana. He mouthed the words silently against her wet skin.

"Felt that," she whispered, weakly flailing a hand up to swat at his arms.

He smirked. "Tough," he whispered back.

He released her and grabbed a towel, then patted her entire body dry. Upon finishing, he quickly dried himself, keeping a close eye on his depleted mentor in case she should start to fall again. He discarded the towel and nudged her forward with a brief kiss upon her shoulder. Together they walked back to the bed, and he carefully laid her upon it. He covered her with a thin blanket before kneeling on the floor beside her.

Bringing his face close to hers, he whispered, "That was beautiful. Thank you."

"You're thanking me?" she asked with a weak laugh. "Pretty sure you've got that backwards."

He smiled and shook his head. "No way."

She tried to sneak another peek at his erection but could barely lift her head off the pillow. "You didn't come?"

"But you did. That's enough for me."

"You're shitting me."

He pressed a quick kiss to her forehead. "Just being with you is more than I could have ever hoped for. Coming is a bonus." He drew back and smirked. "Besides, I came twice before. Remember?"

"Yeah," she whispered. Fatigue finally pounced hard, and she sighed deeply.

"Get some rest, mistress. I'll go get us some"—he glanced at the clock on the wall—"breakfast."

"Not big on breakfast," she muttered, battling to keep her eyes open.

"Some lunch, then," he replied. "You could probably use the extra sleep. I've got some stuff to do anyway."

A brief spark of concern lit in her slitted eyes. "Like what?"

"Just odds and ends. No need to worry."

"Right. That's usually the first sign that I do."

He laughed and stroked her arm through the thin blanket. "Hey, I can take care of myself. I'm a big boy."

She arched one eyebrow and glanced down his body. Licking her lips, she said, "I'll give you that one." He rolled his eyes, and she chuckled softly. "Go on, *git*," she said with a brief laugh. "If you hang around, we'll just end up doing something that'll stick me in medical for a week."

"Can't have that now," he said before kissing her forehead again.

He stood up and walked over to his dresser. Bending over to open a lower drawer, he stopped and glanced back at the bed. Though her eyes were barely open, she was staring at him hungrily.

"Something I can help you with, miss?"

"Yeah. Go get me that potion I left in the bathroom."

He wagged a finger at her. "You need sleep, not a turbocharged gnomish aphrodisiac." Pulling out a pair of black jeans, he stood up and turned to her, his flagging cock pointing to her like divining rod. "Now stop staring at me like I'm a piece of meat and go to sleep or I'll paddle your butt."

"With that?" she asked impishly, eying his cock.

As much as he wanted to pounce on her, he held himself in check with an exasperated groan. Pulling the rest of his clothes from the dresser, he put them on quickly while trying not to make eye contact with his lusty mentor. Finishing, he looked back at her and spread his arms.

"There. All put away."

"Just wrapped up. I can fix that."

He looked back at her in disbelief. "Okay, I'm confused. Why the hell did it take us until now to do this?"

She shrugged and smiled languorously at him. "Cuz we're stupid."

He laughed as he approached the bed. "Point: Kana." Reaching her side, he stroked one finger along her cheek. "Now you get some rest."

She nuzzled his finger. "And you stay out of trouble."

"Deal."

Leaning down, he pressed a brief but heated kiss to her lips. "I'll be back soon," he whispered, brushing his lips over hers one last time.

"No problem," she replied against his mouth.

He stood and walked out of the bedroom, not pausing to look back at her. He was sure she was sound asleep by the time he reached his door.

⸻

Jamyn strolled as casually as he could through the stone corridors. Despite his calm appearance, he was frantically working out the details of the plan that was still evolving in his head. Only a few early risers shuffled about the halls, most of them in search of coffee or something stronger to start their day. The overwhelming elation that had filled him after his encounter with Kana was now a fleeting memory and he set his jaw in determination. A flicker of doubt tried to form in his mind, but he swiftly quashed it.

"If I show the slightest hesitation, I'm dead," he muttered under his breath. Thinking back to Kana's naked body snuggled into his bed, he shook his head. "No way in hell I'm gonna let that happen!"

His path took him on a meandering trek through the halls until he was in one of the unused corridors at the far side of the Sanctum's housing section. "This is it," he said, readying himself.

He strode purposefully down one hall and then stopped near its center. Turning to his side, he faced the blank stone wall. He took a deep breath, clenched his hands into fists, and cast a quick glance up and down the deserted corridor. He reached forward and knocked the stone once.

"Master Donta," he said quietly. "I wish to speak to you."

He waited for a response but received none.

"Master Donta, please. I need to speak to you."

Again, only an eerie silence greeted his words. He sighed impatiently and stole another quick look around to ensure he was alone.

Coming close to the stone he had knocked against, he whispered, "I know who you are."

A ring of flames engulfed him. He stood absolutely still in its center. Space warped around him, and he suddenly found himself pulled through the wall and into the room beyond it. The flames vanished but were swiftly replaced by multiple bands of solid iron that constricted around his body, pinning his legs together and his arms to his sides. The dimly lit room had only one large chair in its center. In the far corner, a spiral staircase led down into the floor. Jamyn recognized it as the one he had raced down during his previous visit. Settled into the chair was a heavily cloaked figure. A carved mask covered the occupant's face. Jamyn nodded at him in respect.

"Master Donta."

The iron bands around him tightened once but then relaxed.

"You will explain your words at once, Siska," Donta said.

"First, I thank you for my mistress's life—"

The bands gave him another menacing squeeze. This time, they did not loosen.

"I do not want your gratitude," Donta said. "I want an explanation."

"I was taken by an Aqiri." Jamyn gasped and squirmed against his bonds.

"And tried to kill Morel while under its influence," Donta said impatiently. "Your life is becoming more of a nuisance every moment you do not answer me."

"Aqiri. Merged with a demon." Jamyn's words came out in bursts limited by his strangled breath. "Found out through it." The bands loosened at last, and he took several deep, shuddering breaths.

Donta stared at him in silence until Jamyn had finally stopped gasping. "You think you know me?" Donta asked, his voice a low rumble.

"The demon only confirmed it," Jamyn replied. "I had suspected it since our encounter down in your chambers." He swallowed hard when he saw Donta's cloaked body stiffen. "Which I sincerely regret," Jamyn said, bowing his head low.

Donta leaped from his chair, strode up to his captive, and growled right in his face. "You are not supposed to remember any of that. Daystar made sure of it."

"I'm sorry," Jamyn said, trying not to cringe at the carved mask now a mere inch away. "I was able to recall the incident afterwards."

"So, you can not only bypass my wards but also counter Daystar's powers *and* escape the grasp of an Aqiri," Donta said in a sinister snarl. "You are now too dangerous to live." He raised one shrouded hand to Jamyn's face and chanted a few arcane words.

Something grabbed Donta's shoulder from behind. His arm was pulled away just enough to redirect the blast of power aimed at Jamyn's face. Instead of removing the acolyte's head, the beam shot from Donta's hand and struck the wall behind Jamyn. Its energy was immediately absorbed by the numerous warding spells protecting Donta's dwelling. Another hard yank sent Donta stumbling back toward his chair.

Path swiftly moved to stand between Jamyn and Donta. She crossed her arms in disgust and glared at the cloaked man.

Instead of flying into an unstoppable rage as Jamyn had expected, Donta merely sat back down. "This is your aspect of the Voice."

Shocked, Jamyn nodded. "Yes."

"Does it have a name?"

"Path."

"Interesting." Donta continued to observe her while her scowl of contempt only deepened. "Have any others seen it?"

"Kana has."

Donta nodded once and fixed his eyes upon Path. "Most interesting. You are supposedly only a novice with the Voice, yet you can manifest your aspect as a corporeal being and reveal it to others."

Path hurled him a withering glare. Reaching back, she swept one clawed hand down through Jamyn's bonds. The iron bands disintegrated at her touch, dissolving into swirls of magic that were swiftly absorbed into her body. Folding her arms across her chest again, she stared at Donta in a silent challenge.

Donta shifted his gaze back to Jamyn. "It seems upset."

"She."

"Excuse me?"

"*Her* name is Path."

"Impudent little beast."

Path lunged, her hands extended forward to throttle Donta, but Jamyn leaped at her and wrestled her back.

"Stop it, Path!" he cried, holding her tightly.

"Problem?" Donta asked, a growing amusement evident in his voice.

Path struggled to break free of Jamyn's grip, but he only squeezed her tighter. "I'm guessing she doesn't like you calling her names."

Suddenly, she stopped trying to escape and snapped her head back, smashing it into Jamyn's nose. His hold loosened and she wriggled free. Instead of launching at Donta again, however, she turned and glared at Jamyn.

Jamyn wiped away the tears in his eyes before pinching his bloody nose closed. "What was that for?" he asked his aspect.

"My words were not directed at it," Donta said.

Jamyn turned to face Donta. By the light tone of his voice, Jamyn suspected the cloaked figure was enjoying this mad exchange. "What?"

"They were meant for you."

Path flailed an arm to her side, gesturing at Donta to indicate her agreement with his words, and continued to frown deeply at Jamyn.

Donta went on in the same relaxed voice. "Curious. You did not know that was the source of its anger? Am I to understand that it also appeared without your direct involvement?"

Path rolled her eyes at Donta before fixing her stare upon Jamyn again.

"No, I didn't call her out," Jamyn mumbled, still holding his nose.

Donta gestured and a sudden blaze of intense heat filled Jamyn's nostrils. When the young man released his grip, he found that his nose was no longer bleeding. "A good thing she did show up, otherwise you would have killed me!"

"You are that unsure of your defense?"

"My magic is locked down by Evrok's anchor spell. I can't cast."

Donta waved a hand forward, casting a spell to analyze Jamyn's body. The scan came back negative, and Donta whispered, "Your aura is not there." He shifted his attention back to Path. "It not only came out on its own but was also able to consume my binding spell. How is that possible?"

"I don't know," Jamyn replied. "Lately, she's been nearly autonomous. As far as her absorbing your spell, that appears to be part of my abilities with the Voice."

"This goes beyond mere willcasting," Donta said. "Do you realize what you are saying, Siska? You have—"

"Another semi-independent being living within me. And, yes, I know what that could mean. It's part of why I'm here."

Donta chuckled once in obvious scorn. "To help allay my concerns?"

"To negotiate your silence."

Donta's cloaked hands gripped the arms of his chair, and he snarled at the acolyte. "You would dare come to me with the threat of blackmail?"

"Of course not," Jamyn said in an unwavering voice. "I'm not that stupid. I just want us to come to an understanding."

Donta bristled beneath his heavy cloak. "The nature of this 'understanding'?"

"I know who you are," Jamyn said bluntly, "and you now know what I possibly am. I'm suggesting that we both keep it to ourselves."

"You insolent little—"

"I am not finished," Jamyn shouted back at the seer. "Aside from our identities, there is one other thing I have come to discover." He bared his teeth and growled. "That Aqiri got into me because of you. You were carrying a shred of demon essence when I attacked you. You released it and it led that damned Aqiri right to me."

Donta took in his words in silence. He released his grip on the chair and looked down at one covered hand.

After several seconds, he looked back at Jamyn. "It appears you are correct."

"Where did you get that essence?" Jamyn asked, the question erupting as a blatant command for an answer.

"From the remains of the lizard demon you defeated on Letron 12-B," Donta replied. "I had retained it for further study."

"So, there it is," Jamyn said. "We both have plenty of things we would rather not have the rest of the Sanctum find out about. I attacked you and you nearly got Kana and I killed. I say we call it even, keep our mouths shut, and work together for a change!" He spread out his arms in supplication. "What say you?"

Donta considered his words for nearly a minute, the entire time slowly sweeping his gaze over both Jamyn and Path. Finally, he stood up and swiftly walked right up to Jamyn. The younger man didn't flinch at his rapid approach. Donta nodded once before rumbling his answer.

"Agreed."

Jamyn fought to keep his expression neutral. He bowed his head once and then looked back at Donta. "Thank you."

Path shrugged and walked over to Jamyn. She gave Donta a playful swat on the behind as she passed him. She turned to him and waved once before disappearing and rejoining Jamyn's mind.

Jamyn swallowed nervously. "Sorry about that."

Much to the acolyte's surprise, Donta chuckled quietly. "Understand this, Siska," he said in the same low voice, "this arrangement relies on your compliance with its terms. Make one mistake and you will know how I gained my title."

"I already know," Jamyn replied, "and I do not wish to remind anyone of it. We are all here to maintain the Balance. Let's focus on that."

"Yes," Donta said quietly, "let's."

He gestured and a ring of flame surrounded Jamyn. When the inferno dissipated, the acolyte was gone.

Chapter Five: Patch Job

The flames obscuring his vision vanished and Jamyn found himself back in the hallway outside Donta's quarters. As before, the corridors around him were vacant. He blew out the breath he felt like he had been holding the entire time of his visit and then resisted the urge to pump his fist in the air in triumph.

That went surprisingly well.

His smile continued to grow. He had initially hoped just to survive the encounter with all his limbs intact. Now that Donta's cooperation had actually been obtained, Jamyn's spirits soared. He took a moment to bask in the victory.

"Next stop on the comeback tour: medical," he said before starting off at a brisk pace down the hall. He chose the fastest route there and went into a loping jog. Speeding around a corner, he nearly collided with a group of neophytes. "Whoa!" He came to an abrupt stop before he could mow them down.

The cluster of two girls in their mid-teens and one older boy gawked at him for a second but then they all quickly bowed in respect.

"Could you please help us, sir?" one of the girls asked timidly.

"'Sir'?" Jamyn asked with an incredulous laugh before shaking it off. "What do you need?"

"We're looking for training room number six," the girl replied, her head still bowed.

Jamyn looked them over in amusement and his giddy mood took over. "Nope. First thing you're looking for is me. Heads up! Let's see who I'm talking to."

The three slowly raised their heads but were still reluctant to look him in the eye. Jamyn waved his hands in front of them and then pointed back at his own face. "C'mon, people. Eyes front." They finally looked directly at him, and he nodded in approval. "That's better. Now who have we got here?"

"Karen," the blond-haired girl who had spoken to him first replied.

"I'm Marty," the boy said solidly.

"Ann," the darker-haired girl mumbled.

"Very good," Jamyn said. "My name's Jamyn. Good to meet you."

Karen started again. "Sir, could you please—"

"Okay, stop right there," Jamyn said, holding up a hand to her. "I'm just an acolyte. No *sir* for me, thanks."

"An acolyte?" Marty asked. "You?"

Jamyn looked to him. "Yeah. And that's so hard to believe because..."

Marty tried to stand firm, but his eyes betrayed his unease. "Well, you're kinda old."

Jamyn stifled a burst of laughter. "I guess you're right. But hey, I only got to the Sanctum about two years ago. I think I can get a pass there."

Karen's light eyebrows rose. "You made acolyte in only two years?"

"Sure did. How long have you guys been here?"

"About three months," Karen replied.

"Nice," Jamyn said with an approving nod. "Keep at it and someday you'll have a master to beat some sense into you on a regular basis too. You said you were headed for training room six, right?" The trio nodded. "Okay. Who wants to hold the map?"

"Map?" Karen asked.

"A volunteer!" Jamyn said. "Great! Give me your hand. Palm up." She held it up at once and he tried to cast a quick spell. Nothing happened and he made a face. "What the-—" His memory kicked in and he chided himself quietly. "Anchor spell, you dope." Seeing the teens' inquisitive looks, he laughed and shrugged. "Plan B it is." He looked up and called out. "Sanctum?"

A disembodied voice replied, "Jamyn."

"Could you help these fine folks get to training room six?"

A glowing line appeared on the floor. It extended up the hall before turning a corner off in the distance. "Route marked."

"Thanks." Jamyn gestured at the line. "There's your path. Who are you guys going to see?"

"Lob the Unmarred," Marty said, obviously impressed with their instructor. "Basic defense."

Jamyn nodded. "Nice. Lob's a lot of fun. Just keep your eyes open around him. He loves sneak attacks."

Marty smiled. "Yeah. He's great."

Ann tugged on Karen's sleeve. "We're gonna be late," she mumbled while giving Jamyn an uneasy look.

Jamyn shook his head. "Don't worry about it. Just tell Lob that I held you guys up. He already knows I'm a troublemaker."

"And your name was Jamyn?" Karen asked.

"Yep. Jamyn Siska."

At this, Ann's body stiffened. "Your master is Kana Morel!" she whispered in awe.

Her friends stood up straighter as well and regarded him with stunned expressions. Instantly, all three of them were bowing again, even lower than before.

"Um, yeah," Jamyn replied, confused by their sudden reverence. "Is that a problem?"

"We're sorry for bothering you, sir!" Karen said in a rapid stream.

"Whoa, whoa, whoa," Jamyn said, holding up his hands to them. "What's with all this *sir* stuff again?"

Ann tugged on Karen's sleeve again and the blond nodded quickly. "We...we have to go!" Karen said in a strained squeak. "Thank you for your help!" In a flash, the trio was racing down the hall following the marked path.

Jamyn watched them go and rubbed the back of his neck.

What the heck was that all about?

He pondered it a moment longer before shrugging and continuing on his own way.

A few minutes of dodging the increasing corridor traffic later, he was at the entrance to the medical wing. Girding himself, he walked in and looked around. As usual, the beds were all empty and the wing seemed likewise free of staff.

Heading back toward the main office, Jamyn called out. "Master Leel? Mistress Tiris?" Walking through the office door, he found Leel sitting on a chair and panting heavily. "Are you all right, Master Leel?" Jamyn asked in concern.

Leel waved a small hand at him and nodded several times, all the while forcing himself to calm down and take in deeper breaths. "Fine. I'll be fine." He took a very deep breath, held it for two seconds, and then blew it out forcefully. "Better." Looking up at Jamyn, he asked, "What can I do for you, Mister Siska?"

"I was hoping to talk to both you and Mistress Tiris."

"Careful with that kind of talk," Leel replied with a faint smile.

Before Jamyn could respond, Tiris's voice sounded behind him. "You just hush, Leely. He can call me *mistress* all he likes." She punctuated her words with a playful pat on Jamyn's butt. Sweeping past him, she went straight to Leel's side. She embraced Leel warmly and planted a loud smacking kiss on his cheek. Turning back to Jamyn, she said, "Well, you look just fine." Sweeping her gaze from his face down to his crotch and then back again, she smiled craftily. "Really, really fine!"

"Calm down, siren," Leel said, wrapping an arm around her waist to prevent her from lunging forward. "What's up, Jamyn?"

Jamyn swallowed, his nerves starting to jostle. "I'd like to thank you both for saving Kana's life."

Leel waved a hand at him while giving Tiris another firm hug. "Pah. It's what we do here. No thanks are necessary."

Tiris giggled. "Besides, Kana already thanked us several times." She nuzzled Leel's ear. "And some of those were quite enjoyable."

"Still, I just wanted to add my thanks," Jamyn said.

Leel considered Jamyn's concerned expression. "Do you know how she got those injuries?"

"Um, yeah." Jamyn winced. "I did it." Before they could respond, he continued. "I was under the influence of an Aqiri. It attacked Kana."

"You have apologized to Kana?" Leel asked in a suddenly stern voice.

"Repeatedly," Jamyn replied, nodding emphatically.

Tiris hugged her husband, stood on her tiptoes, and pressed a kiss to the top of his head. "Calm down, husband mine," she said. "She must have forgiven him; otherwise, she wouldn't have come to get that potion for him. Right?" She turned back to Jamyn. "From the looks of you, I'd say the potion did its job."

"It worked great," Jamyn said. "Thank you both for that too."

Leel chuckled. "Thank her," he said, nodding at Tiris. "She's the one who decided to amp it up for you."

Tiris giggled and released her hold on Leel. "On that note, let's see how it's doing!" She waved a hand at Jamyn and a hazy aura of light surrounded his body. "Hmm. It healed everything that was broken, but why is it—" Her words were cut off as a bright spark coalesced on the surface of the cloud and snapped with the sound of a miniature thunderclap. "Now that's odd. Your aura isn't absorbing the excess the way it should. Have you tried casting since you recovered?"

"Just once, but it didn't work. Evrok's anchor spell has my magic locked down."

Tiris's expression drooped. "Oh, crud."

"What?" Jamyn asked. "What's wrong?"

Leel laughed. "Just that my wife is a little troublemaker and sometimes it catches up with her." he said, swatting her ass in playful reproach. He stood up and commandeered Tiris's spell to analyze the flow of magic around Jamyn's body. "How are you feeling?"

"I feel good," Jamyn said, trying to assure him despite the guilty look on Tiris's face. "I feel really good."

Leel grinned at him. "Like you could bench press Lester or arm wrestle Lob, I'm guessing."

Jamyn shrugged. "Sort of. I just feel kinda...I dunno. *Super* confident?"

Leel laughed again, louder this time, and canceled the scanning spell. He turned and wagged a finger at his wife. "See? *This* is why you have to be careful with potion strengths."

She pouted. "I just wanted—"

"To give him a boost that he could then give to Kana." Leel finished with a crafty grin.

Jamyn tried to muffle a burst of laughter but failed.

The gnome turned to face him. "Something wrong?"

"Um, no," Jamyn said, trying hard not to smile at the flicker of recognition on Tiris's face. "It's nothing."

"You did it, didn't you?" she whispered.

Jamyn's buoyant mood quickly overran his shyness, and his smile erupted in full force. Before he could answer, however, Leel spoke up.

"That is absolutely *none* of our business, my dear," he said to his nosy wife. Looking up at Jamyn, he smirked. "You looking like the cat who got the cream isn't helping."

Jamyn swiftly tamped down his smile. "Sorry, Master Leel." He looked at Tiris. "Sorry for giving you the wrong idea, Mistress Tiris."

"Then you didn't?" Tiris asked in a hurt voice.

Leel quickly pinched her butt. "Stop that, minx!"

She stuck her lower lip out in an exaggerated pout. "You're no fun."

"I will debate that with you at length as soon as we're able," he said quietly as a devilish gleam lit in his eyes. Turning his attention back to Jamyn, he asked, "Where is Kana?"

"In my quarters," Jamyn replied. "She needed some sleep."

Tiris squeaked loudly and looked like she about to explode.

"No!" Jamyn said quickly. "She was just really tired after all that stuff with the Aqiri."

Leel arched an eyebrow at him.

Jamyn fought with all his might to keep his expression neutral. "She gave me the potion and then laid down to take a nap after I recovered. That's all."

"Always leave 'em a tangled, sweaty mess and gasping your name," Leel said with a lecherous grin.

"Hey!" Tiris laughed and stroked a hand down over the front of her husband's pants. "Now who's prying?"

A melodic voice floated in from past the doorway. "Master Leel?"

The three faced the door to see Daystar standing there.

"Oh!" she cried in surprise. "Hello, Mister Siska!"

"Daystar!" Leel said happily.

Tiris gave his cock a firm squeeze before backing away a step.

He cleared his throat and spoke again, this time at a much more restrained volume. "What brings you here?"

"A troublesome reoccurrence," she replied. She stepped to the side and ushered in a dark-skinned teenaged boy. "It seems Bhatal has injured his shoulder."

"Again? I thought Nigel fixed that for him yesterday."

"He did," Daystar replied, "but Bhatal has undone your acolyte's fine work."

Leel stepped forward and cast a spell over Bhatal's shoulder. "Ooh, I'll bet that stings," Leel said, noting the angry splotches of red light hovering over the injured joint.

Bhatal nodded silently.

"What caused this little relapse?"

Before Bhatal could answer, Daystar giggled merrily. "Trying too hard to impress his instructor, no doubt. He tried to block an attack that he should have dodged. Right, Bhatal?"

The youngster bowed his head and mumbled, "Yes, Miss Daystar."

She ruffled her fingers through his short hair, eliciting a shy smile from the youth. "Will he live?" she asked Leel in a playfully dramatic tone.

The gnome grinned. "I think he just might. Just give me a moment. I'll patch him up."

"Mistress Daystar," Jamyn said. "I'd like a word with you, if I could."

"Of course!" she said cheerfully, her aura flaring out around her.

She linked her arm around his and they walked out into the vacant wing, closing the office door behind them. No sooner had the door closed when Daystar cast a privacy spell around them to ensure their conversation would not be overheard. She released his arm and hurried down the aisle between the rows of beds. Jamyn followed her and then stopped when she abruptly spun to face him.

"I have been wanting to speak to you as well, Mister Siska," she said, her carefree tone disappearing.

"I figured," he said, seeing her uncharacteristic look of worry. "You've spoken to Donta?"

"I have not, but he has sent me a message. He told me you were able to recall what happened in his chambers."

"I was."

She took in his contrite look with a flustered frown. "How?"

"I have the ability to record events around myself and then recall them in detail later. I guess your suggestion wasn't able to erase it."

"Impossible," Daystar said. "It should have been completely wiped from your conscious mind."

Jamyn considered this. "Maybe Path had something to do with it."

"Path?"

"My aspect of the Voice." He looked to her side.

Path suddenly appeared standing next to Daystar. The young girl was now wearing what looked like a classic schoolgirl outfit.

Daystar cried out at the abrupt arrival. "Oh!"

Path smoothed down her crisp white blouse and plaid skirt. She curtsied before Daystar and offered her a bright smile. She waved quickly at Jamyn and then stood up straight, giving the appearance of a dutiful student.

Jamyn chuckled at the show. "Mistress Daystar, this is Path. She's being kind of a goofball today." Path stuck her tongue out at him, and he laughed again.

"This is extraordinary!" Daystar looked over the girl now standing at attention again. "Why can I see her?"

"I'm not sure," Jamyn replied. "She seems to have a lot more to her than other aspects. Part of that is being able to reveal herself to others."

Daystar glanced back at him before returning her perplexed gaze to Path. "You mean you're not actively revealing her?"

"No."

Her confusion turned to a deep concern. "But that means—"

"I know. She's a semi-independent entity living within me. And, yes, Donta and I both share your concerns about what that could possibly mean."

Daystar gasped. "Donta knows too?"

"Yes."

"Jamyn, that's not—"

Jamyn cut her off again. "We've come to an agreement. I would like the same from you."

"And that is?"

"Donta and I both know things about each other that no one else really needs to know. We've agreed to keep quiet and work together. I ask for your silence on the matter as well."

Daystar mulled over his words. "I assume that what happened between Donta and I is to be included in this pact."

"Anything going on between you and Master Donta is your business. I have no right to pass that information to anyone, regardless of what you decide." Jamyn sighed and looked into Daystar's eyes. "And I'm very sorry that I intruded the way I did."

"As am I," Daystar said, a hint of fondness in her voice. "My dealings with Donta are...complicated. Others would likely have very strong opinions on them."

"Which is why I shall not divulge them to anyone." He looked to Path, and she nodded in agreement.

"Even Kana?"

"*Especially* Kana."

Daystar cocked her head, and her aura started to pulse faintly around her. "You would keep this from the woman you love?" she whispered.

Jamyn nodded. "I would. She will not be harmed by not knowing."

"And if she did know—"

"It would cause needless problems."

Daystar nodded before canceling the privacy spell. "Then you have my agreement, Mister Siska."

Path clapped and rushed forward. She caught Daystar in a tight hug before taking her hand and pressing a kiss to it. Daystar looked down into the girl's amber eyes and suddenly uttered an astonished cry.

"Knock it off, Path," Jamyn said.

"No!" Daystar protested with a joyous laugh. She swept Path up in her arms, firmly kissed the girl's cheek, and then started to tickle her.

Path opened her mouth in a silent shriek and pried herself from Daystar's grasp, stumbling several steps back toward Jamyn.

Jamyn frowned down at Path's beaming face. "What's with you?"

Daystar swiftly admonished him through her jubilant smile. "Don't scold the poor girl! Her delirious state is merely a reflection of your own!"

"Huh?"

Path poked him in the ribs and Daystar laughed again.

"Come now, Mister Siska," Daystar said knowingly. "You really think you can hide it from me?"

Jamyn puzzled over her words for a second before realizing what she meant.

"Oh," he said, trying not to blush. "That."

"Yes, *that!*" Daystar swept forward and embraced Jamyn. She hugged him fiercely and kissed his cheek the same way she had done to Path. "And where is my sweetling now?" she whispered in his ear.

"My place," Jamyn replied, squirming in her grasp as he felt his cock starting to harden. "Resting."

Daystar pinched his butt. "You unfeeling brute!" Path slipped behind him and tickled his ribs. He opened his mouth to cry out and suddenly found it filled with Daystar's hot tongue. She kissed him deeply, pressing her tantalizing body even closer to his. Just as he was about to protest, she released him and took a quick step back.

"You march right back there and tend to her every last need and desire," she said with a lusty gleam in her eye.

Jamyn reined in his swirling thoughts and mirrored her bright smile with his own. "I fully intend to, once she's rested again."

Daystar laughed. "Oh, so you've tuckered her out. Well done!"

"No! I—" He cut off his words when he noticed that the office door was now open. Leel was standing in the doorway grinning at him. Bhatal stood beside him and stared at them all in shock.

"Do continue," Leel said with a wide smile while stealing a glance at Daystar's lithe form.

Jamyn let out an aggravated sigh and held his tongue.

Daystar laughed at his consternation. "Have you fixed my dark prince?" she asked Leel before nodding to Bhatal.

Leel tried not to laugh at the tiny squeak Bhatal had uttered at Daystar's question. "He's fine. Ready to be repeatedly pounced upon by his favorite instructor." He quickly latched on to Bhatal's arm to steady him, as the youth's body had started to sway dangerously. "Easy there, lad," Leel said with a grin. "No fainting and hurting yourself again."

Daystar looked solidly at her student. "And what do we say?"

Bhatal turned to Leel and bowed low. "Thank you, Master Leel."

Leel shook his head. "Why is everyone intent on thanking me for just doing my job today?"

Two arms wrapped around him from behind. "Because you're just that good," Tiris murmured in his ear before playfully nibbling it.

He smiled. "Yes, I suppose that's true."

The group laughed.

Daystar extended a hand to Bhatal. "Come, Bhatal. Let's not waste any more of the healers' time." He hurried to her side, and she cast a spell over them. The pair disappeared in a bright flash.

Leel looked past Jamyn and cocked his head when he saw Path. "Hello, who have we here? Another injured student?"

Jamyn shook his head. "No, Master Leel. This is Path. She's my aspect of the Voice."

Path took a step forward and curtsied as she had done earlier to Daystar.

"A visible aspect," Leel said, considering the young girl. "You certainly are full of tricks, Mister Siska." Arching an eyebrow at the young girl, Leel smiled. "Nice outfit." Glancing over his shoulder, he asked Tiris, "Don't you have one like that?"

She nipped at his neck. "You know I do, you little demon," she replied, nuzzling his ear.

Leel looked at Path again. "I would very much like to see it again," he whispered, reaching back to grab Tiris's ass. Looking up at Jamyn, he said, "You should—"

"Already gone!" Jamyn said in a rush. "Back inside," he told Path.

After a quick giggle at the tangled healers, she nodded and vanished.

"Thanks again!" he said before breaking into a run straight out of the medical wing.

Chapter Six: Comfort Level

"Are you feeling all right, Kana?"

The teen glanced up from where she sat to see her new master smiling down at her.

"Yeah," she replied half-heartedly. "I'm just kind of tired."

"Not surprising, given the intensity of your workout."

She looked down and shrugged while she continued to pluck strands of tall grass from the field. "I guess."

Qa squatted beside her. "Is something else troubling you?"

She shook her head, keeping her gaze pointed resolutely at the ground. "No."

The older man considered her reply and sighed. "Kana, if there is anything—"

"There's not."

Qa nodded once and stood back up. "Then I shall be going."

Her head snapped upright. "Going? Where?"

"Back to the Sanctum. I have a few things that need tending. I thought perhaps you might want to spend a little more time here. You seem to enjoy this place."

She looked around at the sprawling fields of this section of the fabricated pocket world known as the wilds. "Yeah," she said. "Nice and peaceful here."

"Like back home?"

At this, her expression soured. "Not at all like that crap heap," she grumbled.

"Of course not. My apologies." He reached down and swiftly ran one finger across the top of her right hand. A series of glowing wavy lines appeared on her skin and then faded to reveal Qa's personal glyph.

Her sense of awe at the spell quickly gave way to a burst of outrage. "Hey!" she said before scrambling to her feet. She clutched her hand to her chest and glared at him.

"Once again, I am sorry, Kana. I should have asked first."

"Damn right," she muttered under her breath. She continued to massage her hand as if he had burned it. Looking at the pattern he had left there, she asked, "So what's this?"

"A glyph. Which is..."

"A magical symbol used in the casting or execution of some spells," she replied, reciting the exact definition from her lessons. "I meant, what does it do?"

"It signals the mages back in the Sanctum to open a gate so you can return. Just run a finger along the lines like this." He held up his own hand to show her an identical glyph upon it, then stroked his index finger in the direction of the lines. A few seconds later, a glowing doorway of light appeared beside him. "If there is nothing else, I shall leave you to recover."

"No," she said with a shake of her head. "I'm good." Qa started to walk into the gate but then turned back and arched an eyebrow at her. "What?"

"Greeting and parting etiquette?" he asked with his usual placid smile.

"Oh. Yeah." She straightened up and bowed once to him. "Thank you for the training, Master Qa."

"You are quite welcome, Acolyte Morel," he replied. "And please work on that. Remember that your future instructors may not be quite as forgiving with such a lapse." With this, he went through the gate, and it vanished.

"Yeah, yeah," she mumbled before clapping a hand over her mouth.

Qa always seemed to hear every single comment she made. It didn't matter how quietly she spoke or even if he was in the same room. Somehow, he always knew.

Gotta be careful with that. Don't wanna say the wrong thing and get my ass booted outta here.

Taking in the scenery again, she let herself get lost in the wonder of this made-up world tucked away between planes of existence.

Damn. How cool is this?

She stretched her arms high over her head and drew in a deep breath. The sun was now almost directly overhead, and the summer heat embraced her gangly body. Despite her denials, the nearby forest did remind her a little of the wooded areas around Azure Junction where she had grown up.

"But here there's no good ol' boys or locked-up secrets or none o' all that bullshit!" she shouted.

She listened intently for a moment and smiled at the complete silence. Qa had magically cordoned off this part of the wilds, ensuring that they could train in peace without any of the local denizens disturbing them, so she decided to take full advantage of the solitude.

"The Junction c'n suck mah purty lil' ass!" Kana cried, slipping back into the accent she had tried so hard to hide ever since joining the Sanctum. "Y'all c'n just bite me! Y'hear?" She whooped loudly but then fell silent as she thought she heard the faintest hint of a giggle off in the distance.

In a flash, she was crouched in an attack stance, a pulsing aura of magic surrounding her balled fists. "Who's there?" she said loudly as she scoured the woods for any signs of movement.

She hoped it had just been her imagination, since the glow around her hands was about all the magic she could safely perform, but her rebellious side still yearned for a fight. Only silence answered her shouted question, and she started to feel silly.

"Qa said the critters—" She stopped and set her jaw. "The animals around here are locked out," she said, taking care to form the words. "No one's here but me."

She extinguished the light around her hands and took a deep breath.

Gazing into the woods again, she set off for them at a brisk pace. "You're jumping at shadows again, Morel," she told herself as she walked.

Though she was much less skittish than she had been when she had arrived at the Sanctum two months before, she still found herself spooked by the slightest things. True, magic always came with some element of surprise attached to it. Now that she knew she could command it, however, it was much less of a shock.

Just keep your head, girl. She weaved her way through the tangled foliage. *You'll get the hang of all this magic stuff.* A grin curled the corners of her mouth. *And then watch out, world!*

Her trek had carried her far enough into the woods that she could no longer see the field where she and Qa had worked out earlier. The sound of bubbling water ahead caught her attention and she hurried up a small rise. She fought the urge to break into a run up the slope, which was fortunate as the ground there suddenly ended. Just as she stepped out into open space, she quickly lurched backward, losing her balance and landing on her butt.

She yelled at herself, disgusted with her latest mental lapse. "Pay attention, dammit!" Standing up again, she peeked over the rise to see what lay beyond.

A secluded alcove was cradled a few feet below the rise where she was standing. Centered in it was a large calm pool of fresh water. Kana had found similar ponds near her home and knew them to be fed by underground springs. The promise of a quick swim to fend off the day's heat spurred her feet into a quick sprint down the side of the rise. Soon she was crouched beside the pond and trailing her hand through it.

"Not too cold," she said before pulling off her t-shirt, shorts, and shoes. She started to remove her sport bra but then stopped as a twinge of pain shot through one budding breast. She groaned and carefully rubbed the sore spot.

Damned growth spurts.

She decided to leave her panties on as well and stepped into the water.

Much to her surprise, the ground dropped off after only a few feet. She caught herself and starting treading water in the surprisingly deep pond. The cool water felt great against her skin, drawing a pleased sigh from her. Leaning her head back, she floated in place and gazed up through the dense forest canopy.

"This is awesome," she said as she swept her arms to her sides.

Every so often she kicked a foot out, sending a plume of water high into the air. One especially hard kick sent a splash out into the woods and Kana heard a surprised squeak. Bolting upright, she started treading water again while she searched for the source of the sound.

"Who's there?" She forced the words through the icy fingers of fear clutching at her throat.

There was no response, but she was certain someone was watching her. Fighting back the all-too-familiar wave of terror rising in her mind, she focused her senses on where she believed an unknown watcher could be hiding. Her vision clouded and suddenly the air was filled with hazy swirls of light. It undulated all around like a lazy river except for one point off in the distance. There the light twisted and churned in a miniature whirlpool.

"I can see you," Kana said, directing her words at the spot.

A voice like the tinkling of hundreds of tiny bells replied in surprise. "You can?" The swirl of light dissipated but then reappeared several yards to the right.

Despite the sudden tingling that rushed through her body at the sound of the voice, Kana shouted angrily toward the new vortex. "Stop playin' around! I can still see you!"

"Quite extraordinary!" The voice now chimed from the new spot.

The swirl expanded in size until it formed into the vague outline of a person. The figure snapped into focus and Kana blinked several times to clear her vision. When she opened her eyes, her eyesight was normal again. Someone now stood right next to the pond. Kana's jaw dropped upon seeing the newcomer.

A blond woman a few inches taller than Kana looked back at the teen with a dazzling smile. She was dressed in a flowing garment of sheer white fabric that did little to conceal her lithe body. A faint glow surrounded her flawless skin, wrapping her in a pulsing aura of light. Her abundant breasts sat high upon her chest and her long legs carried her a step closer to the swimming girl.

"Hello!" the woman called out, her jubilant voice making it sound like she couldn't possibly be happier to see Kana.

"Who...who are you?" Kana stammered, completely disarmed by the stunning woman.

"My name is shared only with friends," the woman replied, her tone both teasing and promising. "Are you a friend?"

"I...um...I guess I—" Kana's words stumbled over one another as her mind struggled to right itself. "My name's Kana," she blurted at last.

"Ah, yes!" the bright woman exclaimed. "You're Qa Shon's new acolyte!" Her brilliant blue eyes fixed on Kana's bewildered stare. "You are Kana Morel!"

The words sent a sudden quiver through Kana's belly that quickly dipped even lower. She gasped and clapped a hand over her crotch to help quell the sudden pulsing between her legs. Without her other arm helping to keep her afloat, her head dipped below the water. In her confusion, she inhaled a mouthful of water and started to flail her arms. Suddenly an unseen force thrust down into the water, and something clamped down onto her shoulders. Then all was a blur as her body was yanked out of the pond. She sailed through the air before landing softly on her back on the ground near the water's edge. She coughed and sputtered before a hand gently touched her chest just between her breasts. A soothing warmth spread through her that instantly cleared her lungs and calmed her racing mind. She blinked several times to clear her vision. When it did, she stared up in utter astonishment.

An angelic face framed by cascading platinum blond curls beamed down at her. "I am sorry for startling you so," the woman said in a soothing tone. Looking at the hand still touching Kana's chest, a trace of sadness briefly clouded her radiant expression. "Your heart has been hurt," she whispered.

Kana could only nod in silent reply. A twinge of pain started to surface in her heart, but the strange woman's touch quickly subdued it. The woman broke the subtle contact and Kana whimpered softly at the loss.

"No more," the woman said with a slow shake of her head. Her gaze locked on Kana's silvery-blue eyes. "Your heart is strong, little one. It deserves to be cherished." She seemed to come to a decision and nodded once. "Love will find you, my sweetling," she whispered, her words thick with passion. "Have no fear on that." With this, she stood up and started to turn away.

The unexpected parting spurred Kana's tongue. "Who are you?"

The woman had stopped her retreat just before Kana had spoken, adding to the young girl's amazement.

She looked down at Kana with a blissful smile. "For now, you may call me Daystar. We will speak again."

Kana watched her start to walk away. Though she wanted to sit up to watch her go, her body was content to merely lie there upon the ground. A bolt of urgency rocketed through her mind, and she raised her voice.

"Thank you, Mistress Daystar!"

All at once, Daystar's smiling face was mere inches from her own. "You are most welcome, Kana," she whispered before pressing a gentle kiss to Kana's lips.

Suddenly Daystar's body dissolved into wisps of light that dissipated into the humid air. Kana, eyes wide and heart pounding, stared up into the trees and let the luminous Daystar's words filter into her wounded heart.

Kana woke and stirred beneath the blanket covering her. The dream had fled but the words still echoed in her mind.

Love will find you.

She hugged the thin blanket to her chest. Tears started to gather in her eyes, and she sighed at the awakened memory.

"It did, Mistress Daystar," she whispered. "Thank you."

Opening her eyes, she saw the ceiling of Jamyn's bedroom. Recalling their recent erotic interlude helped to chase her tears and turn her uncertainty back into a glowing passion. The slight sound of a page turning caught her attention. Looking down her body, she saw Jamyn sitting in a chair at the foot of the bed. He was closely studying a tattered, hide-bound book and didn't appear to notice that she was awake. She grinned and opened her mouth to speak but his voice stopped her short.

"How are you?" he asked gently without looking up from his reading.

She wriggled beneath the blanket, enjoying the trapped warmth embracing her naked body. "I'm good. You?"

He closed the book and looked back at her, his eyes bright. "Unbelievable," he said with a smile.

"How's that?"

He gestured to her and then placed the book on the floor at his feet. "Kana Morel is naked in my bed and I'm still alive." He thought for a moment. "Actually, *unbelievable* doesn't quite do it. I'm *out-damned-standing!*"

She laughed at his enthusiasm. "And when I finally get up out of your bed?"

"Same thing, but with a much better view."

She took in the compliment while she snaked her left leg out from under the blanket. Pointing her bare foot at him, she said, "You, my sneaky little acolyte, are trying to flatter me."

He briefly made a face. "Flatter, hell. You are impossibly beautiful, with or without clothes."

She extended her leg straight up and made a show of peeking back at him around it. "Now you're just being silly." She tried to keep her voice steady after his latest bit of adoration.

In one swift move, he shifted from the chair to the bed and sat just past her outstretched leg.

"No, I'm not," he said softly. "Yeah, I'm running hot because of that potion, but it doesn't change anything I said." He leaned forward and planted a soft kiss just behind her ankle. "You are intoxicating," he murmured into her skin.

She fought the tremble in her leg, mostly to avoid accidentally bringing her foot down on his head. "What's that about the potion?" she asked, her entire being focused on the feel of his lips against her skin.

"I talked to Tiris," he said, sneaking in brief kisses upon her ankle and calf between words. "She juiced up the potion. Figured that the excess magic would just filter into my aura. She didn't expect the anchor spell to be activated."

"I get it," Kana replied, her voice unsteady as her body started to respond to Jamyn's nibbling kisses. "Is that why your confidence is in overdrive?"

"Yeah," he said before leaning down and landing a long, wet kiss behind her knee. Her leg did buckle then but his hand flashed up and caught her ankle. Peeking around her leg, he rested the side of his face against her inner thigh and smiled. "I'm hoping I won't die from embarrassment once it does wear off."

Her bottom squirmed as he started to nibble his way down her thigh at a torturously slow rate. "You won't die. I won't let you. And you have got *nothing* to be embarrassed about."

"Yeah?" he asked with a mischievous chuckle. He fluttered the tip of his tongue against the smooth flesh and then looked back at her in expectation. "You sure?"

He was purposely toying with her, but it only made her hotter. "I'm sure, you little dope," she whispered. She started to pull the blanket away, but his free hand came forward and stopped it.

"Just lie back and relax," he said, his soft voice a sensuous rumble against her thigh.

She nodded and withdrew her hand. Reaching both arms up, she laced her fingers behind her head. "I think I like this new you."

"Oh, yeah?" he asked, nipping lower along her thigh. "And what if I go back to being like I was?"

"What do you mean?"

"Skittish. Indecisive. Like that."

"You really think you could go back to being that shy around me?"

He stopped his gentle worshiping of her leg and looked back at her. "I hope not."

She leaned her head back and closed her eyes. Recalling her dream, she smiled. "Don't worry about it. Believe it or not, I was once even twitchier than you. You'll be fine."

"Hmm," he replied, his tone one of disbelief.

He dipped his face down suddenly and pressed a long slow kiss to her covered mound. She drew in a quick breath and then let it out as a pleased sigh. After going without sex for so long, she was finding the sudden deluge suited her just fine. Jamyn's enthusiasm, despite his recently renounced virginal status, was contagious. She idly wondered what other delicious pleasures they could share before she finally forced herself to get up out of his bed. His soft voice roused her from her growing list of possibilities.

"Kana?"

"Yeah?"

"I want to taste you."

One of the entries at the top of her list was swiftly checked off. Her heart pounded at the eager tone of his stated desire. She slowly slid her covered leg to the side, spreading herself wide for him beneath the blanket, and tried to respond. The feel of the blanket being slowly peeled away from her lower body turned it into a broken jumble of noises.

"Was that a *yes*?" he asked, a smile evident in his voice.

Just as she tried to speak again, he kissed the neatly trimmed strip of hair on her mons. He maintained the kiss, despite laughing at the new gasp he had ripped from her lungs.

"Very funny, mister!" she replied in breathless exasperation. She bumped her pubis up against his mouth. "*Yes*, dammit!"

"*Language*, mistress." He snaked the tip of his tongue through the short hairs, tickling her.

She looked down her body at him and whimpered. He idly traced his tongue through her bush and then waggled his eyebrows at her. Her eyes widened in outrage, subdued only by her rising lust. "You keep teasing me and you'll hear some language."

He kept his eyes locked with hers as he slid his tongue down to linger on the bare patch of skin just above her hooded clit. "*Hnn?*" he asked in an inquisitive grunt.

She eased herself up to force his tongue lower. "Uh-huh," she whispered, entranced by the look of hunger in his eyes.

He gave her hooded clit a long, slow lick. Apparently encouraged by both the groan that erupted from deep in her throat and the way her hands were now clutching handfuls of bedding at her sides, he repeated the move. Soon, he was laving his tongue over her flesh in sweeping strokes and trying to follow her movements as she squirmed upon the bed. He constantly varied his attack, running the tip of his tongue just between her swollen lips before flattening it and swirling it up over her pulsing clit.

The gentle ferocity of the assault completely overwhelmed Kana. None of her previous partners had ever given her much more than a cursory lick down there, so the bombardment of sensations now radiating up from between her legs was almost too much to bear. Though she struggled to keep her body still enough to enjoy Jamyn's devotion, her hips kept lurching up off the bed. She forced an annoyed groan between her clenched teeth and firmly pressed her ass down against the bed. He abruptly stopped and looked up at her, his eyes shaded with both lust and concern.

She gasped breathlessly. "No! I—"

"Relax." His slick lips curved into a pleased smile. "I was just going to ask you something."

She settled down just enough for his statement to register in her mind. When it did, she couldn't help the confusion that followed. "What? Now?"

"Yeah." He chuckled and gave her clit a quick kiss. "Show me how you like it."

"Huh?"

He laughed again. "Down here. I'm just thrashing away. I don't know what's working for you and what's not." He winked at her. "You know. *Recovering virgin* and all that."

She laughed, both at his joke and at the sheer impossibility that someone would actually stop in the middle of sex to ask for directions. Her laughter trailed off as he continued to stare up at her in sheer adoration. "You...you're kidding, right?"

"No, I'm not," he said before running his tongue up along her inner thigh. Once again, her ass jerked up off the bed. "See? If I keep stumbling along like this, you're gonna knock out my front teeth with one of those bounces." He very carefully and slowly fluttered the tip of his tongue just over the delicate edges of her lips. "Show me what you like." He pulled a sad face and stuck out his lower lip. "Please?"

"You are such an idiot," she said, running all the words together in a rush.

Despite her words, she quickly reached both hands down between her legs while he backed away a space. Keeping her eyes locked on his face, she carefully spread her lips with her fingers, exposing her innermost delights to his enamored gaze. She pulled up slightly and his eyes widened as her clit was revealed. She dipped the tip of her index finger into her center and then started to gently massage the light pink nub. The ripples of passion streaking through her body made her want to throw her head back into the pillow, but she fought to keep her eyes trained on Jamyn's face. He had the same riveted expression he got during his studies and the intensity of his stare fed straight into Kana's lust. She quickened her movements, the pad of her fingertip flicking her clit over and over while her peak started to rise. Just before the crest hit, he snaked his tongue past her finger. She pulled her finger away but held herself open for him as he started to mimic her actions with the merest tip of his tongue.

Her orgasm was swift and unrelenting, coming for her in waves that tossed her body around like a leaf in the wind. She screamed and started to buck up off the bed, but he suddenly reached up beneath her and firmly held her waist down. She screamed even louder and came, her legs flailing up over his shoulders and her heels pounding against his back. Just as the storm was starting to subside, he lunged forward and wrapped his lips around her clit. He sucked hard and her world ignited in a flash of light behind her tightly closed eyes.

"Gaah!" she cried out, grinding her pussy against his chin as he continued to suckle her overwrought clit. "*Stopitstopitstopit!*" Clutching twin handfuls of his hair, she tried to pull him away. Another orgasm slammed into the trailing end of her first and her body flopped backwards, twitching and squirming under his merciless tongue.

He finally released her tormented clit and gave it one fluttering lick. Her body relaxed at last and went limp. He carefully pulled her legs off his back and then propped himself up on his elbows between them. He ended as he had begun, pressing a long, slow kiss to her now sweat-soaked mound.

Somehow, she found the energy to look back at him. His hair was mussed from where she had pulled it. The lower half of his face was slick with her juices. Despite his disheveled state, he was smiling at her with the most overjoyed expression she had ever seen.

"The hell are you grinning at?" she mumbled, the rest of her body still refusing to obey her commands to move.

"You," he said, his smile continuing to beam up at her.

Trickles of sensation started to return, and she wiggled her fingers and toes. Her training kicked in and she started to channel her chi to revive the rest of her body. "What about me?"

"You are...just...wow."

Her ability to move returned and she arched an eyebrow at him. "Me? What about you? What the hell was that move at the end?"

He shrugged and tried not to laugh. "Improvisation?"

In a flash, she sat up and hooked her hands under his armpits. In the next heartbeat, she fell back again and pulled hard, hauling his body on top of hers. "Fucking *brilliant*, you mean!" She snared his lips in a deep kiss. She continued to plunder his mouth while she wrapped her legs around his waist. Hooking her feet behind him, she bumped her crotch up against his. "You got *way* too many clothes on." She snarled the statement between ravenous kisses.

Despite her actions, he shook his head and pulled away from her voracious attack just long enough to blurt a single word. *"Can't!"*

She chuckled wickedly as she squeezed his erection. "Oh, I think you can."

He smiled briefly but then shook his head again. "We have somewhere to be," he said, trying to ignore her nibbling licks up the side of his neck.

"You mean *you've* got somewhere to be," she said, nudging her pussy up against him again. She started to pull at his belt, but he grabbed her hands tightly.

He snapped at her at last. "Kana! *No!"*

The command slammed into her, and a pang of remorse hit her hard. Bursts of memories raced through her mind, and she yanked her hands back to her sides as she cried out. "I'm sorry!" She was instantly torn between wanting to run her hands over his arms to comfort him and curling her body up into a ball beneath him. "I'm sorry!" she said again, looking away from his concerned expression. "Sorry!"

"Stop it," Jamyn said. He lunged forward and cut off her next apology with a firm kiss. Pulling away, he stared into her eyes. "Kana! *Calm down!"*

The firmness of his tone and the sincerity in his gaze finally quieted her. She nodded in reply and closed her eyes. He reached up to stroke her cheek and she weakly leaned her face into his palm.

"Are you okay?" he asked. "What happened?"

She opened her eyes. "You said *no*," she whispered.

By the stunned look in his eyes, she knew he had finally realized what was going on.

He shook his head emphatically then hugged her tightly. "No, it's not like that. I *want* to. I really do. We just have something else going on this afternoon. After that, I'm all yours." He ended his statement with a kiss on her cheek.

"I get it," she whispered. "I'm sorry."

He propped himself up on his arms, then shook his head and laughed. "Nothing to be sorry about, mistress. We just have to work on our communication a bit. You okay now?"

She nodded. "Yeah."

He knelt on the bed between her splayed legs. "Up with you." He took her hands in his and helped her sit up. They looked at each other in silence for a moment before coming together in a solid hug.

"I got us some lunch," he said. "Let's get to it."

"What have we got?" she asked, not wanting to let him go just yet.

"Cheeseburgers. From that place a few doors down from Evrok's."

"You mean S'ppok's?"

"Yeah."

The glow in her heart was drowned out by the appreciative rumbling of her stomach. "How did you—"

"I asked around," he replied with a laugh. "I stalked you for a long time before we met, remember?"

She nodded and held him tighter. "You're spoiling me," she murmured against his shoulder.

"No way. If anything, we're spoiling each other. Sound good?"

She pulled back and draped her arms around his shoulders. "Yeah, it does."

"Good."

She rested her forehead against his. "Hey."

"Yeah?"

She playfully kissed the tip of his nose. "You get fries too?"

Chapter Seven: Resolution

Kana leaned back against the headboard, being careful not to let the thin sheet draped across her chest fall. "That was great," she said with a pleased sigh.

Jamyn nodded and popped the last bite of his cheeseburger into his mouth. "Mm-hmm," he replied as he savored the last morsel.

She crumpled her empty paper wrapper into a ball and lobbed it at his head. "No talking with your mouth full."

"You're one to talk," he replied after swallowing. "Who was raving about the burgers the whole time she was wolfing her first one down again?"

She mimed a belch and they both laughed. "Can't help it. S'ppok is a damned culinary genius."

"Gotta agree with you there." Jamyn chuckled.

"What?"

"I've never seen anyone polish off food like that before."

"Especially a *girl*, huh?"

He grinned at the term. "Yeah. Something like that."

She shifted her foot under the blanket and gave him a playful nudge. "It's all your fault."

"How's that?"

"Don't forget that you're the one who helped me work up that appetite."

His grin grew into a warm smile. "I'll remember that 'til my dying day."

She recognized the fond gleam in his eyes. "So, this is why you volunteered for that twitch mission with me way back when, huh?"

He cocked his head and looked back at her in confusion. "To lure you to my room to have cheeseburgers in bed?"

"Wild sex and cheeseburgers," she said with a lurid grin. "No, I meant because of that look."

He blinked. "What look?"

"That far-off, million miles away look."

He shrugged. "Dunno what you mean."

"Oh, c'mon. I've seen it just about from the start with you. It's the amped-up version of that adoring gaze I get from my misguided fans."

Jamyn laughed and nodded.

"What now?" she asked.

"I saw the kind of reaction your name gets earlier today."

"What happened?"

"I almost ran over some lost neophytes in the corridor. They asked me for directions, and I figured out where they needed to go. Then they asked for my name. As soon as they heard it, they somehow knew I was the acolyte of *the* Kana Morel. Poor kids went straight into the *I-am-not-worthy* bowing and scraping routine. Ran away from me like you were gonna show up and skin them alive."

Kana smirked. "Get used to it, kiddo. The mere mention of my name around these hallowed halls gives most people fits."

He shook his head. "Nah. From what I've seen, it gets a ton of respect. Back when I was asking around about you, almost everyone I talked to spoke about you like you were royalty."

"Pff," she said with a dismissive wave of her hand. She frowned suddenly and huffed in fake indignation. "What do you mean, *almost* everyone?"

"I'm sure you can figure out the owner of the lone dissenting opinion."

"Oh, let me guess." She pulled the bedsheet up over her head and hunched forward. "Kana Morel is an undisciplined, arrogant child!"

She growled, mimicking Donta's raspy snarl. "She does not adhere to the limits of her rank and refuses to cower in abject fear in my presence!" She muttered darkly under her breath for a few moments before breaking into a spirited laugh.

Jamyn laughed along at her accurate rendition. He leaned forward and poked her forehead.

"Watch it, you. That's the woman I love you're talking about."

She pulled down the sheet just enough to reveal her wide eyes.

Jamyn grimaced and drew back. "Sorry," he said quietly before busying himself with gathering up the trash from their meal.

She uncovered the rest of her face and tucked the sheet back around her chest. She reached for one of his hands and held it.

"It's okay," she replied. She tugged his hand to get him to look at her again. "I'm kinda getting used to it."

He gave her a slight nod. "That's good, right?"

She squeezed his hand. "Yeah."

He raised her hand to his lips and kissed it. "Good."

Cupping his chin, she gave it a playful shake. "And *you*," she said with a grin. "You are just..." She stopped and considered his relieved expression.

He sat up and struck a pose, inclining his head and sticking out his chest. He planted his hands on his hips and flashed her his best smile.

"Gorgeous?" he said with a cocky flair. "Virile? All kinds of wonderful?"

She laughed at his ridiculous pose. "I was gonna say batshit crazy, but yeah, I guess all that other stuff too."

He relaxed and laughed along. "This means you'll keep me a while?"

She sat back against the headboard, shaking her head at the silly question. "Yeah, I guess I won't toss you back just yet."

"Cool."

He stuffed all the wrappers into the empty bag and made a show of aiming it at the trash can on the far side of the room. He launched it in a high arc, but it fell short and bounced off the rim. Before it could hit the floor, Kana snared it with a spell. It floated directly over the can before neatly dropping into it.

"Nice."

"Anything to assist my favorite acolyte."

He started to smile before catching sight of the clock on the wall.

"Whoa! We're gonna be late."

"Late for what?" she asked. "You never did tell me, you know, *before*."

He recalled stopping her lusty attack earlier. "Yeah. Sorry. I just have a reservation, and I don't think we should be late."

"Reservation?" Her heart did a funny little skip in her chest. "You taking me out on a date?"

His eyes widened for a second, but he calmed down and shook his head. "No. I would have asked first."

The notion briefly choked her up. "What, then?"

"Nothing terribly interesting." He glanced at the clock again. "You really need to get dressed."

She looked him over. "You're wearing that?"

He nodded.

"Casual, then." She looked to the bathroom and sighed. "I guess I could scrub up the clothes I have here."

"That'd be fine." He stood up to let her out of the bed.

She considered just walking to the bathroom nude but then had an even more devilish thought. Pulling the top sheet along with her, she got up and started to walk to the bathroom. She held the sheet against her chest but let it trail loose behind her. She tagged Jamyn's cheek with a brief kiss as she passed him and then sauntered to the bathroom, giving him an unrestricted view of her bare backside. She rolled her hips in an exaggerated strut, knowing that she likely now commanded his full attention. Reaching the doorway, she cast a flirty glance over her shoulder before letting the sheet fall away from her body. Blowing him a kiss, she hopped over the pile of fabric and closed the door behind her.

———— ◉ ————

Jamyn hurried to pick up the sheet and groaned as he bent over. "Whew," he whispered after standing back up and slipping a hand into his pants to adjust his thundering erection.

"Problem out there?" Kana called out through the door.

From her tone, he was sure she was smiling. "Yeah. Big problem."

"How big?"

"Wait until we get back. I'll show you."

"Ooh. Promises, promises!"

Jamyn tossed the sheet back onto the bed and smiled at the tangled mess.

I should have the bed bronzed just like that. This is what was left after the first time.

His smile grew and his heart started to beat faster.

The first couple *times.*

He started to adjust himself again when Kana tickled his ribs from behind. He cried out and she hugged him tightly before he could leap away.

"Gotcha," she said, giving him an extra squeeze.

He let his hands rest upon hers and snuggled into her embrace. "Yep. Now whatcha gonna do with me?"

She let one hand dip down and ran her fingers over his bulge. "I know what I'd *like* to do," she whispered into his ear, "but you keep saying we've gotta be somewhere else." She gripped his shaft, teasing a low moan from him. "You *sure* you don't wanna rethink those plans?" Before he could reply, she released him and stepped back. "No, I've gotta start teaching you responsibility sometime. Lead on, acolyte!"

He turned around to face her and saw her wicked grin. "You're mean."

"Hey, I'm not the one who scheduled this little mystery jaunt. I'd rather spend the day pounding what's left of your virginity into the ground, but you had other—"

Her words were cut off as Jamyn lunged forward and kissed her hard. She fell into it willingly and then squeaked when he cupped her mound.

He smiled against her lips and drew back. "You gonna be quiet now?" he asked softly.

"Only until you get me back here."

He nodded. "Then you can get as loud as you like." Taking her hand, he led her out into the hallway.

In minutes, they found themselves outside Evrok's tavern. A small wooden sign hung on the door that read *Closed for private party* in a plain black script.

"Evrok's?" Kana asked.

"Yep."

She eyed him in suspicion. "What's this *private party* stuff?"

Jamyn shrugged. "There's no party. It's just closed to the public." Seeing her look of disbelief, he said, "No, really! There's no party in there."

"There better not be." She raised one hand, and it was quickly shrouded by crackling arcs of electricity. "Surprises like that have a funny way of getting blown up around me."

Jamyn pressed a quick kiss to her forehead. "Calm down. For me?"

The glow extinguished and she relaxed her stance. "You're first to go if you're lying to me."

He turned the door handle and chuckled. "I will gladly submit to your vengeance." He opened the door and bowed to her. "Ladies first." She went in and he followed right on her heels.

The tables and chairs had been arranged in a semicircular pattern facing the rear of the tavern. The bar was populated from one end to the other by several patrons that they immediately recognized. Before they could say anything, several of them turned and issued a booming greeting.

"Kana!" they cried, lifting their respective drinks high.

She turned to look at Jamyn. Her expression upon seeing the entire Inner Cabal gathered before her was one of sheer disbelief. She turned back to the assembled patrons. "What the hell is all of this?"

"Ask the boy wonder," Fangs said from the far end of the bar. He took a healthy swallow from one of the many tankards in front of him and then wiped his sodden beard with the back of his free hand. "It's all his doing."

"And you, of course, were totally against it," Daystar said to him. "Especially when he mentioned free drinks."

"Of course, mistress," he replied, raising his current drink to her. "When I get blitzed, I rather like knowing that I did it to myself!"

Evrok piped up. "Easily rectified. I shall start a separate tab for you, retroactive to when you arrived this morning."

"Hey, no need to be crazy now," Fangs said. He looked to Jamyn. "Right?"

Jamyn laughed. "No worries, Fangs. I'll cover you."

"I knew there was something I liked about you." Fangs flashed him a toothy grin before draining the remains of his current tankard.

"Well, before things get entirely out of hand, let's begin," Jamyn said loudly before gesturing to the tables.

Donta grumbled, hopping up from his seat and storming past Kana and Jamyn. The others filed past, each giving them both a nod of respect.

Tiris started to say something to Kana, but Leel swatted her butt and ushered her forward.

Tiris squeaked in protest. "Hey! I was just—"

"I know what you're up to, little minx," Leel said sternly. "Just keep moving. Save it for later."

Tiris peeked past him and flashed Kana a quick thumbs-up before Leel started tickling her to move her along. She cried out and did her best to fend him off.

Kana looked to Jamyn. "What was that all about?" she asked quietly.

Jamyn shrugged. "No idea."

"Yeah, right."

The cabal had taken their seats. Jamyn noticed that only two others had not joined them. Evrok stood directly behind the bar, looking over the proceedings with a tired detachment. Another figure lurked in the shadows in the far corner. Every time he tried to focus on it, however, it vanished. Kana's hand on his shoulder distracted him enough to stop his futile effort.

He blinked several times and looked back at Kana. "You ready?"

She looked at the seated cabal members and frowned. "I guess."

He took the lead, guiding her around the assembled tables.

"The last time I saw the cabal, they were trying to sanction you," she said in a low, ominous voice. "Time before that, the sneaky buggers promoted me." She poked him in the back. "This time better not suck as bad."

"It won't. I promise."

Jamyn stopped at the table where Qa was seated and turned to face Kana.

The older man gestured to the open chair beside him. "I saved you a seat."

Kana turned her confused expression back to Jamyn. "No. I—"

"Am a member of the cabal," Jamyn said. "Sit down. I can handle this on my own."

"But I—"

"Kana," he said, his voice hardening, "please sit down."

Kana looked to Qa for help, but he only gestured to the open chair again. "Fine," she said, sliding into the seat and shooting Jamyn a sulking frown. He turned and continued forward alone.

Jamyn finally reached the single table that was the focal point of the gathering and faced his audience. Instead of sitting on one of the chairs, he casually sat back against the edge of the table. He raised his voice and addressed them. "Thank you all for agreeing to meet here."

"Ridiculous," Donta muttered.

"Come now, Master Donta," Daystar chimed from her seat beside him. "I think this venue is a refreshing change of pace."

"Agreed!" Fangs cried before diving into one of the several tankards upon the table he now shared with Archdruid Vynael.

"I am sorry for any inconvenience," Jamyn said. "Evrok suggested that it might be best to bring you to the spot where all of this started." He took a deep breath. "Per the cabal's decision, Evrok applied the anchor spell to me here. Immediately thereafter, a demon tried to possess me."

Daystar gasped. "What? How could a demon enter the Sanctum undetected?"

"I unknowingly picked up a piece of its essence during my trip to Letron 12-B. It somehow channeled the attempt through that piece."

———— ◉ ————

Kana fought to keep herself outwardly calm while her stomach clenched into a knot. Leaning over to Qa, she whispered, "What the hell is he doing?"

"I have no idea," Qa replied. "Didn't he go over his plan with you?"

"No!" She looked up and noticed Jamyn had stopped talking and was now looking right at her.

"Problem?" he asked.

"Nah," she replied, trying to sound bored.

"I'll try to make this quick." He scratched the back of his right hand, hiding Kana's glyph. A quick touch of one of the small circles initiated the veiled converse between him and his mentor.

"Don't worry," his mind told hers. *"I know what I'm doing."*

"All right," she reluctantly replied. *"Be careful."*

He raised his voice again. "Fortunately, Evrok had switched off my magic before the attempt took hold, so the demon couldn't use it. Evrok then tried to counter the possession, but I beat him to it."

"What?" Leel asked. "How could you fend off a possession without magic?"

"That's part of the reason I've asked you all here today. I was able to siphon off Evrok's aura and use its magic to break the possession attempt."

"Nice trick," Fangs said between muffled belches. "Too bad it's impossible. With your own magic locked down, you couldn't have cast a proper spell."

"That's true. What I did is part of my willcasting. It turns out I can redirect and repurpose any magical energy around me. That's how I took apart Evrok's bouncer spell. Apparently, I can also do it without my own magic functioning."

Donta growled. "A troubling revelation. If you can still use magic, what good is the anchor spell upon you?"

"A valid question," Jamyn replied. "I can only offer that every time I have used this ability, it was purely for defense and only in what my subconscious mind considered to be a life-threatening event. I took apart the bouncer, I broke the possession attempt, and I gated out of here to get away from the demon."

"Gated?" Vynael asked, breaking his usual stoic silence.

"Yes. The possession attempt kicked in my fight-or-flight response, and I ran. Somehow I was able to restructure the magic around me into a makeshift gate."

"To where?" Fangs asked, the evolving tale tearing his attention away from his many drinks for the moment.

"Near the site of one of my missions with Kana. After that, I started blindly jumping from place to place, each time gathering more magic so I could continue running."

"You weren't in control of your actions?" Leel asked.

"No, I wasn't. As it turned out, something else had entered my mind and was guiding me. The demon that tried to possess me had itself been taken over by a being called an Aqiri."

Fangs suddenly loosed a hearty laugh.

Everyone looked at him in shock and Donta snapped at him angrily. "You find this amusing?"

The snarling query did nothing to dampen Fangs's mirth. "The Aqiri? No." He eyed Jamyn with a wide smile. "Him building a track record of encountering weird critters that rivals his master's? Hell yes!"

"He's got a long way to go to get there," Kana said with a smile, causing most of the cabal to laugh in agreement.

The thoroughly unexpected proceedings to this point had rendered her silent so she was happy at last to be able to say something.

Evrok piped up over the din. "So, the Aqiri took you itself. Move along."

"Of course," Jamyn replied with a courteous nod. "The reason behind all of this was that the Aqiri wanted to use my abilities to free itself from the demon."

"A curious concept," Qa said. "Why did it believe that you could help it in that regard?"

Jamyn took another deep breath. "During one of my trips, I encountered a lesser demon. I siphoned off much of its aura to use for another gate. I found out later from Kana that the demon had become human, partly because of what I did to it."

A stunned silence permeated the bar.

"How?" Leel asked in an astonished whisper. Tiris, wide-eyed and gripping his arm, nodded in silent agreement with his question.

"Kana?" Jamyn asked, gesturing to his master.

Kana snapped fully alert. "I found out that Jamyn had taken off after the anchoring, so I started tracking him by analyzing each of his gates. I talked to the demon he had encountered. It had fallen in love with a young woman before Jamyn showed up. After the demon's aura was diminished, he completed the transformation on his own when he rescued that same woman from an attack."

"You went off on your own to track down Mister Siska without informing the cabal first?" Donta asked.

She faced him solidly. "That's right. He's *my* responsibility. Besides, I work better on my own. I wanted to find him and bring him back here as quickly as possible."

"I'm guessing that you did eventually find him," Fangs said, sneaking a sip of another of his drinks.

Jamyn spoke up again. "Yeah, she did. It was then that the Aqiri tried to cement its control over my mind."

"You mean it didn't have full control of you yet?" Daystar asked.

"No. I got hit in the head during one of the jumps. That dazed me enough for the Aqiri to gain a major hold on me. I guess it wasn't enough to fully take me over because I was still fighting its influence."

"But if you weren't in control," Tiris asked, "how could you know that?"

"The Aqiri told me later. I'll get to that in a bit. Kana found me and the Aqiri attacked her to break my spirit. Fortunately, she got a message back to Master Qa. He showed up to stop the Aqiri before it could kill her."

"And I, in turn, brought Kana to Tiris and Leel so that she could be healed," Qa said smoothly.

"Right," Jamyn said. "After that, Kana found me again and helped me to finally get free."

"Bet that was one helluva fight," Fangs murmured with a toothy grin.

Kana shrugged. "Yeah, it had its moments."

"After a quick word with what was left of the Aqiri, we disposed of it and came back here. I got patched up and then had Evrok lock down my magic again so that I couldn't get into any more trouble." Jamyn spread his arms. "And now we're here."

Donta grumbled impatiently. "The point of this wearisome tale?"

"Full disclosure," Jamyn replied. "The cabal voted to have me anchored so that I couldn't do something stupid again. Well, something stupid happened to me anyway. It wasn't my fault, but I still thought everyone should be made aware of it."

"And now we are," Daystar said. "Now what?"

Jamyn stood up straight and his expression sobered. "I respectfully ask the cabal for another vote. The choices are simple. Either I stay with the Sanctum and try to learn more about my abilities under your guidance or I get bounced back home."

Kana shrieked through the veiled converse spell. *"Are you insane?"*

Jamyn continued to evenly scan the cabal's faces and didn't look at her directly when he replied. *"Just relax."*

"A simple majority vote?" Donta asked deliberately.

"That's up to you," Jamyn replied. "I do admit that I would prefer a unanimous decision. Still, I don't want anyone to doubt their call, one way or another."

"I say he stays," Fangs said. "I want a front-row seat for this kid's next trick!" Jamyn smiled at him, and Fangs raised a tankard in response.

"Stay," Vynael said in his usual tired monotone.

Tiris nudged Leel, who nodded to her in deference, and she giggled. "We say he's staying."

Daystar's aura flashed briefly. "You are staying right here, Mister Siska."

Donta considered the young man's unwavering gaze and rumbled at him ominously. "You will stay, but we will be watching you."

"He's a giant pain in the ass," Kana said, doing her best to hide the swell of relief blossoming within her, "but I guess we should keep him around."

"I believe he should stay," Qa said. "Aside from his budding potential, his presence also seems to have a calming effect on Miss Morel here." He looked to her annoyed scowl and smiled. "That can only be a good thing."

Several of the assembled mages laughed.

"He is troublesome but no more than any of you," Evrok said. "I say he stays."

Donta roared in outrage without looking back. "You are not of the cabal!"

"But I *am* the proprietor of this establishment," Evrok replied. "If I ban him from here, what other reason is there in the rest of the Sanctum for him to stay?"

Fangs laughed while nursing his current drink. "He's got a point there."

"Oh, I think he might find one or two things," Daystar said nonchalantly.

Tiris giggled, earning her bottom yet another pinch from Leel.

The space all around them trembled for a moment before a curious vibration rippled through the air. A voice formed in the emptiness of the shadows and called out.

He stays!

"Your unanimous vote, Mister Siska," Donta said, his voice now strangely calm.

Jamyn bowed low before them. "I thank you all." He held the bow a moment longer and thought to Kana.

"Told ya it'd be okay."

He straightened up.

She stared daggers at him despite her beaming smile.

"You're completely insane."

"Apparently."

"What's next for you, Mister Siska?" Daystar asked.

Jamyn drew in a breath between his teeth and blew it out again. "I want to go back to each of the stops I made while the Aqiri was piloting me around. There are some people along the way that I need to explain some things to. Probably should apologize to a few of them as well."

"And I'll be keeping a close eye on him the whole time," Kana said firmly.

Donta stood up. "Then we are adjourned." He started to turn away, but Daystar reached out to stop him.

"We may be adjourned but that doesn't mean we have to leave right away." Looking over her shoulder at Evrok, she flashed him a winning smile. "Correct?"

"Stay as long as you like." Evrok sniffed, apparently unaffected by the radiant Daystar. "I've already removed the sign from the door. However, I am sure the rest of the Sanctum will remain safely outside once it's known that the entire Inner Cabal is here."

"Very good, then," Leel said. He shot to his feet and hooked arms with his wife. "Shall we, my dear?"

"Indeed, we shall," she replied with a devilish grin, "but let's have a drink first!"

Both Kana and Daystar laughed. The rest of the cabal started to make their way back to the bar. Tiris latched on to Kana's hand and yanked her down to give her a firm hug.

Jamyn easily deduced the intent behind the burst of quick whispers between the two women and shook his head. As he walked over to them, Tiris shot him a quick glance and then nodded once to Kana.

"And what are we up to?" he asked innocently as he reached them.

"Up to?" Kana asked once Tiris had released her hold. "Us?"

"Why would you think we were up to something?" Tiris asked in a hurt tone.

"Because you usually are," Leel said, sidling up behind her.

"Oh, all right," she said. "I was just asking Kana how you did." She looked up at Kana's smiling face. "How did you put it again? Passable?"

"I suppose," Kana replied, stifling a faked yawn. "It was tolerable, I guess."

Leel frowned at them both. "Which is why you needed a nap right afterwards."

Kana shrugged. "I can't help that the kid put me to sleep."

Leel harrumphed. "Women! Horrible, indelicate creatures, the entire lot of 'em." He turned to Jamyn, who had been taking in this entire exchange in stunned silence. "A good thing we're all speaking in hypotheticals, of course, else this would be a rather awkward exchange. Right, Jamyn?"

The acolyte swallowed hard as a measure of relief lightened his expression. "Right."

Tiris laughed gaily and launched herself at Jamyn, clutching his thigh and rubbing it affectionately. "You poor, poor man! I think you should take Kana home and spank her at once!"

Jamyn arched an eyebrow at Kana as if he was seriously considering the prospect. "Not a bad idea." She stared back at him in a silent challenge, causing him to finally back down. "But I think I might want to live until morning."

"Good idea, lad," Leel said. "Never spank 'em unless they want it or seriously deserve it. Speaking of which..." He planted a sharp swat directly on his wife's ass, causing her to release Jamyn's leg and jump back.

"Ow!" she cried, though mostly for show. "Why'd you do that?"

"That would have been under the *seriously deserve it* heading," Leel replied.

She leaped forward, crushing her husband in a tight hug. "Oh, I don't know," she murmured against his lips. "Might have been in the *want it* category too."

"Little temptress," he whispered back before kissing her soundly.

Jamyn smiled at the two gnomes before noticing that Kana was now eying him casually.

"Which category are you in?" his mind asked hers through the veiled converse. *"Want or deserve?"*

"Might be both," she replied, trying to look nonchalant despite her simmering lust.

"I think I'll have to do something about that."

"I think you better."

He smiled and looked over to the bar. Daystar was chatting up both Vynael and Donta, much to the latter's annoyance. Qa was attempting to talk to Fangs, who was starting to wobble a bit on his barstool.

Turning back to Kana, Jamyn asked, "Buy you a drink, miss?"

She looked him up and down, frowning as she did. "I don't know," she replied. "I don't think you're really my type."

Tiris yanked herself away from Leel, much to her husband's surprise. "Oh, yes, he is!" she said breathlessly.

Leel made a face at her rude outburst, only to have it swiftly removed by another of Tiris's passionate kisses. Kana laughed and held out a hand to Jamyn. He took it in his and they started back to the bar together.

"Okay, then. One drink." She gave him a quick wink. "Doctor's orders."

Chapter Eight: Confident

"So how *much is too much?"*

Kana leaned back against the bar and casually eyed Jamyn over the top of her glass. Her acolyte was sitting at one of the small tables with Qa and a group of neophytes. The youngsters were chatting away with Qa, who appeared to be enjoying their enthusiasm.

"Usually once you can't see straight, you should probably slow down a little," Kana replied through the veiled converse.

"Not that. Us."

She continued to calmly sip her drink. *"What do you mean?"*

"I mean I'd really like to kiss you right now."

She swallowed hard to avoid spitting her drink all over the people around her. Despite Evrok's earlier misgivings, the tavern was now packed. She took a measured breath and then coughed hard to clear her throat.

Fangs noticed her distress and patted her firmly on the back. "Easy there, Kana," he said in a jovial roar. "Don't let the beast get the better of ya!"

She elbowed his side. "You should talk," she replied, gesturing to the collection of empty mugs and tankards in front of him. "All your little friends here should be kicking your fuzzy ass right about now."

"Nonsense!" His pupils narrowed to vertical slits, and he leaped straight up. He gripped the high ceiling with his now clawed hands and hung there looking down at them all with a wild-eyed grin. "See? I'm in complete control!" Suddenly a beam of light struck his hands. He lost his grip and fell but landed neatly right where he had been standing.

"I will remind you yet again that the walls and ceiling are off-limits!" Evrok piped angrily from the far side of the bar. His hand glowed with an eerie light that matched the beam that had dislodged Fangs.

"I sincerely apologize to both you and your fine ceiling," Fangs said with a regal bow. Standing up straight again, he stuck out his tongue as soon as the barkeep turned away.

Kana laughed and Fangs winked at her, his eyes now back to normal.

"Sorry about that."

Jamyn's voice in her head brought her mind back to their silent conversation. She turned and saw him staring back at her.

"Knock it off," she replied. *"What the hell are* you *apologizing for?"*

Fangs rumbled into her ear. "You know, some people would consider that terribly rude."

Annoyed at this latest interruption, she snapped at him. "What now?"

Fangs ignored her question and waved to Jamyn. "Hey, kid! Get over here." He pointed to a spot right in front of Kana.

Jamyn hesitantly stood and walked over to them. Once he had moved close enough, Fangs darted around him and gave him a firm shove from behind. Jamyn stumbled forward and Kana braced her hands against his chest to avoid a hard collision.

"There," Fangs said, obviously pleased with himself as he eased back into his spot at the bar. "Now say what you need to say."

A delicate hand slipped over Fangs's shoulder from behind and tugged his bushy beard hard. Before he could turn around, the hand dipped down under his beard.

"Now that wasn't very nice of you, Master Varondis-Mai," Daystar whispered into his ear while she teased her fingernails across his neck.

Fangs growled, a low, menacing sound that caught the attention of most of the patrons around him. "You know I don't like that name," he murmured back, "or claws at my throat."

She dragged her nails across his skin, though not quite hard enough to draw blood. "Perhaps I need reminding," she replied, her own voice dropping to a feral snarl. "At any rate, I believe you've had enough to drink."

The hand over his throat slipped away and he tossed them a toothy grin. "Sorry, kids," he said in a rush. "I'm afraid I need to call it a night." He ducked into the crowd, weaving through the patrons with catlike grace before hurrying out the door after Daystar.

Kana and Jamyn turned their attention back to one another. Her hands were still pressed tightly to his chest. Jamyn glanced down at them and then looked back at her.

"I've had enough here too," he said quietly. "You?"

"Yeah," she whispered. "I'm good." She started to pull her hands away, but Jamyn caught one of them and raised it to his lips.

"Let's go," he said before pressing a kiss to the top of her hand.

Her pulse started pounding in her ears at this small but very public display of affection. They made their way to the exit, oblivious to how the volume level of the crowd around them had suddenly ebbed. The neophytes around Qa took turns glancing at the couple while sharing a burst of quick whispers. Qa smiled to himself and took another sip from his mug.

<hr />

Jamyn panted as he chased Kana through the corridors of the Sanctum's housing sector. Shortly after exiting Evrok's, she had eluded his attempt to hold her hand while they walked. After a quick look around for bystanders, she tagged him with a quick kiss and then took off running. He eagerly joined in the game, sprinting after her while ogling her lithe form. He caught up to her once and grabbed at her ass, but she teleported forward far out of his reach.

"Hey!" he said, pouring on the speed to catch up to her again. "That's cheating!"

"Said the loser!" She laughed back at him and rounded a corner, leaping up and kicking hard off the far wall to retain her momentum.

Jamyn didn't pause to admire the move, though his steps did falter as he nearly took the same turn a little too quickly. Pushing hard against the wall to avoid smacking into it, he called out to her. "When I catch you, I'm gonna—"

"That's the idea!"

Suddenly she disappeared. Jamyn slowed his breakneck pace just long enough to see her reappear up the corridor right outside his quarters. She waved back at him and then slipped inside, slamming the door behind her.

He skidded to a stop outside his door. "Yeah, walk right into an ambush," he said between rapid pants. "Ain't gonna happen, mistress."

He turned the knob and flung the door open. Immediately he leaped forward and fell into a feet-first slide, ducking right under the figure charging at him from the darkness of his quarters. He stood up again and snared Kana from behind. Spinning her around, he clamped his hands on her shoulders. He launched forward again, pinning her against the door as it slammed shut behind her.

"Hey!" She tried to squirm out of his grasp. "What are you—"

He cut off her protest with a ravenous kiss. Tearing himself away, he dropped a hand to her belt and tugged it hard. "Claiming my prize," he said before kissing her again.

———⊙———

A surge of unease threatened to surface within her, but her rising lust easily squashed it. In a heartbeat, her hands were all over him. She raked her fingers through his hair before pulling him even deeper into their kiss. Easing her hands down his neck, she stroked over his chest and back. Dropping a hand to his crotch, she gripped his cock and squeezed. He groaned in appreciation, and she smiled against his rapacious mouth.

He withdrew again and dipped down into a low crouch. Confusion had barely registered in her mind before Kana shrieked in surprise as he hooked his arms behind her legs and back and hoisted her up. Then he was at her again, nibbling and sucking her neck as he carried her to the dimly lit bedroom. Just as she was starting to lose herself to his frantic ministrations, he tossed her into the air. Before she could cry out, she landed neatly on the bed. In a flash, she spun around into a kneeling position facing him.

"Now what, acolyte?" she asked with a wild grin.

"Now?" His voice was a husky rasp of lust. He slowly peeled off his shirt and then carelessly tossed it to the floor. "Now I'm gonna kiss every damned square inch of your body." He fixed her with an intense stare. "Got a problem with that?"

"Maybe I do," she said despite the primal thrill that shot through her. She removed her own shirt in the same teasing way he had his. Instead of throwing it to the floor, she tossed it at his face.

He batted it away. "So, what's the problem?"

She undid her belt and the snap on her jeans. "Ticklish feet."

"Okay. No feet."

She pulled off her low boots and flipped them onto the floor behind her. "And elbows are pretty boring."

He kicked off his shoes. Keeping his eyes trained on her face, he dropped his pants and likewise discarded them. "Anything else, mistress?" he asked in an impatient rumble as he stood back up.

She shrugged as she stared at his naked body and unwavering erection. "Oh, there's a whole list," she said, sitting back on her heels. "Maybe you should write it down." She winked at him and traced a finger beneath one bare breast. "Got a pen?"

He launched forward with a cry of outrage. She recoiled from his sudden advance and then squealed as he latched on to her ankles. A firm yank later, she was lying on her back and struggling to evade his hold on her. He grabbed at her pants and started to tug them down her legs.

"Hey!" she said in a haughty reproach. "Leave my pants out of this!"

"Gladly!"

He finally wrested them from her flailing legs. She nearly kicked him in the jaw, and he clamped a hand on each of her ankles. Holding her legs high, he spread them apart and looked down upon her bare charms. Her pussy glistened in the dim light, and he smiled in triumph.

"I think mistress is enjoying this more than she's letting on," he said before licking his lips.

She folded her arms across her chest and huffed in defiance. "No, she most certainly is not."

In response, he licked a wide swath up the inside of her thigh. He ended the long stroke with a tickling lick behind her knee.

She shrieked and he relented. "Mistress is *ly-ing*," he said in a singsong tone.

"No, she's not!" she replied, trying to catch her breath.

He started to nibble and kiss the wet stripe along her leg, moving down from her knee to mid-thigh. "Yes, she is," he murmured against her skin as he went.

"Well, maybe," she said, internally cursing his slowing pace while her heart rate skyrocketed. "A little bit."

A trail of soft wet kisses ended just shy of her center and had her holding her breath in anticipation. "Just a little?" he whispered, his heated words washing over her delicate lips.

"Jamyn." She gasped, forcing the air from her lungs. "Please."

He smiled at last. "Yes, dear."

The shout that welled up inside her at the unexpected endearment instantly turned into a shuddering moan as he plunged his tongue into her. She tried to gather her thoughts but quickly lost herself to the relentless onslaught that was Jamyn. He seemed to be everywhere at once, constantly alternating between nibbling at her delicate lips and swirling his tongue around her clit. All the while he pressed quick, wet kisses to every part of her he could find. Just as her orgasm started to crest, he pulled away and stood up again.

"Wha...what are you—"

He replied by kneeling on the bed between her outstretched legs. Taking his rigid cock in his hand, he stroked its length up between her soaked folds. She moaned in appreciation, and he repeated the move. This time, however, he ended the stroke by nudging the tip of his cock over her excited clit. Kana threw her head back into the pillow and gasped as electric arcs zipped up her spine. Encouraged by her reaction, he started to rub his cock over her throbbing clit in small circles.

Kana's scream had just bounced back off the bedroom walls when it was instantly outclassed by the one that erupted from her as Jamyn slipped his cock into her. She shrieked as the sudden fullness caused her back to arch up off the bed, her greedy body demanding even more of him. He complied, slowly easing himself into her while he carefully gripped her waist.

When his balls finally nudged up against her ass, Kana uttered a growling moan and hooked her ankles behind his butt. "Come on!" she said between ragged pants.

Her muscular legs yanked him closer, trying to speed up his relaxed thrusts. He resisted her as much as he could, meeting her wild gaze with a look of intense concentration. His strokes were deep and regular, giving Kana ample chance to finally catch her breath.

"Trying to make it last?" She clenched down at the deep end of one of his strokes.

"Mm-hmm," he said in a low rumble.

"Don't!" She pulled his hands from her waist and brought them to her breasts.

His eyes widened and his back stiffened as his peak suddenly hit with unrelenting swiftness. A broken cry slipped from between his clenched teeth. His lean body bucked, jamming his pulsing cock even deeper into her as he came.

The force of his final thrust helped Kana vault over the edge as well. She moaned in pleasure and squeezed his hands. He suddenly pulled away and held her thighs as aftershocks continued to thunder through his body. Her hands fell to her abandoned breasts, and she stroked them lovingly as she eased down from her orgasm.

He softly grumbled under his labored breath. "Dammit."

She opened her eyes to see his were tightly closed. He wore a look of anguish that she quickly knew was not entirely due to his peak. A sympathetic twinge within her made her reach for him.

"Jamyn?"

He jerked at the first touch of her fingers to his chest. Opening his eyes, he tried to force a weak smile but failed.

"Yeah?"

"What's wrong?"

He started to absently stroke her waist. "I just..." He paused to gather his thoughts. "I was just trying to last longer."

The hint of guilt in his eyes told her there was more to it than that. "Don't sweat it. That was awesome. I'm not sure how much more teasing I could have taken." His expression didn't soften at her words. If anything, it grew even sadder. "Come on, Jamyn. What's up?"

He shook off his melancholy with an effort and smiled down at her. "Nothing! I was just trying not to disappoint you."

She made a face. "Nothing you've done so far has come *close* to disappointing," she said, giving his ribs a quick tickle.

He laughed briefly. "Good."

"You still worried about getting shy on me again?" She traced the tip of her finger over the top of his shaft where it met her body.

"A little." He grinned down at her teasing finger. "Though not so much when you do that."

She trailed her finger up his abdomen. "You're not so shy now, are you?"

"Nope."

"Then there's your answer."

"Huh?"

She clenched down on him. Though his cock had started to soften, its girth still filled her enough to tease another groan of pleasure from her. "Want to know a secret?"

He drew in a quick breath at the intimate squeeze. "Sure."

"Tiris drained the potion's excess magic from you."

His eyes widened. "What? When?"

"Back in the bar when she hugged your leg. I told her to." Kana squirmed, enjoying the way his cock suddenly twitched within her. "That whole *wild man* routine when we got here and all the teasing and stuff since?" She flexed her legs, pulling him closer. "That was all *you*, big boy."

Jamyn looked down to where their bodies were joined and started to slowly ease himself forward and back again. "Whoa," he whispered to himself.

"So that's settled," she said with a catlike stretch of her upper body. "No more worrying about it!" She laughed for a moment and then reached for his hands. "Come on. Let's see what you've got." Lifting her ass up to accept his latest thrust, she pulled his hands to her chest again.

Jamyn jerked to a stop and yanked his hands away from her. The way his expression changed told her he immediately regretted the move. He leaned into her again.

This time, she firmly held a hand against his chest to stop him. "Okay, what's going on?" He opened his mouth to reply but she snapped at him. "You tell me *nothing* again and I'll beat it out of you." He stared at her in silence, and she shook her head with an exasperated frown. Bearing down on him, she said, "Tell me or I'll rip your dick off!"

The sadness in his eyes was briefly interrupted by a glimmer of shock. She grinned at his reaction and then shimmied up the bed until his cock sprang free of her. Sitting up, she looked into his eyes and held his hands in her lap. "C'mon. Tell me."

His gaze darted from their joined hands to her breasts and then back again. "I-I just—" He fell silent again.

She sighed and lifted one of his hands to her breast. Instead of pulling him to her again, she laced her fingers with his. "You're still freaked out about what the Aqiri did?" she whispered.

He closed his eyes, and a tear trickled down his cheek. "What *I* did."

She squeezed his hand hard. "Now stop that. You didn't do anything to me. The Aqiri did."

He hung his head and took a deep breath. "But I still see it. Every time I come near them, I see *my* hands tearing you apart."

The confession stunned Kana but only for a second. "Damn that little bastard. You should have left some of him behind for me to beat the shit out of."

"I could never kill him enough for what he did to you," Jamyn muttered solemnly.

"Exactly. What *he* did. *You* didn't do it." Seeing her words had no effect, she tried another tack. "Do you remember anything from the nokturne dreamstate you were in?"

He nodded. "I saw it later during a replay."

"Remember how you were looking at my double?"

His cheeks reddened at the memory. "Yeah."

"And what were you staring at almost the whole time?" Receiving no response, she glanced down at his cock. Despite his sullen state, it was fully erect and pointing directly at her. "Part of you remembers," she said, fighting off the urge to reach for it.

"I do too," he mumbled.

"What's that?"

He lifted his teary-eyed gaze to her. "I love all of you, Kana. But I—" He swallowed hard and allowed himself another quick peek at her chest. "But I *really* love your tits."

She grinned at the term. "And I think they'd love you right back." She pulled their joined hands toward her and rubbed her nipple with the back of her hand. "You've gotta let it go. Remember that I hit you in the balls on our second mission. I got over it." To prove her point, she reached her free hand down and teased her fingers over his scrotum.

"That's a little different."

"Only if you let it be." She cupped his balls and gave them a light tug. "I've got an idea."

"What?"

"Move." She gave him a gentle shove and then swung her legs around, so she was lying on her side facing away from him. She nudged her chin back over her shoulder. "How about a cuddle?"

He took the hint and spooned up behind her. His cock rested between her taut buttocks, and he pressed a slow kiss to the nape of her neck. She squirmed from the attention, cooing softly at the feel of his body pressed up against hers. Reaching down, she grasped his shaft and guided it between her legs. It slipped between her slick lips without entering her body and she eased herself back and forth, sliding over the top of his shaft.

"How you doing?" she whispered back to him.

"Great," he murmured against her skin. He held her waist, guiding her body's movements over his cock.

Reining in her growing excitement, she rested her hand atop his. She pivoted her hips, adding pressure to his trapped erection. He gasped in the middle of a deep suckling kiss and gripped her waist tighter. Sensing he was ready, she pulled his hand up and guided it to cup her breast.

When the soft flesh filled his hand, his body stiffened in shock. She gave his hand a gentle squeeze and stopped her movements over his cock.

"What do you see now?" she asked while she guided his fingers to hold her erect nipple.

His wide eyes scanned the back of her head. Tiny bumps dotted her neck. "Goosebumps," he whispered back.

She clamped her fingers over his, causing him to firmly pinch her nipple. "And now?"

The tiny hairs at the nape of her neck started to rise.

"Somebody liked that," he replied.

"Only a lot," she said, lifting her body up briefly so he could wrap an arm beneath her to hold her other breast. "Still okay?"

He smiled at last and kissed her shoulder. "Much better than okay," he whispered into her ear. "Thank you."

She started gliding along his length again, teasing him. "I'm sure you can find a better way to thank me," she said, releasing the hand she held and stretching her arms out to brace herself.

He started to gently knead her flesh and lightly stroke his fingertips over her nipples. She responded with a loud moan and started to drive herself back over his cock with renewed vigor. Soon her ass was slapping hard against his pelvis, and she was quickly losing control of the pace. Jamyn responded by squeezing her breasts firmly and pressing them hard against one another. Kana stopped her frantic movements for a second, but it was long enough. He dipped his hips down and then thrust up into her body, filling her in a single stroke. She screamed out her pleasure as he started to relentlessly hammer his cock into her.

"Oh!" She gasped, overwhelmed by the force of his attack. "Oh, you little brat!"

He buried his length within her and held it there. "How's that again, mistress?" he asked, licking up over the shell of her ear. "What kind of brat?" He nearly pulled out but then slid right back in up to the hilt.

"Big one." She groaned and reached a hand back to pull his body closer. "*Big* fuckin' brat."

"And don't you forget it," he said with a smug grin.

In a flash, he was at her again, pistoning his shaft into her while massaging her ample breasts. He firmly pinched both of her nipples, launching her headlong into a thrilling climax. He continued to pump into her while her body thrashed through her orgasm. The added heat and pressure on his cock was more than enough to trigger his own release. He held her tightly as his offering jetted up into her body.

Kana struggled to catch her breath. "Oh, my...*hnng!*" Another aftershock hit, rendering her speechless.

"Yeah." Jamyn wheezed against her back. "What you said."

They started to laugh. Jamyn wrapped his arms around her midsection and hugged her.

Kana snuggled into the warm embrace. "Y'know, I think I could get used to this," she said with a languid smile as she traced her fingers over his strong arms.

He tickled her briefly and kissed her shoulder. "And now you've got plenty of time to, since it looks like I'll be here for a while."

She chuckled. "That move with the cabal back at Evrok's was completely insane. You know that, right?"

"Well, not as insane as you think." He leaned up toward her ear. "Want to know a secret?" he whispered.

"Sure."

"I kinda stacked the deck."

"What?"

"I talked to most of them individually before the meeting. Got 'em all on the same page beforehand to prevent the meeting from going sour."

"Who did you talk to?"

"Tiris and Leel. Daystar." He dropped his voice to a low rumble. "Donta."

She looked back at him over her shoulder. "You didn't."

He smiled at her. "Talked to him first."

Kana was stunned. "When the hell did you—"

"While you were sleeping. Remember I said I had some stuff to take care of?"

"And I told you to stay out of trouble." She gave him a playful dig in the ribs with her elbow. "Thanks for following my directions."

"Anytime, mistress." He stretched over and kissed her nose.

She rolled her eyes. "You're lucky you're great in the sack."

"And the shower." He waggled his eyebrows.

"And wherever else I feel like having you," she said in a rush.

Reaching a hand back to him, she traced her fingers over his cheek. She shifted her body up until his cock slipped out of her and then she turned to face him.

Seeing the familiar fond gleam in his eyes, she rubbed the tip of her nose against his. "Go ahead."

"With what?"

She looked him straight in the eye. "I know you're just *dying* to say it."

His eyebrows rose as he caught her meaning. "Yeah, but are you ready to hear it?"

She smiled warmly and nodded. "I think I am."

"Okay," he said hesitantly. "Kana?"

She nipped her bottom lip and girded herself. "Yeah?"

"I gotta pee."

Her eyes widened. "You what?"

He laughed loudly at her reaction, only fueling her outrage.

"Why you little—" She launched at him and tickled him mercilessly.

He grabbed at her as well, poking her midsection to further provoke her. Soon they were wrestling each other and laughing their heads off. Bedding flew everywhere and Kana took at least one pillow to the face. Bringing all her skills to bear, she finally pinned his hands to the bed and straddled his waist.

"Okay, I give!" he said.

"Damned right you do." Both struggled to catch their breath, and she took full advantage of her helpless prey.

Falling atop him, she sucked hard on his chest just above his left nipple. He laughed and kicked his feet, playfully flailing beneath his captor. After a few seconds, she sat up again to admire her handiwork.

Nodding at the darkened patch of skin, she said, "Caught and branded!"

"And one more thing."

"What's that?"

"I love you."

His words caught her off-guard and she started to blush. Shaking it off, she took in his smug grin. "Oh, you are *so* clever!"

"It works better when you don't expect it," he said, trying not to grin.

A renewed fire blazed in her eyes. Releasing his hands, she firmly grabbed his head. He only had a second to ponder the move before she fell forward and plunged his face into her cleavage. She swung her shoulders from side to side, playfully pummeling his trapped head with her breasts.

"Give up yet?" she asked.

He extended his tongue and licked up the center of her chest.

"Not just yet," his muffled voice replied. "Gimme another couple hours."

She dragged one nipple across his face. "Hey! It's a sneak attack. You're not supposed to be enjoying it!"

He snared the teasing nipple between his lips. "Your own fault," he said out of the corner of his mouth, not wishing to release his captive. "You attacked me with something I love." His lips closed around the excited bud, and he licked it with the tip of his tongue.

She closed her eyes and whimpered at the delicate torture. "Sooner or later we're gonna have to get back to work."

He reluctantly released her nipple, then kissed it firmly. "My vote is for *later*," he said with a wink. Moving to the other breast, he gave it a quick lick. "How about you?"

"Later," she replied breathlessly. "You're busy." She thrust her chest forward, mashing her breast against Jamyn's wild smile.

Chapter Nine: Blossom

K ana woke lying on her side with the blanket bunched up around her face. She drew in a long, deep breath, held it for a moment, and then released it just as slowly. Warmth surrounded her naked body, and she snuggled deeper into her cozy little burrow. For the first time in what seemed like ages, both her body and mind felt truly relaxed. As comfortable as she was, however, one small corner of her mind insisted that something was out of place.

Impossible. She kept her eyes closed. *This is just perfect.*

Despite her denial, instinct held her body still. She continued to scan the area around her with all her senses.

The faintest squeak of the bedsprings was all it took. The haze enveloping her mind burned off in a flash. Someone was snuggled up behind her. A hand that wasn't hers rested lightly upon her hip. Her defenses automatically flared but her memory jolted just before she could summon up her magic.

It's only Jamyn, moron! I'm still in his bed.

She relaxed again and rolled her eyes behind her closed lids at her instinctive reaction.

Now recovered from her initial shock, she realized his presence was actually quite pleasant. The heat coming from his lean body mingled with hers in their shared cocoon. His fingers flexed upon her bare hip. Slow, even breaths tickled the nape of her neck. Before long, she found herself smiling. She had never woken up with someone before, but she quickly decided she could get used to it. She opened her eyes and carefully turned over to face him.

His amber eyes greeted her. "Morning, beautiful," he murmured with a warm smile.

She arched an eyebrow at him. "Morning back. How long have you been up?"

"A little while. Sleep well?"

She nodded once. "You've just been sitting here watching me sleep? That's not creepy or anything."

"Hey, it's nice seeing you peaceful for a change"—he gave her hip a playful shake—"and not beating me up."

She poked him in the chest. "Wimp."

"Meanie."

She tossed him a brief frown. "I don't beat you up that much."

"Dunno about that. You ran me ragged last night."

"Is that a complaint?"

"If I *ever* complain about that, I want you to shoot me in the head." He skimmed his hand up along her side. "Twenty or thirty times."

She tickled his ribs. "Deal. So, what are we up to today?" She let her fingers wander down across his stomach and grinned.

"I thought we could start visiting the people I crossed paths with during my jumps," he said quickly as her hand closed in on his morning erection. "I'd like to tie up those loose ends."

"Good idea." She teased her fingertips lower. "Wrap up the old goofs before we start making new ones."

Jamyn grimaced. "Thanks a lot, mistress."

She gave him a curt nod. "You *should* be thanking me, acolyte. I made your first visit easy."

"How's that?"

"Remember the young Arab girl you met? The one with the push?"

"Sort of."

"Her name's Shamara. She's here in the Sanctum."

His eyes widened. "She is? How?"

"I sent her here."

"Why?"

"Her family and friends were all dead. That and the locals found out about her magic and didn't take it well. I talked to Qa and decided to send her here to develop her talents. If she wants, I'll sponsor her for membership in the Sanctum."

His gaze softened. "That was sweet of you."

She smirked at the compliment. "Yeah, that's me. Sweet all over."

He glanced down and licked his lips. "No argument there."

"You naughty little thing!" She grasped his cock and gave him a few teasing strokes. "And here I was trying to behave!"

"Right," he replied through his clenched teeth. "Like you were behaving last night when you left all those love bites on me."

She leaned forward, bumping the tip of her nose against his. "That wasn't behaving. I was marking my territory."

He laughed. "Oh, I get it. That would explain why I feel like the victim of a land rush. How many flags did you plant, anyway? I lost track."

She released his cock and pulled his body closer. "I'll help you count 'em later," she whispered.

"And probably add a few more."

"Maybe. If you're lucky."

He laughed again and pulled her into a solid hug. "I guess I should get used to wearing long-sleeved turtlenecks," he murmured into her ear before kissing the side of her neck.

"Nah," she replied, snuggling into his arms. "I'll get you some concealer."

"From your personal stock, right?"

"What kind of lousy stalker are you? You should know by now that I don't use makeup."

"Why ruin perfection?" He sighed happily and hugged her tighter.

The simple comment sent a tingle throughout her body. "Yeah, right," she said, pressing a kiss to his cheek.

"Hey."

She pulled back to look at his face. His smile was one of complete adoration and she choked down the lump in her throat. "Yeah?"

"Good morning."

"You already said that."

"Not *properly*."

He came forward and kissed her with a passion that stole all thought from her mind. She fell into it willingly, holding him close while he continued to silently worship her. His hands roamed over her body. Though she quickly warmed to his touch, something told her it was not meant to arouse her. It was as if he was trying to gather her in one sensation at a time. A sense of completeness washed over Kana, and she quickly found herself unable to deny the feelings emanating from his entire being. She squeezed her eyes shut and clung to him. All the while, a storm started to brew in the back of her mind.

"What's wrong?"

His voice snapped her mind back to the present. He was no longer kissing her. A brief space now separated his body from hers.

Opening her eyes, she looked back at his concerned face. "Huh?"

"You're crying." He dabbed the wet trail over the bridge of her nose with his finger.

Quickly shaking it off, she forced a smile. "No, I'm fine." She bumped her nose to his. "You're just really sweet."

"You sure?"

"Yeah," she replied, punctuating her words with a quick kiss. "I suppose we should get up and get to it."

"Okay," he said. From his tone, she could tell he didn't quite believe her. "Where is Shamara staying?"

"I told Qa to have her stay with Lob. That way, Lob could check out her abilities."

"Makes sense."

Kana looked up to the ceiling. "Hey, Sanctum."

"Kana," a disembodied voice replied.

"Location of Lob the Unmarred."

"Training room seven. He has it marked as a private session."

"Tell him Kana and Jamyn want to pop by for a visit."

Several seconds passed. Jamyn started to say something, but Kana waved at him to keep quiet.

Suddenly the voice returned. "You have been granted access if you abide by his usual conditions."

"I'd have it no other way," Kana said with a smile. "Thanks." Turning back to Jamyn, she gave him another quick kiss. "Get up, get dressed, and meet me at seven. On the double!" She settled back against her pillow and eyed him expectantly.

"Um, okay." He frowned at her inaction. "What are *you* waiting for?"

"You, of course."

"Huh?"

She waved a hand toward the bathroom. "My turn to ogle you getting up out of bed," she said with a lurid grin.

He glanced down at the blanket. Though his erection had started to subside, he felt it twitch back to life at her suggestion. "No."

"No?"

"Yeah. No."

She cocked her head. "Which is it?"

He tried his best not to go along with her playing. "No, I'm not gonna parade around in front of you."

She sat up, holding the blanket to her chest. "And why not?"

He sat up and his gaze locked with hers. "Because we're never gonna get anything done if we keep tackling each other."

"And that's a bad thing?"

He sighed. "Yeah, it is."

She reached over and tweaked his nose. "Points for your sense of duty, acolyte. Though I should take 'em right back for making your mistress wait."

"Maybe I'm worth it," he said without thinking. He flinched and bowed his head.

Kana considered his words while the tempest in the back of her mind flared. "Yeah, maybe you are," she said softly. Coming forward, she tipped his chin up with her fingers before pressing a kiss to his lips. Her body started to glow. "Get yourself together and meet me at seven," she murmured against his lips. Her body scattered into a flurry of glowing petals of light that quickly disappeared.

———— ◉ ————

Jamyn marveled at the slow dissolve, so different from the abruptness of the usual teleport spell. Once she was gone, he fell back on the bed and stared at the ceiling. "Kana," he whispered to the empty room. Fear crept back into his heart, prompted by the night terrors that had jolted him awake nearly an hour before her.

———— ◉ ————

Kana thumped her fist against the shower wall while the warm spray doused her body. "It's just sex," she said to herself yet again. "He's young, he's hot, and he's a fabulous fuck. No problem." Her heart twitched at her words. She leaned her forehead against the wall and sighed. "And he's in love with me," she whispered. "Dammit."

Grabbing her bath mitt, she soaped it up and forced herself to continue her shower. "So what?" she said, continuing her debate while she lathered up. "He's in love. He already knows I'm not and he's okay with it."

"Is that so?" asked a female voice from outside the shower.

"The fuck?" Kana flung open the shower door.

Eva stood there smiling at her. "Having a little disagreement with yourself?"

"Dammit to hell, Eva! Get the fuck outta here!"

"Some greeting." Eva huffed despite her smile. "Your head is the one who called me out. I'm guessing you're having some sort of earth-shattering moral dilemma."

"Nothing of the kind." Kana grumbled and quickly turned her body under the spray to rinse herself off. She shut off the water and stormed past Eva to grab a towel. "Jamyn and I finally got down to it. That's all. End of story." She brought her hand right up to Eva's face and flexed her fingers in a brief wave. "Buh-bye." She pulled away again and started to towel herself dry.

"You know that's not all."

"It's all that's important," Kana said from under the towel as she dried her hair.

"Then why am I here?"

Kana groaned in disgust. "Stress, most likely. We're gonna start visiting the innocent bystanders he messed with on his jaunt. Might get a bit dodgy."

"Or maybe he stopped fucking you long enough for you to start thinking again." Eva lowered her voice. "Maybe that thinking is scaring you to death."

Kana pulled the towel off her head and glared at Eva. "Maybe you're full of shit." Kana snarled the words through her clenched teeth. Reaching up, she pinched a lock of hair and held it up. "Color?"

Eva sighed. "Black."

"And you know why."

"I do."

"So that's it. End of story."

Eva's body started to fade away. Before she fully disappeared, she whispered, "But for how long?"

Kana turned to look at herself in the mirror. Her memory briefly challenged the sight of her short black hair, and her frown deepened. "It's there to stay," she said before leaving the bathroom to get dressed.

——————⚬——————

Kana jogged up the corridor to training room seven. Jamyn was already there, leaning against the door.

"Hey."

"Hey," he replied with a brief smile. "You okay?"

"Fine." She grabbed the door handle. "Ready?"

He stepped out of the way and nodded. "Yeah."

She opened the door and hurried past him. "Hang back. Remember you don't have your magic."

"Oh, yeah. Good call," he said as he followed her in.

The interior of training room seven was that of an oriental garden, though the buildings were now spaced farther apart, making the enclosed courtyard even bigger. Kana carefully stalked into the open space while Jamyn stuck to the wooden walkway surrounding it. A giant boulder sat in the center of the grassy space. Beside it, the ground bulged up in a small mound.

Kana suddenly sprinted forward and vaulted atop the boulder. Spikes of glowing light shot from her outstretched hands, driving themselves into the ground around the perimeter of the raised area. Crackling strands of electricity arced between the stakes, weaving a net that covered the hill.

"Gotcha, tiny!" she called down in triumph.

The grass became transparent, revealing Lob lying on the ground beneath one of his shields.

"You've got me?" The giant chuckled. "With what?"

He jumped to his feet, forcing his shield and the encompassing net straight up. The magical stakes were yanked out of the ground and the electric arcs drew them all together in a bright ball of magic right above Lob. The sudden movement jostled Kana atop her precarious perch and she fell backwards with a cry of surprise. Lob manipulated his shield to crush the ball of light. He leaned around the boulder to see Kana.

"Not even close. Promotion must have made you soft."

A hand smacked him hard on the ass and Kana's laughing shout sounded behind him. "Who you calling soft, doughboy?"

Lob stood up straight again, thrusting his hands high above his head. "Don't shoot, officer!" he cried in mock distress. "The man was dead when I got there!"

Kana laughed at the ridiculous statement. "What man?" Suddenly her arms were pinned to her sides and her trapped body rose into the air.

Lob turned around just as her face came level with his. "The last one who tried something sneaky like that," he said with a grin. "They said his head was embedded in what looked like a giant butt-print in the ground. The darnedest thing, really."

"Ooh, I bet that stung."

"Sure did. I had a head-print in my right cheek for hours."

Kana shook her head and chuckled. "How's it going, Lob?"

Lob directed his shield to lower Kana back to the ground. He dispelled it and bowed low. "Quite well, First Seer! Out terrorizing the populace again?"

"What makes you say that?"

"A couple of my students ran into Jamyn the other day. I thought they were gonna have heart attacks after their close call with the acolyte of the Sanctum's she-demon." He turned to see Jamyn off in the distance looking back at them. "Why are you lurking in the shadows?" Lob asked him. He jerked a huge thumb at Kana. "Mom ground you for ruining her killer rep and not dying yet?"

Jamyn's bemused smile turned into a stifled laugh. "Nah, Lob. I've got my magic locked down right now. I wouldn't be much of a fight."

"Bummer," Lob said. "Anyway, I'm sure you two are here for the same reason." He cleared his throat and then released a bellowing shout. "Come on out, my little battle maid!"

The doors of the building behind him burst open. A young girl rocketed out and soared through the air. She reached her arms forward, produced a blast of force that slowed her to a stop, and then landed neatly beside Lob.

"Here I am, Mister Lob!" she said before bowing to him.

"Nice entrance, Shammie. Got some people here that want to see you."

Shamara straightened up and saw Kana. "Miss Kana!"

"Hi, Sham—*oof*!" Kana wheezed as the young girl lunged forward and caught her in a tight hug. She looked down to see the neophyte clad in loose pants and a light, airy top. Her long, dark hair was bundled into a single ponytail. "I see Lob taught you some English."

"No, Miss Kana," Shamara replied without releasing her. "Mister Qa took me to see Miss Baba when I first got here."

"Nice." Kana briefly wondered what Qa had to exchange for that favor. "You can let me go now."

Jamyn walked over and smiled at Kana's predicament. "Looks like you've got another fan."

At the sound of his voice, Shamara's entire body stiffened. She stepped back from Kana to see the newcomer. In a heartbeat, she fired the push straight at Jamyn. The blast sent him flying back toward the entrance.

Lob caught Jamyn in a curved shield that gently spiraled the acolyte's body back to the ground. Once he landed, the slide changed into a transparent wall between him and the others.

"Hold your fire there, Shammie!" Lob said. "He's a friend."

Kana had unintentionally broken into a run toward Jamyn. She caught herself after a few steps and skidded to a stop. Gathering her wits, she called out, "You okay?"

"Yeah," Jamyn replied, standing up again. "I'm fine."

Kana nodded curtly and turned back to Shamara. Seeing the look of remorse on the young girl's face, Kana smiled. "Take it easy. That's Jamyn. He's the one I was looking for when I found you."

Shamara instantly fell into a low bow. "I'm sorry, Miss Kana!" she said, her voice a repentant squeak.

Kana looked to Lob, silently mouthing, "Miss Kana?"

Lob grinned and nodded. "Excellent reaction speed, kiddo," he said gently. "Just be sure to identify the target first next time, okay?"

She remained bent over and sniffled. "I am sorry, Mister Lob."

"Now cut that out." He gently patted her head. "It was a simple misunderstanding. Nobody got hurt." He reached one finger beneath her chin and tipped her head up so he could see her teary eyes. "I told you before," he whispered. "No one's sending you away. They'll have to get through me to try. And..."

She smiled despite her tears. "And no one can move Mister Lob!"

"Too true!" He scooped her up off the ground and she shrieked in delight. He sat her on his broad shoulder. Dispelling his shield, he told Jamyn, "C'mon, kid. Get over here and introduce yourself properly."

Jamyn jogged over, keeping an eye on Shamara the whole time. "Hi, Shamara," he said as he approached. "I'm Jamyn. We kind of met before."

She nodded. "I'm sorry for hitting you."

He smiled. "Don't worry about it. These two hit me all the time."

"Hey, I only do it during training," Lob said

"Yeah. Training," Kana said with a sneaky grin.

Jamyn shot them both a look. "Right, guys." Returning his gaze to Shamara, he continued. "Besides, that was a really good attack! What was it?"

"I call it the push," Shamara replied shyly. "I've been able to do it for a few years."

"And it's one of the coolest things I've ever seen," Lob said, patting Shamara on the back. "It's really unique."

"How so?" Kana asked.

"It's not totally magic-based. At least it doesn't act like it when it interacts with my shields or the null rock. I can't figure it out." He looked from Kana to Jamyn and back again. "Maybe you two could help with that."

"Sure," Kana replied. "What do you need?"

"Hit the null rock with a basic force beam."

Kana lifted one hand and fired a shot at the boulder. The magic struck it and immediately dissipated without a sound.

Lob lifted Shamara from his shoulder and stood her back on the ground. "Now you hit it with the push."

Shamara focused on the stone and gestured with both hands. The blast of force hit with a loud thump and the stone budged slightly.

"See?" Lob asked, gesturing to the rock. "It wipes out pure magic but doesn't negate all of the push."

"Huh," Kana said, equally perplexed. Turning to Jamyn, she asked, "Any ideas?"

"Not really." He thought a moment. "Maybe the Voice could give us a clue."

"Good job. That's what I was thinking."

Jamyn smirked. "Another test, huh?"

"Yep. Problem Solving 101. Use all the tools in your kit." Kana tuned her mind until she could see the Voice clearly. "Shamara, hit it with the push again."

Shamara loosed another shot while Kana watched the null rock intently. Once again, the rock shuddered with a loud thump. The surrounding swirls of ambient magic that Kana now saw, however, were undisturbed.

"Hmm," Kana said with a frown. "Not much to go on."

"You're not looking in the right place," Jamyn said, awe evident in his voice.

"Huh?" She looked to Jamyn to see him staring at Shamara. She focused on the girl too. "Do it again, please."

This time, Kana saw the undulating clouds of energy surrounding Shamara suddenly vanish as their power was drawn into the young girl's body. Shamara loosed the push and a faint edge of light billowed from her outstretched hands. The magic flowed back around her as before, replenishing the depleted area.

Both Kana and Jamyn blinked hard, restoring their vision.

"Now *that* was cool," Jamyn whispered.

"So, what have we got?" Lob asked.

"One immensely talented young girl!" Kana smiled brightly at Shamara. "From the look of it, she draws in the ambient magical energy around her and then transforms it into a blast of kinetic force."

"I hit it good?" Shamara asked Lob in an unsure voice.

Lob dropped to one knee and laughed. "You hit it *real* good!" She hugged him tightly, though her arms barely reached around one of his massive biceps. "What do you think?" he asked Kana.

Kana nodded. "I think it's time."

"Time?" Jamyn asked.

She nodded to him, holding up a hand to indicate he should wait. "Hey, Shamara?"

Shamara looked over without releasing Lob's arm. "Yes?"

"How do you like the Sanctum so far?"

"I love it here," she said emphatically. "No one has been mean to me. And Mister Lob and Miss Juushin have been helping me control the push."

Kana arched an eyebrow at Lob. "Crusha is in on it too?"

Lob tried not to look embarrassed. "Er, yes. I asked her to spar with Shammie, but only after I swore her to secrecy."

"Hmm. That's not good," Kana replied sternly. "The Sanctum's not big on secrets." She looked over to Jamyn. "Right?"

Jamyn caught on and played along. "Oh, no," he said in a dire tone. "Secrets are definitely frowned upon here."

"And outsiders too. I think we're gonna have to do something about this."

Shamara clung tighter to Lob's arm and whimpered. "Do I have to leave?"

Kana shook her head. "No, I think there's a better way to fix this. How would you like to be an official member of the Sanctum?"

Shamara turned her unbelieving stare to Lob, who was grinning madly. "She means it?" she asked, her voice a mere whisper.

"Yes, she does," Lob replied gently. He peeked at both Kana and Jamyn, who both smiled back at him. "Even though those two are being total jerks about it. Should be ashamed. Worrying a poor girl like this." He brought his face close to hers. "So whaddaya say? Want to live here? For real?"

"Yes!" she cried before kissing his cheek. She hugged him tightly and hopped up and down in excitement.

Kana chuckled at Lob's flustered expression. "Congratulations," she said. "It's a girl!"

Lob had just started to frown at her joke when Shamara suddenly tore away from him. She ran straight to Kana and enveloped her in a tight hug. "Thank you, Miss Kana!" she said, pressing her face hard against Kana's chest.

Kana gasped through the tight hug. "There's just one thing you have to promise me."

Shamara looked up at her face, but her grip didn't loosen. "What?"

Kana smiled. "I'm just Kana. No *miss*."

"Okay, Mi—" Shamara swallowed hard and nodded emphatically. "Okay, Kana!"

Kana kissed her forehead. "Good deal." She pried herself free and gestured to the others. "So, it's formal introduction time. The big lug there is Lob the Unmarred. Basically, a giant lump of crazy housing the best defense teacher in the Sanctum." She turned to Jamyn. "And that is Jamyn Siska, my acolyte. When he's not out causing trouble and scaring young girls"—she playfully poked Shamara's side—"he's actually pretty useful."

Jamyn shook his head at the description then bowed to Shamara. "Hello again, Shamara. I'm hoping I didn't scare you when we first met."

"I was scared of everything then, Mister Jamyn," she replied quietly.

"Still, I'm hoping I didn't add to it. I didn't hurt you, did I?"

"No, you didn't. You just appeared somehow and said some things I didn't understand. I didn't know your language then." She fidgeted a bit. "I hit you with the push, but it didn't affect you."

"Ah. I probably absorbed it."

"Absorbed it?" Lob asked in surprise.

"One of the energy talents he has," Kana said. "Like when he analyzed your shields."

"I'm just glad I didn't hurt you," Jamyn said to Shamara. "I hope we can be friends."

Shamara turned a questioning gaze to Lob, as if she was looking for his approval.

Lob chuckled at her. "Hey, you can hang around with whoever you like. Even this little troublemaker."

She turned back to Jamyn. "You're friends with Mi—" She fell silent and started again. "You're friends with Kana, right?"

Jamyn looked to Kana.

"Well, are we?" Kana asked, trying not to smile.

Emboldened, Jamyn nodded. "Yeah. We're friends."

"Then we can be too," Shamara said with a shy smile.

"Great!" Lob said. "When's the party?"

"What party?" Kana asked.

"Shammie's official *welcome to the Sanctum* party, of course."

Kana laughed. "Let's get it approved first." She cast a converse spell. "Hey, Qa."

"Yes, Kana?" Qa's voice replied.

"Time to make it real. I'm officially requesting that Shamara be admitted into the Sanctum as a full card-carrying member."

Lob grumbled to himself. "Hmmph. I never got a card."

"Your request has been officially noted," Qa said in a lively tone. "You have five days to bring Shamara before the Inner Cabal for final approval. Until then, she can move about the whole of the Sanctum with the proper supervision." He chuckled. "Tell Lob he doesn't have to carry her around in that backpack anymore."

Kana saw Lob's embarrassed grin. "I'll let him know. And thanks for setting Shamara up with Babbles. I don't think I want to know what that cost ya."

"Just as well, as I'm unlikely to tell you," Qa replied, sounding a bit flustered.

"Over and out." Kana laughed and cancelled the spell. She turned back to Lob. "Backpack?"

"Well, yeah," Lob said. "I didn't want the poor kid to go stir crazy just sitting in here all day. I conjured up a shield bubble on my back so I could show her around the place. I disguised it as a backpack. Qa must have figured out what it really was."

"Yeah, he's funny like that," Kana said with a smile.

"Mister Jamyn?" Shamara asked hesitantly.

Jamyn smiled. "Just *Jamyn* is fine. What's on your mind?"

"Why were you in my village?"

"That's kind of complicated," Jamyn replied. "I got into some trouble. When I first met you, I was jumping from place to place looking for sources of magic I could tap into. I must have sensed your abilities."

"Thank you."

"Huh? For what?"

"If you hadn't, then Kana wouldn't have found me and I wouldn't have ended up in this wonderful place," She ran over to Jamyn. "Thank you!" she cried, wrapping her arms around him.

"No problem," he said, hugging her back.

Kana walked over and ruffled her fingers through Jamyn's hair. "*Now* who's got a fan, smart guy?" she asked with a grin.

Several loud thumps at the entrance door to the room startled them. Shamara looked up at Lob and giggled. "Miss Juushin's here!"

"Crusha?" Kana asked Lob.

Lob nodded. "She was coming over today for another sparring session."

"Then we'd better get outta here," Kana said to Jamyn. "Ready for the next hop?"

Jamyn released Shamara and stood next to Kana. "Ready. Congrats, Shamara!"

"Yeah. Welcome to the madhouse," Kana said with a pat on the young girl's shoulder.

"Thank you both!" Shamara exclaimed.

The door to the room burst open and they heard heavy footsteps rapidly approaching.

Shamara instantly assumed an attack pose next to Lob. "Here she comes, Mister Lob!"

"Let's knock her down today, Shammie!" The giant laughed and likewise readied himself.

"And we're gone," Kana said, casting a gate spell.

Judging by the increasing din, she would have sworn they were about to be trampled by an oncoming stampede of rhinos. Lob and Shamara leaped forward just before Kana and her acolyte disappeared.

Chapter Ten: Roughing It

"Where are we?"

Kana dispelled the gate behind her. Looking around the wooded area, she said, "Site of your second jump. Deep in the heart o' the fucked-up south." She cupped a hand to her ear. "*Der der-der der der*," she said with an exaggerated twang, mimicking a banjo.

Jamyn laughed. "Shore nuff, Daisy Lou?"

"Shore nuff, Bubba," she replied with a grin. "Most of your jumps ended up in places close to our previous mission sites. Shamara was near the dubsov. This is—"

"Ah. Sorry about that."

She wrinkled her nose at him. "Don't worry about it. We're a couple of counties over from the Junction. I'm pretty sure the pair we're looking for were headed *away* from the stupid."

"The girl and the demon."

"Ex-demon," she said. "Be careful about whipping out the D-word when we catch up to them. He might still be having issues with it."

"Gotcha."

Kana took a good look around. "The cabin I found her in is several days' walk that-a-way." She pointed deeper into the woods. Turning her back to it, she pointed ahead. "So, they must be that-a-way. We should be able to pick up their trail as we go. Let's get a move on." With this, she started off at a brisk pace.

Jamyn hurried to catch up with her. Soon they were walking side by side at an impressive rate.

"Where were they going after you left them?" Jamyn asked after a while.

"Dunno. Rayven seemed intent on putting as much distance between her and this place as possible. Wherever she went, I'm sure Eddie followed."

"Eddie? Kind of a weird name for a demon."

Kana smiled. "I named him that."

"Why?"

"Think about it. Eddie. Rayven."

Jamyn groaned. "Really? A Poe joke? That's bad."

"Hell, he might have chosen another name by now." She thought a moment. "Though he did seem to like how it sounded when Rayven called him Eddie."

"He fell in love with her while he was still a demon? That's odd, isn't it?"

"*Odd* doesn't start to cover it. For a demon to think of a human as much more than a food source is way weird." She shrugged. "Just something about her, I suppose."

"They say everybody's got somebody out there. I guess she was his."

Kana glanced over at him without slowing her steps. The uneasy feeling in the back of her mind surged while she struggled to phrase a response. She was just about to open her mouth when Jamyn's voice stopped her.

"Sorry."

She nearly broke stride but kept her steps even with a solid effort. "Huh?"

Jamyn sighed. "You already know how I feel about you," he said quietly. "I shouldn't keep bringing it up."

Kana tried to appear unaffected by his words. "Hey, you're in love. They say people in love do strange things."

"Yeah. I guess."

His tone was sad enough to set off a flutter in her chest. "Come on, then," she said firmly. "Let's pick up the pace. Hopefully they haven't gotten too far ahead." She cast a spell over them both to boost their speed and stamina. The pair streaked forward through the woods, each mired in their own thoughts.

———◉———

Jamyn panted heavily. "Maybe we should call it a night."

Kana stumbled over a tangle of roots in the near-total darkness. The night vision spells she had cast over them earlier were starting to fade, making the surrounding terrain even more impassable.

"Good call," she replied. She cast a quick cantrip. A small ball of light appeared, illuminating the area around them. "Ouch," she said, looking at the thick ground clutter.

"I think there's a bit of clearing over that way," Jamyn said, pointing into the darkness.

Kana squinted at the dark expanse. "How can you tell?"

"Moonlight coming in through the canopy. At the very least, there's no trees."

She shrugged and motioned for the light to follow Jamyn. "Lead on, scout."

———◉———

A short walk later, they were standing in the center of a relatively clear patch of ground. The area was bigger than Jamyn expected, a good eight feet across, and had a sparse covering of grass. The gentle glow of the moon shrouded their chosen spot, making the guide light unnecessary.

"*Ta-daa*," he said with a smile.

"Nice," Kana replied. She looked up through the gap in the tree cover. "No clouds, so no threat of rain. You okay without a tent?"

Jamyn nodded. "Fine with me."

She pulled the stash out of her back pocket and reached an arm into it. She rooted around for a moment before pulling out a rolled-up blanket. Together they spread it out on the ground. She laid down and stretched out across it.

"Not exactly a feather bed but it'll do," she said. Seeing Jamyn staring down at her, she asked, "What?"

Jamyn didn't hear her as he continued to drink in the sight of his beloved. She appeared to him to be a sylph maiden birthed from the forest itself, her tempting form bathed in moonlight. The hunger within him stirred and his body teetered as it cried out for him to pounce.

"Like what you see?" she asked coyly, rolling on her side and drawing one bent knee up. She thrust her chest out and teasingly stroked one hand up over her thigh.

Jamyn whimpered. "Um..."

She cupped a breast in her hand, teasing a finger over her nipple. "You in there?" she asked in a sultry murmur.

"Uh...yeah," he said, his voice barely rising above a whisper.

"Getting kinda lonely down here all by myself," she said, nodding at the empty space beside her.

"Yeah," he said, still mired in his stupor.

She flicked her hand toward him. The guide light shot straight at Jamyn and smacked right into his chest. The ball popped, producing a dazzling burst of sparks. He came alive with a start, swatting at the sparks, which rapidly disappeared. "What the—" he cried, only to be cut off by her spirited laughter. "Why'd you do that?"

"It seemed more polite than dumping a bucket of water on your head. I think your brain slipped into neutral again."

"It had help," he grumbled.

"Yeah?"

"Yeah. You look way too good in the moonlight."

She stretched out again, this time folding her hands behind her head. "How 'bout now?"

His enamored gaze raked over her body. "Even better."

"Why's that?"

"You're smiling. You always look better when you do that."

"Silver-tongued little devil. You trying to seduce me?"

He frowned at her joke.

"Hey, I didn't say it wasn't working," she said, waggling her eyebrows at him. She patted the blanket beside her. "C'mere, you." He laid down, keeping his eyes locked with hers the entire time. Soon they were lying on their sides and staring into one another's eyes.

"Hi," she whispered.

"Hi," he whispered back, quickly falling under her spell again.

She regarded his adoring gaze and sighed. "Has your brain completely turned to mush or are there still some lumpy bits in there?"

The odd question took him by surprise. "What?"

"Hey, there's one now," she said with a grin. Reaching over, she gave him a playful shove. "You really need to work on that."

"Now what?"

"The way your brain seems to shut down every other time you look at me."

"It doesn't shut down," he said quietly. "There's plenty going on in there when I look at you."

"Such as?"

The dim light effectively concealed his blush. "Being with you." Her incredulous look made him swallow nervously.

"So, when it looks like you're spacing out, you're really thinking up naughty things to do to me?" She ran her fingers over his concealed bulge and whistled softly when she felt how hard he was. "Hmm. I guess you are." She cupped his balls through his jeans.

"What sordid little fantasy was running through your mind just now?"

"Cut it out, Kana," he said, torn between snarling at her and wanting to grab her in return.

"No, I really do want to know." Coming closer, she kissed him. Pulling away again, she smiled at him. "Tell me."

"I want to try something," he replied, summoning up his courage.

"Care to clarify?" she whispered in reply, all trace of teasing now gone from her voice.

He kissed her again and reluctantly pulled her hand away from his crotch. Easing forward, he rolled her onto her back. "Just stay there," he said between kisses.

"Mm-hmm," she murmured against his mouth.

He continued to nibble at her lips while he placed her hands at her sides. Propping himself up on one elbow, he started to unbuckle her pants with his free hand. Once her zipper had been pulled down, he slipped his hand into her panties and cupped her mound. Their kisses deepened and she thrust her tongue up into his mouth. He spread out his hand, spacing her panties away from her bare charms, then slid his middle finger down through her folds. Gathering her moisture, he slowly spread it over her outer lips.

She pulled away from his mouth and sucked in a deep shivery breath. "Jamyn."

"Shh," he said against her cheek. "Just relax." He started tracing the tip of his middle finger in an endless circle around her clit.

"That makes it"—she gasped again and squirmed beneath him—"kinda hard to relax!"

"Try. For me," he murmured, kissing her cheek.

He rubbed her clit with long sweeping strokes, every so often dipping his middle finger down to gather more of her juices. He kept her outer lips spread wide with his other fingers, ensuring access to every part of her. All the while, he nuzzled her cheek and neck.

Her orgasm started building up from the tips of her toes. She spread her legs wider and arched her back up off the ground, meeting Jamyn's every teasing stroke. Her lips moved in a wordless litany, broken pieces of sound merging with her heavy breathing. All at once, her arms and legs seemed to lose all feeling, and her body slumped back to the ground. Just as she settled upon the blanket, a spark restored sensation to her entire body in one searing jolt. She started coming, pushing up against Jamyn's touch while her screams pierced the night. She clenched fistfuls of blanket in each hand, twisting and pulling the fabric while her entire body writhed in pleasure. Turning her head, she tried to come forward to kiss him. For some reason, he kept his distance. She gasped and moaned, wanting nothing more than to draw him closer but he still did nothing but look back at her helpless thrashing. The waves of pleasure finally receded, and she fell limp, panting and sobbing in her afterglow.

She was suddenly aware of his lips against her cheek.

"You are amazing," he whispered into her ear. "Thank you."

She blinked several times, trying to steady her vision. The image of the moonlit treetops finally cleared, and she took a deep breath. "What?" She gasped, unable to manage much more than the simple query.

"For indulging me." He moved his face over hers and smiled. "I love you, Kana," he said before kissing her gently.

The burst of unease that usually followed was lost amid the slowing beat of her heart. She closed her eyes and let herself revel in his kiss and his words. She was barely aware of him fastening her pants again and snuggling up beside her on the blanket. The night wrapped around them in a warm embrace, and she fell asleep in his arms.

———— ◉ ————

Jamyn was face down on a cold metallic floor. His entire body was wracked with pain. The taste of blood filled his mouth. Though he could not see a thing, his ears caught every sound around him. The clink of metal. A heavy boot scuffing against the floor. An angry voice that grumbled to itself before rising into a fierce bellow.

"The Soul Flame shall be extinguished!"

Jamyn's eyes popped open. The first rays of sunlight played across the treetops directly above him. His entire body broke out in a sweat that was quickly cooled by the light morning breeze. His thudding heart threatened to batter its way through his chest, but a curious weight there kept it contained. Glancing down, he saw Kana's head resting upon him. Her arm was wrapped around his midsection. The sight of her helped calm him but also strengthened his desire to hide this latest nightmare from her.

What the hell's wrong with me? Why have I been having these stupid dreams ever since Kana and I got together?

He sighed deeply before pressing a kiss to the top of her head.

———— ◉ ————

She jerked awake and her grip on his waist stiffened, but she relaxed again just as quickly. "Jamyn?" she mumbled against his chest.

"Good morning," he said, running a hand through her short hair.

"Yeah," she said. "Morning." She yawned deeply and gave him a quick squeeze. "Sleep well?"

"Like the dead. You?"

She poked his chest a few times. "You're not the worst pillow I've ever had." Lifting her head, she rubbed the cheek that had been pressed against him. Looking up at him, she caught a hint of unease in his eyes. "Something wrong?"

"Nah, I'm fine. Just wondering where our quarry is."

She yawned again. "You and me both. I thought for sure we would have caught up to them by now." Noticing his troubled look hadn't completely faded, she asked, "What else?"

"Nothing."

"Come on. Tell me."

"Nothing. Really!"

"Is it about last night? I did kinda leave you hanging."

He drew in a sharp breath but quickly merged it with a longer inhalation. "No, you didn't. I wanted to watch you come. That's all."

She traced a hand up his leg. "Then you don't want to..."

"Not right now, if it's okay with you. We should find those two as soon as we can."

Her stroke stopped at mid-thigh. "Probably a good idea. I didn't think tracking them down would be..." Her voice trailed off.

"What?" he asked.

She dropped her face back to his chest. "I am such an idiot," she muttered into his shirt.

"Huh?"

She looked up at him again. "It's all your fault, you know."

"What'd I do?"

"You keep turning my body inside out and upside down. Evidently my brain didn't escape unscathed." She laughed at his confused expression. "*Locan*, dammit! He's probably been tracking Eddie ever since the kid called him!"

"Who's Locan?"

"Member of the Palatinae. They're the Vatican's version of the Sanctum. They make sure that God's fan club is kept safe from stuff that goes bump in the night."

"I've heard of them. So, this Locan guy tracked down Eddie?"

"Nah. I gave Eddie his number. I figured a reformed demon could use all the help he could get. I also had Qa put in a good word for him on my behalf. You know, to keep Locan from blowing Eddie's head off when he found him."

"Good plan."

Kana sat up and cast a converse spell. "Hey, Qa!"

"Yes, Kana?" came the tired reply.

Kana winced. "Sorry. I wake you?"

"I was planning on waking up today anyway. What do you need?"

"Any idea if Locan put a tracer on Eddie?"

"I'm sure he did. Shall I check?"

"If you could. Locan usually ignores converse spells, and I don't have a phone handy."

"It's early evening in Rome, so he should still be up. One moment."

Jamyn sat up. "A tracer?"

Kana nodded. "Standard procedure for Palatinae. They like to keep track of critters in case they go sour."

"Kana?" Qa asked.

"Yeah, Qa?"

"He gave me the tracker code, along with a few rather inventive curses."

"Sheesh. What's lodged up his ass this time?"

"They're currently some distance east of the Vatican, so it's much later there. That and he sounded rather preoccupied."

"Oops. I'll have to apologize to him once we get back. Gimme the code."

"One three zero one one one Edward David."

"Thirteen oh-one-eleven ED," Kana said to confirm the code.

"Correct."

"Thanks, Qa." She cut the connection and smiled at Jamyn. "Now we sit back and let tech do the job."

She pulled out the stash and reached inside. After a few moments of feeling around, she pulled out a small black device that looked like a handheld radio. She punched in the code on its keypad and the device's screen blazed to life. "And our little friends are—" she said before gawking open-mouthed at the displayed results.

"What?" Jamyn asked.

"All your fault," she mumbled.

"*Now* what?"

"Your fault," she said again, as if he had never spoken. "Gotta be." She took a deep breath and released it in an exasperated growl. "Y'know, I used to be good at this kind of stuff," she said, wagging a finger at him. "You've officially ruined me!"

He finally lost his patience. "What the hell are you on about?" His anger diffused with a surprised squeak as she lunged at him and planted her hands firmly on his thighs.

"I was the best damned caster in the whole Sanctum," she whispered, staring directly into his wide eyes. "I could track down a grain of sand in a tornado. Then you come along, looking all hot and stuff, and *bam*! I'm a friggin' neophyte again!"

Catching on at last, he smirked. "Oh, I get it." He thought a moment and his smile grew even more crafty. "There *is* a simple solution, you know," he said quietly.

"And that is?"

He brought his forehead to rest against hers. "I could just stop fucking you."

Her eyes widened in outrage. "You wouldn't dare!"

"The Sanctum needs its best caster back on the job," he said, as if he had already made up his mind. "If that means I have to stop turning you inside out and upside down, like you said, then I guess it's for the best."

She snarled at him. "I will beat you until you can't bleed anymore."

He smiled even wider at the threat. "Oh, I dunno. That might make it difficult for me to get it up."

Recalling the previous night, she nudged her nose against his. "You don't even need to do that to shatter me anymore," she whispered.

"Okay, then," he whispered back. "A compromise. I'll try not to carbonate your hormones any more than absolutely necessary until you can get your game back. Agreed?"

"No deal!"

She launched forward, pinning him to the ground while her lips claimed his in a ravenous kiss. Tearing away from him, she said, "You are gonna keep tending to my every want and desire until I say otherwise."

He grinned up at her. "Wanton desire?"

"Yeah, them too," she replied with a saucy smirk. "I'm just gonna have to remember to reboot my head after each session."

"Good plan, mistress." They sealed the deal with another deep kiss. When they finally came up for air, he chuckled. "You keep doing that and I'm gonna have to find newer and better ways to rile you up."

She grabbed at his chest in a rapid-fire combination of pinches and tickles. "Ooh, if we didn't have somewhere else to be."

"Speaking of which, where did the magic tech say they were?"

"Right the hell back in the cabin where I last saw 'em!" she said with a frustrated huff.

Jamyn laughed, despite her look of warning. "Well, we did get a nice little nature hike out of it."

She thumped his chest and then kissed the abused spot. "Some of us got a bit more than that," she said quietly.

"My pleasure." He took one of her hands in his and kissed it. "We gonna go pay 'em a visit?"

Kana didn't budge from her spot atop him. "What's the matter? You uncomfortable with this arrangement?"

He reached down and cupped her ass in both hands. "Are you?" he asked coyly.

"Hey!" she suddenly cried. "I have an idea. Let's go drop in on Rayven and Eddie." She leaped to her feet and looked down at him. "Well, c'mon. Daylight's burning."

Jamyn stood up, shaking his head and laughing at her outburst. "I must've knocked something loose in your head."

"Watch it, junior," she replied, though with her own manic grin. Together they folded the blanket and Kana rolled it back up into a tight bundle. She returned it and the tracker to the stash and then leaped at him, wrapping him up in a tight hug. "Ready to rock?"

He raised himself up on his toes and stole a quick kiss. "Ready when you are, love."

Swallowing down her surging heart, she cast a spell. A brief flash of light later, they found themselves standing just outside the ramshackle cabin.

"Last stop," she said. "All out."

She released him and looked around the fenced yard. Nothing had changed since her last visit, and she silently wondered why they were still here. "Any of this look familiar?"

Jamyn looked around. "No."

"From what Eddie said, you met him somewhere close to here, out in the woods." She pointed to the nearby trees.

The door of the cabin squeaked, and someone stepped out onto the porch. "Hey! What are you two—" Eddie's words stopped abruptly when Kana turned to face him. "Kana Morel!" He gasped and took a step backward. He saw her companion and stumbled away a few more steps until he backed into the door frame. "You!"

"Eddie?" a female voice asked from behind the door. "What's going on out there?" It opened again and Rayven came out. "Kana!" she cried happily before running over to her.

"Hey, Rayven," Kana replied. They shared a quick hug.

"What are you doing back here?" Rayven asked.

"Carting him around," Kana replied, nodding toward Jamyn.

Rayven turned to see him. "Are you the one who helped Eddie?"

"I guess," Jamyn replied with a brief shrug. "Apparently I siphoned off most of his...um..." He looked to Kana in alarm.

"That Locan guy told me what Eddie is," Rayven said. She looked to Eddie, who was still on the porch staring back at them all in shock. "Or what he *was*, I should say. Come on over here, Eddie!"

He seemed reluctant to move. "I...I don't think—" he stammered, continually shifting his wary gaze back and forth between Kana and Jamyn.

Rayven ran back to him and held his hands. "C'mon. Don't wanna be rude." She kissed his cheek.

He seemed bolstered by her kiss and nodded. "Okay," he said, giving her hand a squeeze. "I'm sorry."

"Enough of that," she said. "C'mon!" She pulled him over to where Kana and Jamyn were standing. She stood behind Eddie and pointed him at Jamyn. "This is the guy who helped cure you."

"You did?" Eddie whispered in wonder.

"I guess so," Jamyn replied. "My name's Jamyn. My mind wasn't quite all there when I found you. I only drew away your aura to use it as a source of power."

"Doesn't matter why you did it," Eddie said, finally getting over his shyness. "I'm just really glad you did. If you hadn't, I don't know how Rayven and I could have ever gotten together." He took a step forward and extended a hand to Jamyn. "I could never thank you enough for what you did."

Jamyn took his hand and shook it firmly. "Don't worry about it. I'm just glad I didn't hurt you."

Kana smiled and turned to Rayven. "Why are you two still here?"

"We're getting ready to leave, actually," Rayven replied.

"Weren't you doing that the last time I was here?"

"We were, but then we headed back to town to find a phone. Y'know, to call that *Locan* guy."

"I hope he wasn't too hard on you."

Rayven shrugged. "He was a real grouch at first. Didn't want to believe our story. But Eddie passed all the tests he gave him. That and Locan said something about you vouching for him, so he let us go on our way after a while. He ended up helping us out a lot before he left."

"How?"

"Turns out there was a reward for those shiners that attacked us. Locan talked to the sheriff and got us the money. It should be more than enough to get us somewhere far from here. C'mon, check it out." She tugged Kana's hand.

Kana turned to Jamyn. "You two have some stuff to go over. I'll be right back."

Jamyn nodded. "Yeah, that'd be good. Thanks."

He watched the pair go into the cabin, Rayven chatting away about the reward the whole time. The door closed and he smiled at Eddie. "Women, huh?"

"I suppose," Eddie said with a shrug.

"So, you're a reformed demon now?"

"I guess so," Eddie said with another weak shrug. "According to the tests Locan ran, I'm pretty much human. There is a faint residue of energy within me that I can still summon up to boost my speed, strength, and healing."

"Nice. How did Rayven react when she found out who you once were?"

"She was a little surprised at first, but she handled it really well. Even before Locan ran his tests."

Jamyn was taken by the obvious fondness in the former demon's voice. "Love makes you overlook a lot of things."

"It's not like that with her. I don't know. Sometimes it's like she almost *enjoys* the fact that I was a demon before. Maybe because I was able to give it all up for her."

Jamyn shrugged. "Some women enjoy the idea of changing their men for the better."

"I would have changed anyway just to be with her." Eddie glanced back at the cabin. "I would have done anything."

Jamyn followed his gaze and sighed. "Yeah. I know what you mean."

———— ◈ ————

Inside the cabin, Rayven had just replaced the stacks of bills inside her backpack. "Is that the guy you were looking for?"

Kana nodded as she examined a collapsed section of roof above her. She didn't remember seeing it the last time she was here. "Yeah. It took a while longer than I expected to catch up to him." She nudged some of the heavy fallen rafters with her boot. "Had a hell of a fight with the thing that took him, but we finally got back home."

Rayven eyed her casually. "And it looks like he convinced you not to kill him."

"Huh?"

"You said that he might feel the same way about you that Eddie does about me. I asked if you were gonna give him a shot. You said you might kill him first."

Kana chuckled. "Oh, yeah. Nah, I let him live."

"That's cool. He really *is* in love with you."

Kana raised an eyebrow at the younger woman. "Why do you say that?"

"The look in his eyes. It's the same one I've seen from Eddie a hundred times." Her own gaze went distant. "He tells me he loves me every single day. He scared me a little in the beginning, but now I don't know what I'd ever do without him." She hoisted her pack on her shoulder with a brief grunt.

Kana smiled at the smitten girl. "Good for you two." She reached out and patted Rayven's forearm.

The young girl drew back with a sudden wince of pain.

Kana instantly recognized the reaction, along with the flash of guilt that crossed Rayven's face. "Wait a second." She grabbed Rayven's upper arm and pulled her closer.

"Kana!" Rayven cried. "It's not his fault!"

Kana yanked up the sleeve of Rayven's thin shirt. A nasty bruise circled her exposed forearm. The darkened patch was in the rough shape of a hand. "Why that little—"

Rayven pulled away. "No! You don't under—"

Kana was beyond caring as she ran for the door. Bursting outside, she saw Eddie and Jamyn standing near the iron fence surrounding the yard.

———— ◉ ————

"What's up?" Jamyn asked. The determined look on Kana's face made him assume a defensive stance just in case.

She didn't respond. Instead, she launched from the porch, reaching Eddie in one impossible leap. Upon landing, she smashed an open hand into his chest. He flew backwards and hit the fence hard enough to ricochet right back to her. A spinning kick caught him in the side of the head and his body sprawled out on the uneven turf. An angry glow surrounded her fist, and she pounced at his prostrate form.

Jamyn intercepted her in mid-jump. Wrapping his arms tightly around her, he hit the ground and rolled her away from Eddie. She fought back, landing on top of him and pinning him down. She drew back her glowing fist and aimed for his face. His hand met hers in mid-flight, stopping the strike cold and keeping her from crushing his skull.

"Kana!" He bellowed at her, and his upper lip curled in anger. "Stop!"

He squeezed her fist with all his might. The magical aura shattered into wisps of light that dissolved into the air between them. She tried yanking her captured fist out of his grasp, but he clamped down on it even harder. Just as her trapped fist started to glow again, Jamyn snared her throat with his free hand.

"Stop it!" His fingers started to dig into her neck. *"Now!"*

The combination of his furious demand and the pressure on her windpipe finally broke through her rage. All at once, the anger drained out of her. She instinctively clawed at his hand, trying desperately to escape his hold on her neck.

"Eddie saved me when the roof collapsed!" Rayven cried. She had helped Eddie to his feet and clung to his arm. "If he hadn't, I would have been killed!"

Kana's wild-eyed stare bounced between Eddie and Jamyn. "Killed?" She whimpered, still pulling weakly at Jamyn's hand.

"Yeah. He heard the roof start to give way a second before it did. He grabbed my arm and hurled me out of the way. That's what made the mark you saw!"

The panic in Kana's eyes changed into a look of sheer desperation. Her body slumped and she started to draw in shuddering gulps of air. Before she could collapse atop him, Jamyn released both her hand and her neck. Sitting up, he caught her just as she dissolved into wracking sobs against his chest.

"Shh," he said softly, stroking her hair. "It's over."

Rayven tugged Eddie's arm and nodded toward the cabin. Together they hurried back inside and pulled the door closed behind them.

"Calm down." Jamyn kissed the top of Kana's head. "Just a misunderstanding."

"I could have killed him," she whimpered against his chest. She gasped and pulled weakly at his shirt. "I could have killed you!"

"Like that'll happen," he replied with a smile. "You're not getting rid of me that easily."

She laughed once before falling right back into a weaker bout of sniffles. "I thought he hurt her."

"Yeah, I figured that out." He rested his cheek against the side of her head. "He would never do that. He loves her too much." After waiting a few moments for her tears to recede, he said, "You're familiar with marks like that." Her body stiffened against his. He quickly folded her into a comforting embrace, being careful not to hug her too tightly. "Thought so."

"It was stupid of me, okay?" she said angrily.

Jamyn hooked a hand behind her head and hauled her up so he could see her tear-streaked face. "You're *not* stupid," he said firmly, his jaw set. He waited for a flicker of recognition to ignite in her eyes before continuing, this time in a much gentler voice. "You're not." He stroked the pad of his thumb over her wet cheek. His own eyes misted up and he chuckled softly. "There's another reason I won't let you kill me."

"What's that?" she said, her voice uneven.

He kissed the center of her forehead. "I'm not done teaching you."

"Teaching me what?"

"That not all men are complete scumbags."

She stared at him in utter disbelief. Her mouth opened in a futile effort to respond but only broken sounds emerged.

He chuckled and tipped her jaw up with his finger, closing her mouth.

She swallowed hard and came forward, just brushing her lips over his. "Not all of 'em?" she whispered.

"Nope," he replied. "Ninety-four, ninety-five percent tops." She tried to laugh but it only inspired a new round of tears. They came together in a tight hug and Jamyn nuzzled the side of her head. "Sorry about that."

"You should be," she replied, digging a thumb into his ribs. "Making jokes while I'm being stupid. Should be ashamed of yourself."

He was cheered by the return of her fiery spirit. "Hey, it's what us scumbags do."

"Oh, please. You couldn't be a scumbag if you tried." She clamped her lips on the side of his neck and sucked hard, adding in a few tongue flicks for good measure. "Mm?" she asked while he squirmed against her.

"Okay, okay!" He tried in vain to escape her tickling tongue. "You win! I'm one of the good guys!"

She finally released him and sat back on his lap. "And don't you forget it," she said. "You're..." Her voice trailed off while she considered his smiling face. "You're just incredible," she said at last.

"I've got a great teacher," he replied, winking at her. Nodding toward the cabin, he said, "Let's make sure they're okay."

"Okay," she nodded. They came together in a firm hug, and she sighed. "Incredible," she whispered away from his ear.

Jamyn smiled as he held her close, being careful not to let her know in any way that he had overheard her.

Chapter Eleven: Cover

They walked together onto the porch. Jamyn raised a hand to knock against the door but then hesitated.

"You gonna behave?" he asked over his shoulder.

"Shut up," Kana muttered. "I'll be fine."

Jamyn rapped against the weathered wood. The door opened a crack and Rayven peeked out.

"She's better now," Jamyn said.

Rayven opened the door with more than a hint of reluctance. Eying Kana, she asked, "Why did you do that?"

"I thought he had hurt you," Kana replied, her gaze shying away from the younger woman.

"He would never do that," Rayven said confidently.

"No, I wouldn't," Eddie said quietly as he walked up behind her. Though he was still in obvious pain, the bump on the side of his head from where she had kicked him was now nearly gone.

Rayven noticed his strained voice immediately and turned around. "Are you okay?"

"Wait," he said simply. He drew in a sharp breath and shifted his torso. A brief squeak of pain later, he stood up straight and sighed. "There. All fixed."

Rayven started to hug him but pulled away almost immediately. "Whoa. You're really hot."

He grimaced. "Sorry! I had to fuse the ribs back together. I should cool off in a minute."

"I broke your ribs?" Kana asked.

"Three or four of 'em, I think," Eddie replied. "They're better now."

"You used the residual power you still have inside you?"

He nodded. "Yeah."

She looked into his scarlet eyes. Though his gaze was still wary, it held no malice toward her. "I'm really sorry. I saw the bruise on her arm and thought..." Her voice lost strength and tapered off.

"I yanked her too hard," he said, sounding easily as repentant as Kana. "We were just caught up in the moment and I didn't have time to think first."

Jamyn's eyebrow twitched. "Moment?"

Rayven and Eddie shared a quick smile. "We were right under where the roof collapsed," Rayven said, pointing over at the empty spot of floor. "Like he said, things happened so fast that he couldn't hold back on how hard he grabbed me. He spun me out of the way before it all came crashing down."

"Then it..." Kana motioned to Eddie.

Rayven nodded. "Yeah. It all fell down on him instead."

Eddie came forward and hugged Rayven tightly, his body again cool enough to touch. "I healed it all up fine," he said. "I just wish I could heal you too."

"Cut it out." Rayven snuggled into his embrace. "You saved me. *Again.* And you more than made up for a little bruise." They shared a brief conspiratorial giggle before kissing each other soundly.

"I have something that might help." Kana pulled the stash out of her back pocket. She rooted around in the bag before pulling out what looked like a long blue beanbag.

The couple finally ended their kiss. "What's that?" Rayven asked.

"Let me see your arm."

The couple shared a quick look before releasing one another. Rayven pulled back her sleeve, exposing the nasty bruise. Kana massaged the bag for a moment before laying it on Rayven's arm. The young woman flinched.

"Damn! That's cold!"

"Only for a second," Kana said, holding the bag still. She felt it warm up again and pulled it away. The bruise had lightened considerably. Rayven poked the area in several different spots but felt no pain. "That better?" Kana asked.

"Yes," Rayven replied. "Thanks!" She showed Eddie her arm and he smiled.

"Thanks a lot, Kana," he said.

Kana put the blue bag back into the stash. "The least I could do. And I really am sorry for beating you up like that, Eddie."

He shrugged. "It's not that surprising, considering what I was."

"Now stop that." Rayven smacked him on the arm. "I keep telling you. You're not that person anymore." She rubbed the spot she had hit, and they shared another affectionate smile.

"She's right," Kana said, warmed by the obvious romance between them. "You're way past that." Her voice lowered. "Besides, that's not really why I did it."

"Then what was it?" he asked.

Jamyn stepped in. "She had some rough times when she was younger," he said.

Kana looked at him in alarm.

"But I'm helping her get past them. Right?"

"Um...yeah."

"Anyway, we should get going," he said, motioning Kana to the door.

"Yeah. Right!" she said, snapping out of her discomfort. She forced a smile. "You two stay out of trouble and have a good life together, okay?"

"We will," Rayven replied, wrapping an arm around Eddie's waist. She looked up at him. "Right?" she asked with a grin.

"Right," he replied, kissing her cheek. "You two take care as well."

"I'll try to keep her out of trouble," Jamyn said with a grin. Kana shot him a look and he shrugged. "Hey, I said I'll *try*."

"You're one to talk." She grumbled and headed outside toward the rusted gate. Rayven broke away from Eddie to catch up with her.

———⬥———

Jamyn hung back as the door closed behind them. He came closer to Eddie. "*Caught up in the moment*, huh?" he asked quietly.

A blush crept up the former demon's cheeks. "Yes."

"So, you two literally brought the house down."

Eddie's eyes widened and he laughed. "I guess we did!" He sighed at the blissful memory. "I'm not surprised. She was really wild that night."

"Always leave 'em panting and gasping your name," Jamyn said with a smile, prompting a perplexed look from Eddie. "Friend of mine told me that once."

"Oh. I thought that maybe you and Kana—" He purposely left the rest of his statement unsaid.

Jamyn caught his meaning. "Well, we haven't inspired any structural damage yet."

Eddie laughed again. "Just be careful." He made a show of gingerly feeling along his ribcage. "She hits really, *really* hard."

"Don't I know it! She's hit me more times than I care to remember. I'm hoping she'll go a little easier on me now."

Eddie offered his hand. "Good luck on that."

Jamyn shook it firmly. "You too. And I'm sorry we've both given you such a rough time of it. You know, now and before."

"Don't worry about it. After everything you two did for us, you can come back and punch me in the face whenever you want." The pair laughed together until the door flung open in front of them.

Kana stood there wearing an impatient frown. "What the hell's keeping you?" she asked Jamyn.

"Guy talk," Jamyn replied smoothly. "Tools, football, that kind of stuff."

Eddie played along. "Stock car racing."

Jamyn clapped him on the shoulder. "Yeah! And hot chicks in cutoff shorts and bikini tops."

"How's that again?" Rayven came up behind Kana in the doorway and frowned at the men.

Eddie relented immediately and pointed at Jamyn. "He said it."

Rayven huffed. "Don't care. You stepped in it now, son." She made a show of turning away but then peeked back at him over the pack on her shoulder. "I've got something like that in here, y'know," she said quietly. "You just made sure you'll never see me in it." She walked away, though not too quickly.

Eddie turned his stunned gaze to Jamyn.

"Don't look at me. Run!" Jamyn said. "Do *not* let her reach that gate before you apologize your ass off."

Eddie nodded emphatically and shot forward. Kana barely had time to lurch out of the way as he rocketed past. Jamyn came forward, joining her in the doorway. Together they watched as Eddie stopped Rayven and launched into a heartfelt apology. Only a second or two into it, his babbling explanation was quashed when Rayven leaped into his arms with a joyous laugh. The pair clung together and kissed, officially ending the brief spat.

"I think we're done here," Jamyn said.

———————◉———————

"Think again, acolyte." Kana glared at him. "*Hot chicks in cutoff shorts and bikini tops*, was it? I suppose you want *me* to dress like that?"

"Absolutely not." He came close to her ear. "You look a lot better wearing nothing."

"Damn, you suck," she whispered in reply. He backed away and looked at her in confusion. "How the hell am I supposed to stay mad at you when you say stuff like that?"

He smiled before shrugging comically. "Hey, ninety-five percent, right?"

She rolled her eyes. "You're not gonna let that line go, are you?"

"Not likely. Works too darned well."

She sighed in resignation. "Speaking of which, what say *we* get back to work?"

"Ready when you are, boss."

Kana waved back at Rayven and Eddie as they walked out into the field. "I think they'll be okay now. They've got more than enough cash to get 'em wherever they want to go."

"They've got a lot more than that going for 'em," Jamyn said.

Kana found herself nodding along with his sentiment. Stopping abruptly, she said, "Onward to stop number three. This one might be a little trickier."

"How so?"

"Bystanders, for one. I'm guessing he should be at work."

"Who?"

"Duane, the guy we're seeing next. He works at a university." She looked at their outfits and nodded. "We should be casual enough for that environment. I figure we could pose as students or something to help blend in."

"What's this *Duane* guy do there?"

"Not entirely sure. I know he does maintenance on their radio telescope. He said he was working on one when Zeekar got zapped into him."

"Huh?"

Kana laughed. "Zeekar is an alien. His consciousness got blasted into Duane's head by accident."

"An actual *off-world* alien?"

Kana frowned at him. "Asks the kid who's already been off planet himself."

"Ah. Right. What's he doing here? The alien, I mean."

"Tracking down criminals from his world. They mucked up his equipment so only his mind got sent here. He got stuck in Duane's head so now they have to work together to bag 'em and tag 'em. They were fighting one of 'em when you showed up."

Jamyn swallowed hard. "And?"

"You hit 'em. The one they were after was huge, but you swatted him away like he was a fly. Then you hit Duane and Zeekar. Sent them flying too."

His shoulders slumped. "Crap. Why did I do that?"

"You were drawing power from all of them. With the anchor spell locking down your magic, you gathered any kind of energy you could so you could keep gating from place to place."

He ran a hand back through his hair. "Using the Voice, no doubt."

"Probably." She stopped and looked him over. "Didn't you go over all of this with that replay you did while we were fighting the Aqiri?"

He shook his head. "No. I just gathered basic information about all the people I encountered. My head was still pretty messed up, even after the Aqiri got kicked out of it. I'll try a full replay after we're done."

"Probably a good idea." She thought a moment before casting a spell. They both faded away until they were completely invisible. "Ready to gate out?"

"Uh, yeah," he replied, blindly reaching a hand out to her. His fingers suddenly touched bare skin. "What the—"

"Figures you would go straight for that." She chuckled as his fingers skimmed along one naked breast.

Not to be outdone, he cupped the breast and stroked the pad of his thumb over her nipple. "So, naturally, you just had to pull your shirt up."

"Naturally," she replied smoothly. "Don't want to waste the opportunity." She drew in a sharp breath as he swiped his tongue over her stiffening nipple.

"Certainly not," he murmured, sneaking in a wet kiss on the held breast.

She ruffled her fingers through his hair as he continued to nuzzle the warm flesh. "Hey," she said while her pulse accelerated. "We going or not?"

He reluctantly released her breast, then wrapped his arms around her waist. Pressing his body close to hers, he rested the side of his face on her bare chest. "Ready when you are," he said. His tongue flashed out, leaving a wet trail up the center of her cleavage.

She hugged him and cast her spell. "Easily ninety-five," she muttered before pressing a kiss to the top of his head.

———◉———

Duane shouted up the aisle of towering computer cabinets. "Yo, Jimmy! How's that?"

"Gimme a sec."

Duane heard the frantic tapping of keys for a moment.

"Hey-hey! The zero finally seems right! Let's try firing up the channel." Another burst of keystrokes later, Jimmy said, "Now the active reading is bouncing all over the place. Almost like it's cutting in and out."

"Sonofabitch. Hang on!" Duane poked at the exposed circuit board. Something tapped the top of his hand, and he drew back in a rush. Ever since the accident that placed an alien consciousness in his mind, even the slightest thing would startle him while working on this equipment. "Ease back there," he mumbled, trying to settle down. "Hey, Zeekar," he said in a low tone. "Got any ideas?"

The voice of the alien residing within him replied in his mind. *"A few."*

Kana's voice sounded inside their shared mind. *"Did you try turning it off and back on again?"*

"Shit!" Duane shouted and jumped away from the cabinet. He looked all around but saw no one.

Jimmy's head poked up from behind his monitor at the far end of the aisle. "What happened?"

"Nothing," Duane said quickly. "Almost zapped myself. Maybe we should break for lunch."

"Good idea. Get our heads clear."

Duane nodded, discreetly looking around for any sign of Kana. "Yeah. My head's a little crowded right now."

Jimmy stood up. "You coming?"

"Nah. You head out. I'm gonna close this up so no one else gets hit."

"Okay. Meet you back here about one."

Duane waved him out. "Take your time. It's not like this hunk of junk is going anywhere."

Jimmy laughed and started to walk away. "Careful with that. The old girl might take offense and bite you again."

Duane frowned. "She took a big enough chunk last time." He watched the door close behind Jimmy before speaking again. "All right. Where are you?"

"You mean you can't tell, mister alien hunter?" Kana laughed.

Duane quickly held one hand out. "Zeekar, ready the gauntlet for a stun barrage."

"Stand by," Zeekar replied.

"Okay, okay," Kana said aloud. "Hold your fire, guys." She dropped the spell and became visible. "How's it going, guys?"

"What are you doing here?" Duane cast a nervous glance all around. "I'm working!"

"So am I," Kana replied.

"And how the hell are you in my head again?"

"Veiled converse spell, same as last time. Just added one more to the mix. You ready?" she asked the empty space beside her.

"Just drop the spell and stop screwing around," Jamyn replied. He became visible and nodded to Duane. "Hi. I'm Jamyn."

Duane looked him over. "Wait a sec. Aren't you—"

"He is the one who interrupted our fight with Fahnel," Zeekar said.

"Dammit, Zeekar! Stop doing that!"

Kana smiled. "Still fighting like an old married couple, I see."

"In his defense, he has had a rather trying morning," Zeekar said.

"*Trying*, my ass," Duane said. "It's been one cluster fuck after another." He eyed up Jamyn. "So, you were the one who smacked us when we were busy getting tossed around by Fahnel. Thanks for that."

Jamyn winced. "Sorry. I wasn't really in control of my actions."

"You are a magic user like Kana?" Zeekar asked.

"Yeah, but my magic is locked down right now."

"Why?"

"To keep him from doing anything stupid," Kana said with a grin. "He wanted to go around and apologize to everyone he messed with. Then maybe he'll get himself back off house arrest."

"Apology accepted," Zeekar said.

"Now hold on there a second," Duane said. "I'm pretty sure I'm the one who should accept or reject his apology."

"Why?" Zeekar asked.

"Because I'm the one who got hit!"

"Agreed. My acceptance is withdrawn."

"Ain't these guys great?" Kana asked Jamyn, nudging his side. "A one-man comedy team."

"Oh, ha-ha-ha," Duane replied with a deep frown. Noticing Jamyn's smile, he asked, "What?"

"I'm just trying to figure out which one of you is the funny one. Right now, it's two straight guys just butting heads."

Kana laughed again, only adding to Duane's frustration.

"But hey," Jamyn said, "I really am sorry for hitting you like that."

"You want to make it up to me? Fix this friggin' thing!" Duane pointed at the circuit board sticking out of the card cage in the open control cabinet.

Jamyn looked over the intricate circuitry. "What's the problem?"

"Goddamn thing won't stabilize." Duane grumbled and pointed at two small dials on the board. "We finally got the input channel zeroed out but now the gain is bouncing around like a rabid Chihuahua."

Jamyn took a closer look at the underside of the board. "How old is this board?"

"That's the other pisser." Duane said. "The damned thing's only a couple years old. The one it replaced was in here forever and never had this problem."

"Then why'd you replace it?" Kana asked.

"Main processor blew."

Jamyn motioned to Kana. "Can you magnify this area here?" he asked, pointing at one section of the board just beneath the dials.

Kana traced her finger in the air over the spot. She brought her finger and thumb together and then spread them apart again. Instantly an exploded image of the area appeared in the air.

Jamyn pored over the picture and smiled. "There you have it," he said proudly.

Kana looked over the numerous metallic bumps. "There where?"

"You gotta be shitting me," Duane said in amazement.

"There is an almost total circumferential crack around the pin," Zeekar said.

"Goddamn hippie bastards," Duane whispered, his face finally breaking into a wide smile.

Jamyn laughed.

"What's so funny?" Kana asked.

Jamyn pointed at one solder bump in the magnified view. There was a faint line in the metal that extended all the way around the central pin. "See that little crack?"

Kana nodded.

"Typical failure in lead-free solder. The joint cracks over time and temperature."

"Which, in this case, causes an intermittent signal that gives guys like me fits." Duane looked over Jamyn with a new sense of respect. "You a tech-head?"

Jamyn shook his head. "Nah. My dad is. When the industry switched over to lead-free, that's all we heard about over dinner for months. I finally read up on what the heck he was crabbing about."

"I'm glad you did," Duane replied. "I could've been banging my head against this stupid thing for days. Hey, Zeekar?"

"Yes?" the alien replied.

"How are the power reserves doing? Got enough to pull off the soldering glove trick?"

"We do. Extend your hand."

Duane raised his hand. His skin shimmered, turning from dark brown to a dull bronze. Pieces of silver metal emerged from under his skin, floating to the surface before interlocking into an armored glove. His index finger sharpened to a fine point that started to glow.

"Operating temperature reached."

Duane touched the tip of his finger against the cracked joint. The metal liquefied, pooling around the component pin. He pulled his finger away again and the metal solidified back into a complete joint.

"Instant toolkit," Kana said. "Nice."

"Yeah," Duane replied. "One of the benefits of my unintended tenant. Lose the glove, Zeekar."

"It will be cool enough to retract in another few seconds," Zeekar replied.

Jamyn looked over the gauntlet. "Now *that* is cool. How did you do that?"

"I fabricate the glove using metals I have absorbed into his body," Zeekar replied. *"I can channel our power reserves into his finger to create the heat required."*

Kana grinned at Duane. "I don't think I'll ask where you keep the batteries."

"She always like this?" Duane asked Jamyn, jerking an armored thumb at Kana.

"Pretty much. But hey, if it's a choice between jokes or her beating the snot out of me, I'll take jokes every time."

"I heard that," Duane said. "I've seen her in action."

Kana gestured at the floor. Black tentacles appeared and wrapped themselves around both Duane's and Jamyn's legs, rooting them to the spot. "And don't you forget it," she said with a sinister grin. Another flick of her fingers dispelled the spectral tendrils.

Duane's hand suddenly shimmered. The metal plates vanished beneath his skin, which quickly returned to its normal color. He tested both of his legs to make sure he was truly free of Kana's spell. "Now let's see if that fixed it." They followed him up the aisle to a computer console beneath a nameplate that read *Jimmy Koasper: Engineer Supreme*. He tapped in a series of commands and then smiled. "Solid as a rock!" He pointed at a number on the screen.

"Probably a good idea to inspect the rest of the board later," Jamyn said.

"Definitely." Duane extended his hand. "Thanks a lot, man."

Jamyn shook it. "No problem."

Duane looked to Kana. "What are you two up to next?"

Kana shrugged. "Dunno. This was our last stop on his *everyone-I-messed-with* tour. Guess we could go back home and get his magic restored. What about you? Getting some lunch?"

"You promised to call Dahlia," Zeekar said to Duane.

Duane gasped. "Shit! I forgot."

"Who's Dahlia?" Kana asked.

"My wife," Duane replied in a rush. "Crap! I've gotta run."

"Go," Jamyn said. "Don't keep the lady waiting."

Duane took off for the door and shouted back to them over his shoulder. "Thanks again! I'm sure you two can find your way out."

Kana eyed Jamyn and arched an eyebrow. "Don't keep the lady waiting, hmm? You're one to talk."

Jamyn took the hint. Reaching for her, he snared her waist and pulled her body close. "And what would my lady be waiting for exactly?"

Her eyes widened in surprise. "*Your* lady?" she asked, skimming a hand over his chest. "When did we determine that?"

Jamyn thought a moment while fighting off a blush. "I guess we haven't. So, give me a list of all your current suitors. I'll get to work fighting them for your hand as soon as we get back home."

She drew back like she was about to slap his face. "I'll give you a hand!"

He took her raised hand and brought it to his lips. "I'm sure you will, mistress," he murmured against her knuckles. "Does the rest of you come with it?"

"Enough to make it worth your while," she replied, her heart rate starting to climb.

A voice up the aisle shouted at them. "Hey! Who are you two?"

Kana and Jamyn turned to see a campus security officer coming their way. They released one another before Kana replied, "We were just visiting an old friend. He left a second ago to go to lunch."

"Then he should have escorted you out. Where are your visitor passes?"

"Right here." Kana made a show of digging deep in one pocket before withdrawing her hand. Suddenly a bright flash centered on her palm flooded the room.

Jamyn blinked several times and rubbed his eyes. "Damn. Were you erasing his memory or trying to microwave his brain through his eyes?"

"Whatever works," Kana replied. The flash burst had been a little more intense than she had intended, mostly because of her growing excitement. The guard stood there motionless, held in place by Kana's spell. "So. Home again, home again?"

Jamyn grimaced. "Well, there's one other place we should probably hit before going back to the Sanctum."

Kana thought for a moment. "Ah. Was wondering if you were going there too or not."

"I probably should."

"Then let's get to it." She cast a spell, and the pair vanished.

The holding spell around the guard dissipated, leaving him to wonder why he had been talking to an empty room.

———— ◉ ————

"Are all stations secure?" the taller man asked, his voice an angry rumble.

"They are, sir," replied the shorter man to his left.

The tall man turned to the robed figure standing to his right. "Summon him."

The wizard started his casting. He pulled an empty ammunition magazine emblazoned with a distinctive crest from a hidden pocket and tossed it to the ground before them. "Stand fast for your judgment, Hajis-Corol!" he called out in a thunderous bellow.

The air above the discarded magazine churned and twisted in a swirl of colors gone mad. Suddenly the magazine disintegrated, scattering flakes of metal into the air. The cloud solidified into an almost human shape. A second later, the storm of color and sound ceased, revealing a kneeling man, panting heavily.

"What...is the meaning..."

Several bands of force wrapped around his body before shocking and squeezing him painfully. He screamed in agony while the tall man took a step closer to him.

He snarled at the kneeling man. "Hajis-Corol. Do you know me?"

Hajis-Corol struggled to lift his head. When he did, his eyes widened in absolute shock and horror. "You!" he blurted just before the constricting bands shocked him again.

The tall man nodded in approval. "Now let us talk of the Soul Flame."

Chapter Twelve: Bonds

John was up off the sofa before the knock at the door had even registered in Maria's mind.

"I'll get it," he said, patting her knee as he passed.

Maria smiled. Though he would never admit it, his ability to anticipate events was the one magical trait he had received from his late mother. She settled into the sofa, wondering how the main inheritor of her mother-in-law's *gifts* was doing.

John's voice broke her from her musing. "Honey? It's for you."

She stood up and made her way to the door. "Who is it?" she called out.

"Not sure. Looks kind of familiar."

She turned the corner into the foyer and gasped. Her smiling son stood just inside the doorway.

———◉———

"Hi, mom," Jamyn said simply.

Maria launched forward, catching him in a firm hug. "Jamyn!"

He hugged her in return. "Whoa. Nice grip," he said with an exaggerated gasp. Looking to his father, he asked, "Any chance you could help me out of this?"

"No way," John replied with a grin. "You're on your own there, my boy."

He put up a weak struggle for a moment, but his mother apparently had no intention of letting go anytime soon. "Hey, Kana? I could use a hand here."

"Tough," Kana replied. "Maybe you should visit more often."

Maria opened her eyes and saw Kana standing on the porch behind Jamyn. "Oh!" She drew back and regarded the unknown woman. "Hello?"

Jamyn was confused by her reaction. He turned to his father only to find the same curious look of unfamiliarity on his face. "Mom, Dad, this is Kana Morel."

"Hello," Maria said again hesitantly.

Kana stepped inside and shook hands with each of them. "Maria and John Siska, I believe," she said, giving them both an extra nod of respect. "It's good to meet you properly."

John looked her up and down, causing Jamyn to toss him a brief frown. "Do you work with Jamyn?"

Kana smiled. "A little more than that. I'm Jamyn's new master. I was handed the reins a while ago. Your wayward son likely hasn't been keeping you up to date on current events."

"Not at all," Maria replied. She turned to Jamyn. "This is your new boss?"

"Um, yeah. Sort of. I'm basically her apprentice. She teaches me advanced magic techniques and I accompany her on missions."

John nodded before motioning toward the living room. "Let's go sit down. I'm guessing this might take a while to explain." He walked on ahead with his wife. They leaned into one another and shared several quick whispers.

Jamyn grabbed Kana's arm to hold her back a moment. "I don't get it," he whispered. "Didn't you meet them before? Why don't they remember you?"

"Qa probably wiped out their memories," Kana replied quietly. "After everything that happened the last time we were here, I'm not surprised."

Jamyn swallowed hard as his own spotty memories of that time came rushing back. "Oh. Right."

"Pull it together, acolyte," she said. "You look like you're gonna puke."

"Jamyn?" his mother called from the living room.

Kana fixed him with a hard stare. "Come on. It'll all work out."

———◉———

He straightened up and nodded. Together they walked into the living room. Jamyn's parents were both sitting in chairs, leaving the couch unoccupied. Kana darted ahead of him and sat in the center of the couch. He sat beside her, leaving a healthy amount of distance between them.

"I'm sorry for not calling before now," he said to his parents.

"I'm sure you've been busy." John spoke quickly, as if he was trying to stop an argument before it started.

"He has, but not too busy for that," Kana said. "Part of that's my fault, I suppose. We've been working pretty hard ever since he was reassigned. Still, it's no excuse for not dropping you a line every so often."

"Thank you!" Maria said while shooting her husband an *I-told-you-so* look.

"In his defense, though, we were both here a little over a week ago."

Everyone in the room stared at her, Jamyn with a look of alarm and his parents with confused expressions.

John finally broke the silence. "When?"

"Can't remember the exact day. It was nighttime. Raining pretty good outside."

Jamyn's voice erupted in her mind. *"What are you doing?"*

His thumb was pressed against the glyph circle that established a veiled converse between them. She canceled the spell and continued. "I was tracking Jamyn after a spell went wrong. He ended up here."

"I don't remember seeing either of you here," Maria said.

"Yeah, things got kind of out of hand. Jamyn was being controlled by an outside force. We got into a bit of a fight. Qa Shon came around afterwards and likely erased your memories of the event."

"You mean that older guy who used to be Jamyn's master?" John asked.

"That's him. He was my master too, back in the day." Seeing that their concerned looks remained, she smiled. "Don't worry. Everything worked out fine." She reached over and gave Jamyn a playful punch in the shoulder. "I didn't have to beat him up too much."

"Something was controlling him?" Maria asked, her voice unsteady.

Kana waved it off as if it was a petty nuisance. "Nothing too tragic. It was just a minor annoyance that sometimes pops up." She jerked a thumb toward Jamyn. "Though it did give him an industrial-strength attitude."

"Him?" John asked with an incredulous laugh.

Kana nodded. "Yep. Mister Cool here was being a real jerk. All kinds of harsh language and nastiness."

Maria stared at her son, who appeared to be ready to curl up into a ball and die of embarrassment. "Really?"

Kana looked to Jamyn, whose face was trying on at least its third shade of green. "Hey. Your mother asked you a question. Speak, boy. Say a few syllables."

John laughed at the jab while Maria threw him a disapproving glare.

"Yeah, I was pretty out of control," Jamyn said quietly. "I attacked Kana and then ran off again. I'm not surprised that Master Qa altered your memories, but I am sorry that he had to." He placed a hand on Kana's knee. "I did a lot of terrible things."

Kana bit back a surge of emotion. She patted his hand before casually pulling it off her knee. "Yeah, you did up the whole *acolytes behaving badly* routine pretty well," she said, trying to laugh it off. "In the end, you got your head back together. Just took a few healthy smacks." Turning her attention back to his parents, she continued. "That's why we're here. We've been going around to all the other people he messed with during his little episode and doing a lot of apologizing. Saved the best for last."

"Well, since we don't remember any of your last visit, I guess there isn't much to apologize for," John said with a shrug. "So, no problem."

Maria turned on him. "Always so logical," she said in an exasperated huff.

"Sorry," he replied with a sheepish grin. "I plead *socially inept engineer*."

Jamyn chuckled at the familiar excuse. "Still using that line?"

John nodded. "It works, doesn't it?" They laughed together while Maria fumed.

"Two peas in a pod," she cried to Kana.

"I can see that." Kana looked them both over. Aside from the obvious age difference, they were strikingly alike in both appearance and mannerisms. "At least now when I have trouble wrangling Jamyn, I'll know where he got it from."

Maria leaned forward. "You poor girl. You have my sympathy."

"Hey! I believe we've just been insulted," John cried indignantly to Jamyn.

"I believe we have," Jamyn replied, his laughing voice rising to meet his father's.

John glanced at the frowning women and then turned back to his son. "Can't you do some magic or something to make them, I dunno, more agreeable?"

At this, Jamyn's smile faltered. "Um, no. My magic isn't working right now."

Maria looked to him in surprise. "It isn't? Why not?"

"It's locked down by an anchor spell. I was having that set up when this whole mess started. After we got everything sorted out, I had my magic shut off again to keep me from doing anything stupid."

"Besides that, he knows I don't like anyone casting spells on me without asking first," Kana said. She fixed him with a solid look. "Right?"

"Right, mistress," Jamyn replied. Realizing what he had just said, his eyes widened. "Um, I mean *master*."

"Ease back, acolyte," she said as nonchalantly as she could to cover his gaffe. "I told you either one is an acceptable term."

John stifled a laugh, then he and Maria shared a quick glance. "When does he get his magic back?" he asked.

Kana shrugged. "Probably once we get back to the Sanctum. We've made things right with everyone, so he should be good to go. Besides, having someone with me who can't cast will really limit our mission list."

"What kind of missions?" Maria asked. "That *Qa* person didn't really give us much detail about what Jamyn actually does in the Sanctum."

"Yeah, that's just like him," Kana said with a smile. "Basically, we're the magic police. We get called in when something weird happens or something starts causing problems."

"Like demons?" John asked.

Maria stiffened noticeably at the question.

"Yeah, they're on the list. Fortunately, we don't usually run into a lot of those. Mostly it's just wandering spirits or weird little critters under the bed. You know, simple *bump in the night* kind of stuff."

"Ah. I just mentioned them because—"

A sharp look from Maria silenced him.

Kana nodded. "Because of your mother." Holding up a hand to Maria, who had spun to face her, she said, "I was briefed on what happened. Jamyn handled it great."

"*Handled it?*" Maria asked, her voice taut.

"Mom," Jamyn said in a calming tone. "Take it easy. It all worked out."

She ignored his statement as tears welled up in her eyes. "That...thing could have killed you!"

"No, it couldn't have," Kana said. "He's way too powerful for that."

"Now, maybe, but back then he was just a boy!" Maria whimpered.

John grasped her hand and held it tightly.

"A boy with some extraordinary talents," Kana said. She glanced at Jamyn, who was obviously both concerned and embarrassed by his mother's distress. "Even then, he had some incredible skills, especially for someone so young. With the early training he received from his grandmother and the help he got from Qa, he's grown into a formidable caster."

"Yeah?" John looked at his son, who was now squirming uncomfortably. "He's doing okay, huh?"

Kana laughed. "Yeah, he's doing okay. At the very least, he's not dead yet."

His mother gasped. "Jamyn! What have you—"

"She's just goofing around, Mom," Jamyn replied swiftly, cutting her off. He turned a glare to his grinning mistress and snapped at her. "Knock it off."

His heated reaction caught Kana off guard. "Okay." Turning to Maria, she said, "He's right. I shouldn't worry you like that. It's kind of an inside joke at the Sanctum."

"What is?"

"Kana's reputation," Jamyn said before Kana could reply. "She's probably the most powerful caster there."

Now it was Kana's turn to squirm. "That's a crock," she muttered. "I told you that before."

"And I told *you* that you needed to learn how to take a compliment," he replied smoothly. "Between all the weird critters she deals with on a regular basis and her own lovely temperament, I'll bet most of the Sanctum gave me a life expectancy of about a week tops when I became her acolyte." He gave Kana a playful shove and then grinned at her grunt of protest.

"Joke's on you, kid," she grumbled. "I took *three months* in the betting pool."

"Put me down for four." The others all looked at John in surprise after his outburst. "What?" he asked innocently.

Jamyn laughed at the well-placed swat his mother landed on his father's arm.

"See?" John asked, gesturing back at her. "*This* is the reward we get from the women in our lives for being practical."

Jamyn glanced at Kana and swallowed hard. "She's my mentor, Dad," Jamyn said quietly.

"But she's in your life," he said, ignoring the death stare he was now receiving from Maria. "And she's a she, so *technically*—"

Maria snapped at him under her breath. "Why don't you make yourself useful, Mister Technical, and get us something to drink?"

John stopped abruptly at the low command. A sneaky grin curled the corner of his mouth. "As you wish, mistress," he said, adding a quick bow.

"Jamyn," she said, still staring daggers at his father, "go help him out. Maybe talk him into behaving while you're at it."

Jamyn looked to Kana.

She shook her head. "Hey, I defer to their jurisdiction. Get moving."

He stood up and walked to his father, who remained seated. "C'mon, Dad. We've been dismissed."

"But we're gonna miss all the girl talk."

"That's kind of the point. Let's go."

John grudgingly got up and started to walk to the kitchen behind his son. He stopped for a moment and turned back. "Wait! You didn't ask Kana what she wanted to drink."

"I already know." Jamyn latched on to his shoulder and spun him back around. "Move it!" He ushered him off to the kitchen.

Maria turned back to Kana and sighed. "And he wonders why we don't have company over more often."

"Don't worry about it," Kana said. "He's obviously just trying to rile up Jamyn."

"I know." She sighed again. "We spent so many years waiting for Jamyn to come out of his shell. When he finally did, it's like his life went in fast-forward. Before we knew it, he had graduated from school and was moving out."

"Meaning you missed out on all the normal growing up stuff," Kana said. "Like him bringing home a girl for the first time."

Maria fought to keep her jaw from dropping.

Kana chuckled and nodded. "I could tell your husband was dying to nail Jamyn about that as soon as we showed up."

"I was hoping you wouldn't notice," Maria said with a blush. "He's been keeping a close eye on both of you ever since you sat down. Even had us sit in the chairs so that you two would have to sit on the couch together. I wanted to swat him for it but figured that if I did, you'd be on to us."

"Another thing he and Jamyn have in common. They notice everything." She leaned forward and lowered her voice. "Makes 'em a lot to fun to be around at times, huh?"

Maria laughed. "Don't I know it! They both take in every damned detail and then use them to their full advantage. It's like arguing with a reference library."

Kana burst out laughing.

"What?" Maria asked.

"That's exactly how I described Jamyn to Qa shortly after we met. *A walking reference library.*" She settled back into the couch again. "Is there anything else his father gave him that I have to look forward to?"

Maria thought for a moment. "That pretty much covers it. An over-observant genius who loves cracking jokes to hide a lingering confidence problem."

"Ah. He passed that down too." Maria's inquisitive look drew a smile and a knowing nod from Kana. "Jamyn can be really skittish at times. Getting him to act or to speak his mind sometimes takes a miracle." Her mind wandered back over their tumultuous courtship and her heart did a funny little skip in her chest.

Her lapse did not go unnoticed. "Jamyn's still prone to zoning out?"

Kana snapped from her memories and felt a rush of warmth in her cheeks. "Not so much lately, but early on it was a bit of an issue." All the delicious pleasures they had recently shared tried to shove their way forward in her mind. Only a mighty effort kept them in check. "But once he does set his mind to something, he goes all out."

———— ◉ ————

"So, my boy. How's life in the service treating you?"

Jamyn frowned at his father's question. "I didn't join the military, Dad."

"Dunno about that. You've got ranks and procedures and missions. Sounds pretty regimented to me." He made a show of peeking back toward the living room. "Your new C.O. *is* a lot prettier than the last one."

"Dad!" Jamyn said, trying to keep his voice down.

"Well, she is. That Qa guy seemed nice enough, but this one's got much better legs."

Jamyn sighed and rolled his eyes. "How is it that Mom hasn't killed you yet?"

"Simple. I keep those kinds of observations to myself when she's within earshot." He looked around quickly before clapping a hand on Jamyn's shoulder. "It's just us guys here now, so I say Kana is pretty. And really tall too. Doesn't that hurt your neck?"

Jamyn's stomach was busily tying itself in a knot as he pulled away. "She's only a few inches taller than me."

"Still, standing at attention while looking at her must—"

"Just cut it out, already," Jamyn snapped, much to his father's surprise. Gathering himself, Jamyn grimaced. "I'm sorry. It's just—"

"Hey, I'm only teasing." John grabbed Jamyn's shoulder again and gave him a friendly shake. "Come on. We haven't seen you in how long and suddenly you show up with that cute little number? I've gotta have *some* fun with you about it."

"I know, I know," Jamyn said. "It's just that we've gone through a lot of really nasty stuff since she became my new master."

"Like the fight she said you two had the last time you were here?"

"It was more than a fight." Jamyn fought to keep his voice steady. "I nearly killed her. Even though something else was controlling me at the time, that still put a serious crimp in our working relationship."

"Yeah, some people tend to take stuff like that personally."

Jamyn smiled at the joke. "I think we've finally gotten to the point where we can deal with one another."

"And teasing from the outside isn't particularly welcome. Gotcha." Opening the refrigerator, he asked, "What's her poison of choice?"

"Root beer, if you've got it."

John laughed incredulously. "Root beer? I was expecting something a bit more exotic."

"Nope. Kana's a complex woman otherwise, but not when it comes to that."

John pulled out a pair of cans and handed them over. "One root beer and one neon green neutrino typhoon."

Jamyn laughed at his dad's description of his favorite soda. "Why have you got this stuff on ice?"

"Your mother's doing. Probably reminds her of you. And it's not like it'll ever go bad. That stuff doesn't have an expiration date so much as a half-life."

Jamyn grinned before popping the can open and chugging half its contents. His eyes briefly took on a wild light and he muffled a belch. "Yeah, that's the good stuff," he muttered, much to his father's amusement.

John put the other two cans he had retrieved on the counter. He nodded toward the living room. "You think those two are done ripping us to shreds yet?"

"Not likely. I just hope Kana doesn't tell her all the ways I've screwed up so far. Mom'll have a coronary."

"Nah. Your mom's a tough old bird. She's put up with me this long, after all."

"Just like Kana puts up with me, I suppose."

"I'm guessing she's easily as tough," John said. "From the little I've seen so far, she looks like she could punch out a dump truck."

"Easily," Jamyn replied with a smile. "You did get one thing about her wrong, though."

"What's that?"

"She's not pretty. She's beautiful." Not waiting for his dad's reaction to his statement, he pressed one of the small circles on his hand.

"How you doing in there?" he asked through the veiled converse.

"Wondering where the heck you two ran off to," Kana shouted from the living room. "We're *dying* in here!"

Jamyn laughed at both her words and the surprised look on his father's face. "I think we've been summoned."

"Nope," John replied. "A summons is usually nicer. That was a full-fledged *get-your-butts-in-here* demand." He picked up the sodas and handed Kana's to Jamyn. "You go first."

"Gee, thanks."

"Hey, age before beauty."

Jamyn grinned and started down the hall. "You got me there."

They turned the corner into the living room to see the women looking back at them expectantly.

"You two run out to rob a convenience store or something?" Kana asked with a smile.

"Nah," John replied before Jamyn could open his mouth. "Had to stop by the lab to whip up his drink in the particle accelerator." He handed Maria her soda and sat down beside her.

Jamyn likewise handed Kana her root beer and sat down. She popped the top and raised it to her lips. "You really need to stop doing that," she told him. "Fangs was right. It's considered rude in most cases." She sipped her drink while he stared at her in stunned silence.

"What did he do?" Maria asked.

Kana stopped drinking and raised the back of her right hand to Jamyn's parents. "This pattern on my hand is called a glyph. One of the circles on it sets up what's called a veiled converse spell between Jamyn and me. It allows our minds to talk directly to one another over long distances. He fired it up while he was in the kitchen."

"I thought you said your magic wasn't working," Maria said to Jamyn.

"It's not. The magic is contained within the glyph," he said.

"Courtesy of him." Kana jerked a thumb at him. "He added that new little bit to the glyph himself. Funny thing is that he's not supposed to be able to do that at his current level. Shows how powerful he can be when he puts his mind to it."

"Doing a little extra-credit?" John asked.

"Uh, yeah," Jamyn replied, trying not to think about the exact circumstances under which he modified the glyph.

Kana continued. "He's been doing that sort of thing more and more as we go. He's worked several spells that an acolyte-level caster should not be able to cast." She turned her attention to John. "Any idea what level your mother was?"

"Not really, no. What was it she used to tell us, hon? Just powerful enough to be useful but not enough to get into any serious trouble?"

Maria nodded.

"Somewhere in the high caster to low mage range," Jamyn said quietly. His parents both looked at him in surprise. "I matched up her talents with the Sanctum's ranking system shortly after I got there."

Kana nodded. "Dunno about that. She was talented enough to keep herself hidden from the Sanctum, so I'm thinking more in the low- to mid-mage ranks."

"Ranking system?" John asked.

Seeing their confused expressions, she continued. "Everyone in the Sanctum is categorized by class and rank. Neophytes are the newbies. Once one of those scores a master, they become an acolyte. Graduated acolytes become hierophants. After those come casters, mages, and seers. Each class is further ranked by level of proficiency, five being the lowest and one the highest. A fifth mage would outrank a first caster."

"What rank are you?" Maria asked.

"I'm a First Seer."

John whistled low and turned to Jamyn. "You scored the top of the top, hmm? Good job, boy."

"Cut it out, Dad. Only First Seers can take on acolytes."

"Makes sure the kids are taught by the best," Kana said. "Also keeps the stodgy old farts on their toes. At least I did with Qa."

Jamyn tried his best to suppress a grin. "Yeah, he told me about some of that," he said out of the corner of his mouth.

She turned on him. "Don't believe half of what he said. He likes to exaggerate."

Jamyn chuckled. "Like the first time you tried a replication spell?"

Kana glared at him. "He mispronounced one of the words during the lesson and he *knows* it! I just repeated what he said."

"What happened?" John asked.

"She was trying to make a single duplicate of a piece of wood," Jamyn said.

Kana grumbled. "It was a popsicle stick."

Jamyn laughed. "And instead of one, she produced thousands of 'em!"

"And we were barely able to get our butts out of the room to evade the avalanche," Kana said in a rush to bring the story to a swift conclusion. "Two casters crushed to death by popsicle sticks. Ha-ha-ha. Hilarious." The other three laughed. Kana finally relented and laughed too. "Hey, it set up the perfect scenario for the mages to test out their newer disintegration spells. They spent two days carving through that mess to get to the original piece. Afterwards I was commended for casting such a powerful spell."

"And that's Kana in a nutshell," Jamyn said to his parents. "She can turn the biggest disaster into something good."

She eyed his compliment with open suspicion. "Must be why they assigned you to me."

He spread his arms wide and bowed regally. "Probably."

She shook her head at the overblown display. "On that note, we should probably get our butts back. We still have to present Shamara to the Inner Cabal."

"Crap!" Jamyn exclaimed. "I forgot about that!" Suddenly he clapped his hand over his mouth and looked back to his mother. She was regarding him with a shocked expression. "Sorry!" he said from behind his hand.

Kana held her laughter in check and leaned toward Maria. "I'll wash his mouth out for you when we get back to the Sanctum."

"No," Maria said, shaking off her surprise. "No, that's fine. He's twenty-two, after all." She regarded her son, her eyes getting misty. "He's his own man now."

"Not entirely," Kana said. "He'll be his own when he hits hierophant. Until then, his butt belongs to me." They all laughed before standing up. John turned toward the front door, but Kana's voice stopped him. "No need for the door. We'll just gate out here."

Jamyn hugged his mother. "See ya, Mom."

"Be careful," she said, squeezing him tightly.

"I will."

"And?" Kana asked in a stern tone.

Jamyn chuckled. "*And* I'll call home on a more regular basis."

"Damned right you will," John said. "I'll never hear the end of it if you don't."

Maria flailed an arm back at him which he barely dodged. She finally released Jamyn and frowned at her husband's goofy grin. "Just wait until later, you," she said. She turned again and surprised Kana by embracing her. "Thanks for taking care of Jamyn."

Kana eased into the hug and patted her on the back. "He can take care of himself. I'm just there to make sure he knows it." They released one another.

John spread his arms wide for a hug. Just as he leaned forward, Maria's hand in the center of his chest stopped his advance.

"And *where* do you think you're going?" she asked.

His gaze shifted from her to Kana and back again. "I thought we were doing goodbye hugs," he said innocently.

"You just drop those arms, mister!"

He did as she asked, stepping back and dropping his hands to his sides. "I never get to have any fun." He stuck his lower lip out in a childish pout.

Maria huffed in exasperation. "Honestly!" She turned back to Kana and Jamyn, who were both trying not to burst out laughing at the comical show. "It's like living with a five-year-old sometimes."

Kana came forward and extended her hand to John. "Good to meet you, Mister Siska," she said in a formal tone.

John smiled and shook her hand. "Likewise, Kana." She suddenly darted forward and kissed his cheek before stepping back to stand beside Jamyn.

John stood there with a bemused grin until Maria glared at him. "I didn't do it," he cried, raising both hands in defense.

Kana and Jamyn both chuckled.

"Go get 'im, Mom," Jamyn said.

She turned to face them. "You two go. I'll take care of him after you leave."

Jamyn eased up to Kana until their sides touched. "Let's go, Kana."

She cast the spell, and their combined outline started to glow. "Don't hurt him too badly," Kana said with a grin. "Just singe him around the edges a bit!" A flash of light later, they were gone.

———————⟡———————

Maria turned back to John, who was grinning like a madman. "Any last words, smiley?" she asked, trying to remain serious despite wanting to smile right along with him.

He nodded once. "Yep. Your son is in love."

"What? But she's—"

"The obvious object of his affection." Seeing her look of disbelief, he laughed. "Come on. You mean to tell me you couldn't see it? His eyes were lit up like the Fourth of July the whole time he was with her."

"Kana's his master," Maria said. "He obviously respects her as a teacher."

"*Mistress.* He said it himself. He also corrected me in the kitchen when I said she was pretty. He said she was *beautiful.*"

Maria raised a hand to her trembling lips. "He did?"

"He did. And you missed the most obvious sign." He came forward and held her close. "He was holding her hand when they left."

A tear rolled down her cheek. "Really?"

John wiped it away. "Really. He probably thought he was being slick by pressing up next to her to hide it, but I saw him take her hand and squeeze it." He pressed a kiss to her forehead and then looked into her teary eyes. "Our son's in love."

"Jamyn. In love." She whimpered before burying her face in his chest.

John lovingly stroked her hair. "Hey, it was bound to happen sooner or later." He kissed the top of her head. "What do you think of his intended?"

Maria nodded against him. "She's nice. Got a good head on her shoulders."

"And cute."

She thumped a fist against his back. "Creep."

"Hey, I said *cute.*" He skimmed his hands down her back until they were cupping her butt. "You know there's always been only one *beautiful.*"

She hugged him fiercely. "That's one other thing I hope he got from you."

"What's that?"

She pulled back and looked into his eyes. "You always know the right thing to say," she murmured before kissing him soundly.

———— ◉ ————

Hajis-Corol screamed in agony as another shocking blast ripped through his body. Smoke seeped from the latest wound, and he panted heavily. Yet another surge tore into him and the screaming started anew.

"Progress?"

The robed figure shook his head. "He is remarkably resilient."

Hajis-Corol had nearly lifted his head toward the sound of the voices before a vicious blow smashed into his face. He spit out a mouthful of blood before similar blows started raining down over every part of his battered body. By the time the beating stopped, he was no longer able to cry out.

"If you wish an answer, you may want to leave him in a state where he can still deliver one."

The taller man left his prey and stomped over to the robed figure. His steps did not slow as he passed, but not before delivering a crushing strike to the top of its head. The robed one slumped to the ground.

"He may paint the answer in his own blood, so long as it is delivered. See that my next visit is not wasted."

"Of course," the robed one replied as it scrambled back to its feet. "The Flame shall be yours."

Chapter Thirteen: Career Path

"Well, that was fun," Kana said upon their arrival back in Jamyn's quarters.

"Sure," Jamyn replied half-heartedly. "Rated right up there with root canal work and Lester stomping on your foot."

"Oh, c'mon. It wasn't that bad. Your folks are nice people."

"Who are way too perceptive for their own good. Dad was on me like a rash about you in the kitchen."

Kana laughed. "Figured. Your mom told me that he wanted to tease the hell out of you as soon as we showed up. She did her best to rein him in."

Jamyn smiled. "She usually does."

Kana raised their joined hands and gave his a squeeze. "This probably didn't help your case any. Think he caught it?"

"Knowing him? Yeah." Jamyn sighed. "And now he's probably working Mom into a frenzy about it."

"About what?"

He smiled and pulled her close. "About her son being in love with you."

Kana's eyebrows rose. "You think he figured out that much? You *were* kind of falling all over yourself early on, but what would have given him that idea?"

"Something I said in the kitchen."

"What's that?"

"He said you were pretty. I corrected him."

She pulled a face. "You told him I wasn't?"

"Sure did."

"Gee, thanks."

"I told him you were beautiful."

She considered his words while a warm glow settled in her chest. "How would that have tipped him off?"

"It's something he's done with mom forever. Other women are always *cute* or *pretty* or something like that. She's the only one for him who rates as *beautiful*. I said the same thing about you without realizing that it would be a big ol' red flag for him."

She nudged his forehead with the tip of her nose. "So, I'm beautiful, huh?"

"Yep. My beautiful mistress," he replied before reaching up to steal a quick kiss.

She eased further into his embrace. "Guess that makes you my silver-tongued, hotter-than-hell stud muffin of a troublemaking acolyte."

He frowned for a moment. "You're not big on subtlety, are you?"

She reached down to stroke his growing erection through the front of his pants. "Not so much, no."

He pulled her hand away and held it. Brushing his cheek against hers, he whispered into her ear, "You should give it a try sometime."

Her inner glow started to give way to the unease that had been churning in the back of her mind. Lust stomped it back into submission and she hugged him tighter. "Overrated," she whispered before giving his ear a quick nibble.

He lightly ran one hand down her back, stopping just shy of her butt. "Sometimes anticipation is half the fun."

She reached around him and grabbed a handful of his ass. "More often, it just ends up wasting half the time." She pulled him harder against her body.

Cradling her face in his hands, he kissed her deeply. She continued to grind herself against his bulge and he quickly succumbed to her gyrations. "Maybe you're right."

"*Maybe*," she scoffed briefly.

She cast a spell, and their clothing vanished. Hooking her right leg around his waist, she reached down to help position his cock. He bent his legs slightly, allowing her to nudge her slick lips up over his tip. He slowly straightened up, easing his cock into her. She flexed the leg wrapped around him, urging him on. He complied and started to gently slide his cock in and out of her body.

She held him tightly and pressed her lips to his ear. "Hard," she said between gasps, loving the feel of his girth repeatedly spreading her.

He complied, grabbing her ass and plunging into her. She whimpered into his ear and held on as he continued to plunder her.

"Oh, my God!" She gasped as her peak hit without warning.

His powerful arms flexed, and he easily hoisted her up. She wrapped her left leg around him, hooking her feet behind his back. Closing her eyes, she panted hard as he continued to ram his cock into her throughout her orgasm. She buried her face in the side of his neck, groaning out her passion between deep suckling kisses.

Suddenly Jamyn pitched forward.

She tensed, clutching at his falling body, before landing on something soft. Opening her eyes, she found herself lying on Jamyn's bed. While her attention was elsewhere, he had walked them both into his bedroom. She was about to speak when he slid fully into her and held himself there. She bit her lower lip while releasing a low, passionate sigh.

He propped himself above her. Sweat beaded on his forehead and he appeared to be trying to settle himself down.

"Hey," he whispered, looking deep into her eyes.

"Hey," she replied with a wide smile.

He took a deep breath and then let it out slowly. "Is it always gonna be like this?"

"Like what?"

"Sneak attacks and hot-and-fast tumbles."

Something in his tone worried her but she kept her voice light. "Got something against hot and fast?" She clenched down firmly on his cock.

He groaned at the intimate squeeze. "Not at all. Just wondering what it'd be like."

"What?"

He pulled away a space before feeding his cock back into her at a tortuously slow rate. "Taking it a bit *slower*," he replied, watching her face intently.

She shivered as he hit bottom again. "Slow is good," she said before the feeling of fullness robbed her of breath.

"Not just this," he said, continuing his leisurely rate. "Maybe let things progress naturally a bit before you just pounce." He leaned forward, grinding his pubic bone against her clit.

Shivers raced through her. Her body reflexively bore down on his teasing cock. In a flash, she reached up to him, pulling him hard to her chest.

"Jamyn," she whimpered, desperately grasping at her imminent peak. "Please!"

He pulled his hips away from her, withdrawing over half of his length in one swift move. In the next heartbeat, he slammed it back into her hard. She cried out in surprise and dug her fingernails into his back. He repeated the move once, twice, and then shuddered as he exploded deep within her body. Her peak soon followed, causing her to scream loudly into his ear. They clung to each other, both trembling and trying to catch their breath.

Jamyn started to speak but fell silent. He kissed the side of her head before nuzzling her sweat-soaked hair. "That was great," he mumbled.

The words were so unexpected that Kana could not suppress her perplexed reply. "Huh?"

"It was great," he said again, his voice firming up.

She nodded against him. "Yeah, it was." The absence of his usual sentiment both confused and worried her. Without warning, something deep inside started to ache. She stroked her fingers through his hair. "You okay?"

"Yeah," he said, nodding and kissing her cheek. "You?"

"I'm great," she replied, though she was rapidly feeling anything but.

His cock slipped out of her, and she squeaked softly at the loss. They hugged tightly for several thudding heartbeats before he released her and fell to her side on the bed. She turned and looked at his face. Aside from the obvious fatigue, a hint of worry shaded his expression.

"Something wrong?"

His mood seemed to brighten, and he smiled, shaking his head. "Nah. Just a bit tuckered out. Been a busy day and all. I think I need a nap."

"Oh. Okay." As much as she tried to believe his carefree tone was genuine, something in his manner still bothered her. "Want to grab something to eat later?"

He shook his head. "Not hungry. Besides, I should really clean this place up." He gave the room a quick scan. "Looks like a bomb went off in here."

She laughed, recalling the vigorous loving they had shared in his room over the last few days. "I could get it for you," she said, raising a hand to cast a spell.

He grasped her hand. "I'll get it. Doing it myself will make me appreciate my magic more once I get it unlocked."

She laced her fingers with his. "Okay."

"When are you presenting Shamara to the cabal?"

The question was so unexpected that it took her a moment to collect her thoughts. "I have to gather the cabal, but that shouldn't be too tough," she replied at last. "I should probably go prep Shamara for it now. Thanks for reminding me."

"No problem."

She came forward, nudging his nose with hers. "Want to come along?"

He smiled. "Nah. I think I still scare her a bit."

The ache blooming within her intensified. "Then I guess I'll be going." She cast a spell, and her clothes reappeared on her body. His clothes appeared in a neat pile on the floor beside the bed. "Bye."

"Bye," he replied. He hesitated a moment before pressing a kiss to her lips. She gladly accepted it but held herself back from lunging at him. Closing her eyes, she cast a spell and vanished.

———— ● ————

Once he knew she was gone, Jamyn rolled onto his back. He stared at the ceiling while his heart screamed at him. "I love you, Kana," he whispered to the empty room.

———— ● ————

Kana paced the living room of her quarters. Though admitting Jamyn's reminder about Shamara had indeed been useful, she couldn't help feeling it was more an effective distraction on his part. She flopped down onto the couch and let her head fall back against the cushions.

"He didn't say it," she muttered to herself. "Before, I couldn't *stop* him from saying it. What the hell happened?"

A familiar female voice responded right next to her. "Maybe he changed his mind."

Instead of turning her head toward it, Kana continued to stare at the ceiling. "Shut up, Eva."

"I'm serious," Eva said. She suddenly appeared on the couch, sitting next to Kana in an identical pose with her head thrown back.

"Maybe he finally figured out that being in love with you was a really bad idea."

"Hey, I warned him about that from the start. I can't help it the kid's slow."

"Then you're glad he doesn't love you?"

Kana sighed. "Sure would make things a lot simpler."

"I guess so. Except for that lingering ache in your chest."

"Stuff it, Eva. I'm fine."

"The hell you are."

Kana sat up and glared at Eva. "I'm *fine*."

The aspect turned and smiled at her. "Sure you are. That's why you feel like that."

"What do you—"

"Oh, just stop already!" Eva sat up straight and pointed a finger directly between Kana's breasts. "It's like he ripped you open again and spit in the hole. And why? Because he didn't say the words you claim mean so little to you!"

"It just surprised me when he didn't say it," Kana replied. "That's all."

Eva frowned. "Right. And that's why it feels like Lester is sitting on your chest every time you draw a breath. That's why your heart is playing a drum solo in your ears. Why you're right on the verge of crying. 'Cause you're *surprised*." Eva relented and sighed. "I'm a part of your mind, so I feel what you feel." Her eyes locked with Kana's. "And right now, I hurt."

Kana bit her lower lip and took in a sharp breath. "Me too."

Eva thought for a moment and then smiled weakly. "I wish I could be like Path."

"Why?"

Eva held up an open hand. "I think both of us could use a hug."

Kana nodded before holding up a hand to mirror Eva's. "I think you're right."

Eva's body slowly started to fade away. "So, what now?" she whispered right before she vanished.

Kana took in a deep cleansing breath and then released it in a burst. "Same as usual. The job." Raising her voice, she called out, "Hey, Sanctum?"

"Kana," came the reply.

"Location of Lob the Unmarred and Shamara."

"Lob the Unmarred is currently in the merchant sector. There is no current Sanctum member called *Shamara*."

That's right. Shamara won't be recognized by the Valet until she's an actual member of the Sanctum.

"Is anyone currently with Lob?"

"He is with a young girl recently identified as Lob's guest."

"And that'd be her," Kana said with a satisfied nod. "Tell them both I'd like to meet them at Evrok's place. Tell Lob I'm buying."

Nearly a minute passed. Finally, the Valet spoke up. "He accepts your gracious invitation and warns you that he's a little hungry."

"Which means my account balance is about to take one hell of a hit." Kana chuckled to herself. "Now send the following invitation to all members of the Inner Cabal..."

⸻ ◉ ⸻

An hour later found Kana, Lob, and Shamara sitting comfortably in Evrok's tavern. The table between them was strewn with empty food containers from half of the vendors in the merchant sector.

Kana polished off the last of her drink. "So that's basically it," she said. "They'll hear your story, maybe ask you a few questions, and then you're in."

"It still sounds a little scary," Shamara replied.

"You'll be fine."

"Of course, she will!" Lob said at his usual booming volume. "If you get stuck, just ask yourself what Kana would do." He leaned down to Shamara's ear and stage-whispered, "And then do the exact opposite."

Shamara giggled.

"Ha-ha, big guy," Kana said, chuckling along with them. She looked to Shamara and jerked a thumb back at Lob. "Don't listen to him. I'm not nearly that bad with them."

"Now, maybe," Lob said, "but I've heard tales of your clashes with the cabal back in the day."

"Did you really fight with Master Donta?" Shamara asked, awe evident in her voice.

Kana froze. Leveling a stern glare at Lob, she asked, "You told her about that?"

"I only gave her the highlight reel," he replied before hoisting his mug and taking a healthy swallow of ale. He peeked around the mug at Kana, who was still staring daggers at him, and fought off a huge grin.

Kana sighed and shook her head. "We had a disagreement," she told Shamara in a controlled voice. "We both said and did some things we shouldn't have, but we ended up settling our differences peacefully."

Lob put down his mug at last. Leaning down to Shamara again, he said, "Meaning Donta apologized and learned the hard way that you don't mess with Kana Morel."

"Cut it out, Lob," Kana said as politely as she could. "She's got enough to think about without you filling her head with wild stories."

"Oh, she'll be fine," Lob replied. "Right, Shammie?"

"I hope so," she said quietly. "I really want to live here."

"You will," Kana said. "I seriously doubt any of them will object to you joining us. So, any questions?"

"The whole cabal will be there?"

"Not everyone. Most of inner group should be there."

"And you've seen many of them already," Lob said.

"She has?" Kana asked.

"When I carried her around the campus in that *backpack*." Lob turned to Shamara. "I know you've seen Qa and Daystar. You remember the older guy with that lady in white?"

Shamara nodded. "She was very pretty."

Both Kana and Lob laughed. "That's Daystar," Kana said. "Anyone else?"

"One of the healers. The woman."

"Mistress Tiris," Lob said. "You thought she was a little girl from the way she was darting through the crowd." He poked her side playfully. "And don't forget your buddy!"

"Buddy?" Kana looked to Shamara, who was now squirming in her seat.

"Master Varondis-Mai," Lob said, grinning at the young girl's discomfort. "The first time she saw him, she was tongue-tied for the rest of the day."

"Fangs?" Kana asked incredulously. "What's wrong with him?"

"Nothing!" Shamara blurted. The pair looked back at her, and she grimaced. "He's very handsome," she mumbled while staring at her lap.

Kana and Lob shared a stunned glance. "Fangs is a fun guy," Kana said, trying not to laugh. "Any thoughts on what you'd like to go into?" she asked, deftly changing the subject. "Do you have any particular areas of interest?"

"I never really thought about it," Shamara replied. "Before I got here, most of my time was spent just trying to survive."

Kana nodded, recalling the girl's war-ravaged homeland. "Just something else to consider during your studies. A lot of people in the Sanctum have a specialty. Lob's is defense, naturally. Tiris and Leel are healers. Qa's kind of the level head that keeps everything semi-sane around here."

"Does Mister Jamyn have a specialty?" Shamara asked.

Their recent passionate tangle charged to the front of Kana's mind, and she swallowed hard. "Not so far," she replied at last. "He's showing a tendency for getting into trouble."

"Gets it from his master," Lob said, nudging Shamara's side.

"What does Master Donta do?"

Kana smiled at the slight tremor in the girl's voice. "He's our demon expert. It kind of suits his disposition."

"And Miss Juushin?" Lob asked Shamara, a twinkle lighting his eye.

"Miss Juushin's a fighter!" she replied, smiling brightly back at him.

"She's not *a* fighter," Lob replied. "She's *the* fighter!" The two of them laughed together.

Kana smiled at the exchange. "You've got plenty of people to talk to when you start deciding your future plans." Leaning over to Shamara, she lowered her voice. "Fangs is our animal expert, by the way."

Shamara blushed and her eyes widened. "I like animals," she said quietly.

"See?" Lob asked, leveling one huge finger at Kana. "Troublemaker!"

Kana stuck out her tongue at him.

Shamara pushed at Lob's massive arm and playfully scolded him. "You tease a lot too!"

Kana chimed in with a crafty grin. "Especially Juushin. When you gonna break down and tell her, big guy?"

Lob straightened up in his chair and looked down into his mug. "Empty again? That can't be right." He hoisted the mug, as well as both Shamara's and Kana's glasses, and headed straight to the bar for a refill.

Kana chuckled as she watched him go. "Poor guy. That hit a little too close to the mark."

"Lob likes Miss Juushin," Shamara said quietly. "A *lot*."

Kana nodded. "I know," she replied, keeping her voice low as well. "One of the worst-kept secrets in the Sanctum. Still, I probably shouldn't tease him about it."

"What's your specialty, Miss Kana?" An arched eyebrow was all the reminder she needed. "I mean Kana."

Kana sat back and shrugged. "I'm kind of a generalist. I dabble in a bit of everything." She thought a moment. "There is one thing I'm pretty good at." She lifted a hand palm-up and concentrated. A thin tendril of golden light erupted from her palm, writhing like a tiny snake.

"What is that?" Shamara whispered.

"My soul," Kana replied, keeping her attention riveted to her hand. "I'm able to detach it from my body and use it to do things." Suddenly the strand lashed out, sweeping past the candle in the center of the table. The glowing thread zipped back into her palm. Kana reached out and lifted the top of the candle from its base. It had been cleanly split in half.

Evrok piped at her angrily from behind the bar. "Must you continue to destroy my place?"

"Sorry, Evrok," she called over to him. "My bad." Seeing that his frown was in no way diminished by her apology, she said, "I know. I'm why we can't have nice things." She placed the halves of the candles back together before casting a spell to fuse it into one whole. She gestured at the repaired candle.

Evrok huffed and went back to his business.

"That was amazing!" Shamara said.

"Her soul lash or how she handled Evrok?" Lob asked as he came up behind her. He placed a new round of drinks on the table before sitting down.

Shamara giggled. "Both!"

"She's getting your sense of humor," Kana said with a smirk.

Lob looked over the remains of their meal. "Better that than my appetite."

"Kana?"

Kana looked to Shamara. "Yeah?"

"What do you think you would be if you weren't in the Sanctum right now?"

Kana blinked. Her mind reluctantly traveled back to her youth, and she tried not to wince at the thought of what that continued existence would have done to her. "Not real happy," she said quietly. Shaking off the demons that threatened to overrun her mind, she smiled. "Good thing I'm here now, hmm?"

Shamara nodded her agreement.

A small, folded note suddenly appeared on the table in front of Kana. Shamara jerked away from it in fright.

"Relax," Kana said with a smile. "I bet I know what this is." She unfolded the note and read it. "And there we have it. You two meet me at the central chamber at nine o'clock tomorrow morning." She peeked over the note at Shamara and winked. "I'm thinking you'll be one of us by quarter-past."

"Too right!" Lob wrapped one huge arm behind Shamara. She leaned in and hugged as much of his massive torso as she could get her arms around, giggling all the while.

Kana nodded at the pair and then chugged her drink. She placed the empty glass on the table then stood up and bowed. "Lob the Unmarred. Shamara, the Sanctum's soon-to-be newest neophyte. I will see you both tomorrow morning." She turned and walked out of the tavern. A small part of her mind wondered what Jamyn was doing at that particular moment.

———————◉———————

Kana strode down the hallways of the Sanctum, her ceremonial robes swaying lazily around her ankles with each step. The early-morning hall traffic was light, adding to her good mood. She went over her prepared arguments again, just in case, even though it was unlikely she'd have to use them.

This should be a total slam-dunk.

Coming around the corner, she stopped dead in her tracks.

Jamyn, also dressed in his formal garb, was leaning against the wall right next to the central chamber's double doors. He caught sight of her in a heartbeat and straightened up.

"Mistress," he called out, bowing to her.

Kana forced herself to move again. Walking up to him, she looked him over. "What you all dressed up for?" She masked the flutter in her voice with a brief cough.

"Same thing you are," he replied, giving a pinch of her robe a brief shake. "Shamara's admission hearing."

"How did you know it was now?"

"Qa. He came by my place last night. Asked me if I was going to say anything on her behalf." He gave Kana a long look. "Was I not supposed to show up for this?"

"No, it's fine. I just realized that I never told you when it was. Sorry."

He came a step closer and grasped her hand. "I'm sorry too," he said quietly. "I was a bit short with you yesterday. That whole thing with my folks messed up my head a lot more than I thought."

Kana's mouth went dry. "Um, yeah," she said, trying to shrug it off. "No problem. I figured it was because of that." Though she fully enjoyed the feel of his hand holding hers, she wished she could pull it back to dry her now sweating palm within her robes.

He took another step forward, closing the gap between them. "Kana."

She looked down into his ardent gaze. "Hm?"

"I do love you."

The weight that had been straddling her chest since their return the previous day released so suddenly she took in a sharp and surprisingly deep breath. She started to reply but a jovial call from up the hallway interrupted her.

"And there they are! All decked out in their Sunday best just for little ol' us." Lob's booming voice echoed off the corridor walls. Beside him walked Shamara, clad in a knee-length emerald green dress that accented her dark skin.

Kana backed away from Jamyn in a rush. "Hey, Shamara." she said with a bright smile. "You look great."

"Thank you, Kana." Shamara smiled bashfully.

Lob pouted. "What about me?"

Kana looked up at the giant. "You look adorable too, you big screwball, but not nearly as good as her. Excellent job."

Lob chuckled. "Right. Like *I* could doll her up like this. Mistress Daystar showed up at Evrok's right after you left. Took us on a little whirlwind shopping spree to help out..." He stopped and thought a moment. "How did she put it, Shammie?"

Shamara cleared her throat. "The budding bloom that is the Sanctum's newest desert flower," she said with an embarrassed smile.

Kana nodded. "That's Daystar, all right." Looking to Jamyn, she motioned to Shamara. "Well? What do you think, acolyte?"

"You look incredible, Shamara," he said warmly. "What's that in your hair?"

Lob grinned. "Oh, you're gonna love this. Turn around and show 'em, Shammie."

The young girl turned away from them, a renewed bounce in her step. Her hair had been fashioned into a wide braid that hung down the center of her back. Woven into the braid were small clusters of wildflowers. Atop each cluster rested a tiny silver butterfly exactly like the one Kana had conjured when she and Shamara had first met.

"Wow," Kana whispered. "That's awesome!"

Shamara peeked back over her shoulder. "It was Mistress Daystar's idea to add flowers native to my homeland. I asked for the butterflies because of you."

"Me?"

Shamara turned back around. "It was the first thing you showed me when you told me of what my life could be." She bowed low. "Thank you, Kana. Even if I don't get in." She stood up straight, her wide smile beaming up at the first seer.

Kana lunged forward and caught her in a tight hug. "Oh, you're getting in." She blinked away the tears gathering in her eyes. "Even if I have to convince every single one of them myself."

"Let's try to keep the body count to a minimum," Jamyn said lightly.

She turned to him and made a face. Just then, a single tone sounded from the doors. "That's our cue," she said, releasing Shamara and opening the doors.

They all walked in and quickly arranged themselves four abreast with Kana and Shamara in the middle. They strode to the center of the chamber, which was bordered on the far side by a large semi-circular table. Around the table sat the members of the Inner Cabal, each clad in their own signature robes.

"What is your intention, First Seer Morel?" Qa called out in a solid voice.

"I ask that the Sanctum admit a new member," she replied, her voice cutting through the air like a trumpet blast. She placed a hand on Shamara's shoulder. "This is Shamara. She has already demonstrated skills that would be a great benefit to us all."

"The nature of these skills?" Leel asked.

"She has an ability that she calls the push. It transforms ambient magical energy into a kinetic force."

"How's that work?" Fangs asked, leaning forward in his chair.

"Quite well," Lob replied in a tone as serious as Kana had ever heard from him. "I have been working with her for a while now. Her ability has both offensive and defensive potential."

"Perhaps a demonstration," Vynael said.

Lob nodded and looked down at Shamara. "Let's do one of the routines we practiced," he said quietly.

She nodded. "Which one?"

"How about goofball pinball?"

Her eyes widened in alarm. "That one's silly!"

"But effective. C'mon. Let's give 'em a show. Ready?" He winked at her.

She smiled and nodded. "Ready."

"And we're off!"

Lob leaped straight up into the air above the young girl. He tucked into a tight ball and formed a spherical shield around himself. The encapsulated Lob started to fall back to Shamara at a frightening rate. She gestured and a push slammed into the ball, sending it flying straight back up. She hit it again, this time from the side, and it veered over the cabal. It started to fall again. Right before it crushed Qa, another blast sent it careening away in a lazy arc. Over and over, she hit the sphere, always keeping it just seconds away from disaster. Finally, she hit it with a complex series of strikes that had Lob spinning like a top on the floor right in front of her. One last hit slowed his revolution to a stop so that he was again facing the cabal. He dropped his shield and stood up on shaky legs.

"Tilt!" he called out in a woozy voice. He curtsied before walking back to Shamara and the others. Before he faced the cabal again, he flashed her a quick thumbs-up.

"Nicely done!" Fangs clapped enthusiastically.

Several others joined in, applauding the young girl's efforts.

"Enough," Donta said, his annoyed growl swiftly quashing the fanfare. His carved mask stared at Shamara. "Why do you want to join the Sanctum?"

Shamara's smile evaporated but she took one confident step forward.

"I have been given two great gifts," she said proudly. "The first is the push, which I had always been told was a curse. The second is Kana." She turned to face her. "She helped me to realize that the push is actually a blessing. She also brought me here, a place where she said no one would ever try to hurt me or judge me. I want to join the Sanctum to learn all that I can about my talents and then use them to help people who need it, just like Kana did for me." She turned back to the cabal and stood at attention.

Donta sat back in his chair, apparently considering the young girl's words.

After several seconds of silence, Daystar leaned over and playfully swatted his sleeve. "Stop being so dramatic!" she said with a giggle.

Donta sat forward again. "Objections?" he said harshly.

The others in the cabal smiled in silence, each knowing what was next.

Donta shot to his feet. "Shamara," he said in a low rumble.

"Master Donta," she instantly replied, adding a formal bow.

"Welcome to the Sanctum."

"Yes!" Lob said under his breath, punching a clenched fist into the air close to his side.

Daystar stood and gestured to the young girl. "Bloom!" the seer cried joyously.

A sudden wind swept up around Shamara's body, lifting her hair and undoing her intricate braid. The tiny butterflies all suddenly took flight, surrounding her in a glistening halo of wings and flower petals. The deep green of her dress faded to a bright ivory. Her hair bundled itself into a tight crown surrounded by a braided loop that circled her head. All but three of the butterflies again took up positions on her braid. Two grew to full size and landed, one on each of her shoulders. The last became a glistening brooch that pinned itself to the front of her dress. The wind ceased and Shamara bowed to them all. Another round of applause filled the air. This time, even Donta clapped his cloaked hands together.

"And with that, we are adjourned," Qa declared.

"We most certainly are not!" Fangs cried abruptly.

Everyone gathered looked to him in surprise.

"I believe such an event should be celebrated *properly*," he said, a manic gleam in his wild eyes.

"You are correct, Master Varondis-Mai," Qa replied.

Qa raised his hands and clapped them once. The doors to the chamber opened and a multitude of others from the Sanctum started to file in. Tables appeared along the walls, each laden with various drinks and foodstuffs. A collection of glasses and tankards sprang up on the central table as well, one in front of each member of the cabal.

"Is this what you had in mind?"

"It is indeed." Fangs roared in a lusty growl. Grabbing his tankard, he hoisted it in a toast. "To Shamara!"

"Shamara!" the rest of the cabal echoed.

Shamara turned on her heel, her head swinging this way and that as she tried to take in everything around her at once. Catching Kana's gaze at last, she stopped and whimpered. "All this for me?"

"All for you," Kana replied, wiping away a tear of joy. She fell to one knee and the two came together in a fierce hug. "Your life starts now, kiddo," Kana murmured into her ear. "Make the most of it."

"I will," Shamara replied. "Thank you!"

Kana looked up to see Lob sticking out his lower lip in a childlike pout. She nudged Shamara and chuckled. "I think Lob has something on his mind."

Shamara tore away from her and spun around. She lunged forward and caught Lob in a tight embrace. "Thank you, Mister Lob!"

"Thank *you*, Shammie," he said. "I knew you could do it." Suddenly a large shadow fell over them both. Lob looked up and his eyes went wide. "Uh-oh," he muttered. "We're in trouble now."

Shamara recognized the words and turned without releasing Lob. Above them towered a figure who was nearly as big as Lob and clad in gleaming gold armor.

"Sneaky little devil." The voice rumbled from the massive helmet, giving the words a metallic chime.

"Miss Juushin," Shamara shouted in delight. "You came!"

Juushin dropped to one knee, her armor making almost no sound when it touched the floor. "Of course, I did. You thought you could just sneak into the Sanctum without me noticing?"

Shamara giggled. "No one can sneak by you."

Juushin chuckled then turned to Kana. "Kana," she said with a nod.

"Good to see you, Crusha," Kana replied. "A bit surprised you came." Juushin was an almost total recluse in her free time, preferring to keep to herself.

The massive helmet nodded. "I couldn't let this one pass," she said. Shifting her gaze, she said, "You must be Jamyn."

Jamyn nodded. "That's me. And you're Juushin, the arms master. Good to finally meet you."

"Likewise." She raised one gauntleted hand.

Jamyn shook the proffered hand. Instantly his body went rigid. Pulling away, he flexed his fingers and looked back at her in shock.

"I'm sorry," she said, looking from her hand to his. "Did I hurt you?"

"No," he said almost immediately. He relaxed again and smiled. "No, I'm fine. Just a bit surprised. The metal was kinda warm."

"It's special," Juushin said, a hint of caution in her voice. "A lot of people don't catch that."

Kana laughed. "Yeah, sorry about that, Crusha. They stuck me with a weirdo."

"Lot of that going around," Juushin replied. She reached over and ruffled her fingers through Lob's short hair.

"I'm not a weirdo," Lob said in a weak protest. "I'm a goofball."

"Of course, you are," Juushin replied, "and I'm the weirdo that you got stuck with."

"But he likes you anyway," Shamara said.

Lob opened and closed his mouth several times, but no sound came out.

Recognizing his discomfort, Kana said, "How about a drink before y'all start mingling? I'm buying." Not waiting for an answer, she tapped Jamyn on the shoulder. "Come on, weirdo. You can help me carry 'em." They had gone a fair distance before Shamara's voice stopped them.

"Mister Jamyn!"

They turned back to her. "Huh?" Jamyn asked.

"Come here!"

Jamyn walked over and leaned down to Shamara. A hushed conversation ensued, followed by a round of chuckling from both Lob and Juushin. Jamyn nodded once and patted Shamara's head before walking back to Kana.

"No problem," he said upon reaching her. "Let's go."

As they walked over to one of the drink tables, Kana cast the others a quick glance over her shoulder. "What was that all about?"

"Nothing much."

The tone of his voice made it obvious to Kana that he was lying. "Jamyn..."

He chuckled and reached for her arm, stopping their advance. "Okay, you caught me. Shamara just wanted to thank us."

"Then why did she only talk to you?"

"Because she's incredibly bright and devilishly sneaky. I think it's a female thing." He sent Shamara an inquisitive look and received an eager nod in reply. Turning back to Kana, he smiled at her harsh scowl. "Why the sour look, mistress?" he asked innocently.

"It's a female thing. Happens right before I kick someone's ass for not getting to the point."

"Okay. The point, then." He came closer to her and whispered, "I have something for you."

"You? I thought Shamara did."

"That's the sneaky part. I think she's on to us." He lifted one hand and opened it. Upon his palm sat Shamara's butterfly brooch. "She wanted you to have this."

Kana gawked at the gift. "But then why—"

"She thought it would mean even more to you if *I* gave it to you, so she gave it to me first. Now I'm giving it to you."

Kana's composure shattered. Turning to the side, she saw both Shamara and Lob grinning like fools. Kana was sure Juushin was also smiling under her helmet. A tug on her robes pulled her attention back to Jamyn. She looked down to see him pinning the brooch in the center of her chest.

"I... I don't know what to say," she stammered, her teary eyes flicking between him and the glittering pin.

"But I do," Jamyn replied with a bright smile. He leaned close to her ear and whispered, "I love you."

A wave of emotion, combined with a surge of panic, crashed through Kana's entire being. Without thinking, she cast a spell and vanished.

Chapter Fourteen: Undone

Jamyn walked back to the others, who were all looking back at him in confusion.

"What happened?" Shamara asked. "Where did Kana go?"

"I'm not sure," he replied.

"Did she not like my gift?"

"No, no," he said with a smile. "She loved it. I think it might have been something I did."

Shamara appeared unconvinced. "Really?"

Jamyn dropped to one knee in front of her and nodded. "I'm sure it had nothing to do with you. I'll go track her down and see what's up. You should focus on enjoying all of this." He motioned to the assembled throng. "Roam around. Talk to people. Now would also be a great time to get to know some of the Inner Cabal members. Start with Master Qa. He'll likely end up introducing you to the rest. That's how it worked when I joined the Sanctum."

"Okay," she replied, her voice still unsure.

"C'mon, Shammie," Lob said. "Let's go scope out the food and then rub elbows with the big shots."

"Notice he mentioned the food first." Juushin gave Shamara a playful nudge.

"Hey, I'm a growing boy."

Jamyn chuckled at their clowning before turning his attention back to Shamara. "Do me a favor. Keep these two out of trouble while I'm gone. Okay?"

She grinned at him. "Yes sir, Mister Jamyn!"

He laughed and shook his head. "Just *Jamyn* is fine. And welcome to the nut house."

He stood up and headed for the door. On his way there, he looked back over his shoulder. The trio was making their way through the crowd in the direction of Qa, who looked like he was already anticipating their arrival.

"Good luck, kid," Jamyn said quietly before slipping out the double doors past the people still coming in.

Once in the hallway, he stopped to wonder where Kana might have gone. Her quarters seemed like the most obvious destination, so he decided to go there first. Hurrying down the deserted corridors, he went over the last things he had said to her.

"Idiot!" he said to himself, adding in more than a few mental kicks. "You know she's iffy about the whole *love* thing, but you still had to keep bringing it up! What the hell's wrong with you?"

His reluctance to say it after their most recent lovemaking came to mind and he sighed heavily.

Hell, she's upset whether I say it or not. I can't win!

Arriving at her door, he paused for a moment before knocking sharply. "Kana!" Nothing but silence answered him, so he knocked again. "Come on, Kana. Open up." Still there was no response. He tried the handle only to find it locked. Sighing in exasperation, he decided to take a risk and pounded on the door. "Open the damned door, Mistress Morel!" He waited, his tensed body ready to spring out of range at the first hint of the door opening, but nothing happened.

He stood there motionless, his mind rapidly calculating what she could possibly be doing.

Right. Try to figure out what that woman's ever up to!

He raised his fist to pound on the door again when he noticed the glyph on his hand. The last circle he had added to it caught his attention and he grinned in triumph.

Let's see you ignore this!

He pressed his thumb against the circle and felt the veiled converse spell form.

"Open the door, Kana."

"I'm not there," she replied. By the tone of her words, she seemed to be calm again. *"Get back to the party and be there for Shamara."*

"I left her in Lob's and Juushin's capable hands. It's you I'm worried about."

"Don't be. I'm fine. Just needed a bit of a breather."

Right before he was about to counter her, he felt the spell collapse.

"She hung up on me!" he said in outrage. "Why that stubborn little—"

His words cut off when a faint glow lit the large circle of the glyph and then dimmed again.

She's in the wilds?

Looking around, he shrugged.

It's worth a shot.

He pressed the large circle, and a gate appeared before him.

"Wonder who'll kill me first," he said as he walked into the glowing doorway, "Lester or Kana?"

He stepped out of the gate and into a familiar clearing. Instantly he scanned the area around him, all senses on high alert for an attack. Several seconds passed without anyone trying to kill him so he relaxed his stance.

The pond.

He headed into the tangled growth of the forest. The trek through the dense foliage was uneventful, giving him ample opportunity to go over what he would say when he finally found her. Unfortunately, he drew nothing but a blank.

She's already pissed at me about the whole love *thing, so coming after her when she told me not to shouldn't really matter.*

"She can only kill me once, right?" he said aloud. Climbing over the rise overlooking the pond, he looked down to the water.

Kana was floating in the center of the pond and staring straight back at him. "Don't count on it, dipshit." Her words had regained their harsh snap. "I can think of all kinds of ways to kill you, bring you back, and then kill you all over again."

He considered her threat while noticing that her robes were lying in a pile on the shore. "I see. How many times are you going to do that?"

"As many as it takes to drive the point home. I tell you to do something, you do it. End of story."

"Got it." He thought for a moment. "Will you grant me a final request?"

She glared at him through slitted eyes. "I don't see why I should but go ahead."

"Tell me why you ran."

A lightning bolt split the sky and slammed into the ground right next to his feet.

"First and only warning." The threat barely made it past her clenched teeth.

He sat down at the edge of the rise and let his feet dangle over the water. "Noted. But you didn't grant my request. Why did you run?"

"How fucking dim are you?" Her face reddened despite the cool water.

"Pretty damned dim. I obviously can't get it through my thick skull not to keep harping on..." He paused to choose his words carefully. "Certain matters."

Her enraged gaze locked on him. "The next shot will not miss." Her words were slow and steady with a particular emphasis placed on the last three.

He sighed heavily and stood up. "Fine," he said in resignation, holding his hands before him in a sign of surrender. He bowed to her and took several steps backward.

———⚬———

Kana had barely taken and released a loud, deep breath when Jamyn came hurtling up over the ridge. He had stripped off his robes and was now only wearing a snug pair of briefs. She watched as he held himself in a tight pike, plummeting at her feet-first. He landed a few yards away, his streamlined form slipping into the water with only a brief splash. He surfaced right in front of her and smiled wildly.

"You may fire when ready, mistress!"

She caught his throat in a vise-like grip while she cast a buoyancy charm upon herself to stay afloat. "Don't think I won't kill you!"

"I don't think that for a second," he replied, his voice straining against her choke hold, "but I'm going to die knowing why."

"Why what?"

"Why you're acting like this."

"I can act however the hell I want! You don't own me!"

"Never said I did. I only said—" He snapped his mouth closed as her hand clenched even tighter around his neck.

She snarled at him. "I know what you said."

"And I don't need to keep saying it," he said, pushing his words through the fatigue clouding his mind. Trying to stay above water while she was slowly strangling him was proving difficult. "I get that. But you're upset whether I say it or not. I'll ask again—what's wrong?"

She pushed him away with a cry of disgust. Turning her back on him, she swam several feet away. She abruptly stopped and muttered, "Everything."

He started moving toward her. "I don't—"

The water around him suddenly froze, encasing him in a block of ice from the waist down. He and his personal iceberg bobbed like a cork as she turned to face him again.

Her face was lined with anguish. "It's all wrong," she said. Her tone made it sound like she was trying to convince not only him but herself as well. "I know how you feel. I just don't—" Her words ended in a choked whimper. She bowed her head and stared at the glassy surface of the pond.

"I'm going back," she whispered. She lifted her head and fixed him with a murderous glare. "If you *ever* follow me again when I tell you not to, I *will* kill you." With this final warning, she canceled the buoyancy charm and plunged straight down into the pond. A brief flash of light under the water was the only sign that she had left.

The ice surrounding Jamyn shattered. He made his way to shore and then frantically rubbed his limbs to fight off the lingering chill. Kana's robes had vanished along with their owner.

"I know you'll try," he whispered, his heart aching for his troubled mistress. "Just like you know I will always follow you."

———⟡———

After a quick stop in his quarters to change, Jamyn made his way back to the central chamber. The festivities were still in full swing, as was typical for Sanctum gatherings. It took him quite a while to finally find Shamara. When he did, she was chatting with a mixed group ranging from neophytes to mages.

He crept up behind her. "Getting to know the locals?" he said close to her ear.

She spun on her heel. "Jamyn!" She wrapped him in a firm hug. She backed away without releasing him and looked at him in concern. "Is Kana all right?"

He forced a carefree smile. "She's fine. She just needed a break." He winked at her. "I think she was actually a bit tweaked that the cabal didn't put up more of a fight. She went into your hearing expecting a full battle and got an unconditional surrender instead."

"Why would that upset her?"

He smiled at her confusion as he extricated himself from her grasp and stood up. "I'm just joking around. Kana's got a bit of a reputation around here. Am I right?" he asked the others standing nearby. Everyone nodded, many of them adding in quick bows of respect, which made him laugh. "Guys, come on. I'm not Kana. You don't have to worry about *me* ripping all your heads off." They all joined in his laughter. He turned his attention back to Shamara. "I see you're making a lot of new friends. Meet anyone else interesting while I was gone?"

"Master Qa introduced me to everyone in the Inner Cabal," she replied excitedly. "Many of them were very interested in the push."

"I don't doubt it. Where are Lob and Juushin?"

"They hurried off a while ago with Miss Daystar. I don't know why."

"Knowing those three, some manner of deviltry," Jamyn said. "I'm not sure about Juushin, but the other two are very capable troublemakers."

A voice rumbled right behind Shamara. "Most definitely."

She spun around and looked up. Fangs stood there grinning down at her.

"M-mister Fanghor!" she stuttered.

"Please, my dear," he said, his eyes gleaming despite his wounded voice. "I told you that wasn't necessary!"

Jamyn smiled at him. "Hey, Fangs. What's on your mind?"

"All kinds of things, especially now that I've had a few." Fangs muffled a small belch. "But I was actually going to ask our newest member something."

Shamara squeaked in surprise. "Me?"

Fangs cocked his head to the side. "There were others?" He made a show of looking all around and then shrugged back at her. "I must have fallen asleep after your admission." She giggled briefly, causing him to break into a full smile. "That's more like it! Now, have they burdened you with a schedule of classes yet?"

"No," she replied, shaking her head. "Mister Lob told me it might be a day or two."

"Excellent! Then you should have some free time tomorrow. I noticed from your outfit that you seem to like butterflies."

"I've only seen the one that Kana created," she replied. "But, yes, I like them a lot. They're pretty."

"That they are. Would you like to see more of them? There is a section of the wilds that has a ton of them. It's mating season so it's a constant whirlwind of color in there right now."

Her eyes grew wide at the invitation. "I would love to see that!" she whispered.

"Then we shall." Looking behind her at Jamyn, he said, "I'll check in on Lester too while I'm at it, but this time from a somewhat healthier distance. He's been really grumpy lately." To prove his point, he raised one arm. His sleeve fell to his elbow, revealing a semicircular area of new pink skin on his hairy forearm.

Jamyn looked over the area. "He bit you?"

Fangs lowered his arm, letting his robes fall back into place, and nodded. "Right before he tried to stomp on me. I was able to outrun him, but I'm lucky that he can't climb trees." Turning back to Shamara, he said, "I will pick you up tomorrow morning. The butterflies are more active then. You've been staying with Lob?"

She nodded. "I have, but I've heard I might be moving to regular quarters soon."

He arched a bushy eyebrow at her. "You like staying with him?"

"I do."

He shrugged. "Then perhaps you can continue to do so, if that arrangement works for you both. You'll find that there are always options here in the Sanctum." He peered at the crowd between him and the doors. "For example." He pointed upward and his pupils became vertical slits.

He grinned wildly, exposing slightly pointed canines. He waved a clawed hand at her and leaped straight up. His impossible vault sent him right to the high ceiling. He sank his claws into it and looked down at the surprised group.

"See you around eight!" he cried before proceeding hand under hand toward the exit in a series of loping swings. He waited for a moment upon reaching the far wall and then shot down like a missile when someone opened the doors. He slipped out right over the heads of those entering the chamber, prompting several shocked cries.

Jamyn laughed, both at Fangs's antics and at the awestruck look on Shamara's face. "He's a lot of fun. You two are gonna have a blast tomorrow."

"How...how did he do all that?" she stammered, pointing to the ceiling and then at the doors. "Was that magic?"

"Sort of. Fangs is more than just our animal expert. He can mimic their abilities." Jamyn considered the exit path Fangs had taken. "My guess is that was a rapid-fire combination of kangaroo for the jump, cougar for the claws, ape for the swinging, and seal for the dive."

"It was incredible!"

"Just wait until you get to the wilds. Once he's back in his element, he can really cut loose."

"The wilds is in another place?"

"Yeah. It's a fabricated pocket dimension." Seeing her confusion, he smiled. "It was created by magic. It's not actually on this planet. It's off in its own little space."

"How do we get there?"

"Through a gate."

"One of those glowing doors?"

"Yep. When did you see one?"

"When Kana first sent me to the Sanctum. She created a doorway made of light. When I went through it, I was standing next to Master Qa in Evrok's tavern."

"That's it. Tomorrow you'll go through one with Fangs and end up in the jungle. Wear something light. It's usually pretty warm there."

"You've been there before?"

"Lots of times. I was just there a little while ago looking for Kana."

"And did you find her?" a female voice behind him asked.

Jamyn turned to find Tiris smiling up at him. "Sure did. She decided to go cool off in the pond."

"Figures," Leel said, sidling up behind his wife. "That pond is one of the few places she allows herself to truly relax."

"Are you relaxed now too?" Tiris giggled and cast a knowing eye up at the acolyte.

Jamyn swallowed. "Not like that. I'm just happy to not be crispy around the edges."

"Ah. Kana's in a mood again," Leel said.

"Really?" Tiris asked. "I figured she'd be completely tension-free by now." She gave Jamyn a saucy grin along with an exaggerated wink.

Jamyn grimaced, indicating Shamara with a quick dart of his eyes. "She's fine. Just a little—"

"Uncomfortable around social gatherings," Leel said diplomatically, noticing Jamyn's distress. They shared a quick nod before Leel pressed up against Tiris's back. "Behave yourself for a change," he whispered in her ear.

"Jamyn?" Shamara asked suddenly.

"Yeah?"

"Are you Kana's boyfriend?"

Jamyn fought to keep his jaw from dropping. Seeing both Tiris and Leel also looking up at him expectantly did nothing for his nerves. "I'm her acolyte," he said slowly. Forcing a smile, he leaned down to Shamara. "But I wouldn't mind the job," he whispered into her ear. She smiled brightly at him as he stood up straight again.

"I admire your self-preservation instincts, lad," Leel said. He turned to Shamara. "And *your* keen eye! Ever think about a career in healing?"

"No, Master Leel," she replied. She thought a moment. "Though it would probably be a helpful skill to have."

"Agreed. A pity Kana wasn't a little better at the craft. With as many scrapes as that girl gets into, it certainly would cut down on our workload."

Tiris cuddled up to him. "But then you wouldn't get to examine her nearly as often."

"True." Lob shouted right behind Jamyn's head for effect.

Jamyn held his composure and turned around to find Lob standing there with Juushin and Daystar. "Subtle as always, Lob," he said. "What have you all been up to?"

The giant laughed. "Celebrating, of course! I saw you all chatting away so I thought you might be getting thirsty." He jerked one thumb straight up. "Drinks are on me." Everyone looked up to find one of Lob's shields acting as a large tray. He gestured and the shield fragmented into a multitude of smaller disks, each holding its own mug. They slowly descended in front of every person in the group. As each drink was removed, its disk popped out of existence.

Hoisting his own huge tankard, he peeked down at Shamara. "Getting tired of being toasted yet?" he asked.

She giggled. "Not really. I'll let you."

"Most kind, young miss," he said, nodding down at her politely before raising his tankard. "To Shamara!"

The sentiment was quickly echoed by the others, and everyone drank. Suddenly Shamara gasped loudly and nearly spat a mouthful of her drink right at Jamyn.

Jamyn lowered his mug, which was filled with a curious fruity concoction. "What's wrong?"

"Wong dink!" She fanned her tongue as if it was on fire.

Jamyn took her glass and gave the contents a quick sniff. "What the—" He puzzled at the noxious vapors before taking another careful sniff. He arched an eyebrow at Lob. "Rum?" He quickly handed his mug to Shamara, who gulped down its contents to help extinguish the blaze.

"What?" Lob asked in obviously faked surprise. "Then *you* got the juice? Huh. I must have mixed up your drinks." He raised his tankard for another swallow. "Purely by accident, of course. Not to make sure she was keeping her guard up like I taught her or anything."

Shamara glanced at Juushin and the pair exchanged curt nods. Juushin planted her feet and slammed her huge body into Lob's right side just as Shamara directed a massive push to crash into his left. The remaining contents of his mug sloshed right in his face. Caught between the two unforgiving forces, he was barely able to lower the mug away from his now sopping visage.

"I guess I deserved that," he muttered amid the group's raucous laughter.

———◉———

The pair made their way across the sprawling field, the smaller man scampering to keep pace with the tall, armor-clad figure.

"You say it's here?" the tall man demanded.

"In a hidden spot near the north end," the small man replied at once. Their trek continued in silence for another dozen steps. "He will not live much longer, I think."

The tall man growled. "I care not, so long as he gives me the answers I require before he dies." A curious glint from a small hillock ahead made him lengthen his already impressive strides.

Reaching the knoll, he pulled away the curtain of vines that obscured his prize. Inside a small alcove hollowed out of the earthen mound was a flower encased in a glass dome. The flower's delicate petals were lined with a faint golden light.

"The Soul Flame," the tall man whispered in a combination of wonder and hatred.

"An inscription." The small man pointed at the base of the dome.

At the bottom of the dome was a small, engraved plaque. "Presented to the Scion Letrona by the Sanctum," the tall man read. "May they someday return to you."

He suddenly thrust his hand forward, driving his fingers through the thin glass. He grasped the delicate flower, mindless of the numerous cuts in his flesh, and closely observed its shimmering aura.

"They have not returned, but I have," he murmured. "The Flame shall soon know of my coming."

———— ◉ ————

Jamyn's body thrashed beneath the blanket covering him.

"Kana!"

He whipped the blanket off and hurled it across the room in one swift motion. He sat upright, his mind frantically trying to catch up with his body. He stared wide-eyed at the clock on the opposite wall while he continued to draw in air in huge gulps. The fact it was now morning trickled in past his lessening fear. At long last, he calmed down and let his face fall into his hands.

"Only a dream," he muttered. "Stupid fucking dream."

After a deep cleansing breath, he peeked past his hands to the empty spot beside him. *Good thing she's not here. I'd have to figure out a way to explain it to her.* He released a frustrated sigh. *Yeah, right. I can't even explain it to myself!*

His hands fell into his lap, and he sighed again when they landed on his pulsing erection. Though her being there would be enough to help calm him, he silently admitted having her naked in his bed again could do wonders for calming his nerves in several other delicious ways. He gripped his shaft and caressed it slowly, reminiscing about her last lusty attack. Closing his eyes, he lay back and continued to fantasize about his mistress. He envisioned her standing at the foot of his bed, calmly watching him stroke himself. Even fully clothed, the thought of her mere presence was all the incentive he needed.

Just as the first tingles started to arc up his spine, the vision changed.

A faint shroud of fire bloomed from her body, consuming her clothes in a flash. Her naked body was quickly outlined by the mystical flames. She smiled at him and traced her fingertips down over one bare breast. The fire enveloping her surged, giving her hair the appearance of a fiery halo.

"Please," she whispered before her entire body was engulfed in the inferno.

The tingles changed to a searing jolt as he started to come. Jamyn cried out as the first splash hit his chest. He shuddered, the spasms wracking him causing his head to snap forward. Another jet hit him in the chin and his eyes popped open in surprise. He pulled his cock hard to his belly and the remains of his heavy load sprayed against his navel. He fell backward, landing on his pillow and gasping for breath while his spent cock twitched in his hand. Still panting hard, his mind continually replayed the image of his mistress shrouded in flame at the height of his orgasm.

"The hell?" he whispered to himself, wondering what the odd vision could possibly mean.

———————◈———————

Kana woke up in her own bed. She instinctively reached a hand to her side but found nothing but empty sheets.

"Not here," she muttered to herself while she continued to rouse herself from her slumber. She spread her questing fingers out and smoothed them over the vacant spot. After waking up alone for so many years, she was surprised at how much Jamyn's absence gnawed at her.

She sat up and tried to shake off her melancholy, but her mind was intent on mulling over their current situation.

No problem. He's been okay in the past when I've gone off on him. He'll just keep his distance and wait for me to get my head together. She smirked. *He'll probably say he's sorry a few dozen times too.*

"Kana."

The Valet's sudden query rattled her. She tossed her head back and shouted at the ceiling. "What?"

"You have received a priority message."

She made a face. *Probably Jamyn.*

"Who from?"

"Letron 12-B. Hajis-Corol, leader of Squad Thirteen, First Regiment."

"Hajis-Corol? Why would he be sending me a message?"

"Unknown," the Valet replied.

"Wasn't talking to you. Just play the message."

"It is in written form. It is also marked for your eyes alone."

Her mind quickly started churning.

Why would Hajis-Corol send me a private written message? He would have had to use the emergency contact beacon we left them. Guess there's only one way to find out.

"Lemme have it."

A folded piece of paper suddenly appeared in her lap. Across the fold was a magical seal. She examined it closely for nearly a minute before pressing her thumb against it. The seal started to glow.

"Name and rank?" an unknown male voice asked.

She made sure to speak clearly while also recalling the Letronan custom of swapping first and last names. "Morel-Kana. First Seer of the Sanctum."

The seal disappeared. She unfolded the paper and scanned it quickly. "Come to the bunker near the Sacred Fields," she muttered. "Matter of utmost importance and secrecy. Exercise extreme discretion." As soon as she had read the final word, the paper disintegrated, leaving her holding only air.

Her brow furrowed and she sat there in silence, immediately regarding the strange summons to be some kind of trap. "Hey, Sanctum."

"Kana."

"Verify authenticity of sender."

"Sender of what?"

She frowned. "The message you just gave me."

"I have no record of a recent message. When was it received?"

"Just now!"

"I am sorry, Kana. I have no record of receiving or delivering a message for you today."

Kana growled under her breath.

Extreme discretion, he said. Would explain why he sent an untraceable message. That would've had to have been authorized by 12-B's entire ruling council.

She mulled over the strange message and its cryptic invitation.

"Wouldn't hurt to check it out," she said at last.

Looking down, she sighed when she saw the ceremonial robes she had worn during Shamara's induction ceremony. She had them reappear on her body in mid-gate coming back from the wilds. Afterwards, she had just collapsed on her bed and went to sleep.

"Whatever," she said dismissively. "This shouldn't take long. I'll change when I get back." Raising her voice, she said, "Sanctum, I'm gating out. Keep it to yourself per my authorization."

"Keyword?"

She took a deep breath and released it in a heavy sigh. "Soulscatter."

"Authorization accepted."

"And away we go."

She cast a spell, and a bright doorway appeared. As she stepped into the glowing gate, she paused to look back at her empty bed, wondering what she could say to her acolyte to make sure it wouldn't stay that way for long.

Chapter Fifteen: Seek

Jamyn ambled down the corridors, scanning them up and down for his mistress. Since she had left the previous night's festivities early, he fully expected her to be up and about by now. He chuckled to himself.

Not like some of the others who were there. I'm betting there are drum solos being played in a lot of heads this morning.

Wandering through the training section, he caught sight of a familiar face outside of room number five. "Hey, Lash," he called out.

Lasher stopped and turned to him. "Hey, Siska. What's up?"

"Nothing much. Just taking a stroll and keeping an eye out for Kana."

"Better use both eyes," Lasher said with a grin. "You're in trouble if she catches you off-guard."

"Don't I know it," Jamyn replied. "You only get to be wrong once around her. The second time is usually fatal." They laughed together.

"Well, you're still alive, so you must be doing something right."

"Guess so. Have you seen her?"

"Nope."

Jamyn sighed. "Damn."

"Something wrong?"

Jamyn noticed Lasher looking back at him in concern. "Nah. She was just in a bit of a mood last night. I'm hoping she's past it."

"Yeesh." Lasher chuckled. "Kana in a mood. That takes me back."

"I'm guessing she's always been like that?"

"God, yes. Ever since we joined the Sanctum." Seeing Jamyn's confused look, he nodded. "I got here a day or two earlier than her. Since we were both training at the same time, it was decided to pair

251

us up so we could help one another. Even back then, she'd get a bug up her butt about something and then stomp off until she got her head back together. But, hey, it sure did beat the alternative."

"That being?"

"Her sticking around and just stomping on *me*, of course."

Jamyn smiled. "Yeah, that does tend to suck." He looked at the gym bag slung over Lasher's shoulder. "What're you up to?"

"Some agility training with the derelicts coming up behind you."

Jamyn turned to see Kresh and two others walking toward them. All of them were wearing workout gear that mimicked Lasher's. "Kresh," Jamyn said to the tall mage. He received a courteous nod in reply. He turned to the fair-haired man beside Kresh and recognized him from their brief encounter the medical wing. "Nigel, right?"

The medic nodded. "Good seeing you again when you're not charging down the door."

Jamyn chuckled before turning to the third man. "And you..."

"Danny," Lasher said. "One of the two guys this training is for. Where the hell is the other one this time?"

"Probably slept in," Nigel replied. "Wanker likely got himself right pissed at the gathering last night."

"He keeps that up, they're gonna drum his idiot ass outta here," Lasher said sourly. He looked around the group. "How we gonna work this? Don't really wanna throw Danny into the meat grinder with all of us." Looking to Jamyn, he asked, "You ever play handball?"

"Nope."

Lasher's face lit up in a triumphant grin. "And there's our second novice. We can go doubles and not get anyone killed."

Jamyn looked around at their smiling faces. "What?"

"I think you've been drafted," Kresh said in his low, rumbling voice. "My condolences."

"Ah, don't listen to him," Lasher said, ushering Jamyn into the training room. "It'll be fun! We're just playing a friendly round of handball to help Danny here with his agility and stamina."

"And my casting," Danny said, sounding a bit nervous.

"Just a bit," Lasher said nonchalantly. "Nothing lethal."

"So far," Nigel said.

"No worries," Lasher said, clapping him on the shoulder. "That's why we brought a medic."

Jamyn stiffened, resisting Lasher's eager tugging on his arm. "Whoa. Afraid I'll have to bow out."

"Aw, c'mon! Why?"

Jamyn held up a hand and waggled his fingers. "Magic's locked down. Anchor spell."

"Oh, right," Lasher replied. "Heard about that." Looking around the group, he shrugged. "I guess this round we'll go magic-free and just do agility and teamwork. Sound good?" He looked over Jamyn's t-shirt and jeans and started to frown. "You're not gonna beg out because of *that* now, are ya?"

Jamyn smiled. "Nah. I'm fine in this."

"Good deal. Let's set the stage." He cleared his throat. "Set up the handball court, if you would!" he called out to the empty room.

Instantly, a huge rectangular box appeared in the center of the room, encompassing the court area. Its walls were transparent and bright red lines were marked on several of them. A half-dozen chairs materialized outside the back wall of the court.

Lasher pulled on a pair of gloves and took a small blue ball from his bag. "Into the pit, ladies. Nigel, you hang back this round."

Nigel returned a dismissive grunt and sat on one of the chairs. "Hell, I could have slept in too."

The others entered the court. Once they were all inside, the doorway closed, forming a seamless wall behind them.

"You know the basics?" Lasher asked Jamyn.

"Pretty much. Hit the ball off the wall and don't let it bounce twice. Or hit you in the junk."

"*That* is priority one," Lasher said. "If any of us loses a nut, I would prefer a lady to be involved." The others laughed. Jamyn, however, grimaced at the thought. "Ooh, sorry," Lasher said, noticing his discomfort. "I forgot that's an actual prospect for some of us."

Jamyn smiled, knowing Kana would likely have very different plans where those were involved. Still, he played along. "Yeah, let's not deprive her of the opportunity."

"All right, then. We'll go me and Danny versus you and Kresh. Sound good?" The others nodded and took their positions on the court. Lasher dribbled the ball a few times. "Follow the bouncing ball!" he cried right before serving.

The shot hit the middle of the opposite wall and bounced to Jamyn. Taking careful measure, he set up and slapped the ball hard. It rocketed back to the wall, hitting it low. The ball careened back at a blistering rate, catching Lasher off-guard. He swung wildly but missed.

Danny retrieved the ball and flipped it back to Lasher.

"I think you lost this," Danny said with a grin.

Lasher forced a chuckle while keeping an eye on Jamyn. "Let's try that again."

He served and gave the ball a bit of spin as he did. The return bounced up high, but Jamyn leaped into the air and smacked it. This time, it hit the wall and just died, coming back in a fluttering arc. Lasher swore and made a frantic dive. He hit the floor hard, and the ball dropped an inch from his outstretched hand.

Kresh and Danny both clapped politely. Nigel, on the other hand, loosed a booming laugh.

"Okay," Lasher said loudly from the floor, "who brought in the ringer?"

"That'd be you, mate!" Nigel laughed again.

"Sorry, Lash," Jamyn said.

Lasher rolled onto his side and propped his head up on one bent arm. "Thought you said you'd never played before."

"I haven't," Jamyn said with a contrite smile. "Just got a knack for it, I guess."

Lasher stood up. "Well, tone it down a bit, Mister Knackered. Remember that this is *supposed* to be a training exercise."

Nigel continued his verbal prodding. "He's doing a fine job of schooling you so far!"

Lasher flung him a rude gesture. "Let's just get a simple back-and-forth going. This time, try to remember you're not in the world finals."

Jamyn nodded. "Got it. Fire away."

Lasher bounced the ball a few times. "Third time's a charm," he muttered, putting the ball into play.

A half-hour later, it was clear Jamyn was a natural. His sharp eyes and keen reflexes had him flying around the court like a man possessed. Halfway in, they switched partners. Jamyn and Danny now took on Lasher and Kresh and the younger team was winning handily.

Danny charged for a return but misjudged the ball's path. He missed badly and then stumbled as he stepped on the ball. He landed awkwardly with a yelp of pain. Lasher quickly called for time, and they all rushed to Danny's aid.

"Doesn't look too bad," Lasher said. "Probably just turned the ankle a bit."

"That your professional medical opinion?" Nigel asked, standing over them. He was off his seat in a flash when he saw Danny go down, a direct result of his training. "Clear out, you lot." The others gave him room. He knelt and cast a spell over Danny's ankle. "No worries, mate," he said to the younger man. "No breaks. Just a decent pull.

Best you sit out a round." He looked up at Lasher. "If that's okay with your doctor, of course."

Lasher bowed and backed away. "I concede to your superior talent."

"Damned right you do." Nigel grinned as he helped Danny sit up. "I've heard about your grades for basic medical."

"Hey! Those are supposed to be private!"

"Nothing's private when you're Master Leel's acolyte." Nigel cast a spell to splint Danny's ankle. "He told me all about the cast incident."

Lasher groaned in response.

Intrigued, Jamyn asked, "Cast?"

Lasher relented and smiled. "I tried a spell to form a cast on my little finger. It kinda got out of control."

"As in Master Leel had to stop it from growing before it encased your head," Kresh said, a smile finally cracking his stern countenance.

"Crap. You too, Kresh? How many people did he tell?"

"He tells everyone," Kresh replied, "right before he informs them that teasing another caster is unwise because everyone makes at least one truly boneheaded mistake in their lives."

"At least," Jamyn said. "Some of us are making a career of it."

Nigel helped Danny up to a standing position. "Let's get you out of the line of fire." Together they made their way off the court and back to the seats.

"So now what?" Jamyn asked.

The other two looked at each other. Lasher jerked a thumb at Jamyn and Kresh nodded solemnly. They turned back to Jamyn with sneaky grins.

"A little something called *cutthroat*," Lasher said.

"Sounds unpleasant," Jamyn said, rubbing the front of his neck for emphasis.

"Judging by your talents so far, it likely will be," Kresh said. "For us."

Lasher picked up the ball and then flipped it to Jamyn. "Simple concept. One on two. You against us. You serve."

"Yeah," Jamyn said in an unsure voice as he bounced the ball a few times. "No problem." With this, he wound up and hit a blazing serve.

Nigel regarded the new battle in progress and shook his head. "A good thing you're not in there," he said to Danny as he continued to assess the younger man's ankle. "That's no place for a civilized lad."

A cocky voice sneered behind them. "Yeah, looks rough."

Nigel glanced back over his shoulder. "Well. Mister Kellor finally decided to roust his lazy bum out of bed."

Kellor looked past Nigel and noticed an unknown third fending off Lasher and Kresh. "You guys got another sucker to pinch hit for me, huh?" He watched the frantic trio racing around the court, each of them trying to pummel the ball through the opposite wall. "What the hell? No magic?"

"No, they're not—" Nigel stopped abruptly. "Now steady on!"

He was too late. Kellor's spell took hold on the ball as it headed for Kresh's outstretched hand.

Jamyn's senses suddenly went wild. He made a frantic lunge to intercept the ball, reaching his hand out as far as he could. As the ball touched the tips of his fingers, a cluster of electric arcs flared from it and seized his hand. A burst of darkness surged from his arm, surrounding the ball and extinguishing the sparks. The collapsed magic formed a shock wave that sent the ball rocketing away from him. It struck the side wall hard and flattened into a thin rubber disk, the air inside it releasing with a loud, hollow *thump*.

No one in the room moved for several seconds. Jamyn was the first, slowly rising to his feet. His fatigue turned into a burning rage that flooded his body.

"The hell was that?" Lasher scrambled to his feet. He quickly looked around the room. Shocked faces greeted him from every one of them, but none more so than Kellor's. He was peeking around Nigel, who had stood up at the sound of the ball's sudden demise. Lasher immediately shouted at Kellor. "Was that you, you little numb-nuts?"

"Hey, I was just—" Kellor fell silent in the next heartbeat.

The recipient of his prank had turned around. Jamyn glared at him in furious outrage, exactly as he had during their encounter in Evrok's. Kellor's face paled and he fainted dead away, his body landing in an undignified heap.

Nigel pushed his chair aside to assist, though he certainly didn't appear to be in a hurry about it.

Lasher released a disgusted sigh. "What's his story, Nigel?"

"Not sure. Looks like he's had a bit of a fright." He glanced down Kellor's body. "Bloody hell. He's pissed himself."

Jamyn snarled. "Good."

Lasher walked to Jamyn's side. "What's up, man? You two got a history?"

Jamyn nodded slowly. "He insulted Kana one night at Evrok's. I took offense."

"You straighten him out?"

"I nearly killed him. Kana stopped me."

Lasher arched an eyebrow at him. "Say what? She heard the insult too, but *you* jumped in to defend *her*? Very *knight in shining* of you."

Jamyn took a deep breath to help clear his mind of the last lingering shreds of anger. "She stopped me from doing something stupid. I heard she took care of him after I left."

"*Took care of.* As in beat the living snot outta him, I'm sure." Lasher shook his head and sighed. "As someone who's been on the receiving end of Kana's wrath, I guess I should feel sorry for him." He smiled and clapped a hand on Jamyn's shoulder. "This time, I think I'll make an exception."

Jamyn turned to Kresh. "You okay?"

"I believe I should be asking you that." Kresh pointed down at Jamyn's hand. "You appear to be hurt."

"Yeah. I'm trying not to look at it. Stings like mad."

"Never a dull moment with you around, Siska," Nigel said as he entered the court area. Gingerly picking up Jamyn's hand, he examined it and then cast a spell. "How's that?"

"Better," Jamyn replied in a relieved sigh. "At least it doesn't hurt now." He examined the singed flesh. "How bad, do you think?"

Nigel grinned at Lasher. "At least *he* has the brains to ask."

Lasher threw his hands in the air. "All right! I'll step back! Jeez!"

"Not too bad," Nigel said, turning his attention back to his patient. "Got a few things back in medical that'll sort it out. I've gotta take him back with me anyway." He nodded toward where Danny sat.

"I guess we're done here, then," Lasher said. "Thanks for sitting in, Siska."

"No problem," Jamyn replied. "Thanks for having me." He walked out of the training room alongside Nigel and a limping Danny.

Kresh and Lasher watched him go and then immediately turned their attention to the ruined ball.

"I thought he said his magic was locked down," Lasher said quietly.

"He did."

"Then how the hell did he do that?" He pointed at the ball's remains.

"I do not know. It happened too quickly for me to see."

Lasher raised his voice. "Lose the court, please." The enclosed area vanished, leaving the rubber disk behind. Lasher picked it up and then inspected it closely on his way back to Kresh. "No traces of magic on it."

"Perhaps the shock made his muscles seize up enough to deal it a fatal blow against the wall."

Lasher shook his head in defeat. "Best to ponder this over a drink. Or several." As they walked past him, Lasher flipped the rubber disk onto Kellor's unconscious body. "You owe me a new ball, asshole," he said before following Kresh out the door.

———◉———

"Have you boys been roughhousing?" Tiris asked in a playfully stern tone as she watched the trio enter the medical wing.

"No, Mistress Tiris," Nigel replied at once. "Just a bit of handball. One sprained ankle and some charred fingers."

"Charred fingers? Did you set the ball on fire?"

"Nah. That twit Kellor thought it would be funny to electrify the ball. Siska somehow failed to find the humor in it." He helped Danny sit on one of the examining beds.

Tiris hurried over to Jamyn. "Let's see."

Jamyn raised his hand to let her examine it.

She looked over the charred wounds. "Hmm. Minor heat damage." She looked closer and cast a spell. "Pretty good shock wave damage underneath. What happened?"

"Not sure," he replied. "I suddenly knew that the ball was dangerous, so I tried to get to it before anyone else did. It touched my fingers, and I just swung at it."

"But the wave propagated—" She cut off her statement and walked to where Nigel was working on Danny's leg. "Have you got that under control?"

"Yes, mistress," he replied.

"I told you that you don't need to keep calling me that," she said. "But I suppose I'll keep letting you since it sounds so good with your accent." She patted his butt. "I'm taking Jamyn back to the office. When you're done, be sure to do up a report for Leel."

"Yes, mistress."

Taking Jamyn's good hand, she pulled him toward the office. Once there, she closed the door behind them and pointed to a chair. "Sit."

He sat down and saw her look of concern. "Something wrong?"

"You tell me. From your aura, or rather your lack thereof, I'd guess your magic is still locked down. Correct?"

He nodded.

She carefully took his injured hand and showed it to him. "The spell on the ball shouldn't have burned your skin. It definitely should not have caused any blast damage to the muscles in your fingers. How about telling me what *really* happened?"

"I had just hit the ball, and it was headed for Kresh—"

"The ebony tower," Tiris said with a gleam in her eye. "Absolutely *gorgeous* voice."

"Um, yeah. Suddenly I knew something was wrong with the ball. I don't know how I knew. I dove for it out of pure instinct."

"And then?"

Jamyn closed his eyes and tried to remember. "My hand got closer to it. A spark hit my fingers and then..." His voice trailed off. The more he tried to envision the ball, the darker the image became. "Damn," he said at last.

He opened his eyes and was stunned to find Path standing just behind Tiris and smiling back at him. She quickly brought a finger to her lips, requesting he not reveal her presence.

"What is it?" Tiris asked, looking behind herself but finding no one there.

"Hang on," he said, trying to keep from staring at Path. "I think it's coming back."

Path nodded her approval. She mimed swatting at something with her right hand, then balled her left hand into a fist. She brought the fist against the fingers of her right hand in slow-motion and quickly opened it to indicate a burst. Closing it tightly again, she quickly drew her fist away.

"I think I collapsed the magic back on itself and it exploded." Jamyn's voice was a shocked whisper.

Tiris nodded. "Your injuries seem to agree. But how did you—" She stopped and considered his stunned expression. "I see. You were willcasting."

He swallowed hard. "I guess so. I didn't mean to."

She poked him in the midsection. "Of course, you didn't, silly boy. Willcasting is instinctive most of the time." She shook her head and smiled warmly. "I think maybe Donta's got you gun-shy. There's nothing wrong with a little impromptu magic every so often. Keeps the skills sharp."

"But I'm locked down," Jamyn said. "I'm not supposed to be able to cast."

She answered him without missing a beat. "You prevented someone from getting hurt. That's all that matters." She thought a moment. "But then, if you hadn't, I'd probably be looking over tall, dark, and Kresh right now." She pouted and gave him another poke. "I think you owe me, kiddo."

Path shot him a wink and repeatedly pointed at Tiris.

Jamyn's memory suddenly twitched. "Y'know, I think I do," he replied. He quickly bent forward and planted a warm kiss on Tiris's cheek. He sat back and almost laughed at her wide eyes.

"What was that for?" She barely managed to squeak the question.

"The restorative potion that you gave to Kana. She said you amped it up or something. Right after I woke up, I promised I'd give you that," he said, indicating her now flushed cheeks.

"My pleasure," she said in a husky rumble.

Her diminutive body shivered. A bright glow surged through her before centering on her hands. She pressed her left palm firmly against a breast while her right hand grasped Jamyn's injury. She took a few quick breaths and then sighed deeply. Another surge of light rocketed from her held breast, traveled up her arm and across her chest, and then shot back down her other arm. The glow enshrouded Jamyn's hand for a moment and then dissipated. When she pulled away, his hand was completely healed.

"I need Leel," she whispered before bolting out the door.

Jamyn started to look over his restored hand when he noticed Path staring back at him in utter horror. He leaped to his feet, spurred on by her look of panic. "What's wrong?"

Path was panting hard, as if she had just received devastating news. Her amber eyes locked with Jamyn's. She stared at him helplessly before vanishing as she rejoined Jamyn's mind.

Jamyn teetered where he stood, his mind suddenly ablaze with panic. "Something's wrong!" In a flash, he sprinted out the door.

<hr/>

Kana struggled to focus her mind while ignoring the numerous pains wracking her body. The side of her face pressed hard against a puddle on the cold metal floor. She started to open one eye but then squeezed it shut even tighter when a trickle of blood blurred her vision. She clenched her teeth as her eye started to sting. Pushing aside the nausea and dizziness of her likely concussion, she tried to piece together the events of the last several minutes in her throbbing head.

Kana stepped out of the gate and into the Sacred Fields on Letron 12-B. She gave the entire area a quick yet thorough scan with both her eyes and her magic.

"No one's home," she said under her breath. Getting her bearings, she set off for the command bunker just past the valley's northern edge. "Probably waiting for me there," she muttered, keeping a close eye on everything around her as she strode across the lush field.

A building appeared off in the distance, a squat truncated pyramid of dull gray metal that barely disturbed the foliage around it. Just to the right of its main doors were two all-terrain vehicles, parked far enough apart to easily fit another between them. A large area of flattened grass covered a stretch of land to the building's left. Kana catalogued every detail as she continued to make her way to the entrance.

"Guess I'll ring the bell," she said in a loud, clear voice.

In mid-step, a shot rang out in the distance. At the same time, Kana's body disappeared.

The sniper behind the near truck blinked in surprise. He immediately scoured the area through the high-powered scope on his rifle. Suddenly the tip of a finger pressed hard against the back of his head.

"You missed." Kana held her index finger against the base of the man's skull. Even though she couldn't see him through the camouflaged suit he wore, she could feel him start to shake.

"How—" the man started to ask.

Kana cut off his query, keeping her voice low and menacing. "How many more of you are there?"

She swung around with her free hand, catching an invisible assassin square in the face before he could drive his knife into her back. His nose shattered, sending fragments of cartilage rocketing up into his brain. His lifeless body hit the ground hard.

"Besides him, I mean."

The man responded only with a faint *beep*.

Kana dove into the shadows behind the truck and disappeared. Less than a heartbeat later, the truck exploded in a fiery burst. Kana reappeared in the shadows behind the second truck and flailed her leg out in a spinning high kick. Her booted foot connected with at least two heads. She stood firm as their owners collapsed, their necks broken.

Kana crouched down and felt around for one of the bodies. Finding one, she hauled him up to a sitting position against one of the truck's tires.

"Now let's see what you look like," she muttered.

She gestured and a burst of color sprayed from her hand. The dead man's features were briefly revealed before his suit adjusted and he faded away again.

"Powered active camouflage," she said, concern creeping into her voice. "I didn't think we left any of those suits intact."

She thought back to the Letronan conflict. The attacking army of mercenaries had used similar equipment. To the best of her knowledge, she and the others from the Sanctum's response team had destroyed all the tech left behind after their decisive victory.

And the mercs were history.

Her mind automatically locked down those memories before they could fully surface.

Shaking off that particular demon of her past, she silently made her way to the bunker's main doors. Instead of opening them, she altered her density and walked right through them. Becoming solid again, she turned to examine the explosive charges attached to the doors' handles. She pressed on, scanning the walls and floor for more traps as she went. Though she found none, she felt more and more uneasy with every step down the long corridor that led to the heart of the bunker.

The corridor emptied into a large central room, dark except for some widely spaced emergency lighting coming from sunken fixtures in the ceiling. Within one of the small cones of light lay a battered body. She approached it cautiously while maintaining a constant sweep of the room. Reaching it at last, she glanced down to see a familiar but bloodied face.

"Hajis-Corol!" Her suspicions about his invitation were now fully justified. "What happened?"

"He was unreasonable," a cruel voice said from the shadows.

Kana flew into action, casting a handful of spells at once. The room was quickly ablaze with light. A barrier formed over Hajis-Corol's body. Kana spun on her heel with one hand extended in front of her. Bright darts of energy streamed from her palm, striking a multitude of unseen foes all around her. Their forms shimmered momentarily before coming into focus, revealing rows of troops standing at attention all around her. She recognized their armor, and her lips tightened in hate.

"Mercs." She snarled under her breath. "What business do you have here?"

The cruel voice she had heard replied, "The unfinished kind."

"Bullshit. Your dealings here were concluded when the Sanctum defeated both you and your employers."

"Our clients were defeated. We were not. But you should know that better than anyone, shouldn't you?"

She continued to scan the ranks of impassive faces. None of them appeared to be the speaker. "You were allowed to leave with your lives." She flexed her hands, ready to strike at the slightest provocation.

"Ready?" the voice asked quietly.

"It is," someone replied in the same hushed tone.

Kana felt around in her robes for the stash. In a flash, she withdrew her metallic staff and brandished it before her, its length covered in a crackling sheath of sparks. "Enough of this. You will get off this planet right now or I will obliterate you."

"Now," the cruel voice said.

A smaller robed figure emerged from the ranks of the soldiers before her. He took a solid step forward and tossed something onto the ground right in front of Kana. She looked down and saw a flower surrounded by a very familiar golden glow.

"Stand fast for your judgment, Morel-Kana!" The figure's voice boomed despite his small stature.

The flower on the floor dissolved into a churning tempest of colors, each of them tinged with gold. A paralyzing weakness suddenly seized her body, sending her face-first to the floor. At the same time, her mind was unbalanced by a wave of confusion that quickly muddled her senses. She had barely heard the harsh clang of her staff against the metal floor when something slammed into her midsection. Her breath escaped in one sudden burst and pain exploded across her entire body. She tried to right her unsteady mind when she was hit again, this time in the forehead. Stars exploded before her eyes, and she blinked repeatedly to clear them. When she did, she saw the end of her staff planted firmly on the floor right in front of her face. Its end was now painted with a bright swath of red. Next to the staff was a pair of heavy combat boots.

A cruel voice sneered from somewhere high above the boots. "Welcome back."

Vicious blows started to rain down on every part of her body, a symphony of pain that was only brought to an end by the welcome blanket of unconsciousness.

Chapter Sixteen: Held

"M aster Qa!"

Jamyn's shout resounded throughout the crowded corridor. Many of its occupants instantly darted out of his way, pressing themselves up against the stone walls to either side. Those who didn't found themselves jostled, dodged, or just rudely shoved out of the way as Jamyn streaked toward his former mentor.

Qa took in the acolyte's frantic rush with his usual placid expression, though his feet seemed reluctant to come to a complete stop. "What is it, Jamyn?"

"Kana." Jamyn panted hard. "Have you seen her?"

Qa shook his head. "No, I have not. Is there a problem?"

Jamyn clenched his teeth as he tried to calm his racing mind. "I don't know. I can't find her and suddenly I'm convinced that something is wrong."

Qa shrugged it off. "Kana is prone to disappearing every so often. You shouldn't concern yourself."

"Still, I want to know where she is so I can make sure she's okay." Jamyn set his jaw in grim determination.

Qa considered his fierce visage a moment longer before placing a hand on the younger man's shoulder. Instantly, a wave of serenity spread throughout Jamyn's body. His breathing evened out and his heart stopped its racing.

"Just calm down," Qa said, his voice a hypnotic whisper. "Go check with Evrok. He may know where Kana is."

Jamyn nodded in resigned agreement. "Yeah. I'll check with Evrok."

"Very good."

———— ◉ ————

With this, Qa hurried off down the hallway. As soon as he was out of earshot, he muttered, "He knows."

Daystar's voice whispered back through the tiny mote clinging to Qa's shoulder. "But how?"

"I do not know. Advise the others. That clock is now ticking." His steps took on a new urgency, propelling him toward the Sanctum's central chamber at an impressive rate.

———— ◉ ————

Jamyn watched him go. Though the acolyte's mind was now untroubled, a small part of it suddenly demanded that it shouldn't be. A surge of darkness welled up around him, instantly dispelling Qa's calming effect, and his lips curled in renewed anger.

He knows something. They all do.

Despite wanting to chase down Qa again, he turned in the direction of Evrok's.

He might have answers that they won't give me.

Jamyn stormed off to his new destination.

———— ◉ ————

"Elapsed time?" Qa asked as soon as he entered the central chamber.

Donta growled his reply. "Just over three minutes."

"Then a follow-up should be imminent." Qa looked all around at the tense faces of the Inner Cabal's members. "Has anyone identified the source yet?"

"Given the circumstances, I think that would be clear," Fangs said, his pupils constricted into thin vertical lines.

"Agreed," Qa replied quickly, "but why? The situation there has been stable since their defeat."

"They seem the type to hold a grudge," Leel said. "If word somehow got out—" He stopped abruptly and sighed. "We all know what happened."

The others nodded gravely.

"Incoming communication," the Valet announced.

"Source and location?" Qa asked.

"Unknown."

"Trace it."

A cruel voice sneered from high above their heads. "I assure you that will be pointless."

Qa held his composure at the bypassing of the Valet. "Whom am I addressing?"

"You know who we are," came the angry reply. "You know what was done. You know what we have."

Donta snarled in anger. "And you know we will stop you!" Thick tendrils of darkness seeped out from beneath his robes. Daystar quickly reached a hand over and held his arm. The shroud of gloom slowly receded, though Donta continued to mutter angrily.

"You will not," the voice replied firmly. "You have probed the area. You know what will happen if you try to come here."

"What do you want?" Qa asked.

"What we want, we already have. When our dealings here have concluded, we will leave."

Only his iron will kept Qa's aura from exploding all around him. "You do not realize what you have brought upon yourselves," he said in a measured voice.

"Nor do you. In case there is any doubt, there is something you should hear."

———— ◉ ————

The door flew open with a loud bang and Jamyn stomped into the tavern. He shouted to the thin barkeep at the far end of the bar.

"Evrok!"

Evrok turned to face the enraged acolyte. "You are being unnecessarily rude today, Mister Siska."

His usual piping tones grated on Jamyn's already frayed nerves. "Where is Kana?"

"How would I know?"

"You know, so spill it!" Jamyn stomped forward toward the proprietor.

Flashes of light coalesced in the air around Evrok's rail-thin body. "Mister Siska, I would advise you to calm down. You are without your magic and your master. A fight now would not go well for you."

The bar's few patrons noticed the brewing altercation and quickly exited the premises, giving Jamyn a wide berth as they did.

Jamyn walked right up to Evrok and glared at him in hate. "Tell me!"

Evrok's sunken eyes calmly regarded Jamyn's flashing amber ones. "Have you tried asking the Valet?" Seeing a brief flicker of uncertainty in Jamyn's eyes, Evrok sighed and called out, "Sanctum, where is Kana Morel?"

"Kana is not currently in the Sanctum," the Valet replied.

"Then she gated out. Where did she go?"

"Kana is not currently in the Sanctum."

"Interesting. She gated out but didn't let the Valet record it. She obviously wanted some time to herself."

"She's in trouble." Jamyn snarled through his clenched teeth.

"She usually is."

Jamyn's rage flared anew. He grabbed at the billowing cloud of magic surrounding Evrok, snatched a handful of the swirling light, and then slammed it onto the bar. The glow scattered into a shower of sparks that quickly floated back to rejoin Evrok's aura.

Evrok's dark eyes widened in shock. "When was the last time Kana was within the Sanctum's limits?" he asked the Valet.

"Approximately three hours ago."

"And did anything precede her exit? Orders or a message?"

"There is no record of her receiving a message."

"Really?" Evrok asked, sounding both perplexed and amused. "She received nothing?"

"There is no record of her receiving a message."

Evrok smiled faintly. "Amazing little man," he said quietly.

"What is it?" Jamyn asked.

Evrok turned a heavy eye toward him. "You really are entirely too much like your mistress. Slow down and use your head for a change."

Jamyn barely held himself back from leaping over the bar to throttle its owner. "The hell you talking about?"

Evrok pointed up to the ceiling. "Qa made the Valet as forthright as possible. If Kana didn't receive a message, it would have simply replied *no*. Instead, it pointed out that there was no record of it."

"Meaning?"

"That she *did* receive something, but it was not recorded, foolish boy. Now will you settle down and think about this rationally?"

Jamyn slammed his fist against the bar. "Dammit to hell. I need to find her!"

"I thought as much."

Evrok curled his finger in a beckoning gesture.

The stool floating behind Jamyn's head immediately responded, firing forward and slamming into his skull with a loud thud. The light in Jamyn's eyes flickered out and he collapsed face-down on the bar.

Evrok sighed. "Medical, please send someone to my establishment. I have someone here who desperately needs to sleep one off."

———◉———

"Jamyn?"

"In here, Mom!"

Maria poked her head around the corner and into the open doorway to Jamyn's bedroom. "Studying hard?"

Jamyn looked around himself at the towering stacks of textbooks piled on his desk. "Nope. I'm just sitting real still so that they won't all attack me at once."

She laughed. "You've got entirely too much of your father's sense of humor."

Jamyn spun his chair around to face her, smiling all the while. "You think he'll borrow me his brain while he's at it? I could use it for this calculus stuff."

Her eyes widened. "Calculus? How far along are you?"

He grinned. "Not that far. Still gotta get the last few bits of grade school finished. I was just peeking ahead."

"Well go peek at that English book again," she said, pointing back at the teetering stacks. "He'll *lend* you his brain, not *borrow*."

He grimaced. "Oh, yeah. You lend something to someone, and they borrow it from you. Thanks, Mom."

"No problem. I'm going to the store. Need anything?"

Jamyn thought for a moment. "I'm out of soda."

"Again?"

"Yeah. Finished the last of it before the science final."

"Which is probably how you managed to stay up cramming for it the night before." She shook her head in disapproval.

"Nope," he replied. "I was studying for the math final then. I already had the science one in the bag."

"*In the bag,* huh?"

He nodded. "I'm thinking at least a ninety-six. Maybe higher if I nailed the bonus questions."

She shook her head and sighed, even though a bright smile lit her face. "I suppose you'll have your high school work polished off by the end of the week."

"Nah," he replied with a chuckle. "Middle of next, I think. Gonna take the weekend off."

"Slacker." She came forward and gave him a firm hug. "Just promise me you won't burn yourself out, okay?"

"Or burn the house down," he said, squirming uncomfortably in his mother's grip. "No problem."

She released him and backed away so she could see his face. "Be careful with that, too," she said, traces of worry lining her face.

He nodded. "I will. Don't worry. I'm much more in control of it than I was. Grandma made sure of it."

"Still, be careful. I don't want to ever see a firetruck outside the house again, if that's okay with you."

He swallowed hard. "Yeah. I'm sorry about that."

Maria relented and smiled at him. "Now cut it out. It was a long time ago. How many times can you apologize for the same thing?"

"'Til I stop feeling stupid about it," he muttered.

"Oh, just stop already." She hugged him again and kissed the top of his head. "Love you, Jamyn."

"Mom..." He groaned and tried to worm his way out of her grasp.

"Oh, I'm sorry," she said, letting him go. "I forgot you're *way* too grown up for all that baby stuff."

He frowned at her teasing. "C'mon, Mom. I'm fourteen. Gimme a break."

"Perfect time for your folks to embarrass you at every turn," she said with a grin. "One case of soda for the grumpy old man, coming up." With this, she turned and started to walk out of his room.

"Mom?"

"Hmm?"

"Love you."

She stopped at the doorway and looked back at him over her shoulder. "Love you too, honey." She managed to squeak the words out.

Jamyn stood up and hurried to her side. "Cut it out, Mom." He gave her hand a friendly squeeze. "I'm better now. Honest."

She quickly wiped her eyes with her free hand. "I know. It's just—"

"Hey, I'm not going back. Okay?"

She nodded emphatically. "Okay." She leaned in and kissed his forehead.

"Bleah!" he said loudly.

"Oh, be quiet, you. Mother's prerogative."

"Thanks, Mom. See ya."

"See ya." She turned and walked down the hallway.

He made his way back to his chair, shaking his head and chuckling all the while.

It's been four years. When is she gonna stop tearing up like that?

Sitting down, he thought about his life since his awakening. "Probably have to be up and about for at least as long as I was under for her to be okay." He sighed deeply. "So, another six years. Great." Looking over the stacks of books around him, he smiled. "These should help take up some of that time. That and actually getting outta here and going to school like regular people."

He stopped and thought about the progress he had made so far. Four years of intense home-schooling had him right on the verge of completing the necessary work to receive a grade school diploma. Next fall, however, he was scheduled to actually attend high school. He idly wondered what it would be like having to regularly interact with people outside of his immediate family for the first time in his life.

The possibility of having a normal life both intrigued and concerned him. Though it might be nice going out and making friends, he worried it would interfere with his ongoing magical training. His grandmother wasn't completely free of the binding spell yet, but they had made major progress lately in loosening its grip on her.

"Gotta get her out," he muttered, once again actively trying to figure out a way to help her.

Suddenly his mind touched on something foreign, as if a stray thought he did not own had somehow found its way into his brain. In a flash, he went into a complete and unrelenting panic. He leaped to his feet, looking all around himself to find the cause of his sudden dread. Colors leaped at him out of thin air, surrounding him in a swirling cloud of brilliance. Above it all, he heard a strange churning sound, like a massive propeller cutting through the air. The colors solidified into a winding path leading out of his room. He followed it as fast as he could, charging up the stairs leading to his grandmother's room.

Bursting through the door, he saw a twisting maelstrom of light spinning lazily in the air in the center of her room. His grandmother was seated on the floor beside it, her eyes tightly closed and her lips mumbling a wordless chant. From the center of the tempest, Jamyn was inundated with an overwhelming sense of dread. He concentrated and was suddenly aware of a familiar feel to the mystical portal. Uttering a loud shout, he leaped forward and grabbed at the edges of the gateway. He yanked the magic as hard as he could, pulling the rift shut through sheer will alone. The portal closed and he panted heavily as his eyesight gradually returned to normal.

His grandmother's eyes snapped open. She looked around the room in shock and saw Jamyn staring back at her from right next to where the gate had been.

"Jamyn?" she asked in disbelief.

He wheezed. "Yeah. Don't worry. I fixed it."

"You what?"

She looked from where he stood to the vacant spot before him. Raising a hand to the empty space, she gasped when she found no trace of the portal.

"What in the hell?" she said aloud. "It's gone!" Turning back to Jamyn, her features hardened. "You did this?"

He took a step back in fright, unnerved by her sudden anger. "Uh-huh."

"Dammit!" she shouted, throwing her hands in the air. She bowed her head, and her body quivered in rage. "Why the hell did you do that?"

"I thought you were in trouble," he replied, now realizing that he had just screwed up big time. "I tried to help."

She raised her head and glared at him. "What you did was set me back at least a month, if not more! That portal was going to give me exactly what I needed to get free. Now it's gone and I can't recreate it! Damn it all!"

Jamyn's insides twisted uncomfortably. "I-I'm sorry!"

She was just about to launch into another scathing reply when she stopped and looked at him. This time, concern had crept past her look of fury. "You said you closed it," she said carefully. "What spell did you use?"

"I-I didn't use a spell. I saw the portal there and just closed it."

"Closed it how?"

"I grabbed the edges and pulled it shut."

The anger in her eyes instantly turned to fear. "With your bare hands?" she whispered.

He nodded silently.

She clapped a hand over her mouth to keep from crying out. Her eyes never left his as she carefully stood up. "Did you see the colors? Hear the sound?" she whispered.

He nodded again. "There was a river of light that led me up here. And a sound like something really big spinning around."

"No!" she whispered in sheer horror.

As much as he wanted to walk over to her, fear rooted him to the spot. He finally forced himself to speak. "What?"

His grandmother walked up to him and grabbed his shoulders. Holding his body still, she shouted right in his face. "You must never do that again!"

"Do what?"

"What you did could have killed you!" She clamped down on his shoulders even harder. "You must never, *ever* do that again!"

"What did I do?" He whimpered, quailing under her stern gaze.

She released him in a huff. "From now on, you will only use magic through spells. You must never do what you just did. *Never!*"

"I don't *know* what I did!"

She sighed in exasperation. "You saw a billowing light and heard a strange sound, correct?"

"Yeah."

"That was a raw, unformed thing that some call the Voice. It's related to magic, but it is thoroughly unpredictable and unbelievably dangerous. Casters throughout the ages have tried to master it. All of them died horrible, agonizing deaths." She fixed him with a solemn stare. "Promise me you will never do something like this again. Promise me you will never again go running into the unknown to toy with that horrid thing."

"But I—"

"Promise me!"

He swallowed hard and nodded. "I promise."

Her stern expression didn't fade. "I mean it, Jamyn. You must maintain control at all times when it comes to magic. If you don't have control, everyone and everything around you will pay the price."

"Okay," he said quietly. "I get it. I'm sorry."

She nodded and gestured to the door. "Go. Back to your schoolwork." He quickly left the room, leaving her there to ponder her student's newfound ability.

———◉———

Jamyn woke up with a faint groan. "What happened?" he mumbled, reaching a hand to the back of his head. He gingerly felt his scalp and was surprised to find it free of pain, though he wasn't sure why he thought it should hurt.

"You had a disagreement with a bar stool," a voice replied. "It seemed to take issue with you shouting at its master."

"Huh?" Jamyn cracked open one eye. Qa was looking down at him in concern. "Where am I?"

"Medical. They succeeded in putting your head back together."

Though his head didn't hurt, he still had trouble focusing his mind. "Put it together? What took it apart?"

"I believe what you should be asking is what led to your injury."

Jamyn rubbed his eyes and tried to remember. "I was... I..." He stumbled over his words, his memory refusing to cooperate. Taking a step back, he mulled over Qa's words. "Bar stool," he whispered. "Then I was probably at Evrok's."

"Correct."

"I think I was asking him something." A sudden burst of terror made his breath catch in his throat and he sat up in a rush. "Kana," he shouted. "Where is she?"

"Why do you want to know?" Qa asked carefully.

"She's in trouble!"

"And how do you know that?"

The simple query put a large dent in his pervasive fear. "I-I don't know. But she is!"

"You are correct," Qa said, keeping a close eye on the acolyte. "Kana is definitely in trouble."

Jamyn's eyes locked with his. "What? Where is she?"

"All signs point to her being on Letron 12-B," Qa replied in a slow, steady voice. "She has been captured."

"Captured? We have to—"

"Jamyn, calm down." Qa's words struck with amazing force, completely driving Jamyn's fear and rage to the far corner of his mind. "Kana is still alive," he said, his volume easing back down to normal levels. "We are doing all that we can to ensure she remains so."

"What happened?" Jamyn whispered, his forcibly calmed state robbing his voice of any strength.

"We do not know. What we do know is that she is being held by the same mercenaries that were defeated during the Letronan conflict."

"But they were all killed."

"We believe they may be a closely related faction. They are holding Kana responsible for what happened there."

"After all this time?"

"Yes. No one here knows how or why either. We do know that Letron 12-B has been completely isolated from us. Magical gate traffic to and from the system has been rendered impossible."

"How?"

"We believe they may be working with the same rogue wizards that they previously employed."

"Nihils," Jamyn whispered in horror. "Users of death magic."

"The same. Very resourceful. Even more deadly."

"But we're still looking for a way in, right?"

"Of course, but our options are extremely limited. Every magical way in has been effectively blocked."

"What about non-magical?"

Qa sighed. "Letron is several hundred light-years away. We do not have the time, even at impossibly high speeds."

"We can't just leave her!"

"We have no intentions of doing so." Qa's voice dropped to a low murmur. "Despite Kana's instructions."

"Instructions?" Jamyn asked hopefully.

Qa nodded. "She was allowed to send a message back to us. Its content does not bode well for her rescue." He raised a hand in front of Jamyn's face. "Please try to contain yourself upon its viewing. I will not be nearly as kind as Evrok if you choose to make a fuss again."

Jamyn nodded, his eyes wide. "Agreed."

Qa reached forward and pressed a finger to the center of Jamyn's forehead. Immediately Jamyn's world went dark as he spiraled into Qa's replayed thoughtstream.

When his vision cleared, Jamyn saw the Sanctum's central chamber. The entire Inner Cabal was seated at a large semicircular bench, each of them staring upward with concerned faces.

Suddenly Kana's voice called out to them. "This is Kana Morel, First Seer of the Sanctum." From the uneven sound of her voice, her words were being delivered under extreme duress. "I am being held for my crimes. The planetoid Letron 12-B is now off-limits to all. No spell can reach me. No spell can save me. Do not try." She suddenly grunted loudly, releasing her breath in an explosive burst.

Someone hit her. Horror washed over Jamyn. His anger didn't have a chance to rise before the next words came.

"I mean it, dammit." Kana's growling statement came in halting gasps. "No one is to attempt to rescue me. It will mean not only my death but yours." She cried out again in pain. "You get me?" She was screaming now. "Stay where you are! *Do not save me!*"

Those last four words careened around Jamyn's mind long after he emerged from Qa's memories. "Do not save me," he whispered.

"Kana to the last," Qa said grimly. "She's serious."

Jamyn's panic tried to surge forward again, and he looked to Qa. "Then we're not going to—"

Qa interrupted him. "*We* are. *You* are not. I believe the last part of her message was directed solely at you."

"It was?"

Qa nodded. "She knows that we will do all that we can to help her. But did you notice the words she used? Specifically, when she said that no *one* should rescue her. By that, she meant you."

"But the message was sent to the cabal."

"I'm guessing she believed I would relay it to you." Qa allowed himself a slight smile. "She knows me well enough by now."

"But I can't do anything," Jamyn said in defeat. "I don't have my magic."

"But you would still try to save her if you could."

Jamyn nodded. "Yes. Of course."

"Which is the other reason I am here. I let you hear her message. Now I am telling you to wait here until we bring her home." The question in the acolyte's eyes prompted Qa to nod solemnly. "You will not be allowed to gate out of the Sanctum until this matter is resolved. I'm sorry, Jamyn. You'll have to trust us."

Jamyn clenched his jaw and stared directly into Qa's eyes.

"Please bring her back to me."

Qa nodded. "We will." With that, he stood up and quickly exited the medical wing.

Jamyn watched him go, biding his time until his former master was gone. He thought over what could possibly be Kana's final words, and a growl of sheer hatred rumbled deep in his throat. Suddenly the memory of their last few moments in the pond before she had vanished came to mind, along with her final warning.

If you ever follow me again when I tell you not to, I will kill you.

He clenched his hands into tight fists and tiny fingers of darkness writhed in his grasp.

"Sorry, mistress," he whispered. "I am going to save you whether you want me to or not."

Path suddenly appeared next to the bed. From her excited expression, she looked like she had something urgent to tell him.

"What?" he asked.

She pointed frantically at his right hand. Raising her own, she slowly clenched the hand into a tight fist. She opened it again in a burst and nodded toward it. Seeing his look of confusion, she repeated the move, faster this time.

"I don't get it," he said.

Path tossed back her head and stamped her feet in disgust. Looking at him solidly, she repeated her movements, this time bringing her fist to the outstretched fingers of her left hand before miming it exploding.

Jamyn gasped. "Like the ball."

Path threw both her arms at him in triumph and then starting clapping.

Jamyn nodded while a multitude of preparations suddenly lined themselves up in his mind. His dream came back to him, and he whispered, "Sorry, Grandma. She needs me."

Path huffed and waved a hand at him, shooing away his maudlin sentiment.

With a laugh, he snagged her hand, yanked her to him, and caught her in a tight hug.

"Thanks, Path," he murmured into her shoulder before kissing her cheek. "Let's get moving."

He released her and bolted out of the bed. He never looked back as he streaked out into the hallway.

⸻ ◉ ⸻

Path sat there on the bed, her eyes wide with astonishment. She lifted a hand to her cheek and released a silent burst of laughter. Her body started to fade away as she rejoined Jamyn's mind. Before she fully disappeared, her faint whisper barely disturbed the silence.

"Wow!"

Chapter Seventeen: Declaration

"What do you think of my little spell?"

Kana refused to acknowledge the taunt. Instead, she kept her eyes closed, took in a slow breath, and continued trying to right her unsteady mind. Since her capture, she had been unable to string more than a handful of thoughts together successfully. Only her indomitable will kept her from falling into a full panic.

"No response?" The raspy voice teased. "You're so weak-willed that you cannot even open your eyes?" Something poked her body at random points, each time setting off a new burst of excruciating pain. "And you are the best of your world? How pathetic." The sound of shuffling steps faded into the distance, leaving her alone with only the sound of her breathing for company.

Despite her disorientation, a burst of hatred ignited deep within Kana's being.

The best, her mind whispered. *I am the best.*

Over and over, she forced her mind to repeat those words. A tiny pulse of light flared in the recesses of her mind, intent on breaking free of its dark prison.

———⊙———

"Progress?" Qa asked the assembled group as he entered the central chamber.

"None to be had," Leel said with a disgusted sigh. "All interplanar travel between here and the Letron system has been effectively scrambled. Anything going near it gets shredded."

"Inter-dimensional?"

"Same thing," Daystar replied. "Space has been warped around the system."

A gout of flame erupted from the floor, sending a twisting pillar of silver fire up to the high ceiling. The blaze extinguished, revealing a cloaked figure lying upon the flagstones. Donta struggled to stand up but fell over in a heap.

"Donta!" Daystar cried, rushing to his aid.

"Enough!" he bellowed, forcing himself upright at last. He regarded her outstretched hand with a vicious snarl before relenting and taking a step back. "I am sorry, Daystar," he muttered, giving her a quick bow of respect.

"You have news?" Qa asked hopefully.

"Nothing good." Donta rumbled and turned to him. "It is unreachable."

"Then you tried—"

Donta angrily snapped at him. "Everything I could. All of it for naught."

"Still, your efforts are appreciated," Qa said. "Thank you, Master Donta."

Daystar gripped Donta's arm despite his weak resistance. "Are you sure you're all right?" she asked him.

"I am fine," he replied, struggling to hold his tone in check. "Anything approaching at a level beyond the simplest teleportation spell will be violently repelled from the planet's surface by the wards they currently have in place. The entire planet is surrounded by this anti-magic screen. Gates also refuse to form on any of the other planets in the Letron system."

"Maybe we could airmail Lob the Unmarred over there," Tiris said with a half-hearted smirk while continuing to pore over a particular section of the enormous book on her lap. "Tell him to wedge open the door with one of those shield manifestations he does."

"Not helping, dear," Leel muttered, intentionally bumping into her side as he opened his own massive tome.

"Do not dissuade her, Master Leel," Qa said while he attempted yet another scan of the Letron system. "We need every idea we can get, no matter how farfetched. The slightest thing could help lead us to an answer."

"Unless there isn't one," Vynael said, his morose tone even drier than usual.

"There is and we will find it," Qa replied. "If Kana has taught us anything, it's that there is always a way."

Tiris chimed in. "Of course, there is. And by the time we find it and reach her, she'll probably have mopped up this entire mess herself!"

Qa smiled despite his heavy heart. "I certainly hope so, Mistress Tiris."

"Are your preparations complete?"

"Nearly."

Kana listened to the quiet conversation without the slightest outward sign of recognition. Through a series of meditative techniques she had learned from Qa, she had finally erected a solid mental framework within which her mind could function again. She worked carefully, shielding her thoughts from outside surveillance with a constant litany of what she had taken as her key phrase.

I am the best. Her mind chanted the phrase over and over again. *I am the best.*

The raspy voice returned mere inches from her face. "You may think that all you like, if it brings you peace. But we both know better, don't we?"

"What are you muttering?"

The second voice receded, its owner pulling away from Kana's prone form. "Her feeble mind has been repeating something I said earlier."

"That being?"

"That she is supposedly the best of her world. Utter nonsense."

"It is possible this one eliminated an entire order single-handedly. That is not to be mocked."

The statement captured Kana's attention in a heartbeat. Apparently, the one making the claim knew that as well, as she suddenly found herself yanked upright off the floor by her hair. Her eyes opened to meet the calm gaze of one she had seen only in her most tortured nightmares.

She gasped in horror. "You!"

"No," the man said, "I am not him." He lunged forward, driving his forehead into hers with brutal force.

Stars exploded before her eyes, and she was vaguely aware that she was falling. She landed hard, her body still unable to fully support her own weight.

"Who are you?" she mumbled, the words barely escaping past her lips.

"I worked tirelessly for years," he replied, ignoring her question. "I had to know who had done it. What I found led me here to you."

"Ready," the raspy voice said.

"Now confirm what I have learned."

Kana was bombarded by a torrent of magic. It clawed at her mind, painfully tearing through each thought with brutal efficiency as it dove into one of her darkest memories.

"We're going where?"

"A place called Letron 12-B."

"On another planet?"

"Technically, it's the second moon of the twelfth planet of the Letron system. But yes, you could say it's another planet."

Kana couldn't believe what she was hearing. "But that's impossible!"

Qa smiled at his student. "Really, Kana? After all you've seen so far, this one thing is so unbelievable?"

She thought over her words for a moment and then grimaced. "I guess not," she said quietly. "Sorry."

"No apologies are needed," Qa replied. "Does the thought of visiting another world trouble you?"

She did her best to shrug it off. "Nah. Can't be any worse than this one." She reached under her tangled red tresses to scratch the back of her neck.

"Kana," Qa said gently, "you're doing it again."

"What?"

"The neck thing. And you're scrunching again."

She looked down at her feet. Sure enough, she was repeatedly curling and uncurling her toes, making the tops of her shoes rhythmically rise and fall. She gave her feet a quick stamp and thrust her hands into her pockets. "I'm fine."

"Are you still upset about—"

"I said I'm fine!"

Qa sighed. "Then you are ready to go?"

The brash teen's anger switched right back to apprehension. "Now?"

"The summons went out a few minutes ago. I am to meet the others in the west exit chamber."

"Who?"

"The initial team consists of myself, Mistress Daystar, and Master Donta. I thought perhaps you would like to come along too."

"What're y'all—" She stopped abruptly and took a quick breath. "What are you doing there?"

"There have been unconfirmed detections of high-level magic there. To the best of our knowledge, the Letronans do not use magic. It was determined that we should investigate."

"And you want me going with you?"

"Of course. You are my student, after all. I thought it could be a fine learning experience. Besides that, someday you may have to go off-planet on a mission. This will be a good introduction."

"I guess." Concern briefly narrowed her silvery eyes. "So, what kind of critters—" She stopped again and pounded a fist against her thigh. "What lives on Letron?"

"Why, nothing," Qa replied in surprise. "Letron is the system's sun. I would be rather shocked to find something living there."

"Huh?"

He smiled. "Always be specific, dear. We are going to Letron 12-B, one of the moons. You must learn to be precise, both in your questions and your answers."

Her shoulders slumped and she looked away from him. "Yeah. Sorry," she mumbled.

Qa came forward and placed a hand on her shoulder. "Stop doing that. You'll make me feel bad."

"Sorr—" She gritted her teeth in frustration. "Dammit!"

"Kana, please calm down. In answer to your question, the inhabitants of Letron 12-B are very much like you and me. Bipedal, carbon-based people. There are a few differences between us but nothing easily visible. We'll have a translate spell active so we can talk to them if necessary. So, are you coming?"

Her uncertainly gradually gave way to her curiosity. "Yeah," she replied. "I'll come along."

"Excellent."

Together they walked out of Qa's quarters and into the hallway. "There is one thing I should tell you about the Letronans in case we do meet them," he said as they walked together. "Their custom is to swap and then hyphenate first and last names. To them, you are Morel-Kana."

"Gotcha." She grinned briefly. "Shon-Qa."

Qa chuckled to himself as they hurried to the west exit point. They entered and found Donta and Daystar waiting for them in the center of the room. The gate mages stood at four equidistant points along the walls of the circular chamber.

"What's this?" Daystar asked, sending Kana one of her more dazzling smiles.

"I thought Miss Morel might enjoy tagging along," Qa replied.

Donta grumbled. "Ridiculous. This is not the time."

"I disagree," Qa said smoothly. "This is only a simple investigative mission." He turned to Kana. "Eyes open. Mouth closed."

She nodded and then bowed. "Yes, Master Qa."

Qa beamed at her, pleased at the extra effort she was making just to placate Donta. "And we are away. Invisibility?" The others nodded so he cast a spell over the group, erasing them all from sight. "Stay close, Kana," he said to the spot where she had been standing. "If you would," he said to the gate mages.

The mages stepped forward, each chanting different segments of the same spell. A glowing portal formed amidst the group and started to grow. Kana watched it in fascination, comparing the undulating swirls of magic around it to the ones around the gates Qa had formed in the past. Suddenly she realized something was wrong. Cracks formed in the periphery of the gate and threatened to propagate down into the portal's center.

"Wait! Something's not—"

Her words were drowned out as she and the others were pulled into the gate.

Kana opened her eyes to find herself face-down in a tangle of wide green leaves and thick vines. The simmering air hung heavy around her, as if it had recently rained.

"What happened?"

She looked around as much as she could without sitting up. The terrain reminded her of the tropical sector of the wilds but far more primal. Sitting up, she pivoted her head this way and that.

"Qa?" Receiving no answer, she spoke again. "Mistress Daystar?" Again, her words went unheeded, swallowed up by the lush foliage.

Quickly checking her hands and arms, she was relieved to find that she was still invisible.

Where is everybody?

Her suspicion flared and she grumbled. "This better not be no test!" Instantly her mind kicked itself. "Better not be *a* test," she said carefully, disgusted with her occasional lapses back to her original accent and speaking patterns.

She was still silently berating herself when something nudged her back. Her body went rigid with fright. The thing bumped her again but still she refused to move a muscle. Suddenly she felt something ease around her side and under her arm before coming to rest in her lap. She slowly looked down and was stunned to find the head of what appeared to be a huge iguana lying there. It looked up at her with one pale yellow eye and continued to nuzzle her thigh.

"What the hell are you?" she asked in sheer astonishment. The creature seemed to be able to see her despite her invisibility.

The lizard slipped its head under one of her hands, all the while rubbing the side of its face against her leg. Her memory went back to the dogs she had known back home. Few and far between, they were her least unreliable friends throughout her unhappy childhood. She instinctively petted the smooth scales, much to its obvious enjoyment.

"You like that?"

The lizard almost appeared to nod as it pressed up into her hand. Encouraged by this, she ran her hand back over the top of its head down to its thick neck. A low rumbling vibrated her thigh, and she smiled at the outrageous notion of a giant lizard purring like a cat. Her gaze swept over its pale green body, which was the size of a young crocodile.

"Three, maybe four feet long," she said. "You full-grown or a young'un?"

Her inevitable self-correction went unsaid as the lizard suddenly stopped purring. It looked up at her in shock, making her cringe.

"What?" she asked, fearful for her safety.

The lizard scrambled to its feet, causing Kana to do the same just in case she needed to start running away. She quickly realized her fears were unfounded as the lizard stared off into the distance behind her. Following its gaze, she asked, "Something wrong?" It looked back at her with wide, unblinking eyes. "Show me!"

Spurred on by her words, it started running through the jungle with Kana in hot pursuit.

They both stopped when they emerged from the jungle's edge. A wide valley sprawled out before them. Long stretches of jagged gray rock flanked the vale. An uneven series of shallow depressions flattened out the grassy terrain between the stony borders. Each of the stamped-down areas held one or more of the lizard's kin. Kana stared in awe at the scores of assembled creatures. Many were the size of her current companion, but several were as big as cars.

She gasped in shock. "Holy shit!"

She focused on one family of lizards. Two larger creatures stood watch over three smaller ones. The youngsters wrestled with one another, happily rolling and tumbling in the taller grass surrounding their lair. Suddenly one of them broke from their frolicking and peered off into the distance the same way Kana's companion had. It squawked inquisitively before a searing blast of light tore right through its midsection. Its corpse fell to the ground, leaving its siblings to stare at it in confusion. Similar beams sliced through them as well and their bodies crumpled lifeless into the grass.

"What the—"

Kana gasped in horror and wildly scanned the entire valley. One by one, the other lizards met a similar fate. Numerous dazzling rays of light from an unknown source at the far end of the valley started to mow them all down. Suddenly she realized that her companion was no longer beside her. She searched the ground frantically before seeing it racing through the center of the valley, apparently searching for its own family.

She immediately shouted out to it. "No! Don't go—"

Her words were cut off as a laser ripped through one of her friend's front legs. It stumbled to the ground with a pitiful cry. One of the larger lizards leaped toward it, shielding the smaller one's body with its own. Multiple shots hit the parent, and it bellowed in pain before falling silent. The smaller lizard crawled forward and nudged the enormous corpse, looking for a sign of life. A beam tunneled through the gigantic body and sliced right through the smaller lizard's head.

"Stop," Kana mumbled, overwhelmed by the loss of her new friend. The slaughter continued, despite her weak plea. "Stop," she said again, louder this time, her voice drawing strength from her rising fury. Still the creatures died one by one, cut down by their unseen foes. A storm of magic was suddenly ripped from the air around her, surrounding her thin body with a shroud of raw power. That power took form in her voice which now exploded across the valley.

"Stop!"

Her body dissolved in a bright flash and reformed in the center of the valley where her friend had died. The stench of seared flesh enveloped her, but she stood firm. A wave of force blasted out from her in all directions, pushing away all the corpses within a fifty-foot radius. "What have you done?" She shouted her query in the direction of the unseen marauders.

The incoming fire continued despite her angry shout. Several shots pelted the ground all around her, but none penetrated the wall of energy she had unconsciously gathered around her invisible body. The shield around her expanded but it was too late to protect the last few dying lizards.

———◉———

Donta lumbered out of the jungle on the side of the valley opposite where Kana had emerged. Looking down at the carnage, he zeroed in on Kana's position.

"I've found her," he said to the others through a quick converse spell.

"Is she all right?" Daystar asked.

Donta concentrated and saw the aura of power building around Kana. "That has yet to be seen," he replied, perplexed by what his keen senses were now telling him.

"What do you mean, Donta?" Qa asked.

Donta sensed an abrupt change in the gathering tempest. "I think she may be—"

An unforgiving blast of unformed magic suddenly radiated from the valley's center and knocked him flat on his back. He staggered back to his feet to find at least a hundred men in body armor at the far end of the valley. All of them were also standing back up and several were checking their weapons, which apparently had somehow been rendered useless.

A huge man standing at the front of the group banged a fist against his chest plate, which did nothing but sizzle and spark at him in reply. He roared at the empty valley in hate. "Reveal yourself!"

Kana bowed her head and held her clenched fists tightly to her sides. Her voice thundered over the terrain and slammed into them all with devastating force. "The strong. The powerful. The mighty. Form the world to your wishes. None shall withstand. All will fall."

She opened her fists and tongues of golden fire licked from her fingertips. "No longer!"

"She's declaring!" Donta whispered in absolute shock.

———◈———

The tongues lengthened into writhing ropes, flailing from her hands like snakes gone mad. The golden glow embraced her body, forming a fiery outline that advanced toward the army with slow, deliberate steps.

"The weak have awakened," she said in an enraged growl, letting her anger pour out from every damaged place, every wounded spot on her soul. "The frail stand tall. None shall resist." The wind suddenly kicked up into a tempest that scorched the air all around the glowing spectre. "Know now the burning truth."

Qa and Daystar appeared next to Donta. Together they stared down at the chaotic scene.

Kana's voice exploded deep within the hidden spaces of the minds of all gathered, filling them with her undeniable revelation.

"I am the Soul Flame!"

The lashes she held streaked forward on their own, slicing through the forward ranks of her armored foes. A few of them tried to run but their speed was unable to best the blinding flash of her attack. Kana advanced slowly and the onslaught continued, cutting the men down where they stood.

Daystar gasped. "She's killing them!" She took a step forward, but Donta's cloaked arm barred her path.

"She is not." Donta's voice was subdued by what they were witnessing. "What she is doing is much worse."

"Their spiritual cores," Qa whispered in awe. "She's tearing their very souls."

The army's leader stood firm in the middle of the carnage while his men fell all around him. Despite any obvious signs of injury, they collapsed to the ground, not dead but no longer willing to remain upright. The glowing tendrils landed blow after blow but stayed a mere finger's breadth away from the leader's motionless form, as if they were intent that he be the last to fall. Kana's steady advance brought her just outside of his reach and she stopped. The golden lashes drew back up into her hands and disappeared.

Uttering a cry of outrage, he swung his rifle with all his might at Kana's fiery outline. Just as the butt was about to crush her skull, the entire rifle fell apart in his hands. He stared at the scattered pieces in shock for barely a second when she reached one hand forward. A single point of light exploded from her palm, knocking him flat on his back and pushing the crippled remains of his army off into the distance. She stood over him and looked down at him in silence. He snarled in rage and pain before uttering a loud shout.

"Obliterate it!"

Kana's head snapped upright. A surge of magic billowed from a point far behind where the army had stood. The blast raced at Kana, but she held up one hand and caught it like it was a gently tossed ball. The energy swirled around her hand, wildly bending and twisting in her grasp. She considered the churning cyclone a moment longer before hurling it back at its source. The torrent exploded with a ferocious roar that mingled with the pitiful scream of its now incinerated caster.

Directing her attention back to the man on the ground, Kana growled deep in her throat. She gestured back at the dead lizards, the flames surrounding her unseen arm fluttering angrily. "Do you see what you have done?"

He roared in defiance. "I have done what was decreed!"

"Now hear my decree," Kana said, her voice an ominous rumble. "Never again shall you harm another. Never again will one in my care fall."

Her body started to reappear, beginning with her feet. When her face was finally revealed, it spoke of nothing but sheer resolve. A bright flash of magic briefly surrounded her. When it faded, a fiery glow was left behind that illuminated her long tresses. The glow winked out and her red hair shattered like it was made of glass. Left behind was a close-cropped shock of solid black.

"Never again will my heart suffer," she whispered.

"I will tear it from your shrieking flesh!"

He lunged up at her. Instead of striking her, his gloved hand passed right through her chest like she was only air. Suddenly his entire arm froze in place within her, holding his body up off the ground.

Her now dark eyes bored into his and she whispered, "Never. Again."

A glittering dagger of solid light emerged from Kana's forehead and thrust down into his bicep, running it through. Another shot from Kana's back, piercing his outstretched hand. More and more gleaming shards erupted from her, each plunging into a random section of his body until he could no longer be seen amidst the bladed maelstrom. The blades all shattered as one and he collapsed to the ground. Kana took a step back and released a final sigh. She fell to her knees and stared numbly at the still body before her.

Qa appeared at her side in a bright flash. "Kana. Are you all right?"

Daystar and Donta quickly joined them, each showing up in their own burst of light. Daystar started to kneel beside the girl, but Donta's outstretched hand stopped her.

"Master Donta?" Daystar asked.

Donta rumbled down to Kana. "You saw it, didn't you?"

"I did," she replied, her voice a weak whisper.

"Saw what?" Daystar asked.

Donta continued to stare down at the motionless acolyte. "Qa's student is fluent in the Voice," he said, his tone subdued.

"I have suspected as much." Qa said, still gazing down at Kana. "Her abilities are—"

Kana interrupted him. "They are here."

"Who are?" Qa asked his student.

"*Scion Letrona.*"

They barely had time to ponder her strange words before the relative silence was shattered by the roar of approaching vehicles. Several armored trucks barreled into the clearing and then stopped. Troops in heavy body armor poured from the vehicles, all of them with their weapons drawn. Several of them took up positions around each of the casters and held them at gunpoint.

One stepped forward from the group. "Identities?"

"Peace, *Scion Letrona*," Qa said, raising his hands before him in a placating gesture.

The man hoisted his rifle and took careful aim at Qa's face. "That term," he said firmly. "How do you know it?"

Qa gestured to Kana. "My student just uttered it."

One of the soldiers gasped. "S-sir! The giants!"

The leader looked past the small group to the many dead lizards piled along the rocky outcroppings. Hatred and sorrow flashed in his eyes and his grip on his rifle tightened until his knuckles went white.

He snarled through his clenched teeth. "You have killed the mist giants!"

"We have not," Donta snapped. "Those men destroyed the creatures." He gestured at the disabled men in the distance. None of them had moved from where Kana had deposited them.

"I couldn't save the giants," Kana mumbled, tears running down her cheeks.

One younger soldier in the ring of men surrounding her looked at the defeated army and then down at the kneeling girl.

"You tried?" he asked. "On your own?"

Kana nodded weakly.

"Hajis-Corol," the leader said, "hold your position!"

The young man persisted and faced the other mages. "Is this true? She stood alone against them?"

He received solemn nods from Qa, Donta, and Daystar.

"She arrived before we did," Qa said. "She defeated the men, their leader, and the caster they had with them. Sadly, they had already killed the giants."

Something in the tall grass caught Kana's eye. Reaching beside Hajis-Corol's boot, she plucked a small flower hidden in the fronds. She held it close, her mind reeling at this one small sign of beauty surrounded by so much death. A gentle light streamed from her fingertips, wrapping the delicate petals in a soft glow. She held the flower up to Hajis-Corol.

"May they someday return to you," she whispered.

Suddenly the lizards' corpses all glowed with a similar light before collapsing into nothingness. The body of her small friend was the last to disappear. Its shroud of sparkling light drifted over to Kana's hand, adding its radiance to the flower she held.

Hajis-Corol took the flower in his numb fingers.

"You have acted with honor this day, young one," their leader said, his voice ringing clearly across the valley. "What is the name of the mist giants' favored patron?"

"Morel-Kana," she whispered.

Fatigue pounced hard and she fell to the ground in a deep sleep.

⸺◉⸺

Her strangled gasp ripped through the air as the mental probe released Kana's psyche. She panted heavily, the horrors of that day even fresher in her mind than they had been when they were new.

All thoughts of escape were blotted out by the unrelenting terror that held her tightly. A grim voice trickled into her universe of fear.

"It *was* you."

She fully expected yet another vicious blow to strike her after the solemn declaration, but none came. Confusion barely grazed the surface of her panic, but it gave her mind just enough of a fingerhold to cling to sanity. She opened her eyes to see her captor regarding her thoughtfully.

"The men you defeated were detained by the Letronans." The leader's voice was strangely calm, especially considering the enormity of Kana's revelation. "They were sent home soon after the final peace accord was signed. Their wills had been completely obliterated." Disappointment briefly darkened his face. "Warriors without wills are nothing more than empty vessels. Most died within the first week. None lived past a month."

He stood up and started toward Kana. She flinched as he crouched next to her.

"The one whose face I share was not as fortunate," he said quietly. "His ravaged mind and body barely held the strength to breathe. When he did, he uttered fragments of sound that weren't much more than gibberish." He sighed at the memory. "The recorders in the troops' armor were shattered beyond repair. I was barely able to retrieve a handful of broken words. There were only two things I was able to make out clearly—*Hajis-Corol* and *Soul Flame*. I knew that if I found the first, it would lead me to the second."

Kane decided to press her luck.

"So, you found me," she mumbled. "Now what?"

The man acknowledged her bravado with a slow nod. "My brother led his order into that foolish enterprise, despite the wishes of the rest of the guild. His reward was death. However, the manner of his demise still warrants a proper response."

Kana forced her fear back just enough to get her mind back on solid footing. "Meaning you'll kill me."

"Nothing as simple as that."

A hideous screech split the air, making her body jerk in fright. The leader continued to stare down upon her with a curious look of respect.

"Once he gives us the name, you will know your final fate."

The agonized cries redoubled, leaving Kana to wonder what would happen when they blessedly fell silent.

Chapter Eighteen: Travel Plans

Jamyn paced his quarters like a caged animal desperately looking for a way out. His initial burst of inspiration had been swiftly blunted as he assessed the sheer futility of his situation. He knew where he had to go but had no idea how to get there or what he could do if he did. Since Qa had forbidden him to intervene, it was unlikely he could even request that his magic be unlocked.

So, I'm stuck. No magic and no means of getting there. It's impossible.

That last word tripped something in his mind. "Impossible," he said aloud, the wheels in his mind starting to spin again. "Maybe that's exactly what I need." Straightening up, he took a breath and then said, "Kat, I need your help."

Nothing happened.

Jamyn looked all around for some sign his plea had been heard but found none.

He tried again, louder this time. "C'mon, Kat. I know you're listening. I could really use a hand here." Still seeing no evidence of a response, Jamyn clenched his teeth and snapped. "Kana's in trouble, dammit!"

A small piece of folded paper fluttered down from the ceiling and floated through the air right in front of his face. Jamyn snatched the note, unfolded it, and read it.

Thank you for calling the HMDAO (Help My Dumb Ass Out) Hotline. All our Kats are busy right now. Perhaps you should have a drink and sort it out yourself.

Jamyn stared at the words in wide-eyed disbelief.

"Oh, come on!" he shouted. "I'm serious!"

A postscript suddenly wrote itself on the paper.

So am I. Have that drink. See what you can put together. Or take apart.

Jamyn stared at the cryptic words, then let loose with an incredulous laugh as they suddenly made sense. He dropped the note and streaked out of his quarters, completely missing the second postscript that appeared.

Say hi to Evrok for me.

━━━━◆━━━━

The raspy voice of the mercenaries' spellcaster broke the silence. It was the first sound Kana had heard since the tortured wailing had finally ceased.

"We have it."

The leader acknowledged him with a curt nod. The caster shuffled off, leaving Kana alone with her captor.

"Who will come to rescue you?" the leader asked from somewhere behind where she lay on the floor. As before, his query sounded oddly civil.

"No one," she replied, her eyes still closed.

"You are sure about that?"

Despite her body's continued weakness, her mind quickly tried to decipher his line of questioning.

What is he up to?

"They'll do what I told 'em," she said, keeping her statements both simple and vague to hide her recovering mental state. "Doesn't matter. Planet's blocked. No one can get in."

"They are not powerful enough to break through?"

He's definitely fishing.

"Dunno."

"If they did?"

Kana fought off a grin while trying not to envision that scenario. "Boom."

"Indeed. Who would lead the charge?"

So that's it. He's trying to figure out who's strongest. Probably to hit them with the same damned spell they got me with.

"Dunno. Someone stupid." She held herself still as she listened to his approaching footfalls. Suddenly his voice was directly in front of her.

The leader crouched down beside her. "Interesting. No one there cares for you at all?"

"Nope."

She felt a brief tug on the front of her robes.

"We shall see," he said quietly. With this, he stood and walked out of the room.

Kana opened her eyes and glanced down at her chest. Her butterfly brooch was gone. A wave of panic surged up within her when she realized its significance.

He's after—

She quickly pinched off the thought, wary of any mental scrying that might still be in place. Instantly she redoubled her efforts to bring herself back up to speed.

I am the best, her mind repeated over and over as she struggled to execute her plan.

———— ◉ ————

The first thing Jamyn saw upon opening the tavern door was its owner staring straight at him from behind the bar.

"No," Evrok said, his tone high yet unwavering.

"No what?"

"No, I will not release the anchor spell upon you."

Jamyn closed the door behind him. "Then I guess it's a good thing I wasn't going to ask you to." He raised his hands in surrender as he walked over to where Evrok stood. "And I'm sorry I was a pain in the butt the last time I was here."

Evrok eyed him warily. "I trust you have learned from the experience."

Jamyn made a show of rubbing the back of his head. "Yeah. Those barstools hurt."

"They were by far the softest things I considered hitting you with, given your previous agitation."

"Hey, I was worried about Kana," he said as he sat down. "Gimme a break."

Evrok regarded the acolyte's strangely calm state. "And you're not now?"

"Of course, I am. I'm just trying to be smarter about it."

"An unexpected but welcome change." Evrok reached under the bar then withdrew a tall glass filled with a fizzing green drink. He placed it before Jamyn.

Jamyn looked over the proffered drink. "Not sure it's the best thing for me right now, but thanks." He raised the glass to his lips and took a slow sip, keeping his eyes trained on the barkeep the whole time.

Evrok's sunken eyes returned Jamyn's cool gaze. "If not to cause trouble, why are you here?"

Jamyn put the glass down and shrugged nonchalantly. "Just getting a drink. Having a chat. Trying not to think about certain things."

"You should give up lying. You're not very good at it," Evrok said dryly. "You are here to find out about the cabal's progress, if any."

"Hadn't really thought of it. But hey, if you've got any info, I'm listening."

Evrok released a tired sigh. "You've heard who is holding her? And where?"

"She's on Letron 12-B. Held by mercs related to the ones she defeated there years ago."

"And their defenses?"

"Entire system's shielded by Nihil magic. Everyone and everything is cut off from getting there."

"Which also means—"

"That magic use on its surface may be difficult, if not impossible."

Evrok nodded his approval. "You appear to have a solid grasp of the situation. There's not much more I could add."

Jamyn raised the glass to his lips again. "Now why do I find that hard to believe?" he asked before taking another slow sip.

"Probably because you just *might* be as bright as her."

Jamyn lowered his glass and smiled at the compliment. "So, what would you do if you were in my spot?"

"Start looking for a new master."

Jamyn kept his expression neutral. "Okay. Now what would you do if you were as stupid and stubborn as me?"

"Probably pick a fight and end up in medical."

"Already did that. Next?"

Evrok fixed him with a solid stare. "You are serious."

"You have no idea."

The barkeep reached below the bar and retrieved a small gray mug. Cradling it in his skeletal hands, he peered at its contents for a moment.

"You know I cannot help you directly," he said in a low murmur.

"Never asked you to," Jamyn replied in the same subdued tone.

Evrok drained his mug and placed it back beneath the bar. "A small, non-magical team would likely be helpful," he whispered, the noxious vapors from his drink swirling about his head.

Jamyn's mind dissected the deceptively simple statement, and he nodded slowly. "Casters may not be of any use there. Small to get in and out without a major incident. But there's still the matter of transport."

"Perhaps there is someone who has gone there without the use of a gate."

Jamyn's memory lurched, nearly causing him to spill his drink.

"That might be helpful. Wonder if I could find someone that stupid."

Evrok almost cracked a smile. "I have full faith in your abilities."

Jamyn chugged down the rest of his drink then pushed the empty glass back across the bar. "I think I have somewhere else to be," he said, his voice back at a normal volume. "Thanks for the drink." He started to leave when Evrok's voice stopped him.

"The usual upon your return?"

"That'd be great. Thanks."

"For both of you?"

A shiver ran up Jamyn's spine and he clenched his fists.

"Damned right." With this, he strode out of the tavern, a renewed sense of purpose adding an extra urgency to his steps.

―――◉―――

"Why are you on the Letronan moon, Voyiv?"

Voyiv calmly regarded the infuriated face on the vid screen. "The settling of an old debt, Guild Head Dullk."

Dullk bared his teeth in an unpleasant snarl. "This is about that fool Noark, isn't it?"

"It is, Guild Head."

"You have engaged the Letronans?"

"I have not. Only one of their number has been taken. He was at the final battle."

Dullk's anger seemed to lessen, if only slightly. "You are sure?"

"I am, Guild Head."

"That is fortunate. You know we do not engage a target, even a previous one, without a binding contract. To do so would bring you a swift death by my hand."

"I am well aware of that, Guild Head."

"You have executed the Letronan?"

"I have not. He was not the one."

"Then who was?"

"We have captured the woman responsible. She comes from the group of magic users called the Sanctum."

"You have protection from her magic?"

"I do."

Dullk's expression swiftly darkened. "Then you have enlisted *them*."

"I have."

Dullk growled. "Your death creeps several steps closer, Voyiv. You know I disapprove of dealing with them."

"A necessary vexation."

Dullk snapped at him. "Execute the woman. End the association."

"Soon, Guild Head."

"The cause of your delay?"

"She will die as he did. Nothing that matters to her will survive to see her end."

Dullk silently mulled his words while he firmly gripped the arms of his chair. Finally, he leaned toward the screen and snarled. "Finish it and return here with your order. They are with you, I trust."

"Stationed outside this facility in full cloak. We remain undetected by all."

Dullk sat back in his chair. "Return here immediately upon completion, Voyiv. I would hear of Noark's final justice." With this, he switched off the vid screen.

Voyiv released his held breath in a rush. As much as he feared the Guild Head's wrath, not even his leader would keep him from seeing his mission through to its end. He turned his attention back to the intricate pin he had taken from Kana.

"Now to wait for the coming."

———— ◉ ————

Jamyn burst into his quarters at nearly full speed, barely slowing enough to slam the door shut behind him. He immediately raced into his bedroom, hooking a hand around the door frame to keep from crashing right into the bed. Coming to a dead stop, he quickly scanned the contents of the room. He spied the target of his search and snatched the small, leather-bound book off the floor. Flipping through its worn pages, he found the one he had marked with the thin leather cord woven into the book's binding. He rapidly re-read several paragraphs and nodded.

"Simple," he muttered to himself. "*He* wants to get there. *I* want to get there. Now I just have to convince him not to kill me first." Placing the book on his nightstand, he made a mental note to return the tome to Fangs if he got back.

He stopped halfway to his closet. "*When* I get back," he said aloud. "Not *if*." He thought a moment longer and further revised his statement. "When *we* get back."

Diving into the closet, he retrieved an old training outfit buried within its depths. He laid it on his bed and looked it over. Reinforced panels covered large areas of both the long-sleeved shirt and pants, giving the pure black outfit the appearance of a semi-rigid suit of armor. He quickly stripped and put on the form-fitting garment. He slipped on a pair of boots and then started to tweak the positioning of the armored plates. Once he was satisfied with the suit's fit, he slammed a fist against his chest as hard as he could. The blow barely registered through the toughened panel, and he nodded his approval.

"Let's go gather the troops."

——————⊙——————

"Hold your fire, Shammie!"

Shamara stopped her attack at once, letting the magic she had gathered for her push safely dissipate. "What's wrong?"

"Nothing," Lob said, dropping his surrounding ring of barriers. "I think someone's rapping at my chamber door." He strode over to the entrance to training room seven and opened it just a crack. He peeked outside and then looked back in at Shamara. "'Tis a Jamyn and nothing more!"

Jamyn looked up at the giant and made a face. "Thanks a lot, Lob."

"Ooh, and he's serious too." Lob opened the door wide and stepped out of the way to wave him in. "Well, come on. Join the fun." He looked over Jamyn's outfit as he passed. "You expecting something to hit you?"

"In here?" Jamyn asked without looking up as he continued forward into the room. "Nah."

Lob closed the door and raised one huge fist to crush Jamyn into the floor.

Shamara saw the move and shouted. "Mister Lob! Don't do that!"

Jamyn spun on his heel and looked up. Lob had frozen in place at the sound of her voice, leaving him standing there awkwardly with one fist raised.

"Yeah, Mister Lob," Jamyn said, his frown deepening. "Don't do that."

"What?" Lob asked innocently. He leaned his face over to his fist and then extended one finger to scratch his nose. "I had an itch."

Shamara giggled at his antics. "No, you didn't."

Jamyn smiled at last. "What she said."

Lob dropped his arms and sighed. "Okay, you win. But only because she doesn't fight fair!" He wagged a finger at Shamara's grinning face.

"Women never do," Jamyn said.

"Too true. So, what's on your mind?" Lob asked as they walked over to where Shamara stood. "Looking for more training?"

Jamyn shook his head. "I wish. Got a bit of a problem."

"Do tell."

"I'm about to do something completely insane that could probably get me killed."

Lob and Shamara exchanged surprised looks.

"Sounds like fun," Lob said with a chuckle. "Might I ask what you have in mind?"

"Have you heard about what happened to Kana?"

"Nope." Lob looked to Shamara. "You?"

She shook her head.

"She's been captured."

Shamara gasped.

Lob frowned. "Now who would be that stupid?"

"A group of mercenaries is holding her on Letron 12-B."

"Mercenaries? So, this is about—"

"Yeah."

"What will they do to her?" Shamara asked, her timid voice barely rising to a whisper.

"Nothing, if I have anything to say about it," Jamyn said firmly to help reassure her. "I'm going to get her back."

Lob's brow furrowed. "Has your magic been switched back on?"

"No, but that's actually a good thing. The mercs have their own spellcaster. They locked everything down on their end, so I can't get there via a regular gate. I'm guessing that any other castings might not work there either. If I go while I'm still shut down, I won't have to deal with all of that."

"Okay, but there's still the small matter of you actually getting there."

"I think I have a way, but I'll need help to pull it off. That's why I'm here."

A grin crept across Lob's face. "Ah. You're here on a recruitment drive."

"Yeah. I could really use your help."

"Sounds like fun." Lob gave Shamara a friendly shove. "What do you think, kiddo? Up for a field trip?"

"I only need you for one thing," Jamyn said to her.

"What?" she asked.

"Your ability to gather magic. I'm gonna need you to pull in as much as you can without converting it to a push. I should be able to use that to get through."

"Hold up," Lob said. "You make it sound like she's not coming with us."

"She's not. Only you and I are going."

Lob looked at him in feigned outrage. "What? Boys only? You sexist little jerk!"

"No! I just—"

Shamara joined in, encouraged by a quick wink from Lob. "Yeah. You're being mean."

"Guys, come on," Jamyn said. "I'm serious. I don't want her getting hurt."

"Pssh," Lob said. "Like that'd happen while I'm around." Jamyn opened his mouth to protest but Lob quickly cut him off. "You don't need to worry about her. We've been working on some new techniques with the push. She can do some stuff now that'd probably give most experienced casters a run for their money."

"Still, I—"

Lob raised a hand to silence him again. Turning to his young charge, Lob said, "It ain't up to him. It's up to you. So whaddaya say? Want to help the nice lady who brought you here?"

Shamara nodded emphatically, sending her dark braids bouncing. "Of course, I do!"

Lob turned back to Jamyn. "Now do *you* wanna tell her she can't?"

Before he could reply, Shamara spoke up again. "Please, Mister Jamyn. If there's anything I can do to help Kana, I want to do it."

"Besides, you said that only non-casters need apply. Shammie's powers aren't strictly magical," Lob said.

Jamyn nodded, albeit reluctantly. "There should still be ambient magic on 12-B that she could use. Otherwise, their spells wouldn't work either."

"It's settled, then," Lob said. "When do we leave?"

"I think we—"

"Mister Lob?"

Lob looked down at Shamara. "Yeah?"

"We should take her along too."

"Who?"

A pair of huge metal arms seized Lob from behind. A loud voice rang in his ear. "Guess who?"

Lob created a shield around himself that quickly expanded to pry the massive arms apart. He sprang up off the ground with an agility that belied his huge frame. Turning around in midair, he snared the hulking figure under a dome of force. He landed and laughed loudly at his captive.

"Damn!" he said. "How do you stay so quiet in that rig?"

"Simple," Juushin replied. "You were all huddled in your little pow-wow. I could have blown a trumpet on the way in, and you still would have missed it." She tapped one finger against the surrounding shield. "Gonna let me out?" she asked lightly.

"You had better let her go," Shamara said in a playfully stern tone. She smiled brightly at Juushin and then back at Lob.

Lob grumped. "Okay, but only because Jamyn's here and unpowered." He dropped the shield and watched Juushin flex her huge arms. Snapping out of his admiring gaze, he asked quickly, "What brings you here?"

Juushin shook her head and leaned down to Shamara. "We have *got* to buy him a watch."

Shamara giggled. "Where could we get one with a wrist strap that big?"

Jamyn laughed at their teasing. "Maybe a weightlifting belt. Or maybe just hang Big Ben around his neck."

"Now don't *you* start," Lob told him, a curious flutter in his voice. "These two don't need any help."

"It's nearly one," Juushin said.

"Yeah, I got it," Lob replied, running one large hand over his face in exasperation. "Our usual sparring session."

Juushin chuckled at his discomfit. "What were we discussing so earnestly before I got here?"

Before Lob could respond, Shamara piped up. "We're helping Jamyn rescue Kana. You should come with us!"

Juushin turned to Jamyn. "Rescue *Kana*? That can't be right."

"Afraid it is," Jamyn replied. "Some mercs are holding her on Letron 12-B. I just asked Lob to help me get her back." Seeing Shamara standing there with her hands on her hips, he smirked. "And Shamara too."

"Book one more," Juushin said.

Shamara nearly squealed. "You're coming?"

"Of course, I am," Juushin replied. "Someone's gotta keep that big lug in line." She jerked a thumb at Lob. Noticing that Jamyn was now looking her over, she said, "If that's okay with you, I mean."

Jamyn flinched at the sudden inquiry. "Huh? Yeah. Yeah, that'd be great. Your powers aren't magic based either, are they?"

"Not at all. This is all me. Why?"

"Magic might not work over there," Lob told her. "They've got some casters mucking up the works."

"Then how are we supposed to get there?"

Lob clapped one huge hand on Jamyn's shoulder. "Ask our travel coordinator."

Jamyn shrugged his arm to make sure his shoulder hadn't been dislocated. "I can gate us to the wilds using this." He held up his right hand to show them his glyph. "After that, I'll have to convince someone there to help us get to 12-B."

"Then time's a-wasting," Lob said. He held out a hand to Shamara. "Shall we?"

She gripped one of his fingers. "We shall!" She reached out her other hand and grabbed one of Juushin's.

"You all go in first and I'll follow," Jamyn said. He pressed the large circle of his glyph, and a glowing doorway appeared. The others walked into it, and he took a quick breath before joining them.

They found themselves standing in a wild tangle of vines. "Lovely place," Lob said in an annoyed grumble while trying not to become ensnared and fall over. Juushin was also trying to pull herself free of the lush growth.

"What now?" Shamara asked Jamyn.

"We just need to find—" His words cut off as the group suddenly found themselves standing in shadow.

Lob suddenly bellowed. *"Heads up!"*

A loud thump sounded overhead. Everyone looked up to see an enormous lizard sitting inside the large bowl-shaped shield Lob had created above them. Juushin quickly settled in under its center and braced herself against the shield in case it started to fall.

Jamyn shouted. "Lester! It's me!"

Lester growled angrily at them before his giant body shimmered and he disappeared.

"What was that?" Shamara asked as she clung to Lob's side.

"Lester," Jamyn replied. "Friend of mine and Kana's."

"So, naturally, he attacked," Juushin said sourly, her towering form now crouched and ready to spring into battle.

"He's seriously pissed off right now," Jamyn said. "I'm kinda to blame for that."

Lob reluctantly dispelled his shield as he kept a close eye on their surroundings. "Great. Nothing more fun than a two-ton gecko on the rampage."

"The real bummer is that he's the next part of the plan. We were able to combine our powers to teleport to 12-B before. I'm hoping that I can convince him to do it again."

"And not kill us before then," Lob said.

"Right."

Juushin shouted. "Target behind!"

They all turned and saw Lester charging them, his prodigious bulk thundering through the tangled foliage.

"Watch out," Jamyn said. "He's smarter than this."

Lester got within a stone's throw and his body vanished. A second later, the ground started to tremble again.

"Ha!" Shamara cried out and fired a push behind the group. The wave of force caught Lester from the side, diverting his charge so that he rushed past them harmlessly.

Lob laughed in triumph. "Nice one, Shammie."

Lester skidded to a halt and turned to face the giant.

"C'mon, little dude," Lob told him with a fierce grin. "Care to try your luck?"

"Don't tease him," Jamyn said. "Just immobilize him long enough for me to talk to him."

"On it." Juushin took up a position an arm's length beside Lob. "Bear hug?"

"That'd be great," Lob said, "but let's give him one first. Shammie, give him a little love tap when he gets here. Just enough to get him looking up."

"Ready," she replied, taking up a stance behind the space between the huge fighters and solidly setting her feet.

Jamyn briefly marveled at the coordination between the three. He slipped behind Shamara and called out to Lester. "C'mon, poochie. Come and get me!"

Lester growled angrily and pounced at the gap between Lob and Juushin. Shamara gestured and Lester's head snapped upward like he had just been dealt a sharp uppercut. Lob and Juushin leapt forward as one, snaring Lester's huge body between them. He struggled against their grasp but was unable to buck free.

Lob strained with all his might and asked Juushin, "You got him?"

The joints of Juushin's armor suddenly lit up with a curious glow. The light vanished and her grip intensified. "Got him," she said, her massive arms circling Lester's waist. "Do your thing."

Lob quickly looked up and down the length of Lester's body before crafting several upside-down U-shaped barriers around him, pinning the irate dragon's neck, midsection, and tail to the ground. "No problem," he said with a relieved smile. Juushin released her grip and backed away slowly, keeping a close eye on the struggling lizard the whole time.

Before he could phase away again, Jamyn jumped forward and grabbed at Lester's head.

"Lester! It's me. Jamyn."

The dragon took no notice of his words and continued to thrash against the restraints.

Jamyn shouted again. "Lester! Calm down. I know what you want."

Lester growled in response but didn't open his mouth to bite the human.

Solidly grabbing his muzzle, Jamyn pressed his nose firmly against the dragon's. "It's your egg. You need to take it back home."

Lester abruptly stopped his squirming and stared back at the human. His growling turned into a strangled whine. Suddenly he nudged Jamyn's face as if to confirm his words.

"I know," Jamyn said in a soothing tone, patting one side of Lester's scaled face. "We screwed up by sending you both back here. You have it with you?"

Lester whined again. He barely opened the corner of his mouth, revealing a faint glow.

Jamyn nodded. "I'm gonna put things right. These guys are here to help, okay?" Lester blinked his wide yellow eyes once and Jamyn patted him again. "Lob and Juushin, get next to Lester and put a hand on him. Shamara, stand behind me and hold onto my shoulders."

Lob and Juushin took up positions flanking Lester. Each carefully laid a hand on him.

Feeling Shamara's tight grip, Jamyn told her, "Now gather as much magic as you can and surround me with it."

"Okay," she replied at once. She started drawing in magic, being careful not to convert it to a push and accidentally crush Jamyn.

Jamyn sensed the sudden rush of power flowing all around them. It continued to build, and he focused his senses on the billowing cloud. "C'mon, big guy," he said quietly as he guided the surge into Lester's body. "Let's go home."

A blast of air from Lester's nostrils hit Jamyn right in the face. A second later, the dragon's enormous frame lit up and started to shimmer. The light culminated in a bright flash and the entire group vanished.

Chapter Nineteen: Smash and Grab

Jamyn landed face down on the soft turf, his outstretched arms helping to break his fall. A second later, a knee smashed right into the center of his back. A tangle of limbs inelegantly followed, pressing his face harder against the ground.

"Mister Jamyn!"

The panicked cry in his ear confirmed the owner of the small body now sprawled across his back. "Hey, Shamara," he said as best he could. "Mind getting off me?"

She scrambled to his side. "Sorry!"

He turned toward the embarrassed squeak. Shamara was staring down at him with fearful eyes.

"You okay?" he asked.

She nodded. "Are you?"

He rolled onto his side and worked a few of the kinks out of his back. "I'll live."

"Sorry for landing on you like that."

He shrugged. "Better you than Lob!" He sat up and looked himself over, checking to see if anything was broken. Everything appeared to be intact, so he stood up. "Now where is everybody?" Together they scanned the thick jungle around them, looking for any sign of their comrades but finding none. "No Lester, Lob, or Juushin. That's not good. And I've got no way to signal 'em either. Dammit."

"I have a way!" Shamara said, a sudden burst of enthusiasm bringing her to her feet. She looked up at the dense canopy and then concentrated on a small gap of sky showing through the trees. A sharp snap broke the relative silence.

"What's that?" Jamyn asked.

"I make two small pushes and collide them," she said as another snap sounded. "The noise it makes resonates with Mister Lob's barriers. From that, he can figure out where I am if we get separated."

"Nice," Jamyn said with a smile. "Your own little fox and hound."

She looked at him in confusion. "A what?"

"It's a diagnostic tool my dad uses for electrical work."

"Oh." The third snap was abruptly muted, and she smiled. "He found it!"

"And he found you." Lob walked out from behind a large clump of trees in the distance.

"Mister Lob!" she cried out happily before running over to him.

He hugged her and patted her on the head. "You okay?" Her beaming face and tight hug more than answered his question. Seeing Jamyn grinning up at him, he said, "What are you so happy about, Mister Travel Coordinator? Just wait until I post my review of this trip."

"Hey, it's not entirely my fault."

"How's that?"

"You didn't fasten your seat belt before takeoff."

Lob raised one huge fist and shook it at him. "I'll give you a *takeoff*, you little maniac. You're just lucky Shammie didn't get hurt."

"Have you seen Miss Juushin?" Shamara asked.

Lob shook his head. "Nope. I was tangled up in a pile of vines over that-a-way." He pointed off to his right. "Just pulled myself free when I heard your clicker. Good job, kiddo."

"We should start looking for Juushin," Jamyn said.

"Wrong," Lob replied. "First we find Kana."

"But what about—"

"Juushin would be fine even if you dropped her from orbit. True, she'd probably be pissed as hell, but she'd deal with it. Securing Kana is our top priority. Right?"

Jamyn nodded in agreement. "Right."

"So where to, oh great navigator?"

Jamyn looked all around again but nothing he saw drew him in any particular direction. "I'm not sure."

Lob frowned at his indecision. "Oh, lemme guess. You didn't really have much of a plan past getting us here, did you?"

"Honestly? No, not really."

Lob shook his head at the acolyte. "Great. Kana kept all the tactical brilliance and put you in charge of the *run in first to draw their fire* department, huh?"

"Hey, I figured wherever she was there was bound to be a riot in progress."

Lob laughed. "Yeah, that is her usual M.O." He nudged Shamara. "I guess it's up to us to help out the little lost boy."

"Okay! Eye in the sky?"

"Good call, but not with you. I don't want some giant Letronan bird flying away with you."

"What's *eye in the sky*?" Jamyn asked.

"Aerial recon," Lob replied. "I encase Shammie in a shield bubble and then she uses the push to launch it high enough to get a lay of the land. But I already said *she* ain't going."

"Well then who—"

Lob spun around and snared Jamyn in a sphere of force. The globe was tinted blue to disguise him against the sky.

"Locked and loaded," the giant shouted.

"Fire one," Shamara cried. A push flared beneath the shield bubble, sending Jamyn blasting up through the jungle canopy and high into the air. As he approached his zenith, she asked, "Should I bring him back down?"

"Nah," Lob said with a sneaky grin. "Keep him up there a bit longer. Maybe give him a slow rotate so he can get the panoramic view."

She directed a series of pushes at the sphere, keeping its altitude constant while slowly spinning it around. Once it had made a full rotation, she let it descend again, every so often sending a smaller push to gradually retard its fall. As it gently touched down, Lob dispelled the bubble to reveal a bedraggled Jamyn sitting on the ground. He was holding his midsection and looked like he was trying not to vomit.

"Problem?" Lob asked innocently. "Rough flight? Should have worn your seat belt."

Jamyn took several deep breaths to calm himself. "You two are bad people," he muttered at last.

Lob turned to Shamara in confusion. "Us? Bad?"

She seemed equally surprised. "Not us."

"Yeah." Lob turned back to Jamyn, who had shakily made his way back to his feet. "Overruled two to one. We're awesome!" He and Shamara laughed together. "So whatcha see? Or do we have to send you up again?"

"Don't you dare!" Jamyn quickly held up one hand in protest. "The Sacred Fields are off that way." He turned and pointed off into the jungle. "To one end of it is a small building. Maybe a bunker. My guess is she's there."

"Based on—"

"There were blast marks on the ground outside the building. Something exploded there recently."

"Ah. Kana's calling card."

"That's what I'm thinking."

Lob nodded. "Then we go west, young man. Shammie, you stick with him. I'll bring up the rear in case Juushin or Jamyn's lizard buddy come sneaking up on us."

The three started off, making their way through the tangled growth. The air steadily grew thicker and warmer as they trudged, the morning sun rising high outside of the jungle's sweeping embrace. Using the push, Shamara cleared away or flattened much of the heavier vegetation from their path, making travel a bit easier.

"What are the Sacred Fields?" she asked Jamyn while she continued to work.

"That's where the other phase dragons like Lester used to live."

"Used to?"

"Yeah. There was a war here years ago. An army of mercenaries wiped out the dragons. Kana defeated the mercs and that pretty much ended the war."

"Why did they kill the dragons?"

"Because the Letronans revered them. Unfortunately, the ones who hired the mercs knew that. They figured that wiping out the dragons would crush the Letronans' spirits."

"That's awful!"

"Yep. So now Lester is the last of them. At least until his egg hatches."

Lob piped up. "His egg?"

"Yeah."

"*His* egg. Lester's."

"Yeah."

"Oh, boy. Didn't Kana have *the talk* with you yet?"

Jamyn frowned back at him over his shoulder. "Evidently male phase dragons can produce eggs too, Doctor Love."

Lob thought his words over for a moment. "Huh. That takes all the fun out of it."

Jamyn relented and chuckled. "There was still plenty of other fun. I had to help Lester get the egg out by opening up his birthing fold."

"His what?"

"Split in his scales down over his belly. It has to be cracked open by someone else before the dragon can get the egg out."

"How'd you open it?"

"Shoulder block to his gut."

Lob laughed. "I'm sure he appreciated your gentle touch."

Jamyn tossed the torn remains of a vine at him. "Gentle, hell. It was like running into a brick wall. Had to hit him twice. Dislocated my shoulder in the process."

"You could have hurt him!"

Jamyn was briefly caught off-guard by Shamara's angry shout. "No, I couldn't have. He's way tougher than that. Besides, he was tickled to death when the fold finally came open. He was purring his big green head off."

"Then why was he in such a nasty mood when we saw him?" Lob asked.

"I had just figured that out before this whole thing with Kana happened. When Lester's egg came out, he was supposed to bring it back here. The dragons have some sort of mystical connection to this place. I didn't know that when Kana sent him back to the wilds. Ever since then, he's been *really* grumpy. That's why he bit Fangs."

Shamara made a small, worried noise.

Jamyn fought back a grin. "No permanent damage, but still. He and Fangs really got along well when I first introduced them."

"Then shouldn't we have brought Lester's egg with us while we were at it?" Lob asked.

"We did," Jamyn replied. "Lester had it tucked in his mouth when he attacked. That's why he didn't try to take a bite out of any of us."

"So now he's back where he's supposed to be. Hatching time?"

"I hope so."

They finally emerged from the jungle's edge and stepped into the bright sunlight. Before them sprawled the rock-bordered valley that housed the Sacred Fields. Jamyn scanned the serene ground, his careful gaze immediately zeroing in on the exact spot where he and Kana had fought off the imp onslaught the last time they were here.

And where I first told her that I loved her, he thought with a smile.

"Whatcha grinning at?" Lob asked, now leaning down to Jamyn's ear.

Jamyn spun around to see Lob looking at him inquisitively. Turning, he saw the same curious look on Shamara's face. "What?" he asked.

They didn't reply, instead choosing to just silently stare back at him.

"I was just thinking about when Kana and I were here. We battled an army of imps."

"Why would that make you smile?" Lob asked. "Sounds like a bad day to me."

"It was."

"I think I know why," Shamara said under her breath.

Jamyn saw her shy smile and shook his head. "Yeah, you probably do. You are a little *too* perceptive. You know that?" Before she could reply, he dropped to one knee beside her. "Remember when you asked if I was Kana's boyfriend?"

She nodded, her eyes widening.

"Hey, forget about it," Lob said quickly. "That's entirely your business."

"Mister Lob! That's cheating."

Jamyn looked at them both in turn. "What?"

Lob vigorously waved a hand at him, as if to quickly dismiss the whole conversation. "Doesn't matter. We're here to find Kana, right?"

"Yeah, we are," Jamyn replied slowly, trying to figure out the cause of Lob's sudden outburst. Turning to Shamara, he asked, "Am I missing something here?"

"No, not really," she replied, keeping her gaze solidly on Lob as he tried not to fidget. "I suppose we should get going."

Jamyn nodded. "To rescue the woman I love," he said quietly.

Shamara suddenly leaped up off the ground with a loud whoop.

Lob let his massive arms fall to his sides and grumbled. "You just *had* to go there, didn't you?"

Before he could respond, Jamyn found himself wrapped in a tight hug.

"I knew it!" Shamara laughed into his ear.

He released an incredulous laugh. "You figured it out, huh?"

She nodded on his shoulder and hugged him even tighter.

"And I said you'd never admit to it without Kana getting you into a headlock first." Lob chuckled before clapping a hand on Jamyn's back. "Thanks a lot for proving me wrong in front of my too-smart-for-her-own-good student."

Shamara released Jamyn and looked up at her teacher. "Told you."

Jamyn shook his head before directing her attention down to a certain spot in the valley. "That's where I first told her."

Lob made a show of following their gaze and peering intently down at the spot. "Huh. Can't even see your grave marker from here."

"Yeah, she came close to planting me right then and there."

"Why?" Shamara asked.

"I guess it just wasn't what she wanted to hear at the time."

Lob laid a hand on his shoulder. "Let's go find her so you can tell her again," he murmured. "This time, we get to watch her beat you up!" He took a quick step back as Shamara charged him, then they spent a few moments play-fighting each other as they laughed.

Jamyn shook his head despite his fond smile. "All right, you two. Let's go get her."

Qa looked up from the library desk at the sound of Daystar's melodic voice. "A what?"

"A slight disturbance, Qa Shon," she said. "It lasted less than a second, but it was a definite fluctuation in the chaos field surrounding 12-B."

"Cause?"

"Unknown."

"If it happened again, could we break through it?"

Daystar pursed her lips. "We would have to time it precisely. But to do that, we would have to be able to accurately predict the next disturbance. If the hole collapses during the gate attempt, anyone inside would be obliterated."

"Unless we could somehow wedge open the door," Qa said quietly.

She studied the older man's face. "You have an idea?"

"The beginnings of one," he replied. "Recall what Mistress Tiris said about sending Lob the Unmarred there. Perhaps if we sent one of his magic-repellent barriers into a fluctuation, we could use it to pry open the field."

"We would have to coordinate the spells just right so that the detection and gating would be simultaneous."

"Work with Donta and Fangs on that," Qa said in an excited rush. "I'll speak to Lob." The two turned and raced off to their respective tasks.

———— ◉ ————

"You're sure about this?"

"Quite sure. Something is out there. And moving this way."

"All is prepared?"

"It is."

Voyiv nodded his approval. "Then we open the doors and wait."

———— ◉ ————

Qa burst into the central chamber, the loud bang of the double doors startling all present.

"Qa!" Daystar exclaimed, looking up from her spell preparations. "You have news?"

"I'm afraid I do," he replied in a rush. "I cannot find Lob. And neither can the Valet."

"That's quite odd," she replied. "Is anyone else missing?"

"Yes." Qa raised his voice. "Valet, please list all Sanctum personnel not currently accounted for."

The Valet responded instantly. "Arms Master Juushin. Lob the Unmarred. The neophyte Shamara."

Leel frowned. "Perhaps they are—"

A swiftly raised hand from Qa encouraged his silence.

The Valet spoke again. "Acolyte Jamyn Siska."

Qa took in their shocked expressions and nodded gravely. "As of right now, the Sanctum is on high alert. I want every available perception of Letron 12-B that we can muster. At the first sign of an opening, I want us on that planet en masse."

"On a full combat footing?" Donta asked.

Qa nodded once in silent reply.

"You heard the man." Fangs roared and pulled his lips back in a fierce snarl. "Let's move this party to the exit points and be ready to hit 'em hard!"

Everyone immediately picked up their gear and rushed out of the room, leaving Qa, Daystar, and Donta behind.

"You really think he somehow got there?" Daystar asked.

"He has the power," Donta said quietly.

"Moreover, he has the will." Qa's voice cracked under the strain of keeping it in check. He saw Daystar's look of worry and it was likely mirrored behind Donta's mask. "Someone has the woman he loves. I would not want to be that person right now."

⎯⎯⎯⎯◉⎯⎯⎯⎯

"Now what?"

Jamyn peered down again at the squat building from their elevated vantage point. Lob had created a high platform in the trees and the three looked down at their objective. Sure enough, the front doors of the bunker were opened wide. Moreover, no one appeared to be guarding either them or the perimeter. The entire place looked deserted.

"Beats hell outta me," Jamyn said at last.

"Shammie?"

She shrugged. "I don't see anyone either."

"Maybe Kana already wiped them out and is just waiting inside."

"That'd be great," Lob said. "You think we're that lucky?"

Jamyn quickly started to re-adjust the plates of his suit. "Nope."

"We just gonna go down there and make ourselves at home?"

"No. I'll go myself. You two stay here and keep an eye on things. If I find Kana, I'll get her out. Be ready to cover us with a barrier if things get ugly."

"You're just full of dumb, ain't ya?"

Both Jamyn and Shamara looked up at Lob.

Jamyn frowned. "What do you—"

"I mean you brought us here for a reason," Lob said, sharply cutting him off. "Keep your butt alive while we rescue Kana. How are we supposed to do that if we're up here and you're down there? If something or someone attacks you, it'd be best if we're down there to fend it off."

"But I don't want—"

"Blah, blah, blah!" Lob blocked Jamyn's face with one huge hand. Jamyn tried to evade him, but Lob mirrored his frantic movements, effectively covering his mouth. "Can you believe this guy?" Lob asked Shamara. "Trying to go off on his own while we just sit around?"

Jamyn leaped backward in frustration. Unfortunately, his escape carried him right off the edge of their high perch. He started to fall but instead landed on a plank that had suddenly sprouted from the side of the platform. He clung to the thin outcropping and noticed Lob smiling down at him in smug satisfaction.

"We coming with, or do you still wanna go yourself?" Lob asked. He raised one hand and held his fingers together, ready to snap them. "I can press the *down* button for you right now, if you'd like."

Jamyn gasped. "You win. We all go together."

Lob nodded in agreement. "Now you're making sense." He gestured and the platform and its addition slowly descended to the ground. Both vanished and Jamyn stumbled away a few steps as his support disappeared.

Shamara looked at the expanse between them and the building. "Hamster wheel."

Lob considered their path and patted her on the head. "Brilliant. I was gonna go for the hamster ball, but I see there are a few divots we could get stuck in. Wheel should do nicely."

"Still a long way to go with us being exposed on all sides," Jamyn said.

"And how were you gonna do it, genius?"

"Crawl through the grass. It's tall enough to cover me most of the way there."

"Hmm," Lob said as he thought over the plan. "That's not half-bad."

"You really thought I was gonna just stroll up there out in the open?"

"You never know. You are Kana's student, after all."

"And what does that—"

"Mister Lob?" Shamara said, interrupting their verbal sparring. "Maybe you could mirror the outside of the wheel. Reflect the sky and grasses to help hide us."

"See?" Lob pointed down to his young student. "At least *someone's* trying to prevent us from getting shot."

"You could always stay here like I wanted in the first place."

"And I told you—"

"Hey!" Shamara snapped at them both. "Stop it. We're here to rescue Kana, right?"

The bickering pair looked down at her.

"He started it," Lob said, pointing at Jamyn.

"I don't care. You two are being stupid!"

They stood there in stunned silence.

Jamyn finally spoke up. "Sorry."

"Yeah. What he said," Lob said quickly. "Hold your fire, kid. We're just working off some nerves here. Us dumb guys do that. Right?" He nudged Jamyn, looking for his support.

"Um, yeah. Right."

"Then let's get to it like the lady said."

He crafted a large cylinder about eight feet long and lying on its side. Its invisible surface started to shimmer as Lob adjusted its reflectivity. Slowly the image of the surrounding grasses started to appear up its sides while its upper half turned the color of the cloudless sky.

"Get in there, Shammie. Let's see how much we've got."

She stepped closer, stopping when her reflection started to climb one side wall of the cylinder. A doorway opened in the illusion, and she went inside. The doorway closed again, obscuring her with the reflected grasses around them.

"Can you see out the front?" Lob asked her.

"Mostly," came her faint reply.

The doorway opened again, wider this time. "Get in," Lob told Jamyn. "You walk beside me. I'll carry Shammie on my shoulder, so she doesn't have to keep up with our pace." They went inside and Lob resealed the wall. He hoisted Shamara up and sat her on his shoulder. "Ready?"

"Let's go," Jamyn replied.

Lob pressed one foot hard against the front curve and the cylinder started to roll. It took a while to time their steps but soon they were advancing on the bunker at a moderate stroll.

"When we get there, I'll open up the front wall. You go in to find Kana," Lob said. "I'll stay out here with the engine running."

"Sounds good."

"How we doing, lookout?" Lob asked.

"Nothing to report," Shamara replied. She lowered her voice. "I'm sorry for yelling at you."

"Don't worry about it, boss," he replied, tickling her side with one finger. "Sometimes we all need a little smack in the head to get us back on track."

"Something's not right." Jamyn warily scanned the entire area around them as they walked. "This is *way* too easy."

"Gotta agree with you there," Lob replied. "Whatcha think, boss lady?"

Shamara nodded. "It's too much like home," she said softly. "When it gets quiet like this, people end up dead."

"Then let's see if we can shake 'em loose. Jamyn, just keep walking normally. Shammie, fire up the popcorn."

She gestured to several random spots around the field between them and the bunker. The air exploded in a series of sharp pops as she used the push to create small bursts of force, each pummeling the space nearby with a focused shock wave. A brief shout erupted between them and the bunker's open doors. Without warning, a rifle materialized and fell to the ground directly in their path.

"They're cloaked," Jamyn shouted.

"Time to move," Lob said. He snagged Jamyn in one hand and tucked the acolyte under his huge arm. In the next second, he stomped hard against the front of the cylinder. It lurched forward and started to roll faster toward their destination. He shouted to them as he ran. "Hang on to yourselves. This ain't gonna be a soft landing."

Shamara clung to Lob's shoulder. "I'll clear the way."

She sent alternating waves of force sweeping from side to side across their path. The rifle that had appeared was crushed into the ground by the advancing cylinder and the weapon's power cell exploded beneath them with a muffled *thump*. Every so often a human shape would briefly appear as a push struck it, but then disappear just as quickly.

"The odds all their boys are outside?" Lob asked as he lumbered ahead.

"Not good," Jamyn replied in a grim voice.

"Swell. How good is that suit?"

"It should protect me from their guns and most magic."

"All except your head."

"Right."

Lob shouted as they closed in on the building. "Hang on to your lunches. We're here." They crashed into the structure with a loud clunk. Lob jumped at the last second and braced both feet against the curved front wall of the cylinder. The shield absorbed his kinetic energy, cushioning his impact, and he hopped back to a standing position. He quickly placed Jamyn back on his feet.

"You have reached your destination. All ashore that's going ashore."

"Open it up so I can get in there," Jamyn said.

"Not so fast there, chuckles. Hold still a second." He pointed one finger down and tapped the top of Jamyn's head. "There. Now get in there, find Kana, and get your butts out here." The front wall opened, and Jamyn quickly hopped out. Just as he went through the open doors, a startled cry turned him back around.

"Mister Lob!"

Shamara's shout rang through the cylinder. The sound was followed by the shriek of multiple laser beams striking their hollow transport, fired by the unseen attackers all around them. Cracks started to form in the protective barrier.

"Oh, great." Lob grumbled and reinforced the shield from the inside.

Suddenly the bunker's doors started to slide shut.

"Lob," Jamyn cried.

Lob glanced back at the closing doors and frowned. "Just move it," he said as the outer layer of the cylinder shattered. "Kana should be able to get you back out of there. If not, we'll just bust down the doors when we finish with these goons."

"Be careful!"

The doors slammed shut and locked.

———————⟶ ◉ ⟵———————

"Easy for him to say, huh, Shammie?" Lob continued to expand and then replace the shield's outer wall from the inside as the lasers chipped away at it.

"Stop it!"

Shamara followed her shout with a devastating push straight ahead. The wall of force slammed into their invisible attackers, knocking many of them off their feet. Their bodies shimmered as their camouflaged suits temporarily overloaded but then faded away again when their systems recovered.

"Nice hit," Lob said quietly, awed by the sheer force of the attack. "Hey. I've got an idea."

"What?" She wildly blasted at their foes again despite her growing fatigue.

"Scattergun." He gestured and a pile of tiny stones appeared on the ground in front of their cylinder. A large crack appeared in the curved wall, threatening to breach it. "Hit 'em!"

Shamara summoned her strength and blasted the rock pile with a push, sending the stones flying in a smothering barrage that covered the field before them. The barrier shards pelted the unseen soldiers and became lodged in their gear. One by one, their systems drained. Their cloaks dropped, clearly revealing them all. Despite the loss of their cover, they regrouped and advanced on Lob and Shamara.

"I think we made them mad," Shamara said in a timid voice.

Lob extended a flared tube out of the top of the cylinder. "We see you now," he bellowed into it, trying to sound as menacing as possible. "Back off or we'll stomp your butts into the ground."

The troops continued forward and took aim.

Lob quickly retracted the tube and sighed. "Guess we have to make good on that now. How you holding up, Shammie?" He looked down and saw she was barely able to stay on her feet. Scooping her up with one hand before she could fall, he held her close. "Okay, then." He growled under his breath and looked out at the advancing men. "Time to get ugly."

The terrain shook and at least a dozen men from the back of their ranks were knocked to the ground. The others spun around to find their new attacker. Peering over their heads, Lob was just able to see a large boulder embedded in the ground. Far beyond it at the edge of the valley stood a massive newcomer in a glittering suit of armor. It held a massive tree that looked like it had been viciously torn from the ground.

A metallic voice thundered from the imposing figure. "Back off like he said!"

Despite her fluttering eyelids, Shamara sat up in Lob's hand. "Miss Juushin?" she asked weakly.

The troops immediately opened fire on the new threat, but their shots did little more than fizzle when they hit the metal giant. A booming laugh answered them. The golden warrior launched forward with blistering speed, streaking down upon them like a sprinter.

"Pay attention, kiddo," Lob said quietly, pointing Shamara at the onrushing figure. "All the movies and comic books and chainmail bikini fantasy artists of the world got it all wrong." He gazed fondly at the charging warrior. "*That* is the way a *real* woman goes into battle!"

Juushin met the enemy with a wild laugh, swinging the tree one-handed like an enormous fly swatter. At least twenty men were sent flying before the others wisely retreated out of her range. She laughed despite the smothering torrent of lasers that blanketed her, each having no effect on her bulky suit.

She shouted in her excitement "Come on! I'm bored. Make this a challenge." She flipped the tree back over her shoulder and beckoned to them with her fingers. "C'mere, little boy," she said to the nearest man. "Give us a kiss."

He responded by snatching a grenade from his belt and hurling it right in her face. She moved like a flash of lightning, snaring it in one hand before it hit. The grenade exploded but the blast was effectively muffled by her huge gauntlet. She took one long stride forward and towered over the awestruck soldier.

"Please tell me you're packing something a little bigger than that," she said down to him. He ran away from her as fast as he could, and she sighed while his comrades continued to fire at her.

"Let's make this a little more interesting."

The joints of her suit flashed briefly. She advanced on them again, though now she moved significantly slower. The men continued their circling assault, doing their best to stay away from her while they searched for a weakness in their unstoppable foe.

While the bulk of their forces concentrated on Juushin, several others were again firing at Lob's cylinder. "Oh, give it a rest," Lob said as he continued to reinforce their safe haven from the inside.

Shamara had finally succumbed to her exhaustion and passed out. He cradled her in one arm while he directed repairs with the other.

Suddenly three men slammed face-first into the cylinder and slumped to the ground. Lob was surprised to count four unconscious bodies lying before him. He looked up just in time to see two more crash into the curved wall. This time, however, he saw the cause. A body had been thrown at them from behind. Peering across the battlefield, he saw Juushin pouncing on the men one by one and then hurling them at the troops still surrounding Lob and Shamara, effectively mowing them down.

"Thanks," he shouted. Shamara stirred at the sound and weakly murmured in complaint. "Sorry," he whispered down at her.

With their numbers now reduced, Lob was finally able to go on the offensive. He extended thick rods from the front wall of the cylinder, each of them striking one of the remaining attackers before retracting again. Between his precise jousting and Juushin's relentless attack, the troops were effectively neutralized in minutes.

Juushin stomped over to the cylinder. After tossing aside the unconscious soldiers that had piled up around it, she knocked one huge fist against the translucent wall. "So how many licks to get to the center of this thing, I wonder."

The cylinder shimmered before turning completely clear, revealing the grinning Lob and sleeping Shamara. A small window opened in it and Lob laughed. "Damn, you know how to make an entrance."

"I should hope so," Juushin replied, keeping her voice down to keep from disturbing Shamara. "Is she okay?"

"Just tuckered out." He reached down and brushed a few loose strands of hair from her face. "She fought like a pro today."

"You too, from what I saw," Juushin said. "Where's Jamyn?"

"Inside." Lob nodded back over his shoulder, indicating the closed doors.

She looked over the clear cylinder. "Well, get out of the way and let's go get him." She rapped the curved shield again. "You got a license to drive this thing?"

"Learner's permit," he replied with a goofy grin.

"Nice. Get to steppin' so I can—"

An explosion smashed into her side, sending her reeling away from the cylinder. Lob immediately threw himself to the ground, being careful not to crush his delicate student, and sealed up the hole in the cylinder wall to prevent the blast from incinerating them both.

Juushin tried to stand up, but another blast knocked her flat on her back. "What the hell?" she shouted, trying to get her bearings. Another explosion erupted, this time directly beneath her. The blast sent her sailing into the field where she landed with a loud crash.

A robed figure came around the far side of the bunker. It slowly made its way across the field, its bony hands extended forward as it crafted another spell.

"Interesting," a male voice declared from inside the deep gray cowl. "An ultra-dense metal. You must be very strong to use such a suit."

Juushin scrambled back to her feet and glared down at the much smaller man. "Wanna see how strong I am, shorty?"

The mage took no notice of her challenge. "I see the joints are enchanted. No doubt to enable you to move. If I were to remove them..." He waved his hand, and the joints of her suit lit up with a curious glow before winking out one by one.

Juushin stood up straight and her giant body went rigid.

The mage nodded in apparent satisfaction. "Now that you cannot move, let's see how many ways I can find to kill your friends."

Juushin growled through her gritted teeth. "Boy, you just officially stepped in it."

"Declared the woman bound in the metal casket," the mage replied.

Juushin shouted across the field. "Lob! Gimme a backstop. Full strength."

"*Full?*" he muttered under his breath. "Oh, jeez." Immediately he erected a massive wall of force between himself and where the lone mage stood. He gave Juushin a quick wave before reinforcing the cylinder as much as he could.

The mage looked back over his hunched shoulder. "Some manner of barrier." He tested several random spots on the unseen wall with contained blasts of magic.

"Eyes front, dipshit," Juushin said. She started to raise her right arm at an agonizingly slow rate.

The mage observed her glacial movements with a mocking chuckle. "At that speed, you may reach me in a few months. You will be rotting in your metal shell long before that."

"Is that so?" She continued to lift her arm, her hand now clenched in a tight fist. "Let me clue you in, shorty. That magic you temporarily nullified around my joints? It's not there to help me get around in this rig."

"No?"

"No." Her arm was now level with her shoulder, bent at the elbow with her fist pointed directly at her foe like she was going to punch him. "It acts as a restrictor. Makes it a *lot* harder to move. Now that it's gone, I have to be careful, or I'll go out of control."

The mage raised his hands to attack but Juushin beat him to it. Her massive arm flexed, driving her fist forward in a blinding flash. The shock wave from the instantaneous strike slammed right into the mage, sending him flying backward. Flesh and bone alike were instantly pulverized in midair. His body dissolved into a crimson spray against Lob's barrier wall.

She called out while keeping her body perfectly still again. "Yo, Lob."

He opened a portal in his cylinder. "Y-yeah?" he replied shakily, stunned by the overwhelming display of sheer power.

"Lose the wall, will ya? Looks gross."

"Right."

He dispelled the wall. The collected viscera landed with a sickening splat.

"I really hope Shamara didn't see that."

Lob checked on her. "She's still asleep."

"Good. Anyway, I'm kinda stuck here until my suit reboots."

"Don't wanna take a step and accidentally launch yourself into orbit, huh?"

She laughed. "Yeah. You two can go in without me if you want."

"No, we'll wait. I'm not leaving you out here by yourself."

"World's biggest lawn gnome."

"With one helluva rabbit punch."

"Liked that one, did ya?"

Lob smiled and sat down, keeping his eyes on Juushin's massive form the entire time. "Better believe it. You were incredible." Realizing what he had just said, he grimaced as a blush raced up over his cheeks.

"You were too. Nice backstop, by the way."

He forced a shy smile. "I'll catch for you anytime."

Chapter Twenty: Scatter

Jamyn silently made his way down the darkened corridor, trying his best to ignore the faint sounds of carnage seeping into the bunker from outside. Despite his concern for his friends, he kept his mind focused on both his mission and his surroundings. The hallway fed into a large circular room up ahead, its only lighting provided by a few recessed fixtures in the high ceiling. Cones of radiance painted widely spaced circles upon the smooth tile floor. Faint reflections bounced back from the many blank monitor screens hung upon the walls.

As he entered the main area, his eyes were drawn to one particular circle of light on the far end of the room. A robed figure curled up into a tight ball was lying within its confines. Maintaining his constant sweep of the rest of the room, he cautiously walked over to its only other occupant. Once there, he risked a quick glance down.

Kana was lying on her side. Her eyes were closed. Several dark bruises covered her face. A long line of clotted blood streaked across her forehead. Despite her unconscious appearance, her lips twitched as if she was silently reciting something.

White-hot anger surged up from deep inside Jamyn, threatening to consume him. He kept his movements slow, despite the desire to sweep her up into his arms. He crouched next to her and gently nudged her shoulder.

"Hey," he whispered. "Get up."

Her lips stopped moving and compressed into a tight grimace. They parted just enough to let a single whispered word past.

"Run."

He clenched his jaw, a hundred mind-borne menaces now threatening to leap at him from the shadows. His anger easily overruled his fear. "Not without you."

"Get out." Her heated order barely stirred the air.

His volume rose despite his efforts to keep quiet. "I'm not leaving you."

"No, you are not," a firm voice said from the darkness.

Jamyn stood up, casually slipping a hand into his pocket as he did. "Who are you?" he calmly asked the darkness.

"My name is Voyiv," his unseen opponent replied. "I am—"

Jamyn angrily cut him off. "A mercenary. You took Kana. I'm here to take her back."

"That will not be possible."

Jamyn bared his teeth in an unpleasant snarl. "Possible or not, it's happening."

A blast of concussive force caught him square in the chest, knocking him flat on his back. He opened his eyes and turned to Kana. Her eyes were now open, and she was staring daggers at him.

She growled at him in the angriest tone he had ever heard her use. "You fuckin' idiot!"

"Nice to see you too," he said quickly before scrambling back to his feet. Tuning his eyesight, he started to perceive the swirls of ambient magical energy all around him. A single empty spot off to his left interrupted the tranquil flow of the rest of the room.

"That all you got?" he asked a point straight ahead.

The vacant outline advanced but Jamyn was quicker. Another force blast ripped through the air, but Jamyn fell to a low crouch, neatly ducking under it. In the next heartbeat, he spun and hurled the null rock he had pulled from his pocket straight at his cloaked foe.

The stone smashed into Voyiv's chestplate, destroying his active camouflage system with an electric sizzle and a shower of sparks.

His body appeared, though it was still partially hidden by the surrounding darkness.

"She has taught you well," he said, stripping off the now useless plate and carelessly tossing it aside.

"Didn't," Kana said, her words slurred into a rough mumble. "Jus' a dumb rookie. Not mine."

"Really?" Voyiv asked, his tone disbelieving. "Hajis-Corol seemed to think otherwise."

"You've got him too?" Jamyn asked, his anger flaring anew.

"He was granted release right after he told us about the student of Morel-Kana."

His eyes now fully adjusted to the darkened surroundings, Jamyn looked over his opponent's imposing stature as well as the rifle pointed directly at him. "Then you should also know that I will do whatever it takes to get her out of here," he said in a menacing tone. "I'd suggest getting the hell out of my way."

"Yes, I know you will fight for her," Voyiv replied. "I'm counting on it." He fired again, this time at Jamyn's right leg.

Jamyn anticipated the onrushing blast. He shifted his weight to his left leg just as the shot hit. Rolling with the force of the impact, he let his right leg swing backward. He spun around in a tight pirouette before setting his feet again. He launched forward, aiming a punch at Voyiv's face. Unfortunately, the larger man was much more agile than his bulky body suggested. He easily blocked the strike and gave Jamyn a mighty shove that lifted the young man right off his feet. Just as Jamyn landed, a brutal kick caught him high in the chest, sending him crashing to the ground again.

Despite his suit's reinforcements, each blow hit with bone-jarring intensity. Jamyn stood up and decided to switch tactics.

"What's your deal, anyway?" he asked, trying to buy himself some time to regroup. "Kana beat your guys the last time you were here. This some stupid revenge thing?"

"She did not best them. She killed them."

"Bullshit. I read the reports. They were all returned to you *alive* after the peace treaty was signed."

"And every one of them died soon after. She had destroyed their will to live."

Jamyn grinned cruelly. "Good. Serves 'em right, after what they did to the mist giants."

"That was decreed by their commander," Voyiv said quickly. "It does not, however, justify what happened to those men. If she had simply killed them outright, we would not be here."

"So, it's *her* fault that your guys gave up the ghost?" Jamyn continued, intentionally trying to provoke him. "What? Having their asses handed to them by a lone teenaged girl was too much for them to handle?"

Voyiv charged him, swinging his rifle at Jamyn's head like a club. Jamyn dodged the strike and hit the merc in the face with a series of quick jabs. Unfazed, Voyiv drove the butt of his rifle into Jamyn's gut. The force of the blow lifted Jamyn high off the ground. Before he fell, Voyiv's gloved hand snared the front of his shirt. He held the struggling acolyte aloft and stared into his wide amber eyes.

Voyiv glared at Jamyn. "She took *everything* from those men. Everything they cared for. Everyone they had ever loved or cherished. And all they had fought for, bled for, sacrificed their entire lives for, got to watch them wither and die." He dropped his rifle and started working Jamyn over with his free hand, driving brutal punches into his body while sparing his face. "Now she will feel what they felt. She will watch you die knowing that she could not do a single thing to stop it." He halted the vicious onslaught just long enough to look to where Kana still lay on the floor. "Turn her. She must see this."

A surge of magic hit her, roughly spinning her body around so that her face was now pointed directly at the grappling pair.

"No!" she cried weakly.

"Yes, Morel-Kana," Voyiv replied. "Now you will watch him die."

"But first she gets to see this," Jamyn shouted.

Though the attack had been relentless, his suit had absorbed much of the punishment. He swung both of his arms around in a wide arc, smashing his fists into Voyiv's temples. In a flash, he wrapped his legs around the larger man's waist. Straining with all his might, he arched his body back and broke free of the merc's grasp. In the next instant, he flexed forward again, smashing a forearm into Voyiv's face with enough force to daze the larger man. Jamyn released his grip and flipped backward. Voyiv stumbled away from him before falling to the floor.

Jamyn retreated to Kana's side. "Don't worry about it," he said, trying to reassure her while ignoring the pains wracking most of his body. "You're the only one who gets to beat my ass."

A focused wave of magic slammed him back into the wall. He tried to move before Voyiv could regain his senses, but something kept him pinned to the spot. Looking past Kana, he saw a hunched figure emerge from the shadows. It advanced with its thin hands pointed straight at him, maintaining the spell immobilizing him. While Jamyn struggled, he saw movement beneath Kana's robes.

The skeletal mage cackled. "Foolish little creature."

"Indeed," Voyiv said, blood dripping from his swollen nose. His unsteady steps carried him until he stood beside the mage. "Do it now."

The Nihil canceled the spell holding Jamyn and the younger man fell to the floor.

Jamyn panted, doing his best to catch his breath. "Two on one, huh? All right, then." He gathered his strength and raced straight at the pair, his fist already drawn back to strike.

The mage pulled Kana's pin from the folds of his robes and tossed it to the floor right in Jamyn's path. He straightened up and his gravelly voice ripped through the air. "Stand fast for your judgment—"

"No!" Kana cried.

"Jamsiska-Jamyn!"

Jamyn saw the flood of magic coming for him but recognized that its leading edge was unstable. Suddenly Path's voice tickled the back of his mind.

An imperfect attack. It won't affect you!

The wave slammed into him but crumbled into nothingness as it tried to invade his body. Thinking quickly, he uttered a sharp cry and collapsed right next to Kana's motionless form. He clutched at his abdomen and groaned in agony.

Voyiv started toward him and nodded in satisfaction. "You are now powerless to resist," he said, "same as your master."

Jamyn opened one eye. Kana stared back at him in shock. He arched an eyebrow at her, causing her to release a stunned gasp. "Wanna bet?" he whispered to her. Noticing a light blue smudge on her lips, the corner of his mouth briefly flicked upward. *"Tiris?"* he mouthed. A slight nod answered him just as a hand grasped his collar. "Make it count!" he whispered urgently before he felt himself being lifted off the ground.

Voyiv hauled him upright and stared into his unsteady eyes. "Your power has been turned back upon you," Voyiv said calmly, despite the blood dripping down over his lips and chin. "Your ties to both that pin and your own name have doomed you. The more you struggle, the weaker you will become."

Jamyn made a show of trying to focus on Voyiv's face, his entire body hanging limp in the larger man's grasp. He tried to speak but it came out in a halting gasp. He took in a strangled breath and barely managed to mutter, "There's...something...you missed."

"And that is?"

Jamyn suddenly smiled and shouted right in Voyiv's face.

"Wrong name, asshole!"

Kana's open hand shot from beneath her robes. A burst of focused chi exploded right behind Voyiv's knees, knocking his legs out from under him.

Jamyn shoved forward, adding his weight to their combined momentum and driving his foe hard to the floor. In a flash, he sat upon Voyiv's chest and repeatedly pounded his fist into the mercenary's face. He had delivered nearly a dozen hammer blows before a wave of force knocked him across the floor.

The Nihil cackled and launched another spell from his fingertips.

The new torrent of magic suddenly exploded, igniting in a rush of flame that came back to scorch its sender. He had barely recovered when a swarm of black tentacles burst from the floor. The strands wrapped around every part of his body they could reach, effectively immobilizing him. Once his body was fully engulfed, they lifted him up off the floor.

Kana growled in sheer hate. "You thought I was deluded when I said that I was the best."

The spectral appendages yanked his arms and legs hard, pulling them straight out from his body and fully exposing him to her rage. She stood up and solidly faced her tormentor. A glowing filament of golden light streaked from her palm, forming her soul lash.

"Here's your proof," she screamed.

She swung the lash forward, striking at his exposed body. Each hit sliced away a part of her foe, be it an ear or a toe or a finger. The Nihil screeched in agony while Kana continued to carve him to pieces. Her voice devolved into a wailing shriek as she worked. The whip moved faster and faster until it became a blur of razor-sharp destruction between Kana and her prey. When she had him whittled down to little more than a head on a torso, she gathered the lash back for one final strike. She lunged at him and her soul wrapped itself around what remained of his body multiple times until he was covered in a glowing net of light. She gave the lash a mighty yank. The net tightened, slicing through the dismembered mage who fell to the floor in a pile of bloody bits.

Jamyn stared at his beloved in stunned horror. He had recovered in time to see her final attack. Its sheer brutality rendered him speechless.

Her soul zipped back up into her palm and her voice faded to a whisper.

"I—"

She collapsed where she stood. A storm of magic erupted from her body, lighting up the entire room.

Jamyn started toward her, his enhanced vision telling him something was incredibly wrong. All the ambient magic in the room was racing in and out of her at random, wreaking havoc on her entire body. Patches of her skin ignited and burned into blackened pits before regenerating almost instantaneously. Bones snapped and shattered and then knit themselves back together. Her screams pierced the air, and she writhed on the floor in supreme agony. As her limbs flailed, he caught sight of her hands. Both were stained the same blue color that he had seen earlier on her lips.

"No!"

He followed his shout with a frantic leap over her supine form. His mind lashed out, swatting away the ribbons of energy before they could touch her. He hung in midair over her, fending off the endless onslaught that threatened to obliterate her body. Fear and rage churned in his gut, boiling down to a concentrated mass of will that coiled within him like a snake preparing to strike. His senses suddenly flared, bringing the entire area around them into razor-sharp focus.

"Enough," he said through his clenched teeth.

The predator within him launched itself at the threat and consumed the rampaging magic instead of merely diverting it. Soon all the ambient power around her was channeling directly into him. His hovering body descended until he was kneeling beside her. He roughly hauled her up to a sitting position before enfolding her in a tight embrace. The beast pounced again, this time drawing the excess magic from her body. Her many wounds healed with unnatural swiftness, and she took in a deep, gasping breath. The torrent reduced to a trickle before winking out entirely. A calm fell upon the entire room, only to finally be broken by his weak voice.

"You doubled-up on Tiris's potion," he mumbled into her shoulder. "Bypassed the dosage restriction by pouring more into your hands and drinking it."

She nodded. "Yeah."

He sighed deeply. "That was stupid." Despite his words, he buried his face into the side of her neck and kissed it tenderly.

She nodded again, her eyes getting misty. "Yeah. I—"

"Shh!"

He tensed, nearly crushing her in his iron grip.

———— ◉ ————

Three cascades of raw power closed in on the tangled pair from across the room. Kana's eye's widened when she saw the multi-colored blasts ripping through the air. Suddenly she lost sight of them. Someone had stepped in her way, blocking her view.

Path spread her arms wide, welcoming the barrage of deadly spells. They struck her with incredible force, but her small body did not budge. Instead, she laughed. Her joyous peals rang off the walls, growing in both volume and strength as the tempest churned around her.

Undaunted, the three mages who had attacked poured even more power into their onslaught.

This only appeared to further amuse the young girl. Her riotous laughter stopped, and she started to draw the billowing storm into her thin form.

She shouted at them as she fed upon the maelstrom. "A child of two worlds. Welcome in neither but tied by both. Now all has changed. The bonds have been broken, the rules rewritten." She glanced back over her shoulder at the entangled pair. She winked at Kana before turning back around. "*Less than nothing* without but now more than could be imagined!"

Kana stared at her in absolute shock.

He's declaring! Jamyn is declaring through Path!

Path screamed at their enemies. "Know fear, *they* who have tormented! Know despair, *those* who have dominated! And to *them*, who have sought to rule all, who have built walls that none may breach, now know this!"

Jamyn suddenly vanished, leaving Kana holding only air. He reappeared standing behind Path and quickly absorbed her back into his mind. Taking a step forward to stand where she had been, he pulled in the remains of the tempest while he took careful measure of the trio of perplexed Nihil before him. His lips parted and the entire room shook with the intensity of his words.

"I am the Scatter."

The Nihil suddenly lit up, their bodies outlined in violet fire. Magic poured into them from every direction at once, not wildly as it had with Kana but in even, regular pulses that pummeled them to their cores. They turned in desperation to the pile of bloody viscera that was their fallen comrade, consuming it in a bid to use its energy for their spells. Instead, the gathered life force multiplied a hundredfold and pierced their minds in a final vicious burst. Their bodies dissolved into swirls of blood and magic, each substance repeatedly transforming into the other at random as their lives were violently extinguished. Their essences evaporated without a trace.

Jamyn released a long sighing breath into the pervasive silence that descended upon the room.

Kana stared at him in awe. "Stage three of the Voice," she whispered, hardly believing what she had just witnessed. "You channeled the magic without using spells to guide it."

A beam of energy slammed into the side of Jamyn's head, the blast completely obscuring it from view. Kana spun in horror to see Voyiv unleashing the full power of his rifle upon her defenseless acolyte. The rifle's energy cell drained at last, and the beam ceased.

"Know now the pain of Noark," Voyiv muttered to Kana.

She slowly turned back to her acolyte, despite knowing what she was likely to see there. His body still stood with his arms held close to his sides. His left arm suddenly shot straight out toward Voyiv and his outstretched hand clenched into a tight fist.

Voyiv's rifle crumpled in his hands, crushed by an unseen surge of magic. The merc tossed the ruined weapon aside and glared at his target.

Kana quickly looked up and gasped.

Jamyn's head was intact and still firmly attached to his neck. All around it, however, was what looked like a dome of glass, its surface covered by a multitude of fine cracks. He reached up and removed the fractured headpiece.

———————◉———————

"Nice work, Lob," Jamyn said softly before tossing aside the ruined helmet. It broke apart when it hit the ground, and the pieces vanished. Looking to Voyiv, he sighed heavily. "You should go," he said, his words slow and calm.

Voyiv's battered face reddened with rage. "I will have my—"

"What?" Jamyn cut him off, though his voice was still as tranquil as Qa's. "Vengeance? Honor? You don't get it. None of that matters now. A lot of people have died. You didn't. Take that and run. Last chance."

"You would dare to—"

An unseen force shoved Voyiv back nearly to the hallway that led to the outer doors.

"Yeah, there's a good idea," Jamyn muttered, his tone irked at last. "Just keep running your mouth." He picked up and pocketed the null rock and then slowly advanced on the bewildered merc. "I am in no mood to hear it."

"I will—"

A series of punishing surges struck Voyiv, forcing him up the hall in a stumbling retreat.

———◉———

Kana scrambled to her feet and followed Jamyn from a respectable distance, still unsure of how he was attacking the larger man. She scanned Jamyn's body and saw the constant ebb and flow of ambient magic surrounding him. Suddenly he drew a much larger portion of energy to himself, and her steps faltered in apprehension.

———◉———

An intense blast blew the bunker doors open, shredding the reinforced steel like it was tissue paper. Lob, Juushin, and Shamara quickly looked up from their work. In the aftermath of their decisive victory, they had discovered a cloaked ship in the empty field beside the building. The battered troops were gathered next to the formerly invisible vessel. The men and their now decloaked ship were corralled by one of Lob's barriers. Juushin, her armor's magical limiters once again back in place, tapped the transparent wall at random spots as she kept a menacingly close eye on the huddled men. When the bunker's door exploded, however, the trio immediately took up a defensive stance with the two larger fighters standing in front.

"What happened?" Shamara asked as she peeked between them at the gaping hole in the previously impenetrable wall.

"Kana, most likely," Juushin replied.

Voyiv hurtled outside and landed awkwardly in the open field. Jamyn emerged soon after and slowly closed in on the prone merc. Lob and Juushin were just about to rush to his aid when Kana hurried out of the bunker. She quickly held up her hand, silently commanding them to stay put. They quickly nodded their acknowledgment. Kana flexed the fingers of her open hand and made a brief clawing motion.

"Get ready," Lob murmured down to Shamara, translating Kana's signal.

Voyiv struggled to stand, his mind unsteady and his body aching from the repeated blows that had forced him out of the bunker. "How?" His voice was raw with anger. "How do you still live?"

Jamyn stopped his slow advance right in front of the ragged soldier. "I live because she has not given me permission to die," he replied simply. "Your troops have been defeated, but they still live. Your Nihil sorcerers are gone. It's over. Your move."

Voyiv tried to take a step forward, but his body stopped abruptly as if he had just walked into a wall. He reached for Jamyn and his arm's movement was likewise blunted. He bellowed in rage. "What is this?"

"You will not be allowed to harm me or my friends."

"You think you can stop me with your magic?"

"No," Jamyn said with a shake of his head. "The magic will stop you itself."

Voyiv openly scoffed at the young man. "And why would it do that?"

"Because I asked it to."

"I will have justice!"

Jamyn briefly cocked his head to one side and listened intently for a moment. "Yes, you will," he said before straightening up and taking two long steps backward. "Who was Noark to you?" He asked in a loud, clear voice so that everyone gathered in the field could hear it.

Voyiv bared his teeth in a fierce snarl. "Noark was an honorable man. He was my commander and brother. Your master deprived him of his will to live."

"He earned his fate when he killed the mist giants."

"Those creatures were cut down in the natural course of battle!"

Jamyn remained calm, despite the clenched fists he held tightly to his sides. "No. It was done only to demoralize the enemy. To him, they were merely a thing to be used. Hardly the act of an honorable man."

Voyiv punched forward at the unseen force impeding him. "The beasts were sacrificed for the cause of victory. In his place, I would have done the same!" In his rage, he failed to notice that his body was now covered by a rapidly expanding shadow.

Jamyn nodded once. "By your words, let justice be served."

Lester landed with a deafening crash, his bulk smashing Voyiv's body into the ground while jarring Jamyn up off it. The young man regained his footing and looked back at the dragon, who appeared to be quite pleased with himself. Stepping forward, the acolyte ran his hand over Lester's nose.

"You have avenged your family," Jamyn said solemnly.

Lester stamped his feet in excitement and leaned his face into Jamyn's body.

Kana rushed to Jamyn's side, but her attention was on Lester.

"Hey, big guy," she said in surprise while giving the top of his head a firm scratching. "How'd you get here?"

"He came with us," Jamyn said. He waved over the others who were still holding their ground near the captive army. "We repeated the long-range teleport trick that I used to get here the first time." Catching sight of something moving through the tall grass, he pointed to it. "And that's not all we brought."

———— ◉ ————

Kana turned toward the disturbance. A miniature version of Lester bounded happily across the field and straight for them. Her breath caught in her throat as the memory of the slain dragonling from her youth surfaced in her mind. The little one slowed its approach and looked up at her in youthful curiosity.

Lester briefly broke away from their patting and gently nudged his offspring with his nose. They exchanged a few soft grunts and then Lester looked back at Kana. He nudged her chest and then looked down again. The little dragon ambled forward and sat down right in front of her.

She dropped to one knee. "C'mere, you."

The dragon suddenly leaped up, knocking her backwards with a quick head-butt to the chest. She fell to a sitting position and looked back at the little dragon in surprise. Jamyn laughed and his mirth seemed to be shared by both father and child.

"Very funny, guys," she said before laughing along. She snatched the little lizard and vigorously rubbed his tummy, much to his delight.

Lob's deep voice chuckled directly above her. "Does this make you Auntie Kana?"

"Yeah, right," Kana said without looking up. "Hi, Lob."

Shamara giggled. "I think it does."

Kana spun to face the young girl, who was grinning madly at both her and the little dragon in her lap. Kana's anger focused on Jamyn in the next heartbeat. "You brought Shamara?"

"Ease back, Kana," Lob said. "We didn't give him much of a choice in the matter. And she was awesome on her first field assignment."

"She was," Juushin said, coming up behind him. "An effective little warrior. Those men didn't know what hit them."

Lob laughed. "Neither did that wizard!"

"Wizard?" Jamyn asked.

"Yeah. A wizard attacked us after we took care of the army."

"Probably another Nihil," Kana said sourly. "What happened to him?"

"Juushin," Lob replied with a grin. "Let's just say he's cast his last spell. So, everything turned out fine, regardless of how much you want to yell at us!"

Kana harrumphed and shook her head. "Still, I told you all not to come after me and—" Her voice cut off in a sharp gasp. "Hajis-Corol!" she whispered in horror. She quickly removed the little lizard from her lap and scrambled to her feet. "He's still in there." With this, she turned and raced back to the bunker.

"Keep an eye on things," Jamyn said to the others before chasing after her. He called out to her as they ran. "Kana! He said they released him."

Kana stumbled up the hall, the quick transition from full daylight to the shadows of the bunker temporarily robbing her of sight. Once her eyes had adjusted, she raced from room to room, searching for the missing Letronan.

Jamyn hurried to catch up to her. Skidding around a corner, he darted through an open door and nearly collided with Kana. She had stopped after taking only two steps into the small room. Jamyn peeked around her to find Hajis-Corol's mangled body lying in the center of the floor. Vicious cuts and burns marked every part of his corpse. A pool of drying blood surrounded him. Kana tried to say something but was only able to utter a brief squeak. She collapsed back against Jamyn. He held her up, quickly wrapping his arms around her as she started to cry.

"My fault," she whispered between choking sobs.

"Shh." He turned her around and held her close. "It's not. They did this to him."

She weakly thumped a fist against his back. "They did it to get to me. And to you. They found out about you through him."

Suddenly she straightened up and tried to push him away. His grip held and she pounded a fist against his chest as a shard of anger wormed its way past her grief.

"Dammit, Jamyn! Why did you come here?"

"Because I—"

"Shut up," she cried, hitting him again. "I know! I know exactly why, dammit. That's why I told you *not* to. I knew they would kill you to hurt me." Her resolve crumbled and she lunged forward, crushing him in a tight hug.

"Like they ever had a shot at that," Jamyn muttered. "I was going to get you back no matter what it took."

"Stubborn shithead," she mumbled.

He chuckled. "That me or you?"

She squeezed him hard enough to make him seriously believe she was trying to break his spine. "Probably both," she said at last. She loosened her grip and snuggled against him.

He closed his eyes and sighed. "Sorry for making you worry."

She shrugged, bopping him in the jaw with her shoulder in the process. "Part of my job." She rested her cheek on his shoulder. "Thanks for coming to get me." They held each other in silence, their bodies slowly molding to one another.

"Kana?"

"Yeah?"

"Why did that Nihil call me by the wrong name?"

She released a sharp exhalation that weakly passed for a laugh. "Because that's what I told Hajis-Corol it was the first time you were here."

"Huh?"

She took in a deep breath and then let it out slowly to help her calm down. "They swap first and last names, right?"

"Right."

"Well, I was so off-balance by your little revelation"—she pressed a hurried kiss to his cheek—"that I goofed up when he asked me. Started to say your first name and then gave him the proper form. It ended up being Jamsiska-Jamyn instead of Siska-Jamyn."

"You didn't correct him?"

"Couldn't. Letronans take names very seriously. Whatever they hear the first time you tell them is what they remember forever. You were always gonna be Jamsiska-Jamyn to them, no matter what I said after that."

"Huh." He considered her story for a moment and then smiled. "Thanks for getting it wrong."

She gave his shin a gentle swipe with her foot. "You're lucky I did. If that Nihil had landed that spell, you would've been fucked."

Jamyn made a small, worried noise. "Definitely a good thing, then." He stroked her back and lowered his voice to a whisper. "You do it much better."

Kana's head snapped up off his shoulder and she stared into his wide eyes. He was just about to apologize for his ill-timed joke when she lunged forward and landed a bruising kiss on his lips. He enthusiastically returned it, taking a second to steady himself after her attack. The kiss softened and deepened, each of them giving themselves fully to the other. He pulled away finally, despite his desire to continue.

"We should get back out there. Clean things up and then get everybody back home."

"Home," she said, fondly running a hand along his cheek. "I'd like that."

"C'mon." He pulled her toward the door. She went willingly, lacing her fingers with his and walking beside him.

———◉———

Shamara saw the pair, now walking hand-in-hand, exit the bunker.

"They're coming back," she whispered excitedly.

Lob gave her a stern look. "Tone it down, my little matchmaker. They've both had a *really* tough day. You can tease them to your heart's content when we get back home."

"But only if you're suddenly allergic to living," Juushin said. "Settled down or not, Kana's not likely to put up with that for long."

Shamara's face sobered. "I'm sorry, Miss Juushin. I was just—"

"Playing around," the larger woman finished for her. "No problem. Just remember that some people are sensitive when it comes to matters of the heart." She glanced over and Lob abruptly broke away from the adoring gaze he had trained upon her.

Shamara also noticed his hasty withdrawal and she smiled. "I think you're right," she said softly, giving Juushin a quick wink.

———◉———

Kana and Jamyn finally reached the trio. Lester and his offspring were now off in the distance and appeared to be preparing a new nest.

"Setting up new digs, I see," Kana said.

"This is his home," Jamyn said. "Phase dragons must have an innate bond to this place. That's why Lester got so crabby when we sent him back to the wilds. Something kept pulling him here."

Kana looked to the dragons with a fond smile. "Then the prophecy has been fulfilled."

The others looked back at her in confusion.

"When the phase dragons were wiped out, I wished that they would someday return here. Looks like some day's today."

"Adding yet another chapter to the growing legend of Kana Morel," Lob said in an overly dramatic drone.

Kana frowned at him before turning her attention to Shamara and Juushin. "Ladies? Sic 'im!"

The pair grinned at one another before pouncing. Shamara hit Lob with a push, driving him back into Juushin's waiting arms.

Juushin quickly latched on to him and pinned his arms to his sides. "You know what comes next, big boy."

Lob suddenly looked worried. "No! Don't you dare."

Shamara reached up and started to tickle him mercilessly. He howled with laughter and yanked against Juushin's solid grip.

Kana finally intervened. "All right, you two. Hold your fire. You can finish him off when we get back home."

They reluctantly released him, and he hurried several steps away to avoid another attack.

"You two are in *so* much trouble," Lob told the smiling pair. Turning to Kana, he jerked a thumb back toward the mercenary army. "Speaking of trouble, what should we do with yonder goon squad?"

"We'll deal with them after we check in. I'm guessing Qa and the others are busy freaking out by now. How long will your barrier hold up if you leave?"

"One that big? Only for a few minutes." Lob turned to Jamyn. "How'd the helmet work for you, by the way?"

"Since my head is still here, I'd say it did great," Jamyn replied. "Thanks. I owe you huge for that."

"Nah. Keeping your head around might help me find out more about Priest. Worth it at twice the price."

"Still, I *will* pay you back." He looked to the others. "All of you. Thanks for helping us out today."

Shamara beamed at him. "You're welcome, Mister Jamyn."

"No problem," Juushin said with a shrug of her broad shoulders. "Didn't have anything else on my itinerary today anyway."

"On to the next problem," Kana said. She looked up at the sky to analyze the Nihil's scrambling field and poked Jamyn's side. "Hey, Stage Three. What do you make of it?"

He tuned his eyesight so that he could perceive the swirls of energy isolating the planet. "Hmm," he said as he pondered the chaotic patterns. "Looks like a greater dispel should be enough to break it, but..." His voice trailed off.

"But?"

He faced her. "It might be able to put itself back together after the dispel ceases."

"Very good, acolyte," Kana said, trying to sound like the wise teacher. "It looks like it's self-healing. That thing could be a *real* pain in the butt." She sighed heavily. "Unless, of course, I had someone here who could nullify the energy once I break down its structure." She took a step closer to him and looked down into his eyes. "Know anybody?" she whispered.

"The Soul Flame breaks the wall," he replied softly.

"And the Scatter sweeps away the pieces," she whispered back.

He smiled. "Sounds good, mistress."

Kana raised her voice without pulling away from him. "Not a word, you three!" In the next heartbeat, the two came together in a brief but heated kiss. Coming apart again, they turned to the others and Kana put her hands on her hips. "Well?"

"Huh? See what?" Lob asked while his gaze idly wandered across the field.

"Didn't see a thing," Juushin said with another shrug. "Shammie?"

The girl was a mere hair's breadth away from dissolving into a fit of giggles. "I might have," she said in a brief squeak.

Lob snatched her up off the ground and poked her midsection. "You *really* must be tired of breathing," he said despite her squeals.

She gasped and tried to catch her breath. "I'm sorry! I didn't see anything."

"All right. Knock it off, you two," Kana said sternly despite her smile. She looked straight up and asked Jamyn, "Ready?"

"Ready."

Together they raised their hands to the sky. Kana's spell swiftly tore through the wild surges of magic blocking their way. Jamyn directed each shattered fragment to disperse harmlessly into the background. In less than a minute, the barrier was annihilated. They brought their hands back down and nodded to one another.

"And that there's how it's done," she said quietly in her native accent.

Chapter Twenty-One: Consequences

The entire area exploded with activity. Magical gates suddenly appeared all around them. Groups of casters, each led by a member of the Inner Cabal, leaped from each gate before quickly taking up an attack stance. In seconds, the field was blanketed with mages, all of them ready to strike.

Kana and Jamyn spun all around, taking in the busy scene, before looking at each other again.

"Oh, sure," Kana said loudly so everyone gathered could hear. "*Now* they show up." Their little group started laughing raucously, much to the surprise of their supposed saviors.

Qa hurried over to them. "Am I to understand you've already got things here under control?" he asked Kana. The rest of the Inner Cabal quickly gathered behind him.

"More or less," she replied, settling down again. "Got a few dozen mercs and their ship over there." She pointed across the field at the confined men. "Got a squashed merc leader a few paces back that way." She gestured to the bloody smear on the ground.

"And a wizard in a similar state somewhere over there," Lob said, jerking a thumb back over his shoulder.

"And finally, we've got the next generation of mist giants setting up shop over in the Sacred Fields." She made a grand sweeping gesture to the lizards off in the distance.

"Hajis-Corol's body is in the bunker," Jamyn said in a more subdued tone. "We should alert the Letronans and return him to them."

Qa scanned the entire field before turning his attention back to the group and scrutinizing each face. His inspection ended and he asked, "Any injuries to report?"

Kana shrugged. "Nothing a bit of rest and a stiff drink couldn't cure."

Qa nodded and then turned to the cabal. "Tiris and Leel, please tend to the soldiers. They appear to have had a difficult day. Fangs, check out Lester and his new child. Daystar, to the bunker and Hajis-Corol. Donta and Vines, perimeter check." He raised one hand and cast a spell that sealed off the entire valley. "That will prevent the Letronans from detecting us prematurely. Everyone to their tasks."

They dispersed in seconds, each to their given assignment.

Lob hurried after the healers. "I'll let you into the playpen," he said as he lumbered along. Shamara ran along with him while Juushin went off to help wrangle the rest of the casters.

"You drew *team leader* duties this time around, huh?" Kana asked Qa.

He shook his head. "The others decided that long before we got here, likely due to my ties to the both of you. What has happened here?"

Kana poked Jamyn. "Field report, acolyte."

Jamyn launched into it. "Both Hajis-Corol and Kana were taken by mercenaries led by a man named Voyiv. He said he was brother to Noark."

"The mercenary leader that Kana defeated." Qa nodded. "This was meant to avenge his brother's death?"

"Not his death but the way he died, apparently."

"For honor, then."

"Sort of. He wanted to inflict the same fate upon Kana. Destroy her will to live before finally killing her."

"But to do that, he needed to find something I cared about," Kana said. She sighed and muttered, "Or *someone*."

"Then his intent was to—"

"Lure me here," Jamyn replied. "Yeah. I played right into his hands."

"Despite my direct order that you not intervene," Qa gently reminded him. "How were you able to disrupt his plans?"

Kana laughed, breaking her brief melancholy. "Nice choice of words, Qa. The disruption was provided by our latest declared caster." She jerked a thumb at Jamyn.

Qa's eyes widened. "Jamyn declared?"

Kana put an arm around her acolyte. "Say hello to the Scatter." She thought a moment then grinned at Jamyn. "Is it *the Scatter* or just *Scatter*?"

"I dunno," he mumbled, trying to worm his way out of her grip.

Qa looked over his former students. "The Soul Flame and the Scatter," he said, pride shining in his pleased smile.

"Eww." Kana stuck out her tongue as if she had eaten something sour. "Sounds like a bargain bin comic book."

"Can I design your outfit?" Jamyn asked, bumping his hip against hers.

Qa raised a hand to her before she could retaliate. "First, I would like to hear exactly what he did."

Kana released Jamyn, but not before giving him a playful dig in the ribs. "Later, you."

"You bet," he replied softly.

"Anyhoo," she said, raising her voice, "he took on Voyiv by himself."

"Where were the others?"

"Outside the bunker," Jamyn said. "They dealt with the mercenary army and a wizard."

"And did a heck of a job, by the look of it," Kana said. "So yeah, Jamyn and Voyiv went at it for a while. Kid was doing pretty well until one of the Nihil attacked him."

"Then they did use the Nihil again," Qa said in a grim tone. "I thought that after the last time—"

"Voyiv was acting on his own, so it's not surprising that he employed his late brother's methods. He had five of them total. They all got toasted. I got one, Juushin got one, and Jamyn nailed the other three."

"You defeated three Nihil by yourself?" Qa asked the acolyte in surprise. "Without your magic?"

"Yeah, he did 'em up good." Kana answered for him. "I finally got my act together enough to take out the first one—"

"By doubling-up on that restoration potion," Jamyn said in an admonishing tone.

She frowned at his assessment. "By doing something stupid, like I always do. The potion got me back on my feet again but then the magical overload nearly took me apart. Jamyn jumped in and dispersed the excess magic before it could kill me. After that, the other three attacked us and he wiped 'em out. Pulled in their spells and then returned 'em to sender. That's when he declared."

"Then his willcasting is his ability to both disassemble and then reassemble magical energy," Qa said. "Very much like what the reality wielders do with the fabric of space and time."

Kana eyed her acolyte. "Yeah, now that you mention it. That's exactly what he does."

Jamyn squirmed under their admiring gazes. "Um...ta-daa," he said weakly. He spread his hands out to his sides.

"*Ta-daa*, my ass," Kana replied. "You do realize that when word of this gets around, your butt is gonna have a big ol' bullseye on it."

"I would also advise discretion," Qa said. "We will have to tell the Inner Cabal, of course. They will be sworn to secrecy, but we must assume that it will get out sooner or later. That level of innate magical manipulation is bound to attract attention before too long."

"Already has," Kana said. "Kat, the lizard demon, the Aqiri." She counted them off on her fingers. "This would explain the warning Kat gave us back in the wilds."

To emphasize her point, a folded note suddenly appeared in her hand. Opening it, she read its message aloud. "Always knew you were a bright one. You two be careful. And congratulate the kid for me." The note was signed with a roughly scrawled *K* and three diagonal slashes. Shoving the note into an inner pocket of her robes, she sighed. "And there we have it. My acolyte is now the universe's flavor of the month."

"Yay me," Jamyn said after a brief wince.

"You'll be fine, Mister Siska," Qa said. "Remember that you'll have Kana to guide you." Turning to her, he said, "And you'll have *him* to keep you from doing silly things in the process."

Kana turned to Jamyn to find him smiling back at her. "Well, he can try, I guess," she muttered before returning his smile.

Jamyn was just about to speak when he stopped abruptly. Turning to Qa, he said, "Tiris wants—"

"Master Qa?" Tiris asked through a converse spell.

Qa glanced up at the sound of voice and then looked back at Jamyn. "Yes, Mistress Tiris?" he replied.

"The comms system in their ship just started chiming. I've got a nice young man here who says he's now the ranking officer. He wants to answer the phone. What do you think? Should I let him?"

Qa looked in turn at both Kana and Jamyn. "I think we all may want to speak to whoever is on the other end. One moment." He gestured and the three were instantly teleported to just outside the ship's open hatch where Tiris and a man were standing. He jerked away from the newcomers in fright. Tiris merely smiled at their sudden arrival.

She playfully scolded Qa. "Now stop that. I don't want to have to restart his heart."

"My apologies to both of you," Qa said with a polite nod. Facing the soldier, he said, "I am Qa Shon. And you are?"

The man stood at attention. "I am Hsinoh. I am in command of this order now that Voyiv is dead."

"Is that gonna be a problem?" Kana asked pointedly.

"It will not. My former commander's will is not mine."

"Then what *is* your intent?" Jamyn asked.

"To take my men back to the guild for whatever awaits us."

"I think we may be able to help with that," Qa said. "Tiris said your communications system requires your attention." He looked for the small healer, but she had scampered off and was now working beside Leel.

"It does, sir."

"Then let us go see what they want." He gestured for the man to precede them.

They followed him into the ship where Hsinoh sat before a large screen. Manipulating the controls, he opened a channel. The scowling face of an irate man appeared on the screen.

"Second Hsinoh," the man said angrily. "Where is Voyiv?"

"He has been killed, Guild Head Dullk," Hsinoh replied, a slight tremble in his voice.

"By whom?"

"He was crushed to death by a gigantic reptile."

"Reptile? One of the Letronan mist giants escaped destruction?"

Kana swung in behind Hsinoh. "It had help." She lowered her voice to a growl. "I trust you know who I am."

"I assume you are the one that Voyiv believed responsible for destroying Noark and his order," Dullk replied calmly.

"Both you and he are correct. I am Kana Morel, the Soul Flame. I attacked those men after their genocidal attack on the mist giants. One of the returned giants has killed Voyiv. So where do we go from here, Guild Head?"

"What of the remainder of Voyiv's, now Hsinoh's, order?"

"Your soldiers suffered minor losses. Our healers are repairing the wounds they received while under Voyiv's command. We are prepared to return them to you."

"The Nihil?"

Jamyn stepped into view beside her. "They were destroyed."

"And you are?"

"Jamyn Siska, the Scatter. Acolyte of Kana Morel."

Dullk carefully considered the younger man. "My thanks for removing those horrid creatures. They are unnatural and do not represent our guild in any way."

Kana gave Jamyn a sideways glare to encourage him to hold his tongue. "Do we have any further issue here, Guild Head?"

"We do not," Dullk replied. "Voyiv was not acting per my wishes or those of the guild. He wanted to bring justice to the one he believed had robbed Noark of his honor. He neglected to consider that Noark's death was gained through a dishonorable act."

"Agreed," Kana said. "You will not pursue myself or anyone from the Sanctum beyond this?"

"Not without a binding contract, one which I would be reluctant to accept. I have no interest in challenging the Sanctum's army."

Kana arched an eyebrow at him. "Army?"

"The one that defeated Voyiv's order."

She shot him a thin smile. "There were five of us. One was a young girl."

Dullk's heavy brow bobbed upwards for the merest shred of a second. "All the more reason not to challenge you without a contract. Further, the pursuit of personal vendettas is a profitless venture."

"That is good to hear, Guild Head Dullk," Qa said, coming forward at last. "I am Qa Shon of the Sanctum. There is one other matter. A Letronan soldier named Hajis-Corol was killed by your men."

Kana corrected him. "By the Nihil, under Voyiv's direction."

Dullk clenched his jaw and silently seethed at the screen for a moment. "Unacceptable," he finally replied with a snarl. His expression calmed after a concerted effort, and he nodded gravely. "I will contact the Letronans personally. Proper reparations will be made to his family and his people."

"I thank you, Guild Head," Qa said with a bow of respect. "If there is nothing further, we will prepare your men for departure."

"I await their return, Qa Shon," Dullk said. His stern gaze darted from face to face, finally coming to rest on Jamyn. The pair stared at each other in silence, their stony expressions not betraying a flicker of their respective thoughts. Hsinoh pressed a button, and the screen went blank.

"I think Voyiv got off easy," Jamyn said quietly.

Kana's brow furrowed. "How's that?"

"He only got squashed by Lester. I'm guessing that his boss would have been much less pleasant about it if he had made it back home."

Hsinoh unexpectedly chimed in. "Agreed. The Guild Head would have been very unforgiving with Voyiv, even if he had succeeded." The others turned to him, and he continued. "Voyiv took the order into this venture without a binding contract. That alone infuriated the Head. Voyiv was a dead man in every possible outcome."

"Then why follow him?" Jamyn asked.

Hsinoh straightened up in his seat, his pride obviously stung. "We are mercenaries of the Guild of Dullk. We follow to the end."

"No offense intended, Hsinoh," Qa said. "Mister Siska here has his own issues with loyalty and following orders."

"Yeah, he's dim like that," Kana said. She snagged Jamyn's arm and pulled him toward the ship's open hatch. "Let's go, acolyte."

They all exited the ship to find things well in order. Leel and a few other medics were finishing up the last of the injured soldiers, despite playful protests from Lob.

"Now this one I know was shooting right at me!" Lob wagged a giant finger down at the man Leel was currently working on.

"And where did he hit you?" Leel asked patiently while he completed a spell to mend the man's broken leg. He helped the soldier stand up and then watched as the grateful man tested it for strength and lingering pain.

"Um, well. He didn't actually—" Lob threw his hands in the air. "Not the point! At least give him a limp for a few days."

"A limp, you say?" Leel asked. "Well, I suppose that's simple enough." He turned to Shamara and pointed at Lob's shin. "Kick hard right about *there*," he told her. "That should get him hobbling around to his satisfaction."

Shamara giggled and launched herself at Lob.

He evaded her initial kick and then hopped away from her repeated attempts. "Hey! Cut it out," he cried, stumbling away from the main group.

Leel smiled at the show and then hugged Tiris who had bounded to his side.

"Finished, my love?" he asked.

"All ready to return to active duty," she said. She leaned close to his ear and giggled. "I'm ready for *extended* duty myself!"

"I would ask for a brief delay in your plans, Mistress Tiris," Qa said.

She pouted. "Aww. You're no fun."

Qa smiled and cast a mass converse spell. "All members of the Inner Cabal, please gather near the bunker." His voice resounded from several different places across the field. "All others, you may return to the Sanctum when ready." He canceled the spell and then faced Hsinoh. "Assemble your men. We'll just be a moment." Turning to Jamyn, he said, "Collect your little band of commandos. The cabal would like a word with you all." With this, he swept Kana away before she could speak to her acolyte.

Tiris and Leel looked at each other and then up at Jamyn. "Good luck, lad," Leel said before hurrying off with his wife.

———— ◉ ————

Lob had overhead Qa's command and walked up behind Jamyn. Shamara followed close behind him.

"I'm guessing we're all in trouble now, huh?" Lob asked.

Jamyn looked up at him. "No way. You guys aren't taking any of the rap for this. This was all my doing."

"But Mister Jamyn—" Shamara said, clearly concerned for him.

"I said no!" Jamyn's outburst made her back away in fright. He immediately regretted his brusque tone and forced a smile. "Don't worry about me, you two. Kana's okay. That's all that matters. Worst they can do is kick me out, right?"

"Who's getting kicked out?" Juushin asked as she approached the group. She had noticed the small gathering while the other casters were filing into the exit gates to take them back to the Sanctum. Now she towered over Jamyn.

"Hopefully no one," Jamyn replied, patting one massive metal arm. As before, the simple contact set off a whirl of visions within his mind. This time, however, they revealed several details they hadn't the first time. Jamyn took a quick step back and then stared up at Juushin in awe.

"You okay?" Lob asked.

Jamyn swung his head back and forth, looking at each of them in turn. He finally wrestled his mind back under control and nodded. "Yeah. Yeah, I'm fine." He looked Juushin's armored suit up and down, his eyes wide with wonder.

"Another weird feeling?" Juushin asked carefully.

Jamyn shook his head. "Nah. Just loving the suit."

She shrugged her massive shoulders. "It does the job."

"You really wear it well."

"Doesn't she, though?" Lob laughed. "She moves like someone a tenth of her size."

Just about.

Qa's voice sounded above them all. "Please join us, Mister Siska. Bring your team."

"Team?" Lob asked.

Jamyn chuckled, trying his best to keep the mood light. "Sure. Huddle up." They gathered into a loose circle, and he dropped to one knee. He gestured several times with his right index finger as if he was drawing up a play on the matted grass. "Okay. Let's run the old *please don't chuck my dumb ass out of the Sanctum* play. On three. Ready? Break!" He clapped his hands together once and sprang to his feet before starting off toward the bunker at a brisk pace. The others hurried along behind him.

Lob hoisted Shamara up and set her on his shoulder as they walked. "Rah, rah, rah. Go team, go," he muttered.

"They wouldn't kick him out, would they?" she asked quietly.

"Not if they know what's good for 'em," Lob replied with a low grumble.

"Easy there, killer," Juushin said, laying one huge hand on his empty shoulder. "The cabal didn't get where they are by making stupid decisions."

Lob sighed. "Dunno about that. They still keep me around."

"Like I said."

For emphasis, she gave him a quick pat on the butt. His enormous body jerked in surprise. He quickly regained his composure, though his steps took on a livelier bounce. Shamara stifled a giggle as Juushin gave her a quick nod.

The group stopped before the cabal, who had arranged themselves in a line standing shoulder to shoulder. Jamyn took an additional step forward from the group while Lob stood Shamara back on the ground.

"You four have got some explaining to do," Qa said in a solemn tone.

"I alone am responsible for what happened here today," Jamyn said, his voice deadly serious. "I request that no action be taken against Arms Master Juushin, Lob the Unmarred, or Shamara."

"I don't recall saying anything about actions, Mister Siska."

Jamyn's confidence took a solid hit.

He isn't addressing me as acolyte anymore. Looks like I'm on my way out.

He risked a quick look at Kana. She stood beside Qa with an indecipherable look etched into her passive face. "I am sorry, Master Qa. Please continue."

"You four took it upon yourselves to come here and then not only engage the enemy but defeat them handily. You did this without thought to your own safety, the safety of First Seer Morel, or the potential repercussions of your failure."

"But we got the job done," Juushin said quietly.

"And looked damned good doing it," Lob said while dramatically running his fingers back through his short brown hair. "In for a penny and all that," he whispered to Juushin out of the corner of his mouth.

"Kana needed our help!" Shamara blurted, much to everyone's surprise. She looked around, as everyone's eyes were now trained on her, and nodded once emphatically. "We had to try."

"You didn't *try*, my dear," Fangs replied with a toothy grin. "You *did*. Well done, all of you." Seeing Qa looking down the line at him, he lifted his hands in surrender. "Sorry. Your show." He stood up straight and looked forward with only a few small chuckles escaping from within his bushy beard.

Qa smiled and faced the group. "As it happens, Varondis-Mai speaks for all of us. Indeed, a job well done."

Donta spoke up. "But one that must not be allowed to pass unnoticed."

Daystar chimed in beside him. "Agreed, Master Donta. There are certain ramifications to your actions that must be addressed."

Jamyn's stomach tightened. He looked to Kana for some glimmer of support but found only a blank expression. He swallowed hard and bowed to the cabal. "I am ready to receive your judgment."

Qa nodded. "Your earlier request will be granted. No actions will be taken against the others. This is for you alone, Mister Siska. Now, I believe a listing of the facts is in order."

"You gathered a force to move against an enemy of unknown strength and ability," Vynael said in his usual drone.

"You transported said force to a distant planet despite it being shielded against magical gates," Leel said.

Tiris spoke up after a quick nudge from Leel. "You utilized abilities far beyond your rank in the rescue of First Seer Kana Morel."

Donta growled softly within his cowl. "And you did all of this without access to your magic. Yet, despite your inability to cast, you also were somehow able to declare, something only one other before you has managed to do at your level." He glanced toward Kana but received absolutely no acknowledgment in return.

"Do you have anything to say on your behalf?" Qa asked.

Jamyn nodded. "Just one thing." He looked to his likely soon-to-be former master. "I'm glad you're okay, Kana."

Her only response was a slight tightening of her cheeks as she clenched her jaw.

"Very well," Qa said. "It is the decision of the Inner Cabal of the Sanctum that Jamyn Siska be—"

A brief squeak of alarm from Shamara stopped him.

"You have something more to say?" Qa asked her and her companions.

"Finish your sentence." Lob cracked the knuckles of each of his hands in turn. "*Then* we'll let you know if we have a response." He nudged Juushin's side, and she nodded as their bodies tensed to strike.

"Very well. Jamyn Siska, you are hereby"—Qa risked a quick glance at the two imposing giants—"promoted to the rank of hierophant."

"Oh, that is a total load of bull—" Lob said angrily before Qa's words fully registered in his mind. He stopped abruptly and looked at the others.

Juushin had taken a step back as if she had been staggered by a stunning blow.

Shamara clapped her hands over her mouth and stared at the proceedings with wide eyes.

Lob looked down at Jamyn's shocked face. "Wait. What'd he say?"

Fangs released a clipped burst of laughter.

"He said shut up, you big dummy," Jamyn told Lob in a disbelieving whisper. "I've been promoted!"

The reality of his situation hit home, and Jamyn's heart swiftly sank.

I'm a hierophant. That means I'm not Kana's acolyte anymore.

His body went numb as a relentless flood of sadness enveloped him.

"There is one further item to address!"

The sharp statement was so filled with anger Jamyn automatically turned to face Donta.

The seer's carved mask glanced in his direction for no more than a second before turning away again.

Jamyn's brain clicked back on, and he shifted his attention to the one who had actually spoken: his former master. Kana had abandoned her blank expression and was now staring daggers at him. "There is?" he asked her.

She snarled in reply. "There is. Hierophant Siska was under direct orders from not one but *two* members of the Inner Cabal. Under no circumstances was he to attempt to rescue me."

"Orders from whom, exactly?" Daystar asked.

"Well, I *did* tell him that he would not be allowed to gate out of the Sanctum until we had secured Kana's freedom," Qa said with some hesitation. "I suppose that would qualify."

Kana nodded abruptly. "And in the message that I was allowed to send back to the Sanctum, I made it *very* clear that no one was to try to rescue me. On top of that, I had previously told him that if he ever followed me when I told him not to, I would kill him." Kana scanned up and down the line of cabal members. "That official enough for you?"

"Yeah, that's pretty cut and dried," Leel said. Tiris swatted him and he shrugged at her follow-up glare.

"Very well, First Seer," Qa said with a resigned sigh. "I leave it to you to decide his punishment."

A faint glow outlined her body. "Hierophant Siska. For disobeying direct orders and for a general lack of brains, I hereby demote you one full rank!"

Jamyn stared at her in stunned silence as her aura slowly faded. A giant hand slapping his back finally broke him from his trance.

Lob laughed down at him. "Congrats, kid. You're an acolyte again."

"Acolyte," Jamyn said in a faint whisper as a glimmer of hope ignited in his heart.

"The next obvious order of business is deciding who gets to train this little troublemaker." Judging by Kana's tone, her anger was not yet sated. "Given his discipline record, his proven issues with authority, and an overall lack of control, I believe there is only one real option for his new master. Donta!"

Both Donta and Jamyn jolted to attention at the name.

"What?" Jamyn gasped under his breath in sheer disbelief.

Donta slowly swung his head to face Kana. "First Seer?"

Kana cracked a cruel smile. "I'm taking him as *my* acolyte. You got any problems with that?"

Donta faced forward again. "I do not," he replied solidly, despite the hint of amusement escaping from behind his mask.

"Anyone else?" Kana said in a rough shout.

The others all looked at each other, most of them shaking their heads and trying not to laugh.

"No," Fangs said for the group. "I think we can all live with that."

Kana turned to Jamyn and snapped at him. "Acolyte Siska! I am your new master. That means I tell you what to do and when to do it. I talk and you shut the hell up. You get me, rookie?"

Jamyn nodded and quickly wiped away the tear that rolled down his cheek. "Sounds good, mistress," he replied with a smile. Realizing what he had just said, his smile vanished in an instant. "I—"

It was too late. Kana had already stomped over to him and now stood with her face a mere inch from his.

"What did you say?" she asked in a low, dangerous rumble.

Looking into her dark eyes, he detected the faintest glimmer of mischief. Taking a chance, he replied, "Mistress."

She considered his anxious face for a moment before smiling.

"You got that right," she whispered so only he could hear. "One last thing," she said loudly. "I'm sure by now you've all had some inkling, but just to make it crystal clear." She grabbed two handfuls of Jamyn's shirt and planted a firm kiss on his lips.

"Can I get an order of that to go?" Tiris giggled her question into Leel's ear loud enough for those around her to hear. Most of the others chuckled at her joke.

"Unless you have yet *another* point to make, First Seer, I trust we are finished here?" Qa asked.

Kana pulled away from the kiss and nodded with a breathless chuckle.

"Yeah, Qa," she said back to him and the others while she stared into Jamyn's eyes. "I think we're done."

"'Bout time." Fangs grumbled in faked annoyance. "A man could die of thirst standing around like this."

"You poor thing," Daystar exclaimed, tousling his wild hair. "I'm sure Evrok will help you with that if you promise not to cause him any undue trouble."

"I'll do my best!" He laughed and gave her quick wink. "Wanna check out Lester and his new progeny first? I don't want to leave without saying goodbye." She nodded and they hurried off toward the Sacred Fields.

The others started to disperse as well. Vynael and the healers used their return glyphs, opening doorways back to the Sanctum. Donta shuffled back toward the captive army, most of them now animatedly talking with one another about the strange proceedings they had just witnessed.

Qa walked up to Lob, Juushin, and Shamara. "Well, Lob?" Qa asked. "Are you still going to hit me?"

"Me?" Lob replied, aghast at the suggestion. "No! I'm not gonna hit anybody." He looked to Juushin and grinned. "That's *her* job."

"Oh, so now I get to fight your battles for you?" she asked, hands on her hips.

"You two looked really mad before," Shamara said quietly.

Lob gasped loudly at the young girl's observation. "Mad? Us? No. We were just—"

"They were just looking out for Jamyn, I'm sure," Qa said with a smile.

"Returning the favor, more like," Juushin said. "He put himself right in the line of fire to keep the hammer from coming down on all of us."

"Oh, that's still happening," Qa replied lightly. He smiled at their surprised faces. "You will all receive special commendations for your roles in today's events. From what I've heard so far, you have all done exceptionally well."

"Yeah, well," Lob said, looking away as he rubbed the back of his neck with one massive hand. "Shammie did most of the heavy lifting."

"She certainly did," Juushin said, giving Lob a playful poke in the side. "Tell you what. I'll buy the first round, and we can tell Master Qa all about it."

"I would especially like to hear how our newest recruit performed," Qa said, patting the young girl's shoulder. She replied with a bashful smile. He gestured and the group disappeared.

Kana hugged Jamyn tightly and rested her head on his shoulder. "I'm still mad at you, you know," she muttered into his ear.

"I know," he whispered back. "I'm hoping it'll pass."

"You were a complete lunatic, coming here like you did."

"I couldn't sit back in the Sanctum and do nothing."

"Yeah. You just had to do the whole knight in shining"—she rapped her knuckles against his chest—"um, impact training suit thing."

They chuckled together and he gave her a quick peck on the cheek.

"Seriously, though," she said, her voice subdued. "You all risked so much for me."

"You're worth it," he murmured, running the fingers of his left hand up through her short hair. "Besides, I can't imagine going on without you in my life."

She nodded and closed her eyes. "Me neither," she mumbled against the side of his neck before kissing it.

Jamyn smiled in silence until he felt someone poking his arm. He shooed whoever it was away with a quick flick of his hand and rubbed Kana's back.

"I love you, Kana," he whispered.

She pulled away enough to see his face and nodded in silent reply as tears filled her eyes. He shushed her before coming forward to kiss her tenderly. Again, he felt someone poking his arm.

"Dammit, Path," he grumbled out of the corner of his mouth, his lips still pressed to Kana's. "Knock it the hell off!"

Kana laughed, abruptly breaking their kiss. "What?"

Looking back over her shoulder, she laughed again when Path waved at her enthusiastically.

Kana faced Jamyn again. "What does she want?"

He sighed. "I think they're carrying Hajis-Corol out now. We should probably get over there."

Kana nodded, her smile fading. "Yeah, we should. Thanks, Path."

Path giggled and then rejoined Jamyn's mind. He shivered as she did, drawing a brief chuckle from Kana.

"After that, it's back to the Sanctum."

He nodded. "Yeah."

She brought her cheek to rest against his. "Dunno about you, but I could use a week-long nap."

He nodded again, enjoying the feel of her skin against his. "Me too, mistress," he softly replied.

"And I'd really love to fall asleep in your arms."

He had no time to ponder her words as she had snared his mouth in an all-encompassing kiss. She let her hands roam freely over his body, from his back and down his sides before bringing them around front to skim over the beginnings of a thunderous erection. He held her face in his hands before running his fingers back through her hair. Suddenly she pulled away from the loose hold and took several skipping steps toward the bunker.

"Get a move on, acolyte," she called back to him. "We've got things to do!"

"We certainly do," he whispered to himself as he ran one hand over his face.

Something tickled his nose, and he brushed it away before hurrying after Kana. A single piece of hair fell from his fingertips and the bright red strand fluttered away on the gentle breeze.

The End

Distil Arcanum III

A *ddendum list of spells, abilities and concepts commonly used in the Sanctum and beyond*

―――――●―――――

Blocking – utility spell that can be used to stop the spread of foreign substances (such as poisons) within the casters body.

Declare – occurrence during which a caster's true nature reveals itself. Usually, a declaration is spontaneously triggered during a stressful event. Only magic users of a very high skill level can declare. An additional name for the caster, related to their newly exposed nature, can sometimes accompany the declaration.

Elemental (or Environmental) Screen – utility spell that will protect the caster (along with their clothing or equipment, if desired) from one of the classical elements (air, water, earth, fire).

Privacy – utility spell that will prevent sound from traveling beyond a certain boundary around the caster. All speakers within the spell's area of effect are affected. Anyone outside this area will be unable to see the mouths of the speakers clearly, preventing the reading of the lips.

Restorative – potion composed mainly of distilled life force (chi). When taken at the proper dosage, the potion can heal most wounds, clear the body of toxins, and restore life to those on the brink of death. Imbibing too much of a restorative potion will result in an imbalance in the patient's own life force, resulting in a cascade of magic that will alternate between healing and destroying the subject's body in a perpetual cycle.

Recommended Listening

After the completion of the Kana/Jamyn trilogy, I happened upon several songs that caught the spirit of the characters I had created. This wasn't surprising, as the series itself was birthed from a single word in a song, but I was struck by how well they explained things I had struggled to.

———◈———

Much thanks to Amaranthe, Within Temptation, and Halestorm for these bits of after-the-fact inspiration.

———◈———

Kana's theme – "Invincible" by Amaranthe. *The Nexus* (2013) Spinefarm
This song captures Kana's pre-Jamyn essence – she is a force of nature, completely unstoppable.

———◈———

Kana/Jamyn theme – "Whole World Is Watching" by Within Temptation. *Hydra* (2014) Nuclear Blast America
Beginning of the end of Kana's solitary existence. The walls around her carefully structured world have been breached and Jamyn is looking back at her from the other side.

———◈———

Acceptance – "Beautiful With You" by Halestorm. *The Strange Case Of...* (2012) Atlantic

Kana's transformation continues. She accepts Jamyn's love and finally believes herself to be worthy of it. She sees herself through his eyes and realizes for the first time that she is indeed beautiful.

Don't miss out!

Visit the website below and you can sign up to receive emails whenever B.K. Bilicki publishes a new book. There's no charge and no obligation.

https://books2read.com/r/B-A-LOKOB-MOLDF

BOOKS 2 READ

Connecting independent readers to independent writers.

Also by B.K. Bilicki

Voices of the Sanctum
Stage One: Hear
Stage Two: Speak
Stage Three: Be

About the Author

Writer? Who, me? There must be some mistake...

In real life, I'm an electronics technician residing in the frozen tundra of the American Midwest. I spend a truly obscene amount of my time peering through a microscope at tiny whiz-bangy components and then performing arcane rituals upon them with a soldering iron. I was deemed a miracle worker early on in my career, and co-workers throughout the ages have been rather intent on making me live up to their ridiculous expectations. It pays the bills, I suppose.

Meanwhile, back at the writing thing...

My entire academic life was centered around a very simple premise – *the kid can't write*. Nope. Forget it. Give me a subject to write about and my brain goes into instant and irrevocable shutdown mode. *Werds? Whassat?*

That core tenet was shaken by an odd series of events involving an ungodly hideous short story (written by someone else), the foolish belief that even *I* could scribble something better, and an out-of-control tractor trailer that attempted to flatten me during a sleet storm. Stir all that up, give it a few days, and a weird little snippet came into being that I thought was interesting enough but not something I'd ever get in the habit of producing in mass quantities.

I posted the bit online, and it got what I considered to be an astonishing number of responses. It was the start of what became a disturbing pattern – post a little one-off short story, people start yelling and screaming "but what happens next?", and it somehow snowballs into a book.

Somewhere between bouts of electronic microsurgery and banging my head against the keyboard, I also cocreated a researcher, a wild man with occasional auto mechanic tendencies, and...an

English teacher. Yes, it seems the cosmos is not without a very twisted sense of humor.

I've also got a pair of granddaughters out of the deal that both think I'm pretty cool. I'm in no rush to disillusion 'em. Their mom has also issued an edict to them stating that Thou Shalt Not read my scribbles until the sprogs turn thirty (though I think I might have talked the second one down to twenty-five...).

Facebook: www.facebook.com/bk.bilicki

Email: BK_Bilicki@wi.rr.com